High Water Mark

HIGH WATER MARK

A Novel

Donna Gannon

This is a work of fiction. All names, characters, locations and events portrayed in this novel are either products of the author's imagination or are used fictitiously. Any similarity to actual events, locales or persons, living or dead, is entirely coincidental and not intended by the author.

Library and Archives Canada Cataloguing in Publication

Gannon, Donna Marlene, 1949-, author
High water mark : a novel / Donna Gannon.

ISBN 978-0-9959101-1-9 (softcover)

    I. Title.

PS8613.A48H54 2017   C813'.6   C2017-903247-X

Book layout and design by Ward Edwards (www.BookSmith.ca)
Cover design by Gayll Morrison (www.gayllery.biz)

Sumas Mountain Press
www.sumasmountainpress.com

*To Violet and Audrey
and in memory of Rachel*

Chapter One

Somewhere between Yale and Boston Bar, the late-March blizzard swallowed the canyon. It shrank Gavin McLeod's world outside his Jeep Cherokee to mere metres. He steeled himself against the hypnotic spell of snowflakes arcing into his windshield. Fat and wet, they pasted there till the wiper smeared them into a line of sloppy ice at the perimeter of its sweep. The blade fought a losing battle to keep his porthole view clear. The right wiper had stuck permanently some time back. Through the parabola that the still functioning wiper made on the windshield, he discerned a sheer rock face on the right shoulder. It afforded the only reference in the blinding whiteout.

One of the most treacherous stretches of highway in North America, this section of the Trans-Canada carved through the rugged Fraser Canyon. It clung to granite walls, at times, hundreds of feet above the wild river. Like a colt in its first snowfall, his Cherokee proved skittish. One false move could send it careening over the edge. Tracks leaving the road would go unseen. People had been known to go over and days, even weeks, pass before their crumpled vehicle was found.

Three times in the last half hour he'd opened his side window, lifting and dropping the wiper to knock the ice off it. He did so again. As he closed the window, shivering against the cold, he made a mental inventory of his emergency supplies. Flares; check. Snow boots, never needed in Vancouver; check. Blanket; check. Candle, matches, bottled water; check, check, check.

The transport he was trailing growled through the road's twists and grades well below the posted limits, or rather the limits Gavin knew were painted beneath snow-blotted signs. He glued his eyes to its tail-lights. The rig's pace slackened as it laboured up a long incline. To maintain traction, Gavin shifted to low. The climb seemed endless, with nothing visible to mark their progress. After a bit they levelled out, carving an S-turn, nose to tail in a highway duet. Accelerating downhill, the transport began to pull away. Loathe to lose the beacon of its taillights, Gavin sped up.

Suddenly, the trucker's brake lights flared blood-red. In horrified fascination, he watched the trailer drift sideways. Its massive wheels skidded across the oncoming lane. He leapt on his own brakes but the Jeep fishtailed, slithering on black ice. Resisting the impulse to crush the brakes, he fought to steer out of his own sickening slide. The Jeep refused to respond.

By now the trailer exposed its whole flank to him. Its rear wheels ploughed along the far shoulder and it began to buck. Clawing for purchase, the wheels threw up a hail of stones, which snapped into his windshield. The wheels inched inexorably toward the edge. Any moment now, the trailer would plunge over, dragging its cab and desperate driver with it.

Gavin gaped in horror as he closed in on the trailer. The Jeep nosed toward the space beneath it and would wedge there if he could not regain control. He'd be dragged into the vortex of the transport's free fall. Frantically he worked his brakes. The trailer loomed above his hood, darkening the already feeble light.

Then, as suddenly as it began, the drama ended. The rig straightened. The Cherokee gained traction, while the space between the two lengthened. Relief burst through his lungs. He puffed his cheeks and blew out his breath with a whoosh, only to have it fog up the windshield. He swiped a peep hole with his hand.

The trucker slowed to a crawl and Gavin meekly followed all the way into Cache Creek. Fatigued from the intense concentration, his neck and shoulders aching from gripping the wheel, he pulled off, calling it quits for the day.

After a monster midday meal at a truck-stop, he had nothing to do but kill time. Spinning channels on the motel room television left him bored and restless after a couple of hours. He ventured out again after dark for a light supper. The mercury had plummeted. Snow fell in huge, fluffy flakes, as innocent as they had earlier been menacing.

He cursed himself for not getting a weather report before leaving the Lower Mainland. *He* ought to know better. But he'd been in such a hurry to get away. The cherry trees, already in bloom in Vancouver, had seduced him into forgetting that winter still reigned over the rest of British Columbia. A white wilderness, Canada's westernmost province hunched under more snow than in recorded history.

His destination, the town of Withers in the province's central corridor, nestled in the hundred year floodplain of the Fraser River. Half a century earlier, flood waters inundated the small ranching community. There'd been heavy snows that winter too. This year's record snowpack put

Withers at risk once again come early summer. When Perce Arsenault, his boss at PEP, the Provincial Emergency Program, announced that someone needed to go help the town prepare an emergency plan, Gavin jumped at the chance. The assignment offered his troubled marriage a reprieve, a few months' absence to soothe abrasions on both sides and with luck, rekindle the chemistry that had sparked their early mutual attraction. An added bonus: he loved the upcountry wilderness and its endless hiking terrain.

Back at the motel, the room pressed in on him. Gone was the euphoria of the morning, the sense of freedom and adventure. The storm served as a deadly reminder of the heavy responsibility that lay ahead. He'd seen enough of disaster to appreciate the full might of nature unleashed. He'd pitched in during the Manitoba flood in '97. Before it was done, the Red River spilled across the prairie, forming a lake nearly eight hundred square miles. He remembered the hollow gaze of farmers seeing the fruits of their entire lives swept away, homes, crops—the very soil.

In '99, he'd flown to South America as part of an international relief effort after the Columbia quake. He would never forget the devastation. He still felt haunted by the vacant stare of people, the foundations of whose lives were quite literally, torn loose.

The mindless rot on TV irritated him. He snapped it off. In this crummy budget motel room, he felt trapped by the storm. It left him prey to a familiar malaise—the sense of mattering to no one. Silence and boredom magnified it, gnawed on him, like a wolf on a carcass. Most of the time, he kept the feeling at bay through hard work. Important work. Lifesaving work.

His thoughts crept round to Celeste. Not to the acrimony of late, but to a time when she took his breath away. He recalled the incredulity of discovering himself a significant player in someone else's world. Without conscious decision, he lifted the phone and punched the number to their West Vancouver home. Three times it rang before the voice of a teenaged girl came on the line.

"Hello Amber, is your Mom home?"

"Oh…it's you," she sighed, her tone flat with scorn. "Whaddaya want?"

He heaved a quieter sigh of his own. His step-daughter could be one hard little biscuit. "Just thought I'd call and see how you and your Mom are doing."

"Yeah, we're, like, A-okay." A loud pop sounded in his ear, from gum no doubt.

"Can I talk to her?"

"No." She giggled.

"No?" He heard something that sounded like smooching.

More giggling. Amber shushed someone. "Um…she's out."

"Who's with you?"

"*No*body!"

No point in arguing long-distance. He couldn't win. He explained about the storm and had her take the number of the motel. He asked her to have Celeste call him when she got in. Just as he was about to hang up, she piped up, her tone honeyed. "Dad, will you put me on your credit card?" She only called him 'Dad' when she wanted something.

"Absolutely not."

"Why not?" she spat. "You're gonna be away for *ages* and I'll need stuff."

"I'll be in touch. Your mother can see you get whatever is necessary."

"Oh crap! I'm not gonna, like, run and *ask permission* every time I need to, like, buy *tampons* or something."

Gavin heard a very male snicker in the background. "We'll talk about this later, Amber."

"Fine!" she retorted, slamming down the phone, but not before muttering, "Bastard!"

———

Next morning, the gentle curves of the more northerly Cariboo Highway dispelled the nightmare of his gauntlet run through the canyon. Snow ploughs had been out. While skies were overcast, visibility was good.

The highway rose up and over raised railway tracks and suddenly he was in Withers. Heeding a speed zone sign, he cruised past small war-time bungalows and grander homes with gables and gingerbread from a more romantic era. He passed a hunting-fishing-guiding outfit, taxidermy and the ubiquitous Chinese restaurant, followed by a gas station, hardware and a workwear store. The commercial buildings had false fronts, like an old-style western town, and were adjoined by a covered boardwalk. Dominating the corner was a three-storey vintage hotel, The Winchester.

A sign pointed right for Town Hall. He turned. Snow nearly a foot deep still blanketed the side street. Deep wheel ruts gave evidence that few had ventured out yet. A block down, he found the municipal building, its parking lot unploughed. Fresh tire tracks led to the only two vehicles in it. He parked, got out and stretched, then followed boot prints up half a dozen steps to the door.

At the receptionist's desk, he asked for Mayor Hale.

"He's not in this morning."

"Oh. Is he snowed in?"

She gave a vague head shake. He started to say something more but she interrupted. "I'll take a message." That's when he saw her headphone. He waited for her to finish the call, noting the name on the tag pinned to her lapel, Lorraine Connor.

"He's expecting me," he said when he had her attention again.

She asked his name. "There's nothing in the book," she said with a bland stare.

His boss had assured him it was all set. He'd meet with the mayor and key staff this morning and brief them on the initial tasks. Arrangements were to have been made for him to deliver a presentation to the public within two days. His accommodations were to have been arranged as well. He explained who he was. She shrugged as if the information meant nothing to her.

"Did anyone tell you anything about my arrival?" he persisted, bridling his annoyance.

"There are no appointments in the book," she reiterated obliquely. He asked if any other councillors were in. Not yet, she told him. He asked for various staff. The town planner? The engineer? Yes, the engineer was in if he'd care to wait. He would.

He took a seat, reminding himself part of the attraction for coming here was to enjoy the slower, saner pace of life. Minutes ticked by. He did not see or hear another soul. The receptionist answered a few calls, her conversations mostly social in nature. Twenty minutes passed. He stood up and paced, partly to remind her he was still here. The net result was a feeling of invisibility. He approached her desk and asked how much longer the engineer expected to be. She called through.

Just then, a flashing orange light caught his peripheral vision. He glanced out to the parking lot, a view he didn't have when he was sitting down. A tow truck was hooking up to the back of his Cherokee. With a cry he shot out the front door, slip-sliding down the snow-covered steps and shouting at the operator.

A silver Dodge Ram idled nearby, a man in a Stetson behind the wheel. He leaned his elbow out his open side window in conversation with the tow operator, who laughed as he worked the crane to lift Gavin's Jeep.

"Hey," Gavin shouted again. "What do you think you're doing?" The operator was a young fellow, with ear flaps on his cap sticking out sideways giving him a doltish look. Instead of responding to Gavin, he looked to the driver of the pick-up.

The man in the Stetson gave a wry shake of his head. "They always act like it's *your* fault don't they, Chuck."

Gavin addressed the man in the Ram. "Are you responsible for this?"

A slow smirk curled up one side of the man's mouth. "That your Cherokee?" he asked.

"Yes, it's my Cherokee."

"Then I'd say *you're* responsible."

Gavin scowled. Sweeping his arm in the direction of the building, he said curtly, "I have business here."

"That so?" the other replied, obviously enjoying Gavin's pique.

"What *exactly* is the problem?" Gavin hissed through gritted teeth.

"The problem?" The man rolled his eyes with an expression of despair, as if Gavin were obtuse. It was then he noticed a boy about seven or eight years of age sitting in the passenger seat. When he caught his eye, the boy dropped his gaze with a blush of discomfort.

The truck door clicked and swung toward him. Hand-tooled cowboy boots emerged below the door. The man unfolded to his full height. Gavin stood six foot one but the other man towered half a head over him. He was imposing, with erect, broad shoulders tapering to a trim waist, a powerful body on long legs. He wore a heavy denim shirt, sheepskin vest and form-fitting jeans. His face bore the tanned look of the outdoors despite the time of year. Wide cheekbones, Paul Newman eyes and expressive, if cruel, mouth came together in an impression of a man used to running things.

"The problem?" he repeated, hooking his thumbs in his belt. "You're occupying a reserved parking spot," he explained slowly and deliberately, as if to a simpleton. "*My* parking spot."

Gavin glanced back over his shoulder. There was a sign on a post in front of the Cherokee, he saw now. But it was obliterated in snow. He scanned the near-empty lot. He felt a muscle ripple in his jaw and his fists clench in frustration by his sides. "Yes. I see there was no other place for you to park," he retorted.

The boy in the truck hunched deeper into his scarf. Gavin could clearly see the pink creep up his cheeks. He felt sorry for the boy and regretted his own pugilism. He was about to say something to de-escalate the confrontation when he caught sight of his adversary in the Stetson signal the tow operator to proceed. He wondered suddenly if he was the mayor.

"Wait a minute," Gavin waved a hand at the operator. Turning back to the Stetson, he said, "Perhaps we ought to introduce ourselves. I'm Gavin McLeod. I've been sent by the Province to work with the town council and staff to prepare an emergency plan. Are you the mayor?"

"Not yet," the man replied with a sizzling smile. "However McLeod, you're in my spot. Chuck here is having a busy morning and you're slowing him up. He's been called out to move your vehicle and he's got to get paid for his efforts. If you want to settle up with him, he might be willing to—I can't say for sure now, you understand. It's not my place to be telling him how to run his business."

Gavin felt the blood pumping in his temples. Chuck was clearly taking his lead from this cowboy in spite of the latter's feigned deference. He was either going to have to pay a fine now or walk to God-knows-where and pay the towing charge to get his vehicle back.

He stepped over to the driver, reaching for his wallet. "What's this going to cost me?" he growled.

"That'll be twenty bucks."

He pulled a twenty from his wallet and thrust it at the driver who proceeded to lower the Cherokee. By now the man in the Stetson was back in his truck with the window rolled up. The tow operator drove off. While Gavin backed out of the parking spot, the other smiled ingratiatingly, flicked the brim of his Stetson and pulled into the space. Gavin parked in the centre of the lot where there were no signposts. By the time he got out, the man was heading toward the steps, with the boy plodding behind him.

Just then a muffled cry arose from the boy. Gavin saw him lean forward. Blood splattered the snow. The man turned when the boy called a second time, a panicky note in his voice. "Dad!"

"Aw Christ, boy, don't you ever have a tissue with you?" he scolded. He reached into a pocket, hauled out a handkerchief and handed it to the boy. Then he turned and proceeded up the steps with the boy stumbling along behind him, holding the wad to his nose.

The only customers in the Dream-Catcher restaurant and bar when Gavin entered after dark were two men on stools, nursing beers at the bar. He took a table on the café side. A woman behind the bar broke off her conversation with the men and approached his table, picking up a coffee pot from a hot-plate on her way.

"Back for seconds, eh," she said with a friendly smile. "Coffee?"

He nodded, turning his cup right side up on the saucer. One of the two nuggets of useful information he gleaned from the receptionist at Town Hall was the Dream-Catcher was by far the best place in town to eat. After his fruitless efforts to find anyone the least bit interested in his arrival, the lunch he'd devoured confirmed the café's quality fare. The second tidbit the receptionist surrendered was the identity of his adversary in the parking lot—Blake Logan, Town Councillor.

After getting a room at The Winchester hotel, Gavin had spent the afternoon tramping through snow, familiarizing himself with the town's layout. It wasn't much of a place, total population 3,243 souls including farms and ranches within a fifteen kilometre radius.

Part of his route had taken him toward the river along Station Street, the town's main crossroad. Two blocks past the highway, Station Street took a sharp left bend to run along the base of the rail line's high embankment. Several blocks farther on, the tracks on their elevated bed turned toward the highway crossing and Station Street rose up the embankment to a dead end at a derelict train station. He'd followed the tracks in the opposite direction. They curved north again to follow the river bank. Soon they curved westward once more to cross the river on a trestle.

At this final curve, a dike met the raised rail bed. According to Gavin's information, the dike stretched north along the river for about sixteen kilometres. Beyond that, natural elevation prevented the river from spreading beyond its banks. The town's main defence against flood was this combined structure of dike and elevated rail bed.

At the north end of town, the highway also curved toward the river, rising over the dike to cross its own bridge. The Dream-Catcher sat in a trucker's parking lot on the highway on the town side the rail line-dike juncture.

The coffee the woman poured him smelled fresh and bold. "What's good?" he asked, scanning the menu board over the counter.

"Everything," she affirmed. "Yuh hungry?" He rubbed his stomach realizing he'd worked up a sizeable appetite with the afternoon's walk.

"Depends," he grinned.

She tipped back her head and gave a hearty laugh. "Cautious one arncha? You like venison? We serve prime venison steak." It would be a change from the sushi or Korean cuisine of Vancouver, he thought. He nodded. She put in his order, then returned to set his table. Rings bedecked her fingers, mostly native-style engraved silver. Beaded earrings of native design swayed gently from her ears.

"You the manager?" Gavin asked.

"Manager, owner, bar tender, waitress and sometime-cook. Billy, back there," she tossed her head toward the kitchen where a head bobbled in the steam, "he's my main cook. He's pretty good. Don't mind sayin' I taught him most everything he knows about cooking. You want to walk away from a table satisfied, you just come on in to the Dream-Catcher. My name's Amanda Sky. Most folks call me Mandy." She hustled off to the kitchen.

The décor throughout was a cock-eyed blend of authentic Indian artifacts—a basket cradle, mask, painted paddle and, of course, dreamcatchers, large and small—and New Age. Crystals and glass pyramids swayed in the windows and god's eyes in garish colours of yarn twirled from a dozen places. A framed poster of a tarot card and another of the astrological chart hung on the walls. The paper place-mat Mandy set in front of him displayed the sun signs and horoscope advice on one's ideal love-partner.

Three pillars demarcated the café from the bar. A large rectangular stained-glass lampshade spotlighted a pool table in the otherwise dimly lit bar. Small pedestal bar tables surrounded it. Two men nursing drinks on swivel stools at the bar bore the comfortable slouch of locals. One, clad in denim and heavy checkered shirt, looked like he might be a rancher. The other was better groomed in less rugged, casual attire. Gavin wondered if he ran a local business. He was tempted to saunter over and strike up a conversation but something in their demeanour dissuaded him. Their glances struck him as inquisitive but cool. He was just beginning to badger himself for being paranoid when the door of the Dream-Catcher opened and Blake Logan strode in.

He stamped snow from his boots, removed his Stetson and waved it in greeting to the two at the bar. Logan looked straight at him as if expecting to see him, that same slow smirk curling the side of his mouth.

Mandy came out of the kitchen carrying his steak, still sizzling on a plate.

"Pour me a scotch and soda, Mandy honey," Logan hollered in a familiar tone.

"Hang on, Blake. I'm serving a customer."

Logan's grin broadened. "Now Sweetcakes, you know *I'm* your most loyal customer," he answered. She snorted and set the plate in front of Gavin, then hustled toward the bar. As she passed Logan, he took a swipe at her behind with his huge hand. She dodged but not fast enough. "Keep your paws to yerself, ya big galoot," she snapped. Logan laughed.

One of the men slid to the next stool, opening up the middle one for him. As he sat down, the one who looked like a rancher leaned toward him and spoke in a low voice. Logan's response made him snigger. The other clapped Logan on the back and threw back his head in a guffaw. Gavin suspected it was at his expense.

Mandy poured Logan's drink, set the glass in front of him with sharp rap and returned straightaway to where Gavin carved into the venison steak. "You in town for a while?" she inquired. With his mouth full, he mumbled his assertion. She seemed to hesitate as if wanting to say more, then waved her hand at him. "You'll want to enjoy your dinner in peace."

Enjoy it he did, despite the company. Just as Mandy refreshed his coffee, Logan departed. Gavin finished his meal, paid and left.

Back in his room at The Winchester, he had nothing to occupy himself. Celeste had not returned his call the night before. He tried again. This time she answered. He explained about the storm and how he'd arrived a day late. Impatience in her tone was obvious. He regretted his effort. "I thought I'd give you a phone number where you can reach me."

"In case of what?"

"In case you need me."

She barked a laugh. "Don't you wish," she mocked. He could have choked back his words leaving her an opening like that. "I could've got your number from your boss. No doubt you've already reported in to him."

"Not yet," he answered. "I haven't set up my laptop yet."

She sighed. "Oh well, give it to me then."

He did. "What are you doing?"

"I'm putting on nail polish if you *must* know," she snapped with clear annoyance.

He heard Amber in the background. "Watch it Mom, he's checking up on you." Celeste laughed.

"I'm not checking up on you," he said through gritted teeth. "Can't we at least be civil with one another?"

"Aw… poor baby. He's lonely. Gone two days and already homesick." He heard Amber snicker and pictured the two of them sharing the joke.

"I'll talk to you later, Celeste."

"Bye-ee," she sang, sarcasm sugaring her tone.

Next morning, Mayor Hale greeted him in his office with a strong handshake and expansive smile. He was as energetic and genial as his name implied. He neglected an apology for missing him the day before and expressed surprise at Gavin's expectations about what was to have been done already.

Having hoped to solicit volunteers for a planning committee at the town hall meeting that was to have been arranged, he found himself behind schedule right off the bat. Hale passed him off to the planning and engineering departments for information he sought—water table records, population distribution, historical data on flooding, topographical and local maps including backcountry roads and trails.

He spent the morning gathering materials and making photocopies. Staff provided documents, if they had them, with bored indifference. He was told that some of the historical data would be at the public library next door. He left a stack of materials he'd obtained so far in his Cherokee and tramped across a snow-covered park, past a gazebo, to the Withers' library. The librarian showed him the section he needed.

He didn't notice the other patron sharing the stacks with him until the man took his selection, a rather impressive pile, to the counter. He spoke in a soft voice, which ordinarily would have been difficult to hear. In the stillness of the library though, Gavin heard him ask if the book he'd requested on inter-library loan had come in yet. It was the subject matter which roused him from the reference book he was burrowed into. Ham radio.

He looked up with new interest. The man was an odd looking character. Short and stocky, he had wispy hair circling a prematurely bald skull, whiskers along his jaw line from ear to ear and wire-frame glasses. Clothed in a coat almost to his ankles, he wore galoshes which made his feet look big and awkward, like duck feet. His long, knitted, striped scarf looked like a university student's cast-off.

On learning his request was not in yet, the man stuffed his check-outs into bags and pulled on his toque. It wasn't till he'd opened the door on his way out that Gavin snapped to his feet. "Excuse me," he hollered after him, but the man seemed only to shuffle faster. By the time Gavin reached the door, he was half way down the covered boardwalk to the side steps.

"Wait." Gavin shouted. The man half turned, the whites of his eyes showing, as if he were fleeing a vicious dog. Something fluttered to the ground. "I want to ask you..." he started, but the man hurried on, not answering. Gavin frowned in puzzlement and watched him waddle briskly through the snow across the park.

He was just about to step back inside when he spied something on the boardwalk. He picked it up. It was a library card made out to Will Hahn. He looked up to shout to the man that he'd dropped it, but seeing the hastily retreating figure, he shrugged and slipped it into his shirt pocket.

The following morning Gavin stopped by the small local press and introduced himself to Floyd Hancock, editor of the Withers Gazette. Floyd sniffed a doomsday story that would sell papers. He was eager to do the article Gavin wanted about the potential for flooding. He was helpful in other ways too, printing posters Gavin produced the night before on his laptop. Best of all, Floyd rented him a hole-in-the-wall office next door. It was once a tiny barber shop. As an afterthought, he asked Floyd to put the address in his article so people could find him.

He spent several hours walking around town distributing the posters Floyd printed, and speaking with local business people. He explained about the emergency planning committee he needed to recruit and the upcoming town-hall meeting.

It was hard to imagine the ferocity of the storm only three days earlier, considering the picture-post-card like landscape under its fluffy blanket of snow. Lunchtime found him again at the Dream-Catcher where Mandy agreeably put up one of his posters in her café window.

"How long have you lived in Withers, Mandy?" he asked as she poured his second cup of coffee.

"You gotta be careful how you ask a woman a question like that, Mr. McLeod. You might as well ask her age and a man's skating on thin ice when he does," she laughed. "What do you *really* want to know?"

"You're onto me," he grinned. He reached into his shirt pocket. "You must know a lot of folks in town. Do you know this man?" He handed her the library card.

She took it and peered at the name. "Will Hahn. Oh sure, he lives up on the hill. How'd you get his card?"

"He dropped it outside the library. I tried to go after him but he just ran off."

"Yeah, he's shy, that one. Almost a hermit."

"You said he lives on the hill." Gavin waved his hand across the landscape out the window. "Which hill?"

Laughter bubbled up within Mandy like a spring, soft and pleasant. He wondered how old she was in fact. She had one of those ageless faces that made it hard to tell. She had black hair with the sheen of a raven, wide cheekbones and more than a hint of aboriginal blood, though she was not full-blooded, he was pretty sure.

She bent toward the window and pointed. "Around here, we call that 'the hill'." 'The hill' sat as if representing the scrapings of the valley heaped into a flattened cone on the northeast side of town.

"Is he a ham radio operator?"

"I've heard tell."

"How do you know him?"

"He fixes things, small appliances, clocks, watches—even computers. He's repaired appliances for my restaurant. Anything electric or electronic. It's how he makes his living. He's a pretty smart fellow but he doesn't seem to have any friends. Keeps to himself."

"He in the phone book?"

"No. As I said, he keeps to himself."

"How do people find him? To get something repaired, I mean."

She chuckled at him again in her slow, easy way. "It's a small town, Mr. McLeod. People need someone to do a job, they ask around. You need a job done?"

"I might."

"Go on up the hill. There's only one road. He's at the top. Watch for his sign." He nodded, accepting the card she handed back and returning it to his pocket.

He went back to the hotel as soon as he finished, picked up his laptop and drove out past Town Hall toward 'the hill'. The blacktop wound serpentine up the giant mound through jack pine. Homes appeared here and there in the trees, each with its own careless clutter—abandoned vehicles, worn trampoline, a horse trailer. He shifted down to third to climb the grade and kept an eye out for a sign. Just as the road levelled off, he spied it on the right, an inconspicuous board tacked on a fence post, 'Electric / Electronic Repairs and Service'.

The house sat back from the road, a collection of boxes haphazardly tacked together. It occupied the very summit, with a clear view of the town behind it. A beam antenna towered in the yard, held fast by guy-wires, with a battered Chevy station-wagon nearby. He went to the door and knocked. The curtain in the window moved aside long enough for him to recognize the short, balding individual he'd seen the day before. The door opened, the occupant half hiding behind it.

"Your sign says you do electronic repairs." Gavin pointed toward the road.

"Yes," the little man nodded almost imperceptibly.

"Computers?"

"Some things. I'm not a regular computer service, mind."

"Well, uh, I'm from out of town and I'm having a little problem and there's, uh, nowhere locally I can find help."

The man's eyes flicked to Gavin's hands. "Where's your computer?"

"Oh! It's, uh, in my vehicle." Gavin turned gesturing with both forefingers at his Cherokee. "It's a laptop."

The door opened a little wider, revealing more of the gnome-like fellow, a thirty-something gnome, if Gavin had his guess. "Right," Gavin said to the unspoken invitation and hot-footed it to his car. He grabbed the laptop, anxious to get through the door before it might be closed on him again.

He entered a spacious kitchen. Stacks of books covered the spindle-legged table in the centre. The room was otherwise clean and tidy. On one of the kitchen chairs, a large marmalade cat curled in a tight ball, asleep.

The man shuffled through to the next room, mumbling "Watch your step," at the threshold of what was obviously a 'box' built at a different time in the house's history. Gavin stepped up a one-inch lip into a room surrounded on three sides with a workbench, filled with the guts of small appliances, motors and machines. Tools neatly lined the peg-board walls above the counter. The man drew up a stool and reached for the case in Gavin's hand.

"What seems to be the problem?"

"It keeps freezing up on me and giving various error messages," Gavin lied, watching the fellow deftly open the case, plug in and power up. For the next few minutes, he put the laptop through its paces.

Gavin took in his surroundings. The room's fourth side opened through a wide arch and down a step into another addition. Over the arch hung a sign in rustic lettering on a piece of barn-board, *Ham shack, sweet ham shack.* A bank of radio apparatus lined one wall on several shelves above a desk. A large window on an adjacent wall offered a southwest view over the town and river. The marmalade cat sauntered by, its long tail a question mark, and took possession of the office chair by the desk.

Ten minutes later, Gavin was apologizing for his computer ignorance when the repairman declared his laptop to be operating in perfect condition. The man asked him a few insightful questions and gave him some basic pointers which, while old-hat to Gavin, made him admire the simple way the fellow had of boiling down technical information for the lay person.

When it seemed time to go, he nodded in the direction of the radio station. "You're a ham?"

The other nodded, colouring, as if it were a deeply personal question.

"Do you, I mean, would you mind letting me see your rig?"

The fellow's mouth twitched to one side in what might have been the beginning of a smile, or a grimace, then tipped his head in a motion of acquiescence. Gavin stepped down into the studio. By the microphone lay a magazine, *The Amateur Radio Communicator.* His eyes roved over the complex system. "You're well equipped, Mr. Hahn."

A look of consternation creased the man's brow. "How did you know my name?"

Gavin ducked his head, embarrassed at his slip. He reached inside his jacket to his shirt pocket and pulled out the library card. He extended it. "You dropped this at the library yesterday." Will took it and jerked his head up to meet Gavin's eyes. "I tried to give it to you but you left in such a hurry."

The other man seemed to shrink. An expression Gavin couldn't quite decipher passed over his face. "There never was a problem with your laptop was there?"

He coughed to cover his embarrassment. "Well, not exactly. I wanted to see... to get an idea of your expertise. I'll pay you for your time."

"What exactly are you interested in Mr. ah...?" he said stiffly.

"Maybe I should properly introduce myself." Gavin gave his name and explained his purpose for being in town, his search for volunteers for a citizens' committee to develop a plan in case of severe flooding. "Your expertise in radio would be invaluable, Mr. Hahn. Someone needs to be in charge of the communications piece of the plan." He told him about the upcoming meeting where he would present information to the townsfolk about the risk and the preparedness needed.

Hahn listened without speaking till Gavin finished. He appeared to contemplate the carpet for a long moment then looked up with a note of resignation. "I don't do meetings, Mr. McLeod. Or committees, or anything where there's a bunch of people."

Gavin turned to the wall opposite the radio station. It was filled with QSL cards, postcards from other radio stations verifying reception by a radio amateur. He moved over to the wall and began reading them. They came from all over the world—Japan, the Philippines, Australia, Borneo, Bolivia. "You've communicated with folks in all these places?" It was a naïve question whose answer he already knew. There was only one way to obtain these prized cards.

"Yes," was all Will answered.

"Voice or code?"

"Some of both."

"Handle traffic?"

"A little."

"Ever help out in an emergency?"

"Once. I picked up a signal from a trucker who'd gone off the road in a snowstorm. He'd been there a while. His signal was weak. I just happened to pick him up and got him some help."

He turned back to Will. "That's why we need you, Mr. Hahn. If a flood does occur, your services will be desperately needed."

Hahn moved over to the window and sat on the sill. The cat stretched luxuriously on the office chair and yawned. In a smooth motion it hopped to the floor and onto the window sill, stepped over a pair of binoculars and stood regarding Will's shoulder a second or two. Then the muscles bunched in his haunch and he hopped gracefully up onto it. Will tipped his head forward and the cat straddled both shoulders. It was a dance the two had obviously perfected over time. "Hey, Macbeth," Will murmured softly.

He directed his next comment to Gavin. "In your business, you must have worked with hams before. You'll know something of the code then. The rulebook requires we help out any way we can in disaster situations. If there is a flood—IF—I'll do whatever I can. But I won't join your committee or attend any meetings," he said with finality.

Gavin nodded his acquiescence. He told him the time and location of the upcoming public meeting all the same. "I'd be happy to see you there, even if it's just to be well informed yourself. I have an office in the old barber shop. You know the place?"

"I know it."

"If you should change your mind, you can find me there."

The interview was at an end. "How much do I owe you for your time with my computer?"

"No charge."

With the public meeting still four days off, Gavin took advantage of the slack time to research. At the library the bored librarian took delight in availing him of historical material on the town, stashed in the archives.

He read up on the flood of '48. The damage around Withers had been moderate, mainly because the population was small then, and scattered. One individual who'd been affected was a rancher north of town. His house and outbuildings had been engulfed. The young rancher had not been too concerned that there would be a recurrence during his lifetime, since the house and outbuildings sat in the hundred year floodplain. Not till his son, born after the flood, was grown and attending university was he persuaded of the potential for future threat from the river. Only then did he undertake to have a dike built. He negotiated with the town of Withers for it to be extended southward to meet the raised rail bed, thereby protecting the town as well.

The name of the rancher jumped out at Gavin. For two decades he'd represented the vast interior region in the Legislature in Victoria. Just as he was absorbing this information, a woman entered the library. In the city, he'd have paid little attention to her, but she looked out of place in this rugged, northern town and this distracted him.

She wore a tailored coat which reached nearly to the ankle of her heeled black leather boots. Tall and handsome, she walked with arresting grace. She carried a sheaf of large papers flopping over her arm. "Hello, Nettie," she greeted the librarian.

"Oh hi, Mary. I see the posters are ready."

She laid them on the counter and removed her coat, draping it over the back of a chair. Her dress was similarly smart and conservative. Glancing in his direction, she lowered her voice to a discreet tone. Nettie handed her a tape dispenser. Mary pulled a poster from the pile and returned to the door. She had a way of moving that struck him as regal.

He rose, shouldering into his coat and approached the counter. "Mrs. Snelgrove, you've been very helpful. There's one more thing I wonder if you could tell me?"

"I'll try, sir," she said, pulling her lips back in a toadying smile.

"I've been reading about the construction of the dike and Hugh Logan. Is the town councillor, Blake Logan, related?"

She flushed and glanced nervously in Mary's direction. Having taped the poster to the glass in the door, Mary approached with aristocratic poise. Eyeing him with an air of self-possession neither friendly nor cold, she asked, "What is your interest in Blake Logan, sir?"

Having no wish to step on a local land mine, Gavin carefully explained his purpose in town and how he would be working with both staff and elected officials. "You're familiar with Mr. Logan then, Ma'am?" he finished.

"I ought to be," she responded with aplomb. "He's my husband. And yes, Hugh Logan was his father."

Gavin extricated himself with what he hoped was diplomacy and exited as quickly as possible. Turning to close the door with its glass window, with excessive care, he found himself staring at the poster. *Help Save the Old Train Station*, it appealed. He paused long enough to read how the Withers Enhancement Society had acquired from the railroad the derelict but classic station-house and hoped to restore it for use as an art gallery. It was not till he was half way up the block it struck him why Mary Logan seemed vaguely familiar. The boy with Logan the day he'd locked horns with him in the parking lot, clearly took after his mother.

Several days later, rising early, Gavin set out in his Cherokee with maps of the area's backcountry. He gave himself the excuse that a spell of unseasonably warm weather allowed him to check out the conditions of the snow and streams above the town. But in fact he'd been itching to indulge his passion for hiking.

Following the twisty lines on the map, he found himself churning up a narrow mud track in the hills through pine forest, bouncing over boulders and through pot-holes filled with water. The road, if it could be called such, deteriorated by the minute. He considered turning around but there wasn't a good place to do so. At the next turn, a rocky outcropping rose a dozen metres above the road. His pace slowed to a crawl as the Cherokee struggled to negotiate the mud coagulating at the base of the cliff. The tires clawed several more car-lengths until finally the elements took ascendancy. Forward motion halted and his wheels spun uselessly. He gave up and shut off the engine.

He climbed out. The ruts his Jeep had made were shockingly deep. He brushed aside for the moment a concern that getting out of there might be a bit tricky, and looked for drier footing as he continued hiking uphill. Through the trees, he could hear trickling water.

Following the sound, he crossed a patch of corn snow and entered the woods. A couple of minutes later he came upon a runnel half a metre wide gurgling down the hillside. He made mental notes to record later, then tramped uphill beside the brook. After a while he headed back, mindful that his location was rather remote from assistance should he need it. He had no desire to find himself in need of Chuck's towing service.

He came out of the trees at the base of a steep bank. The road ran along the top, twenty feet above him. He scrabbled up, slipping in spite of his hiker's boots, and clawing for purchase with his hands. Just as his head reached the level of the road, a shadow fell darkly across him. A snort exploded above him. His heart slammed. He gaped up at the black belly of an impossibly tall beast. It twisted on its hind legs and lunged away.

The horse, for he now saw that's what it was, bolted into a meadow the other side of the road, its rider fighting for control. It ducked its head and thrust up from the shoulder, coming down stiff-legged, like a seasoned bronc. The rider arced through the air and struck the ground with a sickening thud. The horse gave a few more feeble bucks and then stood stock still, its ears pricked forward toward its late rider, as if solicitous of its welfare.

For a moment, none of the principals moved. His blood ran cold. But then the dislodged rider rolled over and stood up. With a shock, he saw it was a woman. She approached the horse, limping severely. Horrified at his culpability he hastened to help. But before he even crossed the road, she was back in the saddle and urging her mount toward him.

The horse was a stunning black, with a graceful high-stepping gait. The woman, despite her fall, was obviously at home in the saddle. As horse and rider reached the road, he opened his mouth to apologize, but before any words were out, she cut him off. "Is that your Jeep down there in the mud?" Her out-flung arm held a riding crop which pointed accusingly down the road. He nodded, tongue-tied by her obvious wrath.

"You're not from around here are you?" Her tone stung with challenge.

He was forced to tip his head back and look way up to meet startling emerald eyes, flashing with disapproval. It made him feel like a child in trouble with a parent or school principal.

"No," he managed, "I'm from Vancouver. I'm very sor—"

"You testosterone-riddled city yahoos! You lounge in front of your TV all week sucking beer and getting brainwashed. You think the wilderness is manufactured by General Motors for the express purpose of letting you tear it up with your over-sized Tonka toys, pretending you're a Marlborough man!" she spewed, her metaphors stumbling over one another in an angry torrent. "Damn you urban cowboys! You've no respect for nature."

She wheeled the stallion neatly on its hocks and cantered off before he could say another word. He stood watching her go, embarrassment flaming his cheeks. Yet he was oddly aware that if a man had just delivered him such a dressing down he'd be steaming mad. As he hiked back to his Jeep, it occurred to him he also might have been angry if the woman had not been so drop-dead gorgeous. That thought turned up the side of his mouth in a wry grin.

———————————

For the town-hall meeting, Gavin had prepared a Power Point presentation. The Town was adequately represented by staff and councillors, but public turnout was disappointing. He recognized a few faces from his rounds to local businesses the past week. The two men Blake Logan had joined for drinks the first evening at the Dream-Catcher were also present. Logan himself entered, shaking hands and clapping his great paw on several shoulders as he moved through the group.

For half an hour Gavin clicked through slides, presenting facts, figures and conditions that make for disaster. He explained the need for volunteers to help develop and implement an emergency plan and invited anyone interested to contact him at the end of the meeting or later at his office.

When he opened the floor for questions, Mayor Hale shot up from his chair. "Mr. McLeod, you've said the potential for an emergency must be carefully assessed to determine whether it is necessary to prepare."

Gavin heard challenge in Hale's tone. "It's wise to assume a certain level of preparedness at all times," he replied evenly, "individuals as well as businesses and governments. It's a good idea to carry emergency supplies in the trunk of your car, for example, or keep a flashlight and extra food and bottled water in your home. You never know when the power may go out or a crippling storm cut you off from help and services, such as the blizzard of a fortni—"

"Yes, of course," Hale cut in. "We northerners are used to depending on ourselves to get through all manner of conditions you don't find in the big city, Mr. McLeod. We're a hardy lot." Several heads nodded agreement. "You've suggested, Mr. McLeod, that our town government," Hale continued, consulting a notepad in his hand, "upgrade the dike, erect signage for evacuation routes, purchase communications equipment and stockpile food, water, medical supplies and blankets for potentially hundreds of displaced persons. All this would put an enormous burden on the modest resources of our small community. As a responsible representative of the people, Mr. McLeod, I would need to know such outlay is justified." Hale's frequent use of his name got under Gavin's skin, given its patronizing bite.

He replied, "I'm not suggesting all that need be done at the outset. There are levels of preparation that relate to levels of threat as conditions arise."

Another man was standing, wanting to speak. Gavin signalled him to proceed. "I represent the business community in Withers as chair of the Chamber of Commerce," he said. "My concern is the effect all this *Chicken Little* publicity may have on our economy. This town relies heavily on tourists who come here to fish, hike and enjoy our outdoors. People from all over Canada and the US start right about now to make reservations at lodges and cabins all around here for the upcoming season. Your article has stirred up a hornet's nest. I've had a dozen phone calls from folks whose livelihood is in the hospitality trade. We don't want this kind of news in the paper and on the internet. I hope the provincial government, and you Mr. McLeod, don't kill us with kindness and good intentions."

From the back, another voice cut in. "One thing you didn't cover in your presentation…. How long will you be hanging out here and just how much is it costing us taxpayers to cover your expenses?"

"The length of my stay here," Gavin responded, "depends on how things shape up over the next few weeks and how quickly a plan can be put in place. As for your concern about cost, Mr. ah…" He waited for the man to identify himself.

"Van Dergeest. Hank Van Dergeest. I run the Overwaitea market here. And I can tell you as a businessman, this town's suffering bad from economic recession. We need our provincial government to be putting money into *stimulating* our economy, not wasting taxpayers hard-earned dollars on *contingency plans*." This last was spoken with clear satirical scorn.

"Yes, Mr. Van Dergeest, there is a cost to emergency preparedness. The cost of not preparing though, can be a thousand-fold. Present conditions already pose a moderate threat even for homes and businesses inside the dike. Some areas outside it, below town and across the river are considerably more vulnerable—the First Nations reserve, for example."

Someone in the front row jerked forward. Gavin was acquainted with him, a councillor named Freddie McCormick. "There's been minor flooding of a few homes occasionally," McCormick cut in, "but the, ah, natives manage just fine. I don't see any percentage in getting them all in a sweat over what will likely amount to nothing. The band already has touchy relations with the town government. They expect Council to do things for them for which we have no responsibility. Raising an alarm that their village is *possibly* at risk is only going to exacerbate relations. I hope you're not going to stir up *that* pot, Sir!"

The remark was met with a low growl of assent. Gavin swallowed the bile he tasted at the racist undercurrent and responded in a measured, yet firm tone. "Understand this; the snow lies deeper in the mountains than it has in recorded history. If it continues to snow, if a late spring is followed by a warm spell, if there are heavy rains the ground can't absorb, Withers will be in a situation of *very* high risk."

"That's a lot of what if's and maybe's," Van Dergeest argued.

Gavin eyed him levelly. "Each factor signals a stage of precautions that should be mobilized. For example, the time may come when ranchers and farmers should move their stock to higher ground or ship them to a safe place till the crisis passes."

A man with a weatherbeaten face jolted to his feet. Holding his Stetson by the crown, he shook it menacingly in Gavin's direction. "Are you telling me I should haul my herd of 400 head of cattle by truck and pay someone else to keep 'em during peak grazing season? I'll go broke! Hell man, this town has a dike that's protected us for years."

"Dikes are not fool-proof," Gavin countered. "They can fail, and when they do, the damage can be catastrophic. The flood of '48 in the Fraser Valley was the direct result of multiple dike *breaches*. Thirteen thousand acres were submerged. The disaster left twenty-four hundred families homeless and cost the equivalent of a hundred and forty-million in today's dollars."

"Hrumph! What could you possibly know about Withers and living with the river us folks who've lived here all our lives don't know in spades?" The hall erupted in an uproar of shouts and growled side conversations.

Logan rose languidly. He cut a compelling figure, towering above the audience in his tailored navy suit, silk tie and crisp white shirt. His presence was affable yet commanding.

His gaze swept the gathering with proprietary familiarity. All eyes fixed on him and the buzz stopped. "Gentlemen, what we have here." he flashed a disarming smile, "is a failure to communicate." He delivered the line with Paul Newman-like aplomb. "We residents of Withers are ordinary folk. Indeed, we *are* concerned about our struggling economy. I know you want your local government to put its effort into boosting it, engage in a marketing campaign to promote tourism, keep taxes down and—oh yes—keep the highway, which is our lifeline to commerce, open. For that we need to purchase more heavy-duty snow removal equipment.

"I understand your reluctance to put your hard-earned dollars into preparing for an uncertain prospect. We feel safe behind the dike that has protected this community ever since it was constructed."

He put his palms together as one would in prayer. "But today we have a messenger among us. A messenger sent from on high." His hand gestured toward the ceiling, then he frowned and made a vague lateral sign. "Er, from Victoria." Titters rippled through the assembly.

"In fact, we have a veritable prophet among us," he turned a sizzling smile on Gavin. "Noah himself come to warn us of a great flood." Several chortled openly. "All beasts must be put in an ark, he counsels." Someone guffawed. "For the waters will surely rise and smash through the dikes. All that we know will be destroyed and only the true believers will be saved."

Gavin clenched and unclenched his fists. He locked eyes with Blake. "Noah wasn't a prophet. He was merely a man who listened when a warning was given." But the meeting broke up in a hubbub of heated conversations. No one wanted to hear more from him.

Later, his guts burning, he tramped around town, knowing it was useless to try to sleep. He was discouraged by the lack of progress, but worse, he couldn't shake his seething anger at what had been a public—and very personal—discrediting.

The email from Perce Arsenault waiting for him when he got back to his room didn't improve his mood. His boss was a low-key kind of guy, counting down to his retirement. Gavin liked him well enough. But Perce was an overworked bureaucrat who reacted to the pressures of the job by chafing at his staff. Gavin knew he should shrug it off but he hated the feeling of not measuring up and would he lash himself to try harder.

The chafing was there now in the email. He had been on assignment half a month and had yet to provide a progress report. It was true he'd avoided emailing Perce because he had nothing to report. Now he keyed a message detailing his activities and contacts. He read it over. He hoped it camouflaged the problems. He pushed 'Send' and went to bed, where he tossed and turned for several hours.

It was a crisp, starry night when Blake got home from the presentation. He was surprised to hear music as he climbed the steps to the front door of his rambling one-story ranch house. Usually Mary was in bed or headed that way by this time of night. He paused on the porch, letting the notes float around him. Her music was her essence and when he heard it, he still felt privileged. Yet it stirred in him a bittersweet tug-of-war.

The first time he laid eyes on her she was playing a concert grand for an audience of several hundred. His college roomie was chasing a flute-playing co-ed in the orchestra and had dragged him along to the concert. Blake fidgeted through the first hour; then a dark-haired beauty came on stage to perform a piano solo. She was unlike any woman he knew. And he had known many.

In Withers, by age eighteen Blake Logan had already earned himself a reputation as a young buck who'd slept with every attractive girl in the valley and more than a few married women to boot. His good looks and brash charm had been similarly successful at university when his father sent him off to get a degree in agricultural studies.

For the first time in the concert, he sat up at attention, listening to the performance on stage. He found himself aroused in a way that was novel. It was not lust which stirred him but awe. He admired her as one does a work of fine art. Indeed she could have posed for a sculptor in classical Greece, with her long white throat, cascading hair and patrician carriage. But it wasn't merely her physical perfection which affected him. Her music cast a spell on him, moving him in a way music had never done before.

After that night, he was hooked. But it was four long years before she accepted his proposal of marriage. During that time he pursued her, as a dog chases cars, out-of-control in love with her. But Mary was in love with another, a temperamental cellist, "That nincompoop" as Blake characterized him to his buddies. She tolerated Blake's attentions on a friendship basis but spurned all attempts at anything more. At the conclusion of his undergraduate studies, Mary was accepted at an elite music academy in Europe, on her way to becoming a professional concert pianist.

Depressed, he spent a disastrous summer sleeping with a variety of valley women. Mary was scheduled to begin at the haute école in the new year following the fall semester of his graduate studies. Then fate lent a hand. The cellist, failing an audition for a coveted position, committed suicide.

Blake was at her side in a heartbeat, supporting her through the ensuing months while he studied for his MBA. In the end, she accepted his proposal of marriage, relinquishing forever her ambitions for a profession career in music. He brought her home to the ranch and bought her a concert grand. At first he was deliriously happy, but she never grafted on to the upcountry lifestyle. He had to admit that it was foolish to think a Thoroughbred could thrive in territory that belonged to the mustang.

Their marriage deteriorated over time and through several miscarriages to a civil, passionless stand-off. For months at a time, she would not allow Blake to be intimate with her. He coped with the physical need the way he always had. There were always women eager to receive Blake Logan's attentions.

Her music drifted out to him as he stood on the porch, listening. Almost reluctantly, he came in. Often, when he appeared in the room, she would stop playing abruptly, depriving him on purpose he believed. But tonight she glanced up and continued. He sank into a wing-back chair and closed his eyes. When she concluded the piece, there was silence between them. He looked up and found her watching him.

"I don't suppose you were waiting up for me," he smiled ingenuously.

She sat erect on the bench, one hand gracefully cupping the other in her lap, as if she had just been auditioning. Her hair was swept up in a

French roll accentuating her elegant neck. "As a matter of fact, I wanted to talk to you."

He regarded her with heat in his eyes and his mouth pulled in an indecent smirk but she ignored his innuendo.

"Withers could benefit from some culture," she ventured.

"Withers *has* culture, my dear. It has you," he said, his lip curling almost to a sneer.

"Don't patronize me, Blake. I'm not a trophy for your mantle-piece."

His private amusement lingered about his eyes. With a barely perceptible lift of his chin, he asked, "What's on your mind, my love?"

She held his gaze, seeming to weigh whether it was worth proceeding, but then forged ahead. "It's about the old train station the railroad donated to the Enhancement Society last fall. You know the Society wants to turn it into an art gallery. We'll raise the funds to restore it. We plan to display the work of artists throughout the Cariboo-Chilcotin and sell for them. We want Town Council to donate the property beside the library and help with the cost of moving it from the railway lands."

"I gather you want something from me."

He looked serious enough. She took it as a sign it was safe to continue. "It won't be me who makes the presentation to Council, even though I'm president. It wouldn't look right, with you being on Council. Nettie, as vice-chair will make the request on behalf of the Society. If you speak in favour of it, enough of the others will support the motion."

"I can imagine how much you would enjoy getting in there and restoring the old station. It would be a project to suit your artistic talents."

She leaned forward, her eyes kindling. "It would be wonderful to see it come to life, Blake! The gallery could be a jewel for Withers. Imagine an art gallery here! With quality works, not cheap amateur trash, but *real art* that captures the spirit of the Cariboo."

"And why should I pitch this scheme to my fellow councillors?" he queried, his voice suddenly mean.

She recoiled, seeing his feigned support evaporate. She held his hard stare, not answering. She would not plead.

Her pride touched him in a way her ardour a moment before had not. "I'll think about it, Mary. It's an admirable project. We'll have to see what the budget will allow."

Guarded now, she merely inclined her head in a stiff nod. Then she rose and went in the direction of the bedroom. Blake busied himself at his desk in his study for a few minutes, tending to some of the accounts for the ranch, then turned out the lights and followed her to the bedroom.

Her back was to him as he entered. She had changed into in her nightgown and sat at her dressing table brushing her hair, now unpinned and cascading around her shoulders. A tightness clutched at him and he moved behind her and gathered her hair in his hands. "When will your delegation come before Council?" he asked, his voice low and gritty.

"Thursday."

"Hmm," he murmured. "Time enough for me to be persuaded to be in an accommodating frame of mind," he murmured, lifting her hair. He bent and planted his lips on the back of her neck. She pulled away.

"Blake don't."

But he twisted her hair in a knot and pulled her head back, kissing her hard on the mouth. The hair brush came up and struck his cheek with a sharp smack. His head jerked at the sting. He stood, fingers still coiled in her hair, looking down at her, his eyes narrow and lips thin. Caught in his grip, she glared back defiantly. Slowly, he released her, then wheeled abruptly and left the room. A moment later she heard the front door slam.

CHAPTER TWO

Following the fiasco at the town hall meeting, Gavin intensified his efforts to recruit volunteers for a committee. He canvassed local businesses methodically. The claim of the Chamber of Commerce chair proved accurate; people were hostile about the doomsday implications in Floyd's newspaper article. Time and again, he found himself disparaged and derided or—if he was lucky—merely dismissed. The moniker, *Noah,* leapt like a brushfire through the small town.

Even the weather turned bitter. Snow fell from a slate-coloured sky as he stopped by the hardware store. A bell above the door jangled when he entered. The owner, busy with a customer, glanced his way as he slipped past. He found what he was looking for at the far end of an aisle, a package of push pins to mount maps in his office. The pair up front gossiped about the minutiae of life in Withers. His ears pricked up when their voices muted suddenly. He sensed he was the subject. Despite their hushed voices, he heard, "…bet he's back there looking for thirty cubits of gopher wood." One of them barked a laugh. Gavin squared his shoulders and strode up to the cash register, tossing the item on the counter.

"Find everything you need?" the owner asked, ringing up the till.

Deadpan, he responded, "Couldn't find a tape measure in cubits. I guess you're sold out." The other reddened. He slapped down a bill and left without waiting for change.

Outside, he paused, forgetting for a moment where he was headed. Across the street a woman came out of the Overwaitea with several bags of groceries and struggled across the parking lot. The snow, thicker now, blew from the north. Despite the wintry weather, she was hatless, her blond hair tugged by the wind. He realized suddenly that her awkward gait was not just an effort to navigate the icy lot. Appalled, he shot across the street. "Let me help you with those bags," he cried. Her head jerked up at his sudden appearance. He gazed down into expressive green eyes, wide with startle, then narrowing to hot flame.

"You!"

"You're hurt. I'm so terribly sorry for your fall. Please, let me help you with your bags." He reached for them but she stepped back, her nostrils flaring.

"If you want to do something charitable, Galahad, donate some of your fun money to the Suzuki Foundation. That might offset some of the damage you did to the environment." She detoured around him with fierce determination in her fine cut jaw. He stood stupidly rooted to the spot and watched her put her bags in a pick-up and clamber in. The engine revved and she peeled out of the lot without giving him another glance.

In spite of the chill, he felt his face burn from her scolding. He deserved it he supposed. His Jeep *had* chewed up the logging road pretty badly that day.

Dr. Robbins shoes were visible through the hole in his chiropractor's bench; they were Nike's. He worked his thumbs into the muscles between Dana Oleson's spine and shoulder blades. "Mmm," she moaned. "That feels marvellous." He always massaged her after his adjustments, warming and loosening the tight muscles.

"Okay, girl, up you get," he said, assisting her to sit up. She swung her feet to the side and slid off the bench. While he wrote in her chart, she observed the framed photos on his walls. In one, he stood beside a silver racing cycle in a form-fitting blue and yellow cycling outfit, his helmet under his arm. In another, the photographer caught him with a full head of steam bent forward over the V-bar. A third showed him with a wide grin, holding a silver trophy overhead with both hands. There were other photos on his desk, she knew, but he was sitting on the corner of it and they were behind him.

"Going to see your Mom, today?" he asked.

"Yes."

"Tell her I'll pop in on Wednesday."

"Why don't you come today?"

"Can't. I want to get in twenty K."

"You're gonna ride *today*? It snowed again yesterday. It'll be hazardous."

"No worries. The ploughs have been out." He put down the chart and smiled at her. "Come here."

She approached and put her arms round his waist. He pulled her to him, kissing her. "I worry," she said. "I don't want you to get into an argument with a truck."

"Life is about risks," he chirped blithely. "Besides darling, the shoulders are wide."

She gave him a baleful look. "Are you talking about yours or the road?"

He stepped back and flexed his biceps, glancing at each shoulder. Then he shrugged. "The road of course. Anyway, it's time we *both* stepped up our training," he added, touching the end of her nose with his finger. "Competition season will be upon us in no time."

She put on her coat. "So will the wedding," she replied. "We need to do some planning before you're completely caught up in your calendar of races."

"We will, darling, we will."

———————

When Dana arrived at the nursing home, Viola Cameron was reading a fat novel. She'd grown frail but her eyesight was still good. Every week she would wade through a stack of books.

She brightened into a warm smile when Dana entered. "Hello, dear. It's so nice to see you." She said that every time Dana came, at least three times a week. Dana knew she meant it too. Viola picked up a folded newspaper from the bedside table and tucked it under her arm. "Let's go to the lounge," she said cozily, slipping her arm through Dana's.

Viola always read the paper cover to cover. Dana was generally too busy to read it herself. Her mother kept her abreast of the news on a regular basis. It gave them something to discuss when all other topics were exhausted.

"It might have been valuable for you to go to that meeting to hear what the man said," Viola remarked after outlining an article and voicing her concern.

"Do you really think it could flood again, Mom? I mean as bad as what you lived through? Withers has a dike now."

"You have no idea how powerful a river in full flood can be till you've seen it, Dana. Nothing in the world can resist the constant battering of tons of water. You should go and see this man. Find out what's being done."

"Okay, Mom. I'll stop by and have a talk with him."

———————

Gavin stood facing the wall of his office, a reference book open in his hand. The office was long and narrow, befitting its previous use as a barber shop. A battered desk and file cabinet he'd scrounged from Floyd were shoehorned in at the back. Both side walls were plastered with maps, charts and photos. He studied the text in his hand, then the map on the wall in front of him. Finding what he was looking for, he inserted a push pin.

The door from the street opened. He looked up expectantly to greet his very first visitor. But the welcome he had ready froze on his lips. Simultaneously, the casual entrance of the visitor came to an abrupt halt. Her eyes widened, flicking from side to side. *Looking for a speedy exit,* he thought.

"Oh!" was all she could muster.

Equally flustered, Gavin felt heat creep up his face.

"Are *you* Gavin McLeod?" she queried, holding up a folded newspaper.

He cleared an obstruction in his throat. "Do I have a choice?"

She groaned softly and looked down and away in a manner he found fetching. He wished he'd invested time since he'd last seen her to think of a gallant line to right things between them. She caught sight of his maps. Her eyes widened with sudden realization. "You were *scouting* when I ran into you on the trail."

He gave a self-deprecating shrug. "I guess you could call it that."

"I owe you an apology, Mr. McLeod. It never occurred to me you had business up there."

"No," he said. "I'm the one who should apologize. I did chew up the road pretty good and I spooked your horse. You took quite a fall. I feel terrible that you were hurt."

"Hazards of the job. I train horses for a living. My stallion is still pretty green. It's not the first time he's dumped me. Anyway, it wasn't as bad a fall as it probably looked. A magnificent bruise in a place I can't show. But otherwise, I'm fine."

"But you were limping so badly."

She laughed, lovely lines wreathing her small, sensuous mouth. "You had nothing to do with my limp. It's congenital. I was born with one leg shorter than the other."

"Oh! I'm sorry," he stammered, reddening, "I must have caught something from your horse. Hoof and mouth disease or something."

She gave a gentle laugh. "It's no big deal. It doesn't stop me from doing the things I love."

"Like riding."

"Mm-hmm. It's a much better way to see the country around here than your SUV."

"I don't know how to ride," he admitted.

"I also *teach* riding," she smiled, her rejoinder sounding like an invitation.

"I don't think I'll be around long enough to learn. The extent of my equestrian experience is when my mother would take me to the carnival when I was a boy." He described a tight flat circle in the air with his finger.

"You know those pony rides where they're attached to a big wagon wheel contraption."

She laughed again, the sound of it musical. "How long *will* you be here, Mr. McLeod?"

"Long enough that you can call me Gavin," he replied.

She extended her hand. "How do you do, Gavin? I'm Dana Oleson."

He took her hand in his. "Hello Dana." When she eased her hand out of his he realized he'd been staring into her brilliant green eyes. "I gather you didn't come in here to drum up business for your riding academy."

"No," she said, turning to the maps. "It's about your article. Is the threat of flood this year really that serious?"

"It depends," he said, hooking his thumbs into his pockets. He spent the next half hour talking with her, pointing out features on the various charts. She asked lots of questions and gave him the benefit of some of her own local knowledge.

"My mother lived through the flood of '48," she told him. "She's in a nursing home here in town. She's who brought my attention to your article. My mother's a gutsy lady. She handled the situation like everyone else did in those days, just rolled up her sleeves and did what needed to be done. People had pioneer spirit back then. There wasn't the kind of damage like in the south. Still, it made a lasting impression on her. She has vivid memories of it. "

"People ought to listen to your mother. Things may go just fine this year and the threat be just that, a passing threat. But I worry about the denial I've seen here."

"Denial?"

"So far, people don't seem to be taking the risk seriously." He paused, his eyes falling on a statistical report on the wall. "The depth of the snow in the mountains isn't just a statistic. It's caused problems all winter long. Wildlife is having difficulty finding food. Trees have snapped from the weight. Sure that happens every winter, but not to the degree we've seen. It's so deep it caused towers for high voltage power-lines to crumple like cardboard. All that snow up there has to come down the valley in the form of water. It's all a matter of how quickly that happens. Could be worse than in '48."

"But Withers didn't have a dike then."

He was silent a moment, struggling with something. Finally he spoke. "Friday is predicted to have clear skies. I'm planning on meeting a pilot at the airstrip south of town. I want to go up and take a look around from the air. If you're not busy, you could come along and see for yourself."

Her eyes widened. "In a plane?"

He nodded, holding his hands up to his shoulders, fingers extended sideways and waggled. "Yeah, one of those little twin-engine jobs."

"I...I've never flown before."

"I don't know. You flew pretty good the other day," he grinned.

She pinked beautifully, a dimple appearing when she smiled. "What's the deal?" she asked. "Why are you asking *me* to go?"

He sighed. "I'd like to think I could convince at least one citizen of this town to heed the warning," he said.

She hesitated, then nodded "Okay. I guess I can steal away from the stable for an hour or two."

She left a few minutes later after they exchanged details of when and where to meet. He watched her cross the street. A cyclist, looking out of place in the wintry scene, peddled down from the highway and pulled up beside her. With an unexpected lurch in his stomach, Gavin watched them kiss. He thought of Celeste. Regret and envy wrestled inside him. The cyclist dismounted and accompanied Dana down the street out of sight. Gavin shook himself to dislodge the feelings threatening to darken his mood and turned back to his work on the wall.

Friday dawned clear and cold, black-green hills etched against a dazzling blue sky. Dana appeared at his office on the dot of 8:00 a.m. They climbed into his Cherokee and headed south on the highway. He quizzed her about what she remembered of her mother's accounts of the flood of '48.

"They drove the cattle up into the hills. People helped each other. I always thought she took it in her stride till the other day when she was so insistent I come to see you. Guess I never thought about it much before."

"You said she lives in a nursing home in town."

"Yes. There's nothing wrong with her mentally, thank goodness. But she got really frail. It just wasn't safe for her to be on the farm anymore. It wasn't my idea. She felt it was time to go before things got to a stage where I'd be afraid for her to be at home. It was really sad for me. But when Viola Cameron gets an idea in her mind, no one is going to dissuade her."

"Cameron?" he queried, looking confused. "I thought your name was Oleson."

"It is," Dana nodded. "The Camerons are my foster family. But they're the only family I know—or care to."

In half an hour they reached a small airstrip. They met the pilot in the office. He led them out to a twin engine Cessna and they waited while he did his walk-around. Dana seemed keyed up for her virgin flight, giving Gavin a bright-eyed glance. They clambered aboard, Gavin up front and Dana behind the pilot. In a few moments they were airborne. He turned to get her reaction but she was glued to the side window. The next time he looked back, she must have seen his movement in her peripheral vision for she turned to him. "This is great," she shouted, grinning widely. He felt ridiculous delight.

Their flight path took them north toward Withers, on the opposite side of the river. "There's the reserve," she shouted again. He looked where she was pointing. The First Nations reserve was one area he was concerned about. A gravel road connected the village with the highway where it crossed the river at the north end of town. This side of the river had no dike. The councillor at the town-hall meeting had said a few houses suffered flooding from time to time. From the air it was easy to pick out which ones were most at risk...maybe fifteen. He suspected most had not existed in 1948. The only option for protecting them would be sandbagging. He made a mental note to get more accurate information later.

At Gavin's direction, the pilot flew back to the Withers' side of the river. The town lay in the valley floor between the dike and hills rising to the east. Homes in the eastern hills would be safe from flooding but if the dike did not hold, they would become marooned. As they continued north, Dana tugged at his sleeve and pointed down. "That's my place."

"Which one?" Gavin hollered.

"See the horses in that paddock?"

He nodded and motioned to the pilot to circle around. He grinned at her and she grinned back in appreciation. The right wing dipped and the Cessna slipped around the points of the compass, shaving off altitude. Though the buzz of the plane should not have affected the horses, it seemed otherwise, for just then the whole herd—about a dozen—leapt into mad flight. The paddock was small enough to turn them in a wide circle and large enough to allow a full gallop.

"Oh no!" Dana exclaimed.

"What's wrong?"

"Oh it's just... You see that grey mare?"

"Well, I can't actually see that it's a mare from here." She reached forward and punched him lightly on the arm. He laughed.

"She's a landscape horse," she shouted.

"What's a landscape horse?"

"Nice to look at but not much good for riding. She has bad legs. She shouldn't be running right now 'cause her knees are swollen but she's caught up in the excitement of the herd."

They circled once more. In that time the herd's sprint ended. Gavin said something to the pilot Dana couldn't hear, then turned to her and shouted, "We're heading for the high country now. That's where we'll get a good look at the snow."

They crossed the river again and tacked north-west, over increasingly rugged terrain. Here the vegetation was thicker. After a while Dana shouted, "I know this area. I did a trip up here on horse-back a few years ago. There's a camp nearby with some cabins."

All three scanned the mountains below. The pilot pointed down to the left.

"That's it," Dana cried.

In a clearing were four buildings. Only the top third of them was visible; the roofs shouldered a blanket of snow many feet thick. The road in was impassable. They continued another quarter hour. The elevation of the mountains climbed higher and higher. Granite peaks thrust upward, the saddles between choked with snow. Tracks of avalanches were everywhere.

They crossed a high voltage power-line. After some consultation between Gavin and the pilot, the aircraft veered in and followed the line. After another few minutes, they all sat forward in unison. Ahead, a tower was bent almost in two. A helicopter with a cable hanging down, hovered above it. A second helicopter perched on the ground and a crew laboured nearby. They passed over and circled to return to base.

On the ride back into town, Gavin asked about the camp Dana had pointed out. "That's where it really hit me finally how much snow there is," she said. "From the air, it was the only solid reference I had."

"The camp looked pretty remote."

"It's an equestrian base camp. There're miles of horse trails around there."

"I'd like to be able to look around on the ground when the weather turns. Are there trails around Withers?"

"Loads of them," she replied.

"Accessible only by horseback?"

"You could hike them too, if you're a hiker."

"I am."

She looked over at him and smiled. "Yeah. But horseback really is the best way to see the back country."

"Oh really?" he arched a sceptical brow. "Why is that?"

"One, you can cover more territory. Two, you have a better view from the back of a horse. Three, you've always got company. Four, your feet don't give out. And five, the horse will smell a bear long before you know it's there and tell you to turn around."

Gavin laughed. "Okay, you convinced me. But as I said, I never learned to ride."

"And as *I* said, I teach. Do horses scare you?"

"No," he said. "On the contrary, I was always drawn to them. In the city, mounted police were always around events with crowds. I'd drag my mother over so I could pet them. She used to take me to the Pacific National Exhibition. I always wanted to go through the horse palace and look in all the box stalls. I loved touching them and feeding them sugar cubes when their caretakers weren't looking."

Dana laughed. "I've seen kids like you at the shows. Hanging over stall doors, eyes as big as saucers, wanting to feed them and at the same time terrified of getting bitten. I've competed in the PNE," she added.

"No shit. That's a pretty big horse show isn't it?"

"Yeah, it's an important event."

"Win any ribbons?"

"Some."

"I'm impressed."

"To tell the truth, I'm not that big on the competitive side of the business, at least not for myself. It's teaching I really like. Especially the kids. They're a ball. I get a lot more kick out of seeing one of *them* get a ribbon. It's such a thrill for them. They're so proud. It's really what gives me a sense of accomplishment."

Gavin smiled with new appreciation. The more he listened to her, the more he really liked this woman. He tried to stop his train of thought when he realized he was comparing her to Celeste.

"You think you could teach me enough to get by?"

"Yeah. I could... if you want a few lessons. I could take you out on some of the trails when the snow melts."

They topped the hill where Gavin had got his first view of the town when he'd arrived in Withers. As they coasted downhill, he eased the speed back to the posted limits.

"Gavin?"

"Yeah."

"Each time you told me about your experience with horses, you mentioned your mother. Didn't your Dad ever take you places?"

"Not much. My Dad was away a lot when I was little."

"What did he do?"

"He was a boxer. When he wasn't on the road, he was training. And when he wasn't training..." he trailed off, a grim set to his jaw.

Finding the unfinished sentence more uncomfortable than what it might hide, she prompted, "When he wasn't training...?"

He rolled his eyes in a rueful look. "Sometimes I don't know when to shut up. But since you ask, when he wasn't on the road or training, he was apt to be on a bender, or in jail."

"I'm sorry."

"Don't be. It took me a while, but I eventually realized his failings are no reflection on me." Silently, he wondered how true that was. Intellectually he believed it, but at a gut level...?

He turned down the street by The Winchester and pulled into the parking space next to Dana's truck.

"Thanks for asking me to go flying, Gavin. It was a real thrill for me."

"I may draw in a favour from you for it."

"What? Free lessons?"

"No. Those I'll pay for. I may ask you to lend your voice to the cause, though. Help people grasp how much frozen water is sitting uphill from them and to not put all their trust in the dike holding it back."

"No problem. Be glad to."

Back at his room, he checked his email. There was only one, from Perce. And he didn't sugar-coat his displeasure over the tab running up on Gavin's assignment with no appreciable progress made.

Gavin combed his fingers through his hair. Perce was right. He hadn't had any response to his call for volunteers. The town council was taking no initiative; staff and councillors humoured him but took no real action.

He stepped next door to the Withers Gazette. A half-wall with windows above it separated the front office from the back room, where a small press turned out the weekly paper. In the back, Floyd acknowledged him with a nod. When he finished what he was doing, he came forward, wiping his inky hands with a cloth. A crease split his forehead. "What can I do for you, Mr. McLeod?"

"Hi Floyd. How's business?"

"Okay I guess. Is there a problem with your office?" He felt a reserve from Floyd that hadn't been there before.

"No, no, the office is fine. It's just what I need. I came to see you about publicity."

"Publicity?"

"I was hoping you could do another story and get some press on the heavy snow conditions. I took a flight over the mountains above the basin this morning and—"

"More press on the notion of a flood isn't a good idea," Floyd cut in, shaking his downcast head.

Gavin's mouth still hung open on his unfinished sentence. He collected himself. "Why's that?"

Floyd shifted from one foot to the other. "Well, we've done that story. People want to move on."

"Move on? People may not want to hear about it, but they need to. And *I* need volunteers."

Floyd grimaced, his mouth in an obstinate line. He shook his head. "Now Mr. McLeod, I'd like to help you but I'm a businessman."

"Gee I must be misinformed," Gavin said grimly, "but I was always under the impression that bad news was good business for newspapers."

"That's true in the large presses. Selling newspapers in the big city is an impersonal affair. You'll go back where you came from and after a couple of months no one will remember your name. But I gotta live here."

Gavin studied Floyd through narrowed eyes. The newspaperman struck him as an amiable guy, but something—or somebody—had got to him. "Well, maybe you're right," he back-peddled. "Another story might be too 'in your face' for folks at this point." Floyd's expression relaxed, reinforcing his hunch. "Maybe there's a more unobtrusive way to proceed," he said.

Floyd's brow creased again. "For who to proceed?"

Gavin chuckled gently. "Easy Floyd. I've no wish to drag you into a partisan conflict. Maybe I could pay for a classified ad. Ads don't represent the views of the newspaper and they get buried in the back. How 'bout it?"

Floyd eyed him uncertainly, then curled his mouth in a friendly grin. "You make it sound kinda clandestine. Sure," he said, sitting down at his desk, picking up a pen. "Tell me what you want it to say."

Gavin dictated a brief solicitation for volunteers. As Floyd scratched the last sentence down, Gavin turned away, clearing his throat. "There are one or two locals who *are* concerned about the possibility of a flood," he said casually.

Floyd's head came up. "Who?"

"One is a long time citizen of Withers," he added, turning back.

"Who?" Floyd repeated.

"Mrs. Viola Cameron, for one."

Floyd's eyes widened, perhaps in recognition.

"And her daughter, Dana Oleson. Miss Oleson took the flight with me this morning. She can attest to the amount of snow up there in the mountains."

"Really?" Floyd responded with apparent interest. He seemed to be considering something, then shook his head and stood up. "Your ad will be in this week."

Gavin flashed a smile. Floyd shook his hand more warmly than he expected. He returned to his office thinking there was more going on in this town than he could figure.

The newspaper ad still brought no response to his call for volunteers. Deciding to take a break from the problem, he called Dana at the number she'd given him and booked a riding lesson. Hanging up, he felt more jaunty than he had in days.

He found her place easily from her directions, north of town. He knew its approximate location, having seen it from the air. He drove down the lane toward a well-kept white clapboard house with dark green trim.

She'd told him to look for her around the stable or indoor arena. Inside the stable's open double-wide doors, a corridor was flanked by opposing rows of box stalls. The stable emanated a pleasant horsey scent. The iron grating above each stall door was fastened back in the open position. Rustling sounds suggested that some stalls were occupied and when Gavin hallooed for a human response, a couple of curious equine heads emerged. He meandered down the row, stopping to observe several more occupants that had not been drawn away from their breakfast. They appeared well fed and contented. He stopped to rub the face of one hanging its head over its stable door. It lipped the front of his jacket, leaving a greenish smear. "Hi there, fella," he murmured softly. As an afterthought he leaned to one side and peered down over the door. "You *are* a fella, aren't you?"

He continued to the far end where the corridor opened into a cavernous interior space. He heard the rhythmic sound of hoof-beats in a gentle canter. As he approached, horse and rider passed by the opening. Stepping inside the enclosed arena, he saw bleachers to the right, behind a board fence. He climbed to the top and sat in the shadows.

He recognized Dana's mount from the first day he'd encountered them. They worked their way round in front of him again, then cut across the diagonal in a figure eight. The black was a looker all right, powerful muscles rippling under his sleek haunch, his neck curved in a smooth arc, nostrils flaring, his blown breath audible with each stride.

They described three more figure eights. At the centre of each, the stallion's forelegs changed leads in a motion as lovely as ballet. Gavin knew Dana had to be sending him signals to guide his seemingly effortless performance, but he never saw any movement that betrayed her.

They circled the arena once more, then turned straight down the centre toward him. The black halted at some unseen signal about thirty yards from the fence directly in front of him. Dana reached forward with a gloved hand and gave the animal several sturdy pats. The reins relaxed and the horse shook his head as if to get the kinks out. It was then she spied him.

"Hi," she called, the sound hollow in the cavernous shell above the ring.

"Hi," he answered. As he climbed down, she urged her mount forward to the railing.

"You're early," she said.

"Yeah, I didn't know how much preparation there might be. I'm glad I got here early. That was quite a show."

She patted the stallion again. "He's very talented, this guy. He's doing really well for still being so young."

Gavin reached an outstretched palm to the horse's muzzle, then pulled back slightly. "May I?" he asked.

"Sure. He's got a nice disposition to go with his talent."

"And his looks! He's stunning. What's his name?"

"Nefarious."

"Nefarious? Oh hey!" he said, letting the velvet muzzle graze his palm. "You're not wicked are you, boy?" He slid his hand up the horse's jowl, finding a spot behind his ear and scratched. Nefarious stretched his neck slightly toward him, drooping his eyelids in rapture.

Dana chuckled. "He'll be your friend for life. You've found his erogenous zone."

Gavin grinned a lop-sided grin. "You like that do you, big boy?"

She swung down off the saddle. "I'll put him away and get you set up." She led him back into the stable, cross-tied the black in the aisle and removed his saddle. As she brushed his coat, Gavin had a view out a side door to a paddock. A grey mare ambled into view. Nefarious lifted his head and let out an ear-splitting whinny. The grey halted, head erect, ears pricked.

Gavin let out a laugh. "He seems to be rather enamoured of her."

Dana snickered. "Now you know why he's called Nefarious. Nefertiti is his mother."

"Hah! You should've called him Oedipus."

She brought out the gelding Gavin had introduced himself to on the way in. She handed him a brush and gave him some pointers on grooming. "It's a good way to get acquainted with a horse you're going to ride. Jake here, is a what-you-see-is-what-you-get kind of guy. Nothing sneaky or unpredictable about him. You two will get along fine."

She brought out a western saddle and handed it to Gavin while she put a blanket on Jake. She showed him how to adjust the saddle and check the cinch for tightness. Back in the arena, she snapped a lunge line onto the halter ring below the horse's chin.

Simply in getting his foot in the stirrup and hauling himself up, Gavin gained a new respect for the apparent ease with which Dana had sprung onto Nefarious after her fall. His heart fluttered a little when he saw how far away the ground was. He was grateful she seemed in no hurry for anything to happen. She explained about ergonomics, of finding natural good posture, something he could relate to from keying at his laptop. Her easy way of speaking mirrored what she was explaining, about quietness of body and hands. She put him at ease.

Stepping back and letting out a length of the lunge line, she asked him to do nothing but experience Jake step out and walk around her in a circle. She gave all the signals to Jake, letting Gavin concentrate on how it felt to be transported. He enjoyed the rocking motion and how his spine undulated.

"How y'doing?" she asked.

He realized foolishly he was grinning like a kid. He let go of the reins. "Look Ma, no hands."

An hour later, he gratefully climbed down from the saddle, feeling a weakness in his inner thighs he knew would give him grief tomorrow morning. But he was amazed at how much he'd learned in an hour, albeit, all at a walk. They put Jake away. Dana told him to come up to the house; she'd give him a receipt. He went to retrieve his wallet from the glove-box of the Cherokee.

He knocked on the screen door; she'd left the inside one ajar. "Come on in," he heard her call from nearby. Closing the outside door behind him, he stepped into a spacious hallway. Every available space on the walls was filled with framed photographs of people, some in colour, some in black and white. "I'm in here," she spoke. He followed her voice to the doorway on the left. She was writing in a ledger. He laid cash on her desk. "Thanks. I'll get your receipt in a sec." He returned to the hallway and perused the photos. Most were of boys, adolescent and younger. Each one had a date hand-written on them, presumably when the photo was taken. He found Dana's picture as a teenager among them.

He heard her tear off the receipt and come out. She handed it to him. "Thanks," he said, pocketing it. "Who are all these kids?"

She smiled. "Welcome to the rogues' gallery. My foster family."

"All these?" he exclaimed, incredulous.

"Mm-hmm. My foster parents had no children of their own but they loved kids so they took in foster children. Some came for a short while and went back to their families. But many lived here till they were old enough to be on their own—me included. Thirty of us, all told."

Gavin gave a low whistle. She stepped up beside him when he got to a black and white of a woman standing in front of the house in a house-dress and apron. "That's my foster mother." She looked like the mother of everybody's dreams. Gavin could almost smell the apple pie baking in the oven. "And this is my Dad, my foster Dad." A man in baggy pants held up by suspenders clutched the lead shank of a draft horse with a wide white blaze. Sitting astride the gentle giant was a curly headed elf. Gavin glanced at Dana who peered at the picture with soft eyes.

"Is that you?" he asked.

She smiled wistfully, a sentimental pout playing around her mouth. She nodded. "He's the one who got me started on horses, as you can see."

"Who? The horse or your foster father?"

She chuckled. "Both, actually. But I meant Dad. This was taken just a couple of weeks after I arrived."

Gavin focused in on the face of the child. He could see the resemblance. The blond curls had relaxed but the bright eyes above a determined chin were unmistakable. "How old were you?"

"Four."

Gavin noted the date and did a quick calculation in his head. That put her age now at seven less than his own thirty-four.

"Where are they all now?" Gavin asked, waving at the wall full of boys.

"All over. Prince George, Calgary, Vancouver, Montreal, even New Zealand. Mom gets phone calls and cards from all over."

"All boys but you?"

"Yes."

"Yet you're the one who's taken over the farm."

"It just worked out that way. I'm a country girl at heart. I had no desire to leave. This place is all I've ever known, all I remember. I was still here when Dad died. I stayed on to be with Mom. I had ambitions of breeding horses and having a riding academy and was able to get my business started here. Then when Mom got so frail, she insisted she wasn't going to be a burden to me. She came up with the scheme. I would never have been able to afford to buy this place at market value. She had her lawyer draw up this arrangement. I augment her pension that covers the cost of her care at the home and the farm is mine. I had to go into debt to turn the barn into a horse stable and get the indoor arena built. It's tight, but I'm managing."

Gavin felt a sick sensation in his stomach. He didn't let on, though. As he drove away he wondered what would happen to Dana if the town didn't heed the signs and was unlucky come early summer. She stood to lose her home and stable—her dream, her living.

The message on his voice mail when he got back to his office was curt, "Gavin, it's Perce. Call me." Feeling guilty, as if he'd been playing hooky, which his riding lesson certainly might be construed, he called his boss's direct line at PEP. "What the hell is going on up there, McLeod?"

He gulped. "Going on? What do you mean?"

"Don't play cute with me, wise-ass. The director is coming down on my backside because of complaints streaming into Victoria."

"Complaints?"

"Complaints!" Perce bellowed. "To every department you can think of—Tourism, Agriculture, Air, Land and Water, not to mention PEP."

"Withers people are making calls to Victoria about what I'm doing here?"

"That's what I'm saying isn't it?"

Gavin winced. "What are they upset about?"

"You tell me, Buster!"

Gavin ran his fingers through his hair. Perce could blow a lot of hot air when he was under stress—like pressure from higher ups.

"Look Perce, we've seen this sort of thing before, people initially responding to the threat of a disaster with denial. Folks in small towns don't trust outsiders explaining about their environment that they think they understand."

"I don't need your excuses, McLeod. It's costing the department several thousand bucks a month to put you up there to get a plan together. You haven't even got to first base yet."

"I just need a bit of time."

"You ain't got time! The river will crest anywhere from nine to ten weeks from now and you better hope that town is prepared. If it's not and things turn ugly, your ass is grass."

"I've made a connection here and there and—"

"You've made enemies too! Screw up again and you'll be back here flying a desk. I'll send a man who can do the job right."

"It'll happen, Perce. I promise you," he said with more assurance than he felt.

"It better!"

After he hung up, he paced his office. He hadn't realized people's reactions were this bad. Sure, some individuals had been kind of hostile but Perce said there were *numerous* callers. Or had he? He tried to remember his exact words. He'd said there were calls to various departments, including his own. Were different people making a single call each or was it the work or one or two disgruntled locals?

Whatever the source, he needed to get a committee together somehow, and soon.

Snow in the valley disappeared over a few days of spring-like weather. Good Friday dawned one of those glorious clear mornings. Businesses were closed, as was Town Hall and the library. Earlier in the week Gavin had intended to take the opportunity of the four day weekend to get home, but another disagreeable telephone conversation with Celeste caused him to think better of it.

He awoke early. Still in pyjamas, he drew back the curtain in his east-facing room on the second floor of The Winchester. Wisps of cloud hung in a sapphire sky, painted rosy pink along the horizon by the sun, not yet up from behind the hills. He decided to take the day off along with everyone else and indulge himself. He would go hiking, exploring some of the trails he'd made note of on maps he'd been poring over.

He showered, then breakfasted at Mandy's café, persuading her to pack him a sandwich in a bag to take on the trail. The Cherokee pulled out of the back lot behind the hotel shortly after eight a.m. His destination was the hills northeast of town. He sped past a church. Suddenly, he jumped on the brakes, coming to an abrupt halt. He reversed fifty feet or so, scrounged in the console for a pencil and scrap of paper. He scribbled something down from the church signboard and then continued on his way.

He sauntered down the trail along the edge of a marsh. The last few hours had done much to restore his mood. He'd trekked a trail winding through a mix of forest and meadow; the unspoiled landscape had a rejuvenating effect. On the return hike, he felt renewed in spite of the effects on his legs from the hours of hiking.

The marsh opened onto a pond. At the far end of it, the trail divided. He was just about to swing onto the left fork when movement caught his eye. He halted, peering through the trees. With the next motion, he realized it was a horse's tail, switching at an insect. He crept toward it. It was a grey and saddled, but riderless.

When he neared the horse, he spotted a child squatting low to the ground. He was staring at something, oblivious to Gavin's presence. Not wanting to startle the boy, he deliberately stepped on a twig, snapping it. The child turned abruptly, still crouching and stared at him. Gavin recognized him at once. He was the boy who had been with Blake Logan the day he'd arrived in Withers.

"Hi there," Gavin smiled. "I noticed your horse. Is everything alright?"

The boy didn't reply. He met Gavin's gaze with the unselfconsciousness of a child. He didn't smile, but neither did he appear frightened. "You okay?" Gavin asked again.

After a second's hesitation, the boy gave a slight nod.

"What are you looking at that's so interesting?"

Again the hesitation, then he replied softly, "A beaver."

"Really?" Gavin remarked, hushing his voice. "May I see?" The answering nod was more eager and Gavin came and crouched beside him.

"It's workin' on a tree," the boy whispered.

Sure enough, about 50 yards away through the underbrush he spotted a fat beaver gnawing on a branch of a small, felled tree.

"Did you see the tree come down?" Gavin spoke softly.

"Yes! That's how I noticed him."

"He'll use some of that tree to reinforce his dam or lodge I bet, and the rest to feed his family."

The boy turned to look at him. "How do you know?"

"Beavers use all parts of the tree."

"Do they eat the wood?"

"No, just leaves and bark. They like plants that grow in the water too."

"How do you know he has a family?"

"I don't really. In fact, *he* could be a she. Beavers mate for life though, and have babies every year that may stay with the family for several years before going out their own. Considering the size of the lodge and dam we can see, there's probably been a colony here for years."

Just then the beaver began dragging the now mostly stripped trunk to the water where it propelled it toward the dam.

"Do you know they can close their lips behind those big teeth?" The boy shook his head, eyebrows arching in surprise. "That way they don't drown when they do what he's doing or when they dive with sticks to build their dams. They also have special see-through eyelids and valves in their ears and nose that close under water."

"How long can they stay under water?"

"A lot longer than you or I. Up to 15 minutes." They watched the beaver climb up onto the dam, dragging the trunk.

"Do they ever break a tooth, you know, like people sometimes do?"

"They're pretty well equipped in that department too. Their teeth keep growing all their life and they have a lot of iron in them that make their teeth very strong."

The boy looked up at him. He met his open, curious gaze. He was a lovely child, eyes like pools of rain, deep chocolate brown with lashes his teen-aged step-daughter would kill for. After a moment, the boy turned back to the pond. "Hey, he dived!" He leapt to his feet. Gavin stood up too, stretching his cramped legs.

Looking up at him, the boy asked, "How come you know so much about beavers?"

Gavin's mouth curled up on one side at the boy's hungry curiosity. "Partly because I'm interested in creatures that live in the wild and partly because it helps to know a lot about ponds and rivers and the habitat around them for my job. Do you know what I mean by habitat?"

"It means the surroundings where things live, doesn't it?"

"Exactly."

"Do you have to know in case the habitat gets flooded?"

It was Gavin's turn to be surprised. "It sounds like you've heard about me already. I have to apologize for my manners," he said. "I haven't properly introduced myself."

"You're Mr. Noah."

Gavin snorted a laugh which was half amusement, half chagrin. "Actually my name's not Noah, it's Gavin McLeod." The boy hung his head as if caught doing something wrong. "That's okay," Gavin added softly. "People have a hard time understanding my job. Sometimes they don't like things they hear from me. They're making fun when they call me Noah."

The boy lifted his face to him. "What exactly is your job, Mr. McLeod?"

"You can call me Gavin."

A pause ensued and then the boy spoke again. "What is your job, Mr. Gavin?"

His funny bone was tickled unexpectedly and he laughed aloud. "Whoa, young fellow, I've told you my name. What's yours?"

"Todd."

"Todd Logan?"

A nod.

Gavin placed his hands on his hips. He liked this boy's uncomplicated way. "My job, Todd, is to help people handle emergencies and to make plans to try to prevent disasters. You said something just now about a flood. What have you been hearing about that?"

"That you've been saying there's going to be bad flooding. But my Dad says it's not true."

Gavin pondered how to respond. Giving a young boy reason to have nightmares wasn't in his job description. And he certainly wasn't about to set a child up to oppose his father—especially a man like Blake Logan. But he knew he was looking into intelligent eyes and this boy would not be put off by a snow job, so to speak.

"I don't know if there will be a bad flood, Todd. I do know there was a lot of snow this winter. Nobody knows how fast it will melt. When it does, the river will rise like it does every spring. Some years, the river floods, sometimes a lot, sometimes a little. There's lots people can do to get ready in case it floods badly. That's why I'm here, to help people make plans, just in case."

Todd looked back in the direction the beaver had disappeared. "Will the beaver be alright if it floods?"

"Our friend over there is an expert at coping with water from snowmelt and rain. In cities or towns their dams can be a nuisance, flooding homes and property. But in the wild, they create a habitat for all kinds of creatures—fish, amphibians, insects, birds. Their dams actually help *prevent* problem flooding because they flood an area gradually. The marshes make the land spongy so it can soak up a *lot* of water. No worries for the beaver. I do have some advice for *you*, though, Todd, and I hope you'll listen to it."

The young eyes fastened on him again. "In these next few weeks, the river and streams will be dangerous. You need to stay well away from them. Promise me you will."

"Okay, Mr. Gavin."

"It's just Gavin, Todd," he said with a grin. "By the way, the horse you're riding looks an awful lot like Dana Oleson's horse, Nefertiti.

"It is Nefertiti!" he said joyfully. "She lets me ride her 'cause she knows I won't make her run. 'Cept, she's not Miss Oleson's horse, she's Dr. Robbins'."

"Who's Dr. Robbins?"

"Miss Oleson's boyfriend."

"Her boyfriend?" Gavin narrowed his eyes. "Does Dr. Robbins ride a bicycle?"

"Yes! He's a racer." Todd declared with enthusiasm.

"I see." He pointed over his shoulder in the direction of his Jeep. "Are you headed this way?"

"No. I go that way," Todd answered, pointing down the other fork.

"Need help getting on Nefertiti?"

"I usually find a rock or log to stand on, but if I can put my knee in your hands I can get up."

"Okay cub, let me give you a leg up."

Gavin waved goodbye to him and made his way back along the trail. Todd struck him as the kind of kid he wished he had, a boy or girl to take hiking, tell the secrets of the universe and tuck into bed. It had been a crushing blow when he'd been told that the mumps that made him critically ill in university also stripped him of any possibility of fathering his own child.

He'd been candid with Celeste before they married and she'd assured him it didn't matter; she didn't want another child. He'd had such hopes when he'd married her that her daughter would form a bond with him. Amber had been about the age then that Todd was now. But Amber had never seen him as anything more than a source of pocket money and an unwelcome intruder in the manipulative relationship she had with her mother.

An hour later, he gratefully yanked off his boots in his room and stretched out on the bed with a sigh. He lay motionless for a moment feeling the pleasant ache in his body seep into the mattress. Abruptly, he sat up and turned to the night table by the bed and opened the drawer. He pulled out the thin phone book for Withers and half a dozen other Cariboo communities. He flipped open the yellow pages. His finger ran up and down columns till it came to rest on what he was looking for. He stabbed the spot with his finger. *Dr. Jeremy Robbins,* he mused, snapping the book shut, *Chiropractor.*

CHAPTER THREE

The moment he passed under the Gothic arch of the open church doors, the scent of Easter lilies swamped Gavin's senses. Memories surfaced from an almost forgotten time; sitting in a church pew in short pants, hair combed and greased, bored and uncomfortable, his mother's hand on his knee to stop him swinging his legs. He couldn't remember his father ever going to church but his mother had insisted her son attend, even long after his father had left them. In his late-teens he finally won the contest of wills and refused to attend anymore.

He found a seat on the outside end of a long pew near the back. The discomfort of a suit and tie on this warm day, with a two hour service ahead made him feel just as confined as he had all those years ago. He wondered why it had seemed like such a good idea two days ago. The conversation with Perce had made him desperate.

As he watched the seats fill up, he was glad he'd arrived early. It seemed like all of Withers turned out on this holiest day of the Christian calendar. Both men that Blake Logan joined at the Dream-Catcher on his first day in town arrived. He'd since learned their names and a little about them. The one steering his wife by the elbow, two teenaged boys following disconsolately behind, was Seth Colville. Turned out, he *was* a rancher. The other, Clint Murdock, strolled with his wife toward a pew up front. Murdock owned the Withers Gazette. He was reported to be fairly wealthy, having made his money in mining. He had two grown daughters, both married and moved away.

He noticed Mayor Hale, with his family, and Lorraine Connor the receptionist at Town Hall with her husband. Noel Conner was the Town's manager of Engineering. Gavin's pulse quickened at the sight of a now familiar limp. Somehow he hadn't expected to see Dana here. Dr. Robbins escorted her. Gavin felt a stab at the comfortable way she clutched his arm. It came as no surprise to see Logan, or to observe him glad-handing his way down the aisle. What did surprise him was that Logan was alone.

Just then the background organ music surged into the first strident chords of the processional hymn. It ushered in the choir, singing as it filed in from the back of the church. The congregation rose and joined in. The first five pairs in the choir were children, among them, Todd Logan. In a white choir gown, he looked artificially angelic. He was glad he'd already seen the boy in a more natural setting.

Junior and senior choir members took their places in the loft at the front. At the conclusion of the hymn, they sat in unison. Less orderly, and noisily the congregation followed suit. At a signal from the organist, the children's choir rose again. The organist stood to lead them in an unaccompanied hymn. That's when Gavin noticed her; it was Mary Logan.

The warm April sun streamed through the windows and as the morning wore on, turned the sanctuary into a stultifying sauna. Gavin longed to remove his jacket, comforted only by the knowledge that every other male was suffering the same torment. He'd hoped that by coming to church on Easter Sunday, he would advance his ratings with at least some locals. But no one had acknowledged him, even though he saw quite a few familiar faces. He felt invisible and increasingly out of place. It had been a dumb idea to come. Long before the final hymn, he decided to slip away as quickly as possible.

But he'd overlooked the tradition of having to shake the reverend's hand at the door. He got caught in the queue. Making the best of it as the line shuffled forward, he tried to catch people's eyes but to no avail. Two more steps, one more, then it was his turn; a hasty explanation to the pastor that he was a visitor and at last—freedom. He cut across the lawn dodging clumps of people conversing and made a beeline for his Cherokee.

But then he heard his name called. He turned. Waving at him to wait, Dana stood on the top step, her below-the-knee dress billowing slightly in the breeze. He groaned inwardly. He was in no mood to meet her fiancé and wished he'd pretended he hadn't heard. She started across to him, walking more awkwardly than usual. The slender spikes on her shoes sank into the soft lawn with each step.

"Stay there," he called. "I'll come to you."

When he joined her, she asked, breathless, "You're not leaving are you?"

He gave her a sardonic grin. "Almost had a clean getaway."

"But it's Easter."

He looked at her quizzically, then she laid one of those delicate hands on his sleeve and laughed musically. "Of course, you wouldn't know. There's always a luncheon after the Easter Sunday service. You *will* stay, won't you." She leaned forward conspiratorially. "It's a good way for you to meet people who might help out on your committee."

He would have gone anywhere she asked as long as she kept that hand on his arm. Besides, she was right; it was a golden opportunity and was what he came for. "Will I be permitted to remove this dam…ah, I mean my jacket?" he pleaded.

She laughed again, "Tell the truth, Gavin. You don't do church as a regular thing, do you?"

He gave a wry look, "True confession time? No, I don't" He offered his arm to steady her up the steps and down another flight inside, to the basement. In the banquet hall, preparations were well underway. Tables placed end to end formed three long rows. People poured into the room and children dashed among them, releasing pent-up energy from the past two hours of sitting in hard pews.

Dana craned her neck peering this way and that, then spotting what she was looking for, she tugged Gavin's arm. He followed her through the throng, nodding to people who seemed to notice him for the first time. Dr. Robbins headed their way, with a woman on his arm. She was advanced in years, her grey hair pinned up in a roll below her hat.

"I want you to meet someone," Dana said to them. "This is Gavin McLeod. He's the man I told you about who's working on an emergency preparedness plan for Withers." He took the hand that relinquished Dr. Robbins' arm and reached toward him. Dana gestured to the woman. "Gavin, this is—"

"Mrs. Cameron," he interjected. "I recognize you from your picture."

"You've been to the Cameron gallery, then," she said with a smile that reached her eyes; eyes, that evinced a sage and perceptive mind.

"I didn't notice you come in with your daughter this morning," he remarked. "Were you able to attend services?"

"Oh yes," she said, her grasp lingering. "My dear friend, Floyd Hancock, brought me." Gavin recalled Floyd's expression when he'd mentioned Viola Cameron's name and, abashed, reminded himself how small a community this was.

Dana edged around to Dr. Robbin's other side and slid her arm around his waist. "Gavin, I'd like you to meet my fiancé, Jeremy Robbins."

Jeremy pumped his hand. "Soon to be her husband—in this very church if we ever get around to making an appointment with the pastor. Since you took her flying, Mr. McLeod, Dana has talked of nothing else." Gavin was just pondering whether this opening gambit was a territorial warning, when Jeremy turned to regard her with a baleful expression. "It's about time Dana got a broader perspective of the world." She rolled her eyes.

They sat together, Gavin beside Mrs. Cameron with Jeremy opposite him and Dana opposite her mother. The two men exchanged pleasantries about their favourite hobbies. Jeremy expounded on his passion for cycling, and racing in particular.

"Do you do anything competitively, Mr. McLeod?"

"No. I lean toward solitary activities, though I don't mind sharing the trail with a good companion who enjoys nature too."

"I love a good contest," Jeremy enthused. "I get high pushing my body to its limit. Competition is great for that."

The rapping of a spoon against a china cup drew everyone's attention to the head of the room where Pastor Hildebrand smiled beatifically at his flock. He welcomed everyone and asked the congregation to stand and bow their heads while he said grace. Afterward, when the thunderous scraping of a hundred and fifty chairs had settled, Viola turned to him.

"Mr. McLeod, tell me your opinion on how serious a problem we're going to face here when the river rises."

He'd been itching to ask her about the flood of '48 but been unsure whether to broach it. He was grateful she'd given him an opening. "So far, it's fifty-fifty whether the weather will be for or against us, Ma'am. Hopefully this weather will hold and give us a long, gradual melt without torrential rainfall in May or June. 'God willing and the crick don't rise,'" he grinned, "we'll squeak through without too much trouble, if you don't mind me saying 'we'. When I work with people to avert disaster, I start to feel personally invested."

Viola snorted. "It seems you've been a good deal more invested than folks in town so far. Are you getting any co-operation at all?" Gavin glanced over at Blake Logan on the far side of the next table where he was forking baked salmon into his mouth. *Careful of the political landmines,* he heard Perce warn.

"It takes most folks a while to gain a real appreciation of the potential. Raising awareness is a part of my job." He canted his head with a questioning look. "Mrs. Cameron, I'd very much like to get some historical perspective on the last serious flood here from someone who experienced it first hand. Would you mind me asking you some questions?"

"Ask away, Mr. McLeod. If an old woman's stories can do anything to help folks wake up and smell the coffee, I'll tell you anything I can." Gavin fired question after question, finding her memory remarkably detailed and her knowledge extensive and useful. This was not someone who had been a *victim* of disaster that had left her and dozens of others homeless for a time. She was a survivor, as Dana had attested, a woman of pioneer spirit.

So engrossed was he, he hadn't noticed Dana leave her seat. He was surprised therefore when he spied her at the end of the far table, leaning down to speak into the Pastor's ear. He remembered Jeremy's remark about needing to make an appointment to arrange their wedding. He felt an unexpected pang. In a town like Withers, Dr. Robbins was no doubt a good catch. Physical excellence was important to him, yet in love, he was apparently blind to *her* physical limitation. They were lucky to have each other.

Dana returned to her place, meeting Gavin's eye with a brief smile, while Viola finished telling about the dust that plagued their home for half a dozen years after the water receded.

Dessert was served and devoured. The ladies from the kitchen worked their way up and down the aisles with pots of coffee and tea. Gavin brought his cup to his lips for a sip of coffee just as the rapping of a spoon on a china cup sounded again, stilling the buzz throughout the hall. Pastor Hildebrand said he had an announcement.

"We have a visitor in our midst who is staying in Withers for several months. He is working with Town Council to put preparations in place in case of exceptionally high water this spring and summer. It's very important for citizens to get involved in helping with these preparations."

Gavin regarded Dana. Like everyone else in the room just then, her attention was focused on the pastor. Perhaps she sensed Gavin watching her, or perhaps she was anxious to see his reaction, but in any event, she turned her head his way. Their eyes met and held. He offered a nod of gratitude. She gave the merest shrug, as if to say, *It was nothing.* But when she smiled, her eyes danced and he was left feeling out of breath.

"Mr. McLeod is recruiting volunteers," Hildebrand went on. "There are a number of tasks to be done I understand. If you can give of your time to help with these important matters, you are invited to attend a meeting. Is that right, Mr. McLeod?"

"Yes, Reverend, that's right."

"And will you be meeting at Town Hall?" Involuntarily, Gavin shot a look at Logan. He was jolted by the black look Logan made no attempt to hide. He had to clear his throat. "Ah...no. No, actually the meeting will be..." in a millisecond his mind scanned and rejected both the library and Elk's Hall. The church would have been more neutral, but he didn't want to be in the embarrassing situation of asking at this juncture. "It will be at the Dream-Catcher, Tuesday evening at seven." He hoped Mandy would not kibosh his claim for her restaurant as the venue. It would further discredit him, and he'd have only a day to find an alternate.

Todd sat at the kitchen table chewing on the end of his pencil, the long division figures in his scribbler swimming. His gaze drifted to the window, sheeting with rain. Though it was pitch black outside, if there had been something to see, it would not have registered. Instead he saw an outdoor arena encircled by stands thronged with spectators. He glanced down at the sawdust base from the back of his horse... Nefarious. Everyone in the stands leaned forward watching his execution of the dressage set. This would be the tie-breaker. He'd won the most points of the event, he and Nefarious, except for one other who equalled him. Now they competed to take home the blue ribbon.

He squeezed his legs against the stallion's sides and Nefarious responded, moving out in a smooth rocking canter, his nose tucked toward his massive chest. His mane rose and fell like a black flag billowing in the wind. Todd eased him back a gait, then asked him to lengthen. Applause broke out as Nefarious stretched to an extended trot, floating along the arena. Just then a gate opened and a judge entered the ring.

"Todd!" The angry bellow brought him crashing back to the present with a lurch in his stomach. His father shouted from the front door. His legs shaking, he dashed to the foyer, skidding to a halt before his father's towering frame. His oiled Aussie slicker made him seem even taller than normal. Rain dripped from it.

"Where's your bike?" Blake snapped.

Todd opened his mouth to answer but nothing came out. Just as he was about to say, *in the barn,* he remembered dropping it in the dust of the yard because he'd been desperate to get to the bathroom.

"I asked you a question."

"I...I...."

"Well?"

He couldn't hold his father's burning gaze. His eyes fell to the floor. "I forgot," he said, barely above a whisper.

"You forgot," his father scorned. "*What* did you forget?"

"I...I...for...forgot—"

"Don't stutter!" His bellow made Todd's heart explode. He heard his mother's footsteps clicking down the hall, coming to his rescue. He didn't know which was worse, his father's rage or the belittling that would follow her intervention when his dad would make him feel like a baby.

Hiding behind Mommy's skirts. Momma's boy.

She entered the foyer at precisely the same moment blood gushed from his nose in a fountain, soiling his shirt in a big splotch before he squeezed if off between his finger and thumb. She whisked him away to the bathroom, clucking at his father.

"I nearly ran over it," he growled in disgust, "lying there in the mud."

———————

Half an hour later, Mary pulled the blankets up to her son's chin, settled in bed at last. She leaned over and kissed his forehead.

"Mommy?" he murmured, "Will you play me to sleep?"

"Yes Dear, close your eyes now." She turned off the lamp and left the door ajar. Down the hall, she seated herself at the piano, breathed deeply and began a run up the keyboard gathering passion in the wake of her fingers, ending in a trill. Soon she was lost in the music.

The notes carried to Blake in his study. The music aroused an ache in him. He went to his liquor cabinet and poured himself a bourbon. The first sip trickled down his throat, warming it. Then he threw back the rest in a swallow, his throat constricting against the sear. He returned to his desk, determined to shut out the feelings hounding him. He pored over reports and documents his job on Council required of him, but after a quarter hour he gave up.

He stepped into the hall. His son's door stood open a crack. Todd would have asked her to play him to sleep, he knew, else his door would be closed. He approached and pushed it open further. The boy lay motionless on the pillow, his blanket rising and falling rhythmically. Blake shut the door. He closed in on the music. Mary looked up when he appeared in the arched entrance and leaned against the frame.

"He's asleep now; you don't need to go on playing," he said coldly.

She halted mid-phrase, the notes hanging in the air between them. He stared brazenly. For a long moment she held his look, then with a sudden motion pushed back the bench and hurried past him out of the room. Almost lazily, he turned his head watching her pass by, then leonine, he uncoiled from his position and trailed her to the bedroom.

She escaped into the ensuite, where he knew she would change into her nightgown. Leisurely he removed his tie, shoes and belt. He was unbuttoning his shirt when she emerged. She whipped back the covers on her side of the bed and got in, turning her back to him. She reached and snapped off the lamp on her side.

He took his time undressing. Naked, he crawled between the sheets, turning off the lamp on his side. He lay on his back, his arm thrown carelessly under his head, and listened to the rain. It pattered steadily in the already soaking yard outside. It drummed on the roof.

He felt her rigid beside him. After a bit, he rolled toward her. He slid his hand down her side into the curve of her waist and over the swell of her hip.

"Don't!"

He left his hand on her hip. After a moment, he traced a slow circle with his palm.

"Blake, stop it."

"Come on, Mary. You have to give in to your needs some time."

She thrust his hand away with her own. "Not with a bully."

He gave a grunt of amusement. "A bully? Am I being a bully to you?"

"Don't play me for a fool, Blake. You're a bully to your own son."

Anger rose in him. "Why? Because I expect him to act responsibly?"

"No. Because you terrorize and shame him. You punish him for not being like you."

"I ride him because he has to toughen up. He's a rancher's kid and he needs to have his wits about him. His forgetfulness could be fatal in this country." She didn't respond. "Come on, Mary," he whispered, moving his body against hers. "Let's not quarrel." His answer was cold silence. "We voted on the train station project tonight," he said, nuzzling her neck. "I got you what you wanted." He slipped his arm around her and felt himself getting hard. So did she apparently, for she wrenched away, sat up and snapped on the lamp.

"If you don't leave me alone, I'll sleep in Todd's room."

Behind her, Blake's lip curled in a snarl. "I'll leave you alone," he spat, flinging back the covers and getting out of bed. "You'll have all the solitude you desire." He dressed hurriedly, while she sat unmoving, her back to him. He pulled on his boots and strode to the door, opening it. With his hand still on the knob, he turned to her, now able to see her face. "But you can't keep this up forever, Mary. You're my wife. I expect to be able to have sex with my wife."

The wipers in the Dodge Ram slapped away the sheeting rain on the windshield. It was coming down so hard, Blake couldn't see the edge of the blacktop. Only the worn centre line and occasional light from a farmhouse were visible to guide him, but he barely needed these. He knew the way. Lorraine Connor's husband, Noel, had left right after church on Sunday to attend a conference down south. Lorraine would be alone.

He passed Mandy Sky's home. Perhaps it was the desolation of the stormy night together with the beacon of the light on her porch which brought the memory so sharply to mind. Or perhaps it was Mary's rejection.

The young half-breed had been like a warm kitten when he'd first taken her. He and Mandy were in their teens. Both had reputations for being a little wild. He'd been no more serious about her than any other girl he'd parted from her bra and panties. But Mandy was one of those comfortable females, with a ready laugh and ready to spread her legs. He'd returned to her again and again when he was between women.

But the summer between undergraduate and post-graduate studies, the time he really needed the distraction, she suddenly slammed down the portcullis. He was furious. She'd taken a tumble for a drifter, a guitar-toting cowboy in an ancient rusted-out pick-up. He'd billed himself to The Winchester as a wandering minstrel and got a job playing gigs in the bar. Mandy waited tables there.

Blake had come home from university with a degree and a sick heart. For three years he'd pursued Mary Harlow. He learned her schedule and waylaid her after classes, teasing, charming and harrying her into going for a drink with him, though she never drank anything harder than soda water. He stalked her, seeking her out in the music building where she practised in one of those soundproof cubicles. He talked with her for hours on the telephone. He'd gone to the same parties, even danced with her. And he proposed a dozen times. She always laughed, not taking him seriously. He took her out rowing on the lagoon near the campus and once, persuaded her to go to the carnival where he'd pressed her into consenting, reluctantly, to go on the Ferris wheel. As they were swept up over the midway, he put his arm around her. For once she didn't object, shrinking against him in fright. And at the highest point, he kissed her. With the wind in his hair, against the whirling lights and the mad sounds from the midway, he felt intoxicated by her. But Mary had not shared his ardour; she'd simply been too paralyzed to resist.

She tolerated him as an entertaining, impetuous, somewhat undisciplined friend. But time began to run out. Mary planned to go to Europe to study in the fall. In the weeks before graduation, in desperation, Blake threw aside his façade of bonhomie. Backstage, after a performance that was to be her last that final semester, he intercepted her hurrying down a deserted flight of stairs. In anguished need, he professed his love to her, proposing with all the intensity he felt.

"Dear Blake," she said, kindly enough, "You know you don't mean it."

He did mean it, he insisted, with everything that was in him. Her gaze, straying below him on the stairs, made him turn. The cellist, *The nincompoop* leaned against the wall, with a supercilious sneer curling his lip. He had witnessed his abasement. Blake searched her face and realized with finality he had no hope. A disastrous summer preceded the fateful change in their fortunes.

He returned to Withers and threw himself into a dissolute existence of indiscriminate sex. It became an obsession to seduce every female who got caught in his crosshairs. He took it as a challenge to wear down the demure, the faithful and the uninterested. As with every other summer, Mandy Sky was available—until that drifter arrived.

Blake showed up at The Winchester one night at closing time to take her back to her house and fuck. She was just cashing in. Though she said no, he told her he'd be back by the time she finished up and he ducked into the men's room. When he returned, she was leaning into the chest of the musician, both of them all smiles. Blake contained the slow burn inside him and left, unseen by either of them. Perhaps he wasn't good enough for Mary, but this slut dared to reject him at her peril. He wasn't about to brook competition in his own valley, *especially* from another musician.

The summer unwound in a cat and mouse game. As he had once stalked Mary, he now stalked Mandy and Wayne Ashton. Once he found them smoking weed. His hackles rose when he heard Mandy's unfettered, stoned laughter. It made him feel shut out. He stepped up his espionage, scouting around the shack in the woods where Ashton was staying. With grim satisfaction, he found what he was looking for—several healthy seven-foot marijuana bushes. Concentrating his focus on Ashton's activities after that, it was not long before he observed a few drug deals transpire. He had his ammunition. Blake moved with the swiftness of the law itself. He ambushed Wayne in the parking lot after midnight one night when Mandy was off. He told Ashton he'd better leave town or he'd set the law on him for growing and dealing pot. By the look on Ashton's face, Blake assured himself he'd seen the last of him.

The next day, he encountered a mournful Mandy wiping tables at The Winchester. She wouldn't tell him what was wrong but the bar tender confirmed that Mandy had discovered what Blake already knew from stopping by Ashton's cabin. He had cleared out, with no forwarding address.

Blake showed up on her porch that night, the same porch he'd driven by, a mile back. He was hungry to close in for the kill. It was for this that he'd gone to weeks of trouble. But Mandy wouldn't co-operate. She pulled away from him when he wrapped his arms around her. She asked him to go. He teased, he charmed; he cussed and insulted. She looked him in the eye and stood firm. She didn't want him.

He couldn't bear it. No woman would reject him again. He became forceful, grabbing her and kissing her roughly. If she'd fought back, he might have enjoyed the contest. But she no longer resisted. She just wept silently, huge, wet tears spilling over those wide cheekbones and streaking down her face. He wrenched away and left her house. He hadn't been inside it since.

The light was on in Lorraine's kitchen window. He saw her peer out it through the rain, which had eased off to a steady drizzle. He got out of the truck and sprinted to her door. It opened before he reached it. She watched him shuck out of his wet slicker and hang it on the peg. Without a word, she crooked her finger and led the way into the darkened interior. He followed her.

The rain ended somewhere around midnight. The sun redeemed herself, smiling down on Withers and thickening the buds on the trees. She had long since sunk below the rim of the western hills however when Gavin entered the Dream-Catcher to grab a late bite before the meeting he fervently hoped would materialize. In the far corner of the bar by the pool table, three people shared a jug of beer. They were all from Town Hall, Councillor Freddie McCormick, who had shown so little concern for the First Nations people living in the floodplain, Lorraine Connor and a staff person Gavin recognized from the Planning Department. They were shooting the breeze with a pair of pool players, Clint Murdock and Seth Colville. On a stool at the bar, a rough looking customer hunkered alone over his drink, like a dog guarding a bone. Gavin recognized him as a regular he'd seen several times at the Dream-Catcher's watering hole.

Gavin negotiated a monstrous steak, still sizzling when Mandy set it in front of him. The only other patron in the restaurant side, he guessed correctly, was a mill worker. And he was conning Mandy, or at least trying to.

"Go 'way with you, LD." She swiped at him good-naturedly with the rag she'd been using to wipe tables. "I'm not going on that over-sized tricycle with you."

"Aw come on, Mandy. You'd like ATVing." She shook her head, adamant.

"What'sa matter? Scared you might have fun?"

"What fun? Gettin' my insides scrambled like an egg in a blender."

"Okay, then I'll take you out in my truck."

She straightened up from wiping the table beside him and leaned her face toward him for emphasis. "No!"

"You *know* you wanna to go out with me."

She let out a bark of a laugh and stood regarding him with her fists on her hips. "You don't give up do you?"

"No," he leaned back, patient but undeterred. "And I won't, till you go out with me."

She walked toward Gavin, shaking her head. "How you doing, Gavin? More coffee?"

"Not now Mandy. Maybe later." She began clearing away his empty plate. "I want to thank you again for agreeing to let me hold a meeting here. You really bailed me out."

"You're new around here, arn'cha?" drawled the fellow who'd been razzing Mandy. He wore a plaid hunter's jacket and jeans, a mop of brown hair and a boyish face, though he was by no means young; perhaps it was his open, pleasant face—*a Cocker Spaniel face*, Gavin thought.

"You could say so," he replied.

"Tell her she ought to go out with me."

Gavin exchanged wry looks with Mandy and asked her, "Is this a frequent request from this gentleman?"

"Gettin' to be that way."

"But you're not interested."

"LD's a nice kid, don't get me wrong." LD watched this interchange with interest, awaiting the outcome.

"Kid?" Gavin echoed, he leaned around Mandy, busy gathering the detritus of his devoured meal, assessing LD. "He doesn't *look* like a kid."

Mandy gave a grunt of a laugh. "Anybody who was still running around pulling girls' skirts up in the playground when I was riding in cars with boys is a kid in my books." She stepped back, laden with dirty china.

"She says you're too young," Gavin reported to LD.

"So that's your excuse this week," LD lamented. Mandy whisked by, heading for the kitchen.

Just then the door to the restaurant opened. A man Gavin took to be in his sixties trundled in. Spying Gavin, he marched smartly to his table. "Mr. McLeod. I'm here for the meeting." Gavin stood and extended his hand. The man might once have been his equal in height but his neck didn't hold his head erect anymore, if it ever had. Gavin found himself regarding a face lined with what looked like a perpetual frown.

"Wonderful," he replied. "And you are...?

"Ellwood. Foster Ellwood. I heard Reverend Hildebrand's appeal for volunteers for your committee. I'm retired now so I've got time to help out."

"That's great, Mr. Ellwood. Sit down. Can I buy you a cup of coffee?"

"No. I never drink coffee after noon. Keeps me awake." Foster had arrived on the stroke of seven. For the next ten minutes, Gavin sought to engage him in conversation, though it was hard going with the taciturn man. He learned Foster was a retired home-and-farm insurance salesman, widowed with grown children who lived down south and that his hobby was fishing.

"I thought this meeting was supposed to start at seven. Are you expecting others?" he groused.

"Frankly, I don't know, Mr. Ellwood."

"Well, why don't we get going. I like to be on time. You can tell me what we need to do."

"Alright. Why don't we?" he agreed and began laying out the work ahead. In the midst of this, Mandy, unbidden, brought a tray with a pot of tea to the table. He looked up quizzically. "No charge," she said. "Just thought you might want something while you two work. By the way, how you going to feed all those people?"

"What people?" he asked.

"The ones you're talking about. People displaced in the flood."

It was then it registered on him she'd been hovering, making no effort to disguise her eavesdropping.

"I don't know yet. It's all part of what the committee needs to arrange, hopefully with support from the town." She grunted and retreated to the table LD still occupied, sitting opposite him. Gavin turned his attention back to Foster. Communications would be vital, he went on. There needed to be the means and skills at hand to communicate in the event that the power went down. They'd need generators.

He paid no attention to the door opening till he heard one of the pool players holler to the newcomer and address him by name. Gavin shot a look over his shoulder. Logan made his way over to the group in the bar.

Foster began to warm up to the task. He had questions, which Gavin took to be a good sign. One of them was where was he staying while he was in town. When Gavin told him, he remarked disparagingly, "Smack dab in the middle of the floodplain."

"Well, yes—"

"What kind of an example are you?"

"It's the only game in town," he countered.

"Kind of expensive, isn't it, I mean as a regular thing?"

"I suppose. But it's on my account."

"You work for the government, don't you? I'd say it's on my account!" Foster grumbled, the permanent vertical frown lines between his brows deepening.

Gavin groaned inwardly, recalling a similar challenge in the town hall meeting. He didn't want to get into an argument with his one and only committee member, or worse, lose him before they really got started. He could hear Perce now.

"Look here, McLeod," Foster was saying, "why don't you rent my fishing cabin? It's fixed up with all the amenities. Did that so my wife would come along, but she's passed on now. It's not far from town, a fifteen-minute drive is all. I wouldn't charge you much and..." Foster gave a short laugh, his first, "At least it's not in the floodplain. It's up above Stayner Creek. Even if the creek spills its banks, the cabin will stay high and dry."

Gavin wondered what "all the amenities" meant. He pictured trying to run his laptop in a place with a leaking roof and smoky cook stove—even supposing there was a phone line. "That's a very generous offer, Foster. I appreciate the thought. One of the things critical to my job is having the ability to communicate by email."

"There's a phone line there. I told you, it's all fixed up, as good as my house in town. I'd live there myself but it's too far out in the winter with the snow and all. At my age..." he trailed off, his meaning self-evident.

So engrossed was he in this turn in the conversation, Gavin didn't notice Blake saunter over till he towered above him. He looked up, uncomfortably aware of Logan's advantage of height.

"It's rather a dynamic committee you have here, McLeod," he said with a sardonic grin.

"Pull up a chair, Councillor. There's room for one more," he replied, equally sarcastic.

"Sadly, I must decline. I'm with the Philistines," he said, smiling still as he turned to Ellwood. "Foster, I know you for a frugal man. This talk of preparation for a phantom flood sounds costly to me. You know I'm committed to keeping property taxes down."

Foster scowled but did not reply.

Blake went on. "You don't really think we're going to have any problems here in Withers do you? We've got a very good flood management system. With my ranch right on the river, I'd be the first one to be concerned, if there were anything to worry about."

"Well, it doesn't hurt to have a plan," Foster qualified. "Just in case."

"Quite right. That's why we have a plan at Town Hall."

Foster looked confused. "You *have* a plan? Then how come the Province sent this guy here."

Gavin leaned forward. "I'll tell you why, Foster. Because the town's plans don't include dealing with a full-scale catastrophe. They haven't set aside the money or the supplies to deal with one."

Foster looked from one to the other, not sure whom to bank on.

Blake turned back to Gavin and clapped a hand on his shoulder with the informality of an old friend. "Well Noah, save me a place on that ark of yours for my prize bull. I'd hate to lose the son-of-a-gun." He winked at Foster and sauntered away.

Gavin raised his voice to his retreating back, "I can only take him if he comes with a heifer."

Logan laughed uproariously. When he passed by Lorraine's chair, he put his fingertips on her throat and ran them along her jaw line in a manner Gavin thought was awfully familiar, sensual even. His gesture ended in a friendly tug of her hair, to which she reacted with a smirk. Blake plucked his jacket off the back of his chair, bid goodbye to his friends and departed.

A pronounced "hmph" from Mandy as soon as the door closed betrayed her sentiments. "And that big lunk keeps gettin' re-elected," she said to no one in particular. To Gavin she said, "If a lot of people get flooded out, there'd have to be a reception area, you said. You mean some kind of refugee camp?"

"It's a possible scenario, Mandy, providing of course we can find a suitable location."

"You need a cook?"

He saw her drift and nodded. "Somebody has to organize feeding them. Could be several hundred."

"Well, sign me on. If Blake Logan thinks this committee is a bad idea, that's reason enough for me to join."

Gavin kept a keen eye on Foster during this interchange. He feared Logan's soft intimidation would cost him Ellwood's participation. But this was dispelled by Foster beating him to the punch in saying, "Atta girl," and pulling out a chair at the table for Mandy.

No sooner had she plunked herself down, when LD piped up. "I don't mind helping out. Can I join too?"

Mandy rolled her eyes in exasperation. "LD you're just volunteering because I'm going to be attending the meetings."

"So?" he answered innocently.

Gavin scratched his head, a little perplexed. "Look LD, it's a nice offer and I don't mind having you. But there is work involved; it's not just meetings. Each of you will have tasks you'll have to carry out."

"That's okay," he grinned. "I got nothin' to do after work and on my days off."

Gavin looked at Mandy. She shrugged as much as to say, *It's your call.* "All right then," Gavin replied, clapping his hand on the table. "Pull up a chair."

Blake needed a cigarette. He'd been a confirmed smoker in his youth but quit because of Mary, who abhorred cigarette smoke. He'd never really given it up entirely, accepting a light occasionally from his two-pack-a-day best friend Seth. Instead of walking back to Town Hall where he'd left his truck, he headed to the Hasty Mart to buy a pack.

This McLeod guy was getting under his skin. Why the hell did the bureaucrats down in Victoria have to waste good money sending an outsider up to the interior to tell them how to handle their affairs? Lord knows, they ignored you the rest of the time. He'd find a way to deal with McLeod. Hell, he was just a cog in the government machinery, an underling.

He paid for his pack of DuMauriers and lit up outside the store. He drew the smoke deep in his lungs, feeling the drug relax him. Needing to unwind, he strolled down the side street to take a roundabout route back to his truck. He cut through the empty co-op lot past a dumpster and into the parking lot behind the clinic. Under an ancient cedar, a thick log divided the two lots. He rested on it, pulling on his cigarette till the end glowed in the dark moonless night.

A light was on in the clinic. A solitary vehicle sat in the lot, a pick-up. He knew who owned it. He finished his smoke and ground it out under the toe of his cowboy boot, getting up just as the rear door of the clinic squeaked open. Light flooding out from it, momentarily silhouetted the person leaving. He was between her and her pick-up. He shrank into the shadows under the cedar.

She had a stunning figure, curvaceous, a flat stomach and a butt that begged to be grasped in his two hands. The face did justice to the body too. She was a looker, all right. He watched her cross the lot with her odd, exaggerated limp. He found it strangely erotic, as if he were a hunter and she a wounded doe. It made her seem helpless and that was enough to stir a twinge in his crotch.

"That's a mighty enticing shimmy, you got there," he said as she passed within three feet.

She let out a cry, throwing up her hands to ward off her unseen assailant.

"Whoa, young filly. No need to be skittish."

"Who...?" Her eyes, wide from fright, narrowed as she recognized him. Her lips thinned in anger. "Do you always hang out in dark alleys to ambush women who are alone, Mr. Logan?"

"I'm minding my own business, having a smoke." He ogled her in an indolent up-and-down examination. "I'd say you're the one setting an ambush, sashaying by with a wiggle that would set my prize bull to pawing the ground," he said, making a second reference that evening to his prime stock.

Dana tried to quell the trembling caused by a combination of sudden fright and outrage, hoping it wasn't noticeable. She wondered if he were drunk. She turned on her heel thinking she wouldn't grace his crude innuendo with a reply. But in spite of herself, she retorted, "Your prize bull and you appear to have much in common, Councillor. Horny beasts, likely to end up in a stew." She climbed in her truck and locked the door. As she drove past, he tipped his head with a smouldering smile and touched the brim of his Stetson.

Chapter Four

When Gavin arrived for his second riding lesson, early again, Dana was teaching a class in the outdoor ring. He watched from a bleacher. None of the riders looked over twelve. Peering under their helmets, Gavin guessed four were girls. The fifth was Todd Logan.

Near the centre of the ring, Dana stood hatless, her hair pulled back in a pony-tail. Riding boots and jodhpurs accentuated her trim figure, with curves in all the right places, he couldn't help notice.

The class trotted their mounts over a low cross-pole. One horse balked and pulled out around the jump.

"Try again, Kayla," Dana called. "Bongo needs to mind you." The girl pulled her mount around to come at it again. This time he rushed at the fence and Kayla nearly got left behind. Once over the jump, Bongo ran off with her and she lost her stirrup. They flew past Gavin, Kayla looking pale and frightened.

"Don't worry about your stirrup, honey. Just get your seat," Dana spoke calmly. Bongo thundered around the ring once more. "Now squeeze back the reins and arch your back. There, you did it!" Dana approached them. She rubbed Kayla's leg reassuringly. "Well, that got you both a little excited, huh." Kayla nodded, giving a nervous smile. "Do you know what happened there?"

"I didn't expect him to run at the jump," she said.

"Well, you got him over! Try to stay balanced on the balls of your feet, then no matter what Bongo does..." she continued talking in a relaxed way, helping the girl analyze the experience, all the while keeping her gloved hand on Kayla's boot. The girl relaxed visibly, then smiled. Dana had the whole class do the jump once more and the lesson ended. The children dismounted and led their horses to the stable as parents arrived. She approached the fence where Gavin sat. "Hi," she said. "Ready for round two."

"Depends. You're not going to make me jump that cross-pole, are you?"

She grinned, "Not on horseback, anyway."

After his lesson, Gavin led Jake to the stable. He was surprised to find Todd mucking out a stall.

"Hi cub. Say, you look pretty good out there in the arena." The boy flushed with pleasure. "How come you get to do chores after the others have gone home?"

"I work for Miss Oleson," he said with downcast eyes, "to pay for my lessons."

"Well, now that's mighty impressive." Todd peered up, uncertainty in his bearing. When he saw genuine admiration in Gavin's expression, he squared his shoulders and smiled. "Well, I can't stand here yacking," Gavin said. "I have to take care of ol' Jake here."

He put the horse in cross-ties and removed the saddle. Dana came in while he brushed Jake's coat. She leaned back against a stall door, looking on. "Did you have any luck with volunteers?" she asked.

He paused, brush in hand, giving her a rueful look. "Depends on your definition of luck." She raised her eyebrows quizzically. He wondered if he should say anything about Logan. The man obviously had a following. The only person he'd met so far who clearly didn't think much of him was Mandy. He decided he wasn't ready to jeopardize his nascent friendship with Dana by disclosing the animosity between Logan and himself. Instead he described the modest beginnings of a committee.

"More volunteers are going to be needed, ideally some with special expertise or resources."

"Such as?"

The brush in his hand paused on Jake's shoulder as he considered where the animal would be if the valley flooded. "Well, for one thing, we'll need a pet shelter. We can't have folks keeping pets in the same place people will be lodged. Farms offer possible facilities but most of them are in the floodplain too. Those that aren't would be more helpful taking in livestock."

"Mrs. Millhouse has a kennel. Her place is high up." Dana and Gavin turned in the direction from whence came this observation. Seeing the two adults staring at him, Todd reddened and pulled his head in, tongue-tied.

"Who's Mrs. Millhouse?" Gavin asked.

"She's an old lady who raises Shih Zhu's and Jack Russell Terriers."

"Have you seen her kennel?"

Todd nodded. "My school bus goes by there. One time I saw a sign saying 'Puppies for sale.' I rode back on my bike. I was hoping my Dad would let me have one..." His face fell and his voice trailed off. "But he said no."

While Todd contemplated the floor, Gavin stole a look at Dana. He could see by her expression how she was drawn into the boy's unhappiness. He steered the conversation back to safer ground. "What can you tell me about her kennels, Todd?"

The boy shrugged. "Like what?"

"Could she take large dogs too? And cats? How many could her place handle? Is it clean?"

"Go easy, Gavin," Dana laughed. "How many questions do you think he can handle at once?"

Todd looked from one to the other as they spoke. He replied, "There's kennels for big dogs. She boards them. Cats too. She has cats of her own, a bunch of them. She has room for lots of dogs. Thirty I bet. It's spic and span." This came out in a stream and ended with both Gavin and Dana laughing.

"It seems he can handle multiple questions just fine," Gavin observed. He gave Todd a thumbs-up sign. "Thanks for the info, Todd. I'll check her out."

––––––––––

When Gavin awoke the next morning, his legs and back protested his effort to move. He pushed back the covers and rolled painfully to his side, groaning. The effects of his riding lesson on his thighs would wear off in a day or two. But he must have wrenched his back when he made his ungainly dismount. He forced himself upright, wincing, and hobbled into the bathroom. After a shave and shower, he wrapped a towel round his waist and lurched to the phone in the kitchen of Foster's cabin. Thumbing through the phone book, he found the page he was looking for and dialled a number. When a woman answered, he asked for an appointment.

––––––––––

The receptionist escorted Gavin into an office and left him alone. Beside the desk, a glass cabinet held thick volumes on anatomy, physiology, skeletal pathologies and chiropractic. Dr. Robbins' degrees hung above the case. On each of the other three walls, in a touch of narcissism, photos exhibited him indulging in his passion for cycle racing. But it was the photos on his desk that arrested Gavin's attention.

In a landscape ten by twelve, Nefarious stood with nose tucked, a blue rosette fluttering from his bridle. In a black formal riding habit, Dana sat erect astride the stallion's glistening back. The second photo was a close-up of Dana and Jeremy caught in an affectionate moment, his arm thrown round her neck. She was laughing. His finger pointed at her, a smirk pasted on his face. Their obvious happiness caused a catch in Gavin's throat.

The third conveyed a wistful mood. He picked it up to examine it. Dana leaned back against a slanted tree, her hands pressed against the trunk behind her. The late afternoon sunlight bathed her face, making her skin glow. She wore a faraway look. He wondered what had transpired before Jeremy caught that look on film.

He started guiltily when the door flew open and Dr. Robbins entered.

"Mr. McLeod!" he said with an open smile. "What brings you here?"

With a sheepish look, Gavin held up the framed photo. "Your fiancée's riding lesson has taken its toll on me," he explained, carefully setting the picture back on the desk. "I seem to have pulled something in my back."

Jeremy chuckled. "You're not the first patient I've had thanks to Dana's lessons." He opened a manila folder and took down a brief history. "Let's have a look at you then," he said closing it. He had him lie face down on the chiropractic bench. Gavin felt deft fingers expertly probe various tender spots in his back.

"I'm not much of a rider myself," Jeremy admitted.

"But don't you own one of the horses at her stable?"

"The mare with the bad knees. Yes. I never intended to ride her. She's from excellent stock though and I was told she'd make a good broodmare. She did too. I had her bred down south. The colt was my gift to Dana. She could never have afforded to buy a blooded stallion like Nefarious," he said, running his fingers the length of Gavin's spine. "I wanted her to have a mount to match her ability. That horse will take her places. The photo over there with her on him was taken last fall in Williams Lake. She took the Grand Championship."

Gavin let out a groan when the doctor's fingers found a painful spot low in his back. "Yes, you've done a nice number here, haven't you," Jeremy acknowledged, then reverted to Dana. "Maybe she'll get to some important competitions further afield, thanks to you," he added.

"Thanks to me?"

"She always dragged her feet when I tried to get her to enter shows back east or in the States. If she's going to advance, she's gotta get onto the circuit of the *big* shows, away from this one-horse town, so to speak. I figured she was afraid of flying. But she came back pretty excited from the flight you took her on."

"Really? I had the impression she's fearless," Gavin remarked, thinking of his early encounters with her.

Jeremy laughed aloud. "She's spunky alright. Never did let her disability get in her way. She used to get teased something fierce when we were kids for the way she walks. You know how it is; kids can be cruel. But

Dana just held her head high and decided to show 'em all by becoming a great equestrian."

"You've known each other a long time."

"We were high school sweethearts." He chuckled again. "I'd stick up for her when other kids teased her. Then she'd rag at me for it. Told me she could take care of herself, thank you very much." Gavin thought of the scolding she'd given him the first time he saw her. He had no trouble picturing her, a feisty teenager, bawling Jeremy out for emulating a dragon-slayer.

Dr. Robbins told him to take a deep breath and expel it. Gavin felt a sudden crunch and let out a yelp. The doctor sat him up. "That ought to do it. Ice it and don't do anything strenuous for a couple of days—like riding," he grinned.

Gingerly, Gavin got to his feet, his muscles still sore but the sharp pain eased. "Thanks, doc."

"She's a great kid, isn't she?" Jeremy smiled indulgently.

"You're a lucky man," Gavin answered earnestly.

He found the Millhouse kennel from the directions she gave him over the phone. The sign in the front yard, visible from the road, advertised dog and cat boarding and championship Shih Zhu and Jack Russell Terrier breeds at stud. He pulled into her driveway behind a woody-panel station wagon that had to be at least fifteen years old. It bore a faded bumper sticker with its clarion protest, 'Ban the leg-hold trap.'

His knock on the door set off a cacophony of barking and higher-pitched yapping. He noted the kennel across the back yard, with individual chain-link runs adjoining it. These were covered with a sloping roof, affording shade from sun and shelter from rain. Farther back was a barn, but judging by the height of last year's grass around it, not in use. The paddock beside it had not seen livestock in years.

He heard a voice. The door opened and he found himself looking down upon a dumpy woman of uncertain age with close-cropped thinning reddish hair. She wore shapeless pants and a grey sweatshirt with a print on the front, of a kitten playing with a ball of wool. A Jack Russell terrier scurried past her feet. Making a sound between a whine and a growl, it sniffed at Gavin's boots.

"Jojo, it's the man who phoned earlier. You *are* Mr. McLeod, aren't you? Don't worry, he doesn't bite. Jojo's just protective; he looks after me, don't you Jojo." All this was said without once lifting her eyes from the dog.

"Mrs. Millhouse?"

"Yes, yes. Come on in then, so I can close the door. Dolly will try to get out and I just bathed her." She hustled him in. "There you are!" she declared, pouncing on a white long-hair making a dash for the opening. "You thought you'd get away, didn't you, sweetie-pie," she purred to the blue-eyed Persian whose sour face she held up to her own. She nestled the cat lovingly in her arm, petting her with her free hand. "So what kind of dogs did you say you have Mr. McLeod?"

"Dogs?" he echoed. "Oh, no, Mrs. Millhouse, I don't *have* dogs. As I explained to you on the phone, I'm the emergency preparedness coordinator. I'm checking out resources in the town for pet care in the event of a flood."

She scowled at him, tipping her face up for the first time, "I thought you said you wanted to see my kennel for your dogs."

"No. I'm sorry for the misunderstanding. It's just that I—"

"What flood?" she interrupted, her tone accusatory. It crossed Gavin's mind maybe Mrs. Millhouse's kingdom was not of this world, but as he looked around he realized that her house, like her yard and at least the outside of the kennel were neat as a pin. The animals appeared healthy and content. And animal welfare was, after all, the reason he was here.

"Maybe I should begin at the beginning, Ma'am." He felt something touch his pant leg and looked down at a small, shaggy mop that had snuck up to assess him. "Hi there, fella." As soon as he spoke to this new dog, it backed away, yipping warningly.

"Barney, he won't hurt you. He's just nervous. He likes dogs. He doesn't take to strangers." She spoke this in a stream, her pronouns so intermingled that Gavin wasn't sure when she was addressing him and when she was talking to her pets.

"Well, you might as well come in and explain yourself." She led him to a sitting room crammed with antiquated furniture. Every square inch of every piece was covered with crocheted bric-à-brac. Coasters, antimacassars, cushion covers and Afghan throws in various patterns of riotous colours, assaulted the eye. A whole shelf was dedicated to Kewpie dolls in crocheted skirts of mauve, lime, turquoise, chartreuse and orange. Even a box of tissues was disguised as a crocheted house, with the emerging tissue simulating smoke.

A grey cat slept on its back in an impossible L-shape in the corner of a settee, its front paws suspended in mid-air. From its throne on an Ottoman, an enormous ginger cat blinked at him with its paws tucked beneath its Farouk bulk.

Gavin squatted on the edge of a chair matted with animal fur. He explained the potential for flooding and his role in emergency planning for Withers. "In the unlikely event of the town being flooded and people being evacuated, pets will need to be lodged away from the reception centre. If you would be willing to take in some animals, compensation would be provided to you, Mrs. Millhouse."

"Sadie,"

"I beg your pardon?"

"Sadie! That's my name." Her manner and tone seemed more parry and thrust than conversation.

"Sadie. Would you be available to help in an emergency?"

"Well, the poor beasts have to go someplace! But I'll need help. And if the town's flooded, what about food? How we going to feed 'em, eh?"

"The emergency preparedness committee will include in their planning that provisions are set aside. Are you on a well, Mrs. Mill…Sadie?"

"Course I'm on a well."

"Then you have a reliable source of water. Is the supply sufficient?"

"Don't see why not. There's enough water for a hundred dogs. Cats too. There be more than a hundred, you s'pose?"

"I don't know yet what the potential need would be. I don't know if there are other kennels either."

"There aren't. I'm the only one. Unless you count that dreadful puppy mill in town," she spat. "I've been after the Town for months to close that place down. It's criminal the way they been keeping those poor creatures. The owners ought to be lined up and shot. Anyway, they're as apt to be in the flood as not, so they're no good."

He wanted to steer clear of Sadie's personal politics. "Well, it sounds like we can count on you, Sadie."

"Well, so long's you get me some help if there get to be a lot. I can't give decent care and attention to more than two or three dozen creatures on my own."

"I take it there's no Mr. Millhouse."

She gave a hoarse laugh, showing her funny bone for the first time. "Oh yeah, there's a Mr. Millhouse, not so's he'd know anymore. He's in a home in Kamloops. He's got the dementia. He doesn't know who I am anymore. Mind you, that's no surprise. He was hardly ever home, worked on the railroad for years, married to it, I always said. I liked it that way. He's fifteen years my senior. We never had a whole lot in common, no kids. I kept house for him to come home to now and again. He sent his cheques and I built this place up. The kennel I mean. You want to take a look at it now?"

"Yes. Please."

The inside of the kennel proved to be as well laid out and maintained as the outside promised. Her people skills may have been lacking polish but he didn't think the animals would have complaints.

Jeremy lounged against his canary BMW as Dana decended her front porch. When she was within reach, he straightened, pulling her into his embrace. "You look lovely," he murmured, kissing her.

She stepped back, extending her arms to the side, showing off her sleeveless sea-green dress, a matching jacket slung over an outstretched arm. "It looks alright?"

He nodded approvingly. "It looks stunning. I knew you'd do it justice."

"You have good taste."

"In women," he winked, opening the car door for her to slide in.

"I'm amazed you found time to shop during the competition."

"We were prowling around downtown. Seattle's such a vibrant city. I wish you had come with me."

She leaned back and closed her eyes. There was so little time for them to just relax and have fun together. Between her hectic round of chores, classes, clinics she taught and regular visits to her mother, her time was at a premium. Add Jeremy's practice, his jaunts to races and training schedule, little time was left between them for romance.

But tonight he insisted she make a real date with him. He promised a drive to a place they both knew, to watch the sunset. "I'm cooking dinner," he declared.

Dana twirled the stem of her wineglass between her thumb and finger, content for the moment. Jeremy bustled about in the next room, preparing dinner. He'd banished her from the kitchen to a bed of thick cushions piled on his Persian rug. His small living room eschewed conventional furniture, its décor a funky mix of Turkish brassware, tapestries, post-modern paintings and posters for major international cycle races. His bike hung from a hook by the door.

Half a dozen candles on a heavy, low circular coffee table were all that lit the room. The clatter from the kitchen was muffled by strains of classical music. Jeremy banged about the kitchen in a kind of frenzy. She watched him fondly.

Jeremy... always a bundle of energy, a man with dreams and ambitions. So many of the guys from high school had ambitions only for hunting, ice-fishing, snowmobiling, getting drunk and getting laid. They were the same oafs who used to make fun of her walk. She'd worn braces on her legs in grade school. With a show of bravado and pride, she endured their taunts about her awkward gait. But on many days she'd retreat to her room to cry. As an adolescent she despaired that any boy would ever want her. The summer before grade ten, the Robbins family moved to Withers. Jeremy became her defender, telling the other boys to take a hike. He was her cheerleader too, championing her efforts to overcome the restrictions of her disability. She could no longer imagine a world without him. After his grueling chiropractic training, he'd established his practice back in Withers to be near her, long after his parents had moved to sunny Spain.

"Now we wait," he announced from the doorway, wiping his hands on a towel. He tossed it on the counter and changed the music, something moody from the fifties. He took her wineglass and set it on the low table. Reaching for her hand, he pulled her upright. He was the only one she'd ever danced with, the only one she trusted not to shame her for her ungainly way of moving.

She closed her eyes and let him guide her around his small living room.

"I'd like to whisk you away to the life you deserve," he murmured in her ear.

She tipped her face to look at him. "I deserve?"

"Don't you ever wish for a more cosmopolitan life—theatre, concerts, intellectual friends, fine dining."

"I never had those things. I don't miss what I don't know."

"But darling that's just the point," he stopped and clutched her upper arms. "There's so much of life we're missing! Nothing ever happens here. No wonder they call this place Withers. You just wither away. Lord, I can't even take you to the movies. There's not a cinema for miles."

"My horses are my life—my work."

"People in the city ride too. There are stables nearby where they keep horses. Near Seattle, a whole development is designed just for equestrians. You could still teach. But we could also sail and swim and go to a major league ball game."

"I guess. I've never really thought about it."

"Never mind," he said quickly, "we can talk about it another time. I have some news." She looked up, catching the excitement in his voice. "I've been invited to join a team of athletes as their chiropractor while they're on tour. Some of them will go to the Olympics. I may even be able to go along then."

"Jeremy! What a wonderful opportunity. When will they want you?"

His grin slipped. "In three days."

"Oh!" she exclaimed. "How long will you be gone?"

"Till August…maybe September."

Happiness deserted her. She meant to give him a brave smile, but brightness came to her eyes instead of her lips, and shimmered there.

"Oh darling," he caught her in his arms, "You know I'll miss you too."

She brushed away an errant tear. "I'm sorry. It's just so sudden. I'm glad for you Jeremy, really I am. It really is an awesome opportunity for you."

"It'll be fantastic," he enthused. "And you'll get away for a few days and come meet me. We'll go sightseeing." She gave him the smile she had wanted to the first time.

"That would be fun," she agreed.

Gavin peered out the window of his office, briefcase in hand. Rain fell in a curtain from the overhang. Heavy cloud cover brought on an early dusk. By now it was almost dark. He flipped off the lights, locking the door behind him. He dashed for his Jeep and drove to the Dream-Catcher.

Foster was already at the table where they held their first meeting. Through a pair of owl-eyed spectacles, he perused the newspaper. LD loitered at the counter, his gaze following Mandy as she tidied up. On a stool at the bar, Gavin recognized the souse who frequented the place. He wore the same red lumberman's jacket, baseball hat and scuffed, steel-toed boots.

Gavin opened his briefcase and set papers on the table. Mandy produced a generous pot of tea with fixings and set out mugs. With a disparaging sigh, Foster made a show of folding his newspaper. He set it aside and checked his watch. Reflexively, so did Gavin. It was three minutes past seven.

"Well, let's get down to work, shall we?" he said, spurred by Foster's impatience. "We need to keep minutes of our meetings. Will someone volunteer? I can type them and you'll all receive copies."

LD flashed a boyish grin. "Don't look at me; I can't hardly read. My fourth-grade teacher gave up on me. 'Lionel Darwin Metcalfe' she'd say, 'the doctor what delivered you musta give you your middle name, 'cause you're a throwback to the monkey.' Kids started calling me Lionel Darwin, laughing at my middle name. I liked it a lot better when they shortened it to LD. Wasn't till I was in seventh grade I found out LD stood for 'learning disabled'. By then, nobody ever called me Lionel anymore." He shrugged, a grin still plastered across his face.

With such an easy going attitude, few insults would stick on LD, Gavin thought. "Okay, LD you're off the hook for minutes."

"I'll do them," Foster fumed, pulling a pen from his breast pocket and clicking the plunger on it. "Do you have paper?"

Gavin slid a blank writing pad over, then handed out a prepared agenda. "I'm going to give you some possible scenarios to help you understand the scope of our job."

He was interrupted by the door crashing open. "Mercy, what a dirty night!" A squat figure, whose gender was discernible only from her voice, bustled in, puddling water around her feet. She wore man's trousers, the legs stuffed into the tops of rubber boots, and toted a plastic shopping bag. Her wispy, short-cropped hair stuck out from beneath a baseball hat. A 'Michelin Man' down jacket hung open for lack of a functional zipper, exposing a sweatshirt filled out by a dumpy chest. On the front was a print of an orange cat curled up on a cushion with the caption, 'Have you hugged your cat today?'

"Ah, there you are!" she addressed Gavin. "I've been all over town trying to find out where the meeting is. Floyd at the newspaper finally told me."

"Mrs. Millhouse!" Gavin stood as she waddled over. "What are you doing here?"

"Whaddaya mean what am I doing here?" she practically shouted. "I'm here to take care of the plan for the animals."

"Oh! Well, that's ah, wonderful," he stammered, taking in her queer attire. He pulled up a chair for her from another table. She sat and immediately pulled a ball of wool from her plastic shopping bag and started hooking around a square of crocheted material. Mandy slid her agenda to Sadie and took LD's since he wasn't using it anyway. Gavin asked everyone to introduce themselves and brought Sadie up to speed. He remained standing, sensing a need to keep a short rein on the motley group.

"Some homes on the other side of the river will need to be sand-bagged," he was explaining some time later. "On this side, the dike protects all areas in the flood plain. If the dike does what it's supposed to, folks on this side of the river will be fine. If a problem does arise, it'll be one of two kinds. The water could get so high it could overtop the dike. In that case, there'll be plenty of warning to get everyone out. The more serious event would be if the dike is breached. That could come with little or no warning."

"Whatta we do then?" asked LD.

Gavin eyed him soberly. "We run away, LD. We run away." The members regarded one another with dawning concern.

LD pressed forward with his unfolding thoughts. "How will everyone know to run? I mean, if they see the water, they'll know but by that time it's kinda late ain't it ? Shouldn't there be some kind o' signal?"

"You're quite right," Gavin replied. Chatter broke out but he silenced them saying, "We'll work on that aspect another time."

"In the event of disastrous flooding," he went on, "the Province will come in with aid. But we have to plan on roads being out. If there's flooding in other areas, the Province could be occupied with several disasters, so for the first seventy-two hours we need to assume we'll be on our own. We will need food, safe drinking water and shelter, the ability to provide medical first aid and, assuming there'll be power outages, a communications system that doesn't require land transmission."

Foster put down his pen. "Anyone who doesn't get up the hill south out of town, or over the bridge to the north before floodwaters hit town is going to get trapped in the eastern hills. From there, there's no road to the outside. That could be half of Withers. Where are we going to house that many people?"

"And how are we going to feed them?" Mandy wailed with a note of panic.

LD said, "If the power is out, you're gonna need an alternative. You can use generators but that's a lotta people. A couple o' generators ain't going to take care of everyone, 'specially if they're scattered all over."

"What I want to know is who's gonna rescue the animals? And how will we feed them, eh? Nobody's thinking about the animals." Sadie scowled, her crochet hook jabbing furiously at the woollen piece she was working on.

"Whoa, everyone," Gavin broke in, holding his hand in a stop sign. "One at a time. Foster, let's deal with your question first. The total population living in the floodplain *inside* the dike is a little shy of two thousand. Some of those need to be evacuated during high-risk time. There's a nursing home for example. It should be cleared out. Anyone elderly or disabled or who couldn't move in a darn hurry needs to be persuaded—and assisted if necessary—to find alternate temporary lodging. Anyone who has the chance to move to higher ground should be encouraged to do so. Assuming a third of the rest could be billeted in homes above the flooded area, we could plan on having to accommodate maybe five to eight hundred. Many can be air-lifted out within a few days or a week perhaps. A core, no doubt, will stay, wanting to get to the clean up as soon as possible."

"Five to eight hundred! Why, that's impossible," Foster protested. "How on earth can we shelter that many people?"

Gavin put a foot up on the seat of his chair and leaned an elbow across his knee. "Well Foster, I don't see that we have a choice. Do you?"

"But Gavin!" It was Mandy's turn to protest. "There's no place around here where that many people can congregate. Are they supposed to just sleep on the ground? And you haven't said how we'll set up a kitchen! There just isn't any place."

"There's a place."

For a moment, no one at the table registered where this observation had come from. They'd forgotten the souse at the bar who sat immobile with his back to them. He had the look of someone on a binge, with a three-day beard, reddened eyes and dishevelled hair spiking out from under his cap.

Gavin drew himself up, alert. "What place?"

"Don't pay any attention to him," Sadie hissed in an indignant whisper, easily audible to the object of her disgust. "He's drunk."

"What place?" Gavin repeated when there was no response. It took a moment, but the bar stool swivelled slowly, its occupant extending a near-empty glass vaguely in Mandy's direction.

"I need a refill."

Mandy sighed. "The bar's closed, Cutter. You know I'm not open late till Thursday."

He tottered to his feet, staggering sideways before he caught his balance. "Well, you got a hell of a crowd in here for bein' closed."

"We're having a meeting. I closed the bar a half hour ago. You should be gone."

He wove unsteadily toward them till he swayed over the back of Sadie's chair. She hunched her shoulders in repulsion and leaned to her side, away from him.

"Sir," Gavin addressed him, "if you know of a possible place to lodge evacuees, I wish you would tell us."

"Won't do you no good. The hoser what runs the place wouldn't take you in if the devil himself were chasing you."

"Still, I'd be grateful for the information."

The man swooped his glass in Mandy's direction. "You gonna pour me another?"

"I'm closed, Cutter. Go home and sleep it off."

He tipped his glass back and drained the dregs, nearly toppling backward in the effort. He belched loudly and plunked the glass down in front of Sadie and tottered toward the door.

"Reprobate!" she muttered. Without turning, Cutter waved his hand with an inebriated flourish.

———

A steady rain fell as Gavin drove to his office next morning. He set up his laptop to key Foster's minutes of last night's meeting. He scarcely got beyond entering the heading and date when Foster's opening gambit left his fingers suspended over the keyboard and his eyes bulging. He snatched up the pages and read through them with increasing dismay. Without reaching the end, he let them slip through his fingers and spill onto his desk. Pushing his laptop away, he leaned on his elbows and let his head sink into his hands.

The entire exercise was rapidly disintegrating into abysmal absurdity. After Cutter's exit, the agenda had been swallowed up in chaos. Each member jockeyed to trump the other with their pet concerns. None seemed capable of co-operating to dwell on one issue at a time. And now Foster's minutes.

They couldn't be printed. They were a madcap cataloguing of the perceived faults of everyone present. Gavin's transgressions included starting late and failing to "run a proper meeting". Foster had recorded LD's admission of a learning disability. He took exception to Sadie being added to the membership without a formal vote, complained that her "infernal knitting" was an annoying distraction and quoted her attributions of Cutter as a vulgar drunk. Foster also 'minuted' that he'd been assigned the duties of garnering supplies, cots and bedding—a matter that in fact, had never been discussed.

He was still holding his head when the door swung open. A wiry man in work clothes thrust his upper body in, still gripping the doorknob.

"You McLeod?" he demanded.

"I am."

"Well, I've got some advice for you, Bud." His voice was hard, cold, his rage barely contained. Slamming the door, he strode to the desk where Gavin sat. He leaned over it, his face close enough for Gavin to feel his breath.

"You keep that renegade out of my camp or so help me I'll sue him, you, the government and anybody else responsible. You get me?"

Gavin felt his heart pumping. He wanted to reach out and push the man's chest to get him out of his face, or shove his chair back and retreat. Instead he said, "I don't believe we've met."

"Name's Malloy. I run the logging camp up at Jackson Ridge. And your boy waltzed in there this morning and starts telling me I gotta turn my camp over to the government for some goddamn relief effort."

"My...boy?" Gavin replied, confused.

"Yeah, your boy!" Malloy fairly shouted now.

"I'm sorry, I don't understan..."

"A member of your *committee*," he retorted with biting sarcasm.

Foster? "Did he give his name, Mr. Malloy?"

"He didn't *need* to. I know who the hell the cunt is."

Gavin flinched at the epithet. "His name, sir?"

"Johnson! Don't you know who you've sent to do your business?"

Gavin shook his head, not in answer to the man's question but to clear it. "I don't believe I know a Mr. Johnson."

"*John*son," Malloy repeated, belligerent in tone and carriage.

Gavin stared blankly.

"*Ralph* Johnson."

He shrugged. Malloy reared back and rotated his whole upper body round to the front again, as if to hammer home how obtuse Gavin was being. "Cutter!" he roared.

The picture snapped into focus. Cutter. *There's a place,* he had said. Gavin recalled the flick of Cutter's wrist when Sadie pronounced her appraisal of him. He wondered if there'd been some deliberate sabotage in Cutter's action this morning.

"This man said you had to turn your camp over for a relief effort?"

"That's what I said, isn't it. And I told *him,* the hell I do! He started cussin' and mouthin' off. I told him to get off the property or I'd set the police on him. The no-account buzzard tried to take a poke at me. Woulda got me too, 'cept he was so pissed he couldn't see straight to land it. I run him off."

Gavin eased himself to his feet "Mr. Malloy, I'm afraid there's been a mistake. Mr. Johnson is *not* a member of my committee. His action may have been well intended, but misguided. I apologize."

"You didn't send him?"

"No."

Malloy straightened up and pulled at the lapels of his leather vest. "Well!" he puffed. "I shoulda known. That cantankerous ol' buzzard. Good day, sir." He wheeled and stalked out, shutting the door sharply on his way.

Gavin collapsed in his chair and dropped his head in his hands again.

Chapter Five

Not everything about the committee meeting had been a disaster. When Gavin touched on the matter of homes at risk on the reserve, Mandy asked what discussions had taken place with the band about protecting themselves. The truth was Gavin felt stymied by Town Hall. They said *they* would approach the band leaders, not to do so on his own. But every time he asked about it, nothing had been done. "I'll take you to see my grandmother," Mandy offered. "She's an Elder. She'll introduce you to the band Council."

The next afternoon, he met Mandy at the Dream-Catcher. She left her part-time assistant, Rosie, to handle the late lunch customers and climbed into his Cherokee with him. They crossed the bridge heading out of town. The river had risen several metres since his arrival in Withers.

"Did you grow up on the reserve Mandy?"

"Me? No. Till I was sixteen, I lived in the Lower Mainland…Burnaby, New Westminster."

"I never took you for a city girl."

"A lot you know," she laughed. "It's taken me twenty years to live down my 'city girl' reputation."

"You make it sound like a 'bad girl' reputation."

The warmth of her chuckle was disarming. "You got that right. I lived alone with my dad there. My mom took off for parts unknown 'cause she felt he couldn't accept her Native ways. I don't think he could fathom his half-Native daughter either. In any case, we didn't get along. First time I ran off, I was fifteen. Did the street scene a few weeks till the police picked me up and brought me home. I decided the next time I'd have a better plan. I knew I had a grandmother up here, so I stuck it out another couple of months till I turned sixteen and hightailed it up here to check out my Native roots. Best thing I ever did. Turn left up there, Gavin."

The wheels crunched on gravel as they left the highway. "Must have been quite an adjustment when you came here."

"I'll say. For my grandmother!" She chuckled again. "Still, she was the first person in my life to love me unconditionally. No matter what wild and crazy things I did, she accepted me. At eighteen I moved into town and got a job at The Winchester."

They passed the occasional house, mostly two-tone clapboard. Yards sprouted a haphazard collection of rusted out cars, children's toys or forgotten blankets on clothes line or fence. Some were better tended. Mandy directed him into the yard of a small house with a deer fence around a vegetable garden. A curtain moved in a window. Mandy waved. Before they reached the door, it opened and a wizened but remarkably erect elderly woman appeared.

"Hello Grandmother. It's good to see you."

The Elder responded in Native tongue, her voice papery thin. Nut brown skin stretched over high cheekbones, her eyes almost lost in creases. Mandy bent to kiss her on the cheek. The woman patted her affectionately on the arm. "Grandmother, I want you to meet someone. This is Mr. McLeod. He's the man I told you about." She spoke louder than usual, from which Gavin gathered the old woman's hearing was fading. "Gavin this is my grandmother, Emma Toms."

"You come in," she said. "I make you some tea." She ushered them into a neat kitchen with a table covered in green checked oilcloth in the centre of the room. She put a tea kettle on the stove and set out cups.

Mandy asked about her garden and people on the reserve. She had coached Gavin on the importance of waiting for the right time to approach the purpose of his visit. "White people are always in such a hurry to talk business," she had explained. "It's not our people's custom." Emma broached the subject after they relaxed awhile over tea. She would take him to people who would be interested in talking to him.

They rode in the Cherokee, while Emma directed. She spoke of their experiences on the reserve with high water. At the band council hall, she introduced him to several members. Three of them piled into a pickup and led the way to several low areas along the river. They visited homes and spoke with the residents. In all, fourteen houses would need sandbagging.

The last one was closest to the river. Mandy shadowed Gavin as he conversed with the men and checked out the area. The group dispersed finally, the band councillors leaving in their truck. Mandy looked around. "Where's grandmother?"

They spied her by the riverbank and strolled over. Emma stood staring down at the fast flowing water. Reeds bent in the current.

"Grandmother?"

The old woman canted her head toward the sound of Mandy's voice, but seemed distracted.

"Are you alright?" Mandy asked.

"The river spirit spoke to me."

Mandy exchanged glances with Gavin. He wondered if the old woman was having a moment of senility. She was in her eighties after all. Trooping around all afternoon must surely have tired her. "What did it tell you, Grandmother?"

"The answer to your heart's longing tarries at the water's edge."

Mandy furrowed her brow. "My heart's longing?"

Emma nodded. "A wound will heal your wound."

"What does it mean?" she asked, but looking up, Emma said only, "You will know, my child. In time you will know."

On the ride back to town, Gavin asked, "What was that all about?"

"My grandmother has the second sight—what white men call clairvoyance. Our people don't scoff at it the way white people do."

In the eastern hills above the town, Gavin coasted along a gravel road, peering at numbers on mailboxes. He'd memorized the address he got at Town Hall from property tax records. He thought the next one should be it. It didn't have a number, but the name 'Johnson' was discernible in chipped, faded paint.

He pulled into the yard. A house, shack really, was tucked back in the trees. He got out, half expecting a junk-yard dog to lunge out from under the porch. But there was no dog.

He knocked on the door and looked around. A cord of wood was stacked neatly against the cabin wall, with what appeared to be freshly split logs on top. Tire tracks led around behind the house. The yard was otherwise devoid of any human imprint. He was about to knock a second time when the door opened the width of the face that peered out. Cutter didn't look surprised to see him. Gavin thought he detected a ghost of a smile.

"Howdy," Cutter greeted him.

"Hello Mr. Johnson. May I come in?"

The door opened wider. "Be my guest."

The interior of the cabin was rustic but not in as much disarray as Gavin had anticipated for a man he'd only ever seen drinking. No more than average for bachelor quarters. Johnson didn't ask him to sit down, coolly waiting for him to explain his presence.

"Mr. Johnson, the other night you indicated you knew of a place capable of lodging a large number of people in case of emergency." Cutter's countenance did not flicker. "But you didn't say where."

He stuck his jaw out in defiance. "Why should I tell ya?"

"I'm not asking you to tell me. What I will ask you is why you took it upon yourself to approach the camp foreman?"

The corner of Cutter's mouth twitched, giving Gavin the impression again of a smirk.

"Who says I did?"

"Mr. Malloy. I had a visit from him. He wasn't too pleased."

"Hmph! Don't believe everything Malloy tells you. He's a liar and blowhard."

"Nevertheless Mr. Johnson, I don't understand why you approached him about this."

"Maybe I was trying to help," he answered thrusting out his chest.

Gavin stuck his hands in his pockets, leaned forward slightly regarding his boots, then peered up again at Johnson. "You believe this logging camp could house several hundred people with facilities to feed them?"

"Absolutely. For a short time in warm weather anyway. It would take some upgrading and maybe some tents. But there's a big kitchen, dining hall, rec hall and office. It's got bunkhouses, showers and a first aid station," he said, becoming animated. "There's a generator in case of power outage. More could be brought in. There's plenty of open area for a helicopter to land."

Gavin nodded, digesting this information.

"I could help you out on your committee," Johnson added eagerly.

Gavin regarded him, pondering something. "There seems to be a history of animosity between you and Mr. Malloy."

"Hmph! That hoser."

"He claims you tried to strike him."

"Why would I want to do that?" he said, his tone belligerent.

"I don't know, sir. But under the circumstances your confrontation with him may have cost us the only potential emergency lodgings for townsfolk if Withers floods this spring."

"Blame Malloy. That arrogant son-of-a-bitch wouldn't give you the sweat off his ass! He's the reason I can't work anymore. That bastard ruined me."

"Did you try to punch him?"

"Hah! The hoser had it comin'. I was only actin' for a good cause."

"Perhaps you were. But your intervention was monumentally unhelpful."

He looked chastened. "I'll make it up to you."

"How?"

"By working on your committee. I'm a hard worker. See if I don't do a bang up job."

"I need people I can depend on, Mr. Johnson, people who can gain the co-operation of others without getting into a confrontation."

Something that looked like hunger seeped into Cutter's eyes. "Mr. McLeod, I *need* something to do. I sit around all day every day twiddling my thumbs. I worked hard all my life. I was proud to pull in a day's pay and fall into bed at night with my body achin' from hard labour. Now I got aches and pains and nothin' to show for 'em."

Maybe it was the shift from belligerence to desperation, maybe it was the faint breath of alcohol, maybe it was the macho pride his father had made familiar, but Gavin felt his gut wrench.

"No. I'm sorry." It was hard to see the disabled logger's expression cave in. He didn't argue and Gavin left quickly to leave the man some vestige of pride.

The weather forecast called for a drying trend, sorely needed. Creeks were already swollen and the unrelenting rain was making people irritable. Despite being used to the soggy West Coast, even Gavin suffered cabin fever, so when Dana called early next morning suggesting they take advantage of a dry day to go hacking, he eagerly agreed. "There's a trailhead above Stayner Creek on your road," she said. "Your cabin must be near it. Why don't I trailer the horses over to you?"

An hour later, they saddled up in the yard in front of the cabin. Side by side, they rode down the gravel road several hundred metres to a bridge crossing the gushing flow of Stayner Creek. Beyond the bridge, Dana eased Nefarious' nose down the right embankment onto a trail. Jake followed and Gavin leaned far back to keep his balance. Once on the level, Dana turned in the saddle. "We'll go single file in the woods. Jake will follow Nefarious. Don't interfere with his head and you'll be fine."

They rode in silence. When next she turned to look back, she caught him grinning. "What's so funny?"

"It's my first time out of the pony ring." Her answering laughter rang out through the trees.

For the next half hour he watched Nefarious' swaying haunches through the scope of Jake's ears. Talk was limited since they had to shout to make themselves heard over the rushing creek. The trail wound away from it finally, through a stand of birches. These thinned out to a meadow where Dana pulled Nefarious up to let Jake come alongside.

"Do you want to see the conditions higher up? If you're up for the ride, we can get to the headwaters of the creek... unless we run into the snow line."

He arched an eyebrow. "What does, 'If you're up for the ride,' mean?"

"It's probably an hour and a half up and there's some climbing to do. The horses do most of the work, but if you're not comfortable in the saddle going up or downhill..."

He pondered. "It *would* be useful to know if the melt has reached the headwaters." He grinned at her, "And it is, after all, why I let you talk me into lessons."

For the next hour, the trail alternated between woods and open meadow. Sometimes the horses had to scrabble over rock where Gavin marvelled that Dana could follow the trail. Other times they followed a well-worn, muddy track. They stopped at noon in the open by a tarn. They sat on the rocks beside the outflow and he dug out sandwiches he'd prepared for them. They had a panoramic view down the mountain and up to the craggy top.

He breathed in deep relaxation. So much tension had built up in him over the last few weeks, it felt good to let it slip away. "It's amazing, isn't it?"

"The view?"

"The view, the space. You realize we haven't seen another human being all morning?"

"Mmh," she mused and looked around. "I love it up here. I spent a lot of time riding back in these hills as a child."

"I envy you."

A nostalgic smile touched her mouth briefly. "That part was nice. But it wasn't always a picnic for me back then." She wrapped her arms around her knees and turned her face from him, purportedly looking down the mountain. "Kids at school weren't very kind to me because of my disability."

He greeted her admission with silence. After a long moment, she glanced up to see him regarding her. "What disability?" he said softly. Her gaze fell away to the surface of the water, but he saw the corners of her mouth give the slightest curve.

He scanned the peaks above them and spoke in a gentle cadence. "'Unto the hills around do I lift up my longing eyes. Oh, whence for me doth my salvation come, from whence arise?'"

"I thought you weren't a church-goer."

He rolled his eyes. "A reluctant one. My mother insisted." He leaned back on his elbows and gazed uphill again. "I remember singing that hymn. I know it's supposed to be about God, but for me it truly *meant* the hills…the mountains. Even from the dingiest street in Vancouver, they were always visible. As a youngster, I used to dream about escaping to them. When I was older, I'd take a bus to the north shore and do exactly that."

"What was it like for a boy growing up on the dingiest street in Vancouver?" she asked.

He paused, looking bemused, then said, "We lived in the neighbourhood where my father grew up. I had to contend with his reputation as an Irish street-fighter turned professional boxer. Every kid in the neighbourhood wanted to fight me. Truth is, I didn't have the mettle for it."

"Were you bullied?" she asked sympathetically.

Again he took his time responding. "One day my father saw me get beaten up by a bigger kid. He didn't stop it. Afterward he dressed me down for not trying to land a few punches of my own. He took me down to the gym, strapped a pair of gloves on me and stood me up in the ring. He kept egging me to hit him, but every time I tried, he boxed me. What hurt the most was, he taunted me in front of his cronies, calling me a cry baby and sissy. I had a bloody nose and couldn't see for tears, but he just kept hitting me till I snapped and started flailing in a blind rage. My mother was furious when she found out what happened but he overrode her opposition. He kept up those lessons till I learned some moves."

"Did it give you better odds on the street?" she asked.

"Better…and worse. Every tough for miles around wanted to see if they could get a piece of Donnie McLeod's son." He felt her eyes on him but couldn't bring himself to meet them.

"I was eleven when he left for good. We heard through the grapevine he fought this or that fight across the States, that he spent more time in jail. When it became apparent he was never coming back, my mother packed up and moved us to another part of town. That was the end of my fighting days. From then on she instilled in me her own code. 'You need to learn words, Gavin,' she'd lecture me. 'Real men solve conflict with words, not fists. If you're going to succeed in life, get an education.'"

"Your mother sounds like a smart woman."

"Smart, yeah. And tough. She's gone now."

"Did you ever see your father again?"

"No. And believe it or not, I really missed him. I felt guilty too."

"Guilty?"

"I thought he left because of me."

"You know that isn't true," she said softly.

He grimaced. "Yeah, I guess." He picked up a stone and tossed it into the tarn.

When the ripples ceased, a chilly breeze disturbed the water's surface. Dana sighed loudly, as if to break the somber mood. "We must be near the snow line. Shall we press on?"

They continued uphill another half hour. As she'd promised, the trail got considerably steeper and rockier. The horses scrabbled in places, making him grab the saddle horn to keep from sliding off over Jake's rump. He admired how Dana seemed part of Nefarious.

They reached a sloping alpine meadow laced with tiny rivulets. When they stopped, they could hear them making soft gurgling sounds. Crystalline snow blanketed the upper part of the meadow. The horses sank up to their fetlocks in oozy mud. Not liking the footing, they shuffled around, their hooves making loud sucking noises with each step.

"It's too slippery to go on," Dana said.

"I've seen what I need to see," he replied. "There's a lot of water still up there." He peered up at the sky. "We've lost the sun."

They started back down. The horses, eager to return to their stable, clipped along at a lively pace. In the trees, the shadows were deeper than on the way up. The wind picked up. Gavin turned his collar against it. Halfway down, as they crossed an open area, the first big drops of rain fell. "So much for a drying trend," he hollered. He saw her nod but she didn't turn her head.

It was raining in earnest when they entered the trees again. At first they offered some cover but after a few minutes, the leaves acted more like funnels than umbrellas. Rain soaked through his jacket. His shirt pasted to his back. He shivered and wondered how Dana was faring.

By the time they reached the road, it was a downpour. They trotted across the bridge, then urged their mounts to a canter the remaining several hundred metres. Gavin barely dismounted and loosened Jake's saddle before Dana had removed and stowed Nefarious' tack and trotted him up into the trailer. She took Jake to load him while he stuffed the second saddle away.

"Come inside and get dry," he yelled into the trailer.

"You go ahead. I'll be there in a minute."

Inside the cabin, he kicked off his boots, peeled off his sodden socks and rolled the bottom of his pant legs. Only then did he venture across the carpet, thinking of the deceased Mrs. Ellwood as he did so. He went straight to lighting a fire in the wood burner he always kept ready. Once it caught, he closed the glass doors, grateful Foster had put in 'all the amenities'. The rain pattered steadily on the roof.

He grabbed a couple of fluffy towels from the bathroom and was towelling his hair when the tempo of the rain suddenly went from steady to fierce. Seconds later he heard a squeal outside. First he froze, then took three strides toward the door, when it flew open. Dana, vocalizing still, bolted in and slammed it behind her. He stared at her. Simultaneously, they burst out laughing. Her hair hung in strings, she held her hands away from her body in a helpless sort of pose, water dripping from fingers, nose and sleeves. And she was smeared from chest to toes in thick, oozy mud. She shrugged apologetically. "I slipped."

A grin split his face. "So I see. You don't suppose I'm letting you in here like that do you?"

She giggled. "What do you suggest?"

"I suggest I dig out a dry shirt and pair of jeans you can borrow. And that you take off what you're wearing and head into the bathroom," he thumbed behind him, "and get into a shower." He put a kitchen chair near her and draped the second towel over it. "Here, take this. I'll put some duds in the bathroom. Then I'm going into the bedroom to change as well. I won't come out till I hear the shower running."

A few minutes later, in dry clothes, he put on a pot of coffee. He gathered her muddy shirt, jeans, socks, bra and panties by the door and put them in a plastic bag. He rearranged the wood in the fire with tongs, to get a good blaze going. The bathroom door opened. Dana emerged wearing his jeans and blue flannel shirt. Her breasts pushed against the fabric in pointy mounds. A desire to pull her into his arms shot through him like low-voltage current. He reminded himself she was engaged and he was married. He turned instead and poured two steaming mugs of coffee, extending one to her. She accepted it gratefully, wrapping both hands around the mug, apparently oblivious to his adulterous impulse.

They sat in the kitchen with the table safely between them. "How are things going with the committee?" she asked.

He groaned, so pathetically that she laughed a crooning sort of laugh in sympathy. "That bad?"

"Nah," he shrugged.

She raised a sceptical brow.

"Okay," he conceded, "so it's the committee from hell." Her intent gaze loosened his tongue. He hadn't meant to divulge the quirks and eccentricities of his volunteers and their separate one-track agendas, but he did. He told, anonymously, of his failed attempt to recruit Will Hahn, and of Cutter, the wannabe member. He regaled her with Cutter's presumptuous approach to Malloy, ending in violence, and how it caused him to suffer Malloy's rage. He imparted the gist of Foster's offensive minutes. By the time he finished, she was laughing helplessly.

"You can laugh," he said with a rueful look, "but my boss is gonna have my ass in a sling if I don't start making progress and stop getting complaints."

She regarded him thoughtfully, a sympathetic smile still lingering. "In a small town, things don't happen the same way they do in the big city, Gavin. You work with what you've got."

He nodded introspectively. "I'm just worried. Chances are there'll be nothing worse than a few wet basements come early summer. On the other hand, things could get very ugly."

"Maybe I can help."

He met her gaze with a questioning look.

"Not in a big way. But it sounds like you could use a secretary at your meetings. Now that Jeremy's gone till fall, I have some extra time. I could take min..."

"Jeremy's gone?"

Looking abashed, she waved her hand, as if this information were nothing newsworthy. But Gavin sensed it was more important than her gesture implied. He regretted his blundering observation. The silence was awkward.

"He had this great opportunity," she said brightly, filling it. She explained briefly, finishing by saying, "He'll be gone a few months. Between running my riding academy, taking care of my mother and spending time with him, I'm normally really busy. But I'll have extra time now. I could come to your meetings and take minutes. I took typing in high school and I used to be the secretary for a pony club I belonged to. It would be one less thing for you to worry about."

"I'd be most grateful for your secretarial skills," he said sincerely.

"Good," she flashed a broad smile.

The rain lessened to a light patter. "I need to get the horses home," she said. Promising to return his clothes to him at his office, she left in the gathering dusk.

The rain continued in pulses through the night. At his office next morning, Gavin made some calls about the logging camp at Jackson Ridge. He pored over maps to locate it and studied the pattern of roads in the area. A steady drizzle pattered in the street. Rain fell in a beaded curtain from the eaves beyond the covered boardwalk. He didn't hear the door open but suddenly the rain sounded more immediate. He looked up. A man stood framed in the doorway, frozen there.

"Mr. McLeod?"

He leapt to his feet. "Mr. Hahn!" He strode to the front of his office extending a hand. "How nice to see you. Come in out of the weather."

Hesitantly Will Hahn entered, closing the door behind him. He avoided Gavin's eyes, cautiously taking the hand thrust in front of him.

"Would you like some coffee?" Gavin indicated the pot on the shelf by the wall. "You look wet through, man. You must be chilled."

"I've been walking. Yes, thanks. Black, please."

He took the chair opposite Gavin's desk and reached under his jacket and shirt for a dry corner of undershirt to wipe his wire-frame glasses. Gavin handed him a steaming mug and poured himself one. He dragged his chair out from behind his desk and they sat. Will hugged his mug in both hands, warming them.

"How can I help you, Mr. Hahn?"

The man reached into his pants pocket and pulled out a damp, folded sheet of paper. He handed it to Gavin. "I received this in my mailbox yesterday."

Gavin carefully unfolded it. The side of his mouth curled up in gratified recognition. It was a flyer he'd created on his laptop and reproduced at Town Hall. It condensed information from various sources on what supplies to have on hand and how to respond in the event of a flood. His contact information was on the bottom. He'd taken stacks of them to the committee meeting the other night. He told the committee they needed to go out to every household. LD jumped right in, offering to deliver them to every one of the seven hundred-odd homes in urban and rural Withers. He'd even coaxed Mandy to ride along on the back of his ATV to stuff the mailboxes.

"When I read it," Will said, "I agonized over what to do."

"Agonized?" Gavin echoed.

"Yes," he murmured, lowering his gaze to the floor.

When he looked up again, Gavin offered a perplexed frown.

"After I turned down your request for my help, my conscience plagued me. I began following the news about the snowpack and the high risk it poses this year." He contemplated the depths of his mug with an expression of misery. He sighed, seeming unable to go on.

Gavin waited, unsure how to help. Hahn raised his eyes, his gaze searching. "I hate being around people, Mr. McLeod. I don't seem to fit in."

"Will…May I call you Will?" The other nodded. "Will," Gavin went on gently, "your display of QSL cards suggests to me you have friends all over the world."

"It's different on the airwaves. People don't really know the face behind the handle."

Gavin gave his head a tiny shake and blinked. "So? What's with your face? Is it plastered on a wanted poster or something?"

That produced a sheepish grin. "Hardly. I've never been in trouble with the police."

"Then what's not to fit it?"

There was an awkward silence. Finally Will admitted, "I don't normally talk about myself."

"We all have insecurities, Will. Believe me, I have mine."

Hahn smiled faintly, his whole demeanour tentative. "I admire the work you do, Sir."

"Forget the 'Sir'. I'm fine with 'Gavin'."

"Okay…Gavin." He seemed to vacillate, a pause stretching between them. "The kind of work you do, is it just the planning, or do you get involved in disaster relief?"

"I've taken part in many relief efforts."

The other nodded thoughtfully. "Relief work is common among Mennonites."

"Are you Mennonite?"

He nodded. "I was raised in an Old Order community. I left when I was barely out of my teens."

"That must have been hard for your family."

"I have not spoken with them since. They shunned me." Will answered, shamefaced.

"That's tough," Gavin said gently. "I'm sorry."

Will fell silent again. Gavin waited and soon he spoke up. "I feel I can trust you Mr. M—Gavin. I'll tell you why I refused your request that day and why I'm here now.

He took a deep breath. "You see, as a child, I had an insatiable appetite for knowledge. In the Old Order, no one receives an education beyond grade eight. More than that isn't considered necessary for our lifestyle. Reading, of course, is permitted and I devoured books. But often my father censored what I wanted to read. I developed a keen interest in electronics and radio. Radio, of course, is forbidden. My father forbade me to read such subjects. Alas, I defied him. More than once, I was caught and severely punished. One time I had a terrible argument with him, which itself was considered a sin on my part, because in arguing, I was not honouring him. In the heat of the argument, he told me if I could not submit to the Ordnung—the rules of the people—and of his house, I should leave. In my foolish pride, I didn't back down. He refused to speak to me. It turned our household upside down. I packed up and left.

"I had grand illusions of life in the outside world, of getting a university education. But for a farm boy who has lived apart, it is very hard to break in. Wherever I went, people thought I was odd. Peers can be very cruel. I wanted to be accepted but it seemed the harder I tried, the more I became the object of ridicule. I once tried to visit my family, but my father refused to acknowledge me. My family could not go against him. I knew I could never return to my former life. I was never able to scrape together enough money for university. But I discovered libraries, books. I love the classics—Shakespeare, Kipling, Byron. I also discovered ham radio. Now these are my life."

"How did you come to be here, in Withers?"

"I travelled, wanting to see more of the world. In the end, I sought out the same solitude and segregation I ran away from. I earn enough with my repair business to get by. It allows me to buy my radio equipment.

"Although I've not ventured into the aspect of ham that involves helping out in disaster, I'm very aware of the duty. It's something ham has in common with my Mennonite upbringing. Whenever anyone in the community or a neighbouring community suffered a calamity, everyone pitched in to help out."

Gavin nodded to encourage him to continue, which, momentarily, he did.

"When I was a young boy, a flash flood swept through a nearby town. The people were not Mennonite, but my father and many other able-bodied men went to help out. They were away for weeks, clearing debris, setting up tents to feed people, repairing and rebuilding homes. I remember how utterly exhausted he was when he came home and how proud I was of him." Will heaved a sigh and sank back into his chair, seemingly exhausted himself from probably the most he'd spoken for a very long time.

Gavin got up and refilled Will's empty mug. He sat down again and leaned forward. "Are you offering to join the volunteers on my committee?"

"If something terrible were to happen and I did nothing to try and prevent it, I don't think I could live with myself."

Gavin reached across the space between them, offering a handshake. "I could sure use you, Will."

Will accepted his grasp, evincing a shy smile.

Gavin awoke the next morning to the riotous sound of birds. He stepped outside with his coffee mug, soaking up the sun that streamed down. Steam rolled off the cabin's sodden shake roof.

Twenty minutes later, the Cherokee purred up a gravel road into the eastern hills. He dodged logging trucks barrelling down to the mill. The drivers must have nerves of steel or strong suicidal tendencies, he thought. A large sign heralded the entrance to the logging camp. Soon he came to a clear-cut area accommodating the camp. He counted fifteen buildings. Two of the larger ones were probably a dining hall and recreation facility. Most others were likely bunkhouses. On one side of the camp, logs ready for transport, were heaped in piles. A mammoth machine lifted one as he watched, loading it onto a truck. On the other side, a field of rough cut grass looked like a sports field.

He shifted into low, cruising past buildings till he came to one with the company logo over the door. A man in work clothes and hard hat emerged just as he pulled up. Gavin leaned out the window.

"Where can I find Mr. Malloy?"

The man hooked his thumb over his shoulder, indicating the door he'd just exited. Without a word, he strode away.

Gavin went in. He found himself in a rudimentary office. Behind the desk, Malloy looked up from papers. His eyes registered recognition. His mouth hardened in a thin line.

Gavin removed his hat. "I'd like to talk with you, Mr. Malloy."

"Likely won't do you no good."

Gavin indicated an empty chair with his hat. "May I sit?"

"I'm a busy man."

"I won't take much of your time."

Malloy gave a curt gesture toward the chair. Gavin sat.

"I want to apologize again for the aggravation you suffered the other day when Mr. Johnson misrepresented himself to you."

Malloy absorbed this stone-faced.

"You thought the government was…well, expropriating the camp." Gavin paused for a response, but none came. He plunged on. "I *do* work for the government. My job is to help people prepare for or deal with disaster situations."

"I know what your job is."

"Good. Then you're probably also aware there is a heightened alert for possible severe flooding. The town of Withers is vulnerable."

"I'm in the logging business, Mr. McLeod, not the navy. What is that to me?"

"If the town is inundated, this camp will be cut off from the outside world. The mill you transport your product to will be under water." A brow in Malloy's forehead arched almost imperceptibly. "There would also be people trapped in these hills, possibly a thousand or more."

"So your employer, the government, can send in some rescue helicopters and take 'em out."

"Yes, sir, the government or the armed forces will no doubt evacuate some people—eventually. However if Withers is under water, it may not be the only populated area experiencing a state of emergency. Marshalling resources to provide aid could take days. There could be significant medical emergencies. People will require food, water and shelter, or the death toll will rise."

Malloy's eye contact broke as he took in his message. Gavin pressed his advantage, leaning forward. "We all hope Withers survives the high water mark without crisis. In such a case, you'll experience little if any disruption to your business. But if the worst happens, I believe your camp could serve as a much-needed refuge, with only minor upgrades. At no cost to you of course."

Malloy glanced up sharply, squinting with suspicion. "Why here?"

"Where else would you suggest, Mr. Malloy?"

Malloy regarded him grimly. "So basically, Cutter had it right. The government expects me to turn over my camp for a relief effort."

"I'd like to think of it as the government—and the citizens of Withers—making some enhancements, with your permission, that most likely will never need to be used by them."

"Enhancements?"

"A communications centre and radio room, extra bunks, temporary water reservoir, stocks of food staples, bedding, medical supplies, that sort of thing."

Malloy mused. Then his mouth pressed into a thin line again and he shook his head. "Nope, I'll be damned if I'm letting that miserable bugger waltz in here, insult me in front of my men, take a poke at me and out-manoeuvre me just to try to prove I don't control my camp. Not after all the hell he raised around here." Malloy sprang to his feet, spurred by remembered grievances. "No siree! That bastard would have to *crawl* back here before I was to agree to something others would see as him getting the upper hand," he snarled, jabbing his finger on the desk.

Gavin sat back with a sigh. Once again he was conscious of the role of history and relationships in a small town, in trying to get things done. It seemed he was always tripping on them. "Would you mind telling me about the events that led to the animosity between Mr. Johnson and yourself?"

Malloy's raised brows registered surprise, then knit together in a puzzled frown. "Didn't he tell you? His version anyway."

"Truthfully, sir, I don't know the man. He was drinking in the bar while I met with my committee. He listened in and offered some information. The next thing I knew, you were burning a path to my desk in my office."

Malloy's jaw-line softened in sheepish acknowledgment. He sat down again, sighing heavily. "Cutter was a good man in the woods," he said. "Married, happily, I'm told. He was vying for the job of foreman, wanting better pay to be able to build his wife a nice house. But I beat him out in the competition. He probably would have got over it, but his wife took sick shortly after. She got pneumonia and died. He took it hard. I sent him home a couple of times because he came to work with alcohol on his breath.

"Round about then, I hired my nephew. Cutter was the best I had. I wanted Jeff to learn from him, so I put him on Cutter's crew. I didn't find out till later that Cutter rode Jeff, rode him rough. Jeff never came to me 'cause he didn't want it to appear as if he was the subject of favouritism. Apparently that was one of the things Cutter rode him about.

"One day there was an accident. Jeff felled a tree; Cutter got trapped beneath it. Lucky he wasn't killed, but his injuries ended his days as a logger. In the ensuing investigation, he accused me of mismanaging the camp, practising nepotism and allowing Jeff to do things he wasn't properly trained to do.

"Jeff took it pretty hard. In the course of asking the men on the crew my own questions, it started to come out about how Cutter had been treating him. I asked more questions and learned he'd been drinking on the job. The guys liked Cutter and they felt sorry for him on account of his wife. That's why nobody told the investigators he was drunk and that he failed to heed the warning Jeff hollered. I took Jeff aside and he admitted he knew Cutter had been drinking. I put the investigators onto it. They got the hospital records which confirmed there was alcohol on his breath when he was brought in. Unfortunately the doctor didn't do a blood alcohol test. As for assigning fault, the investigation ended inconclusively. To this day, Cutter has it in for me, holding me responsible for him being unable to work."

Gavin nodded when Malloy ended his story. "Thank you for sharing that with me, Mr. Malloy. I can understand your frustration. Notwithstanding, I hope you can put the welfare of the citizens of Withers ahead of a feud Mr. Johnson has chosen to carry on with you."

"You told me it's only a *chance* the camp would be needed in an emergency."

"Yes."

"Well, the pomposity of Cutter Johnson is a sure thing. If I give you the go-ahead, he'll make my life miserable. I'll take my chances with a flood, Mr. McLeod. Sorry. It's no deal." Malloy stood again to indicate the interview was over.

Gavin rose to meet the other man's eyes on the level. "Mr. Malloy, he won't even be involved."

Malloy bent over the desk toward Gavin, leaning on his knuckles. "That son-of-a-gun is going to have to own up and apologize before I'm turning my camp over, after he demanded I do just that."

The two men eyed each other in silence a moment. Then Gavin sighed in defeat. "Thank you for your time," he said. He walked to the door, opened it and put on his hat.

"Good luck to you," Malloy called after him.

Gavin kept on going. Not till he got into his Jeep did he expel his pent-up breath. "Bloody hell," he swore, thumping the steering wheel.

———

Cutter was splitting kindling when Gavin pulled into his yard. Gavin sauntered over, hands in his pockets. "Can I talk with you a minute, Mr. Johnson?" he asked.

Cutter leaned his axe against the chopping block and drew a rolley from his pocket. He struck a match and lit it. Eyeing Gavin warily, he waited for him to speak, taking a long drag and blowing a stream of smoke.

"You were right about the camp, Mr. Johnson. It would serve very well for what we need."

"Hah!" Cutter exclaimed. "I told you so."

"Unfortunately we won't be able to use it."

"Huh? Why not? Malloy?" Gavin said nothing, letting silence answer. "That cock-sucker! I told you he was a hoser."

"Mr. Johnson, there may still be a way."

Cutter's brow furrowed. "How?"

"Mr. Malloy seems to think you owe him an apology."

"Hah!" Cutter exploded again. He spat a wad to his side. "That'll be a frosty day in hell."

Gavin continued evenly. "And he wants you to own up to what really happened when you were injured."

Cutter's gorge rose; his eyes narrowed to slits. Gavin was acutely aware of the axe within Cutter's reach. He flashed on the thrill of fear he used to get when his father impaled him with the same look.

"That sleaze-bag can kiss my arse. His patsy nephew broke my back. Malloy is to blame for putting a boy on a man's job and letting him screw up."

Gavin locked eyes with Cutter, confronting but not judging. "Were you intoxicated at the time?"

Cutter's eyes blazed. "He tell you that? He's a goddamn liar!"

Gavin shook his head wearily. "I don't know what the truth is, Mr. Johnson, but I do know this. Because of your feuding, the welfare, and indeed the lives of a great many men, women and children may be put at risk in the very near future. I've asked him and I'm asking you to consider that. I hope one of you comes to your senses before it's too late." He turned and headed for his Jeep.

———————————

By the time he got to the Dream-Catcher that evening for the committee meeting, Gavin was in a foul mood. In the afternoon he'd suffered a dressing down from Mayor Hale on the telephone. Two committee members, notably Foster and Sadie appeared before Council the evening before, demanding financial backing for a long list of supplies, including cat food and pet crates. Their solicitation was disorganized and testy. It sparked sharp negative reaction from council.

No doubt, Gavin thought, furious. He was running late but chose to hoof it from his office on foot to burn off some of his simmering rage. He'd been looking forward to the possibility of a more productive meeting, with both Will and Dana contributing. But the walk had minimal effect on his temper.

If he hadn't paused to take a last calming breath, he might not have noticed the vivid, swirling colours of the poster in the window of the Dream Catcher. Etched across the dark clouds of the Van Gogh print was its title, *Starry Night*. The name had been appropriated for the event the poster advertised. To raise funds for the restoration of the old train station for an art gallery, Withers Enhancement Society was holding a community dinner and dance. Dismissing it instantly, he headed in. Foster, Sadie, Mandy, LD and Dana were assembled. But no Will.

He swung his briefcase on the table, snapped it open, withdrew a writing pad and tossed it in front of Dana. "Need a pen?"

"I've got one," she replied.

"Right. Let's get down to business."

On the far side of the room, a figure in the bar broke his focus for a moment. It was Seth Colville, nursing a beer. "I thought the Dream-Catcher was closed," Gavin addressed Mandy almost sharply.

She glanced at Seth. "It is. He's just finishing his drink."

He sat. "The first item of business is the matter of an irate phone call I received from the mayor." Committee members looked from one to the other, except for Dana. She kept her head down and wrote on the pad on her lap. "Does anyone want to hazard a guess as to what he's upset about?"

Sadie hooked ferociously at her crocheting. A guilty look passed over Foster's face, quickly replaced by an irritated scowl. "Why should he be put out? The citizens of this town have a right to expect their town council to put some resources aside for… well, a rainy day, you might say."

"Yes Foster, you're right. Council also has a right to be approached in a professional and organized way by this committee."

"Well, gosh darn it, we need to get crackin'! Time's passing."

"Wait a minute," LD protested. "Will someone explain what yer talking about?"

Gavin placed both palms on the table and stared at the space between them, exhorting himself to calm down. "You're right, LD," he said, looking up. "I'm getting ahead of myself. The mayor called me this afternoon. He was quite upset by a delegation from the committee appearing before Council last night, without the customary advance request."

Mandy turned to Foster. "You went to the Council! On your own?"

"No Ma'am," he said haughtily. "Sadie went too."

"Somebody's got to look out for the animals," Sadie protested, her jaw thrust forward.

"But Sadie," Mandy wailed, "we haven't even got food for *people* yet."

"Or blankets," Foster added, glowering at Sadie.

"Well, if I don't speak up for the poor beasties, you'll all put them to the bottom of the list," she sulked.

Suddenly everyone was talking at once. "Hold on, hold on everyone," Gavin had to practically shout to make himself heard. "We have to be organized here. We can't be running off in all directions. We need to make decisions as a group and know who's doing what. Before we go asking Council for money, we ought to have a clear idea of what we're going to need from them. We may be able to get a lot of things donated. We should be going to Council for necessities we can't get other ways. Before we acquire supplies, we need to have a place to store them. At this point, we don't even have a reception centre or place to lodge people."

"What about what that guy said when we had our last meeting?" LD asked.

"Hmph! That nasty old fart!" Sadie huffed.

"Cutter!" Mandy lit up. "Yes. I figured out where he must have meant. It's the logging camp."

"Yeah," LD exclaimed in unison with Foster's "Of course!"

They all looked expectantly at Gavin but he shook his head, his countenance stern. "It *is* the logging camp. But I'm afraid using it is out of the question." He was greeted with a howl of protest. He held up his hand for them to listen. He explained about Cutter approaching Malloy and how it became confrontational. He summarized his own visit to the camp and his failure to persuade Malloy to reconsider. He omitted the historical feud and his visits to Cutter.

"Why that detestable scoundrel!" Sadie snorted indignantly. "I move this committee write him a sharp reprimand and *demand* he rectify the damage he's done."

Dana peered up, her pen suspended over her notepad and caught Gavin's eye. He shook his head at her.

"I understand your frustration," he responded to Sadie. Looking around the table, he continued. "But this committee has no authority to require anything of citizens. In any case, such a letter is not going to accomplish its aim."

"I agree," Mandy nodded. "It would just create a lot of negative energy. If we all think charitable thoughts about Cutter and Mr. Malloy and visualize the white light of protection shining on them, they'll probably have a change of heart," she said brightly.

"The white light of protection?" Foster guffawed. A wounded frown furrowed Mandy's brow.

"Hey Foster, don't you be making fun of Mandy," LD protested.

The restaurant door opened. "I'm sorry sir," Mandy called out. "We're closed."

Gavin shot a glance over his shoulder. "Will!" He jumped up, almost knocking his chair over backward and strode to meet him.

"I'm sorry I'm late," Will mumbled, cringing like a truant. Gavin gripped his shoulder with one hand and pumped his hand with the other. "I almost didn't come," Will confessed in a whisper. "I had to summon my courage."

"Never *mind*, man, I'm delighted you're here." He drew him over to the table. "I want you all to meet Will Hahn. He'll be joining us."

On the far side of the room, a stool scraped noisily. Seth Colville donned his hat and departed without a word or glance to anyone.

For the next hour, Gavin attempted to have the group develop a plan covering evacuation, rescue, reception, first aid, lodging, feeding and communications. It was like herding cats. Most talked too much, interrupted each other and argued. Will kept pretty quiet, though he gave sound, useful input on the topic of communications. The possibility of a sudden breach of the dike raised again the necessity of a signal for immediate evacuation.

LD sprawled on the table like a school boy, his chin propped on his stacked fists. He peered up at Gavin tentatively. "Gavin? Don't get mad, okay?" The others mirrored Gavin's cautious gaze at LD. For the first time in an hour, the group fell silent.

"What is it, LD?"

"I realize you didn't want us going off and acting on our own ideas without talking things over here." His beseeching tone alerted Gavin to an unspoken plea for forgiveness.

"What did you do?"

"Well...I got to thinking about how to get the message out to people real quick that they need to head for the hills. Supposing people patrolling the dike had cell phones and if it is breached they phoned the mill—there's someone there twenty-four seven—the mill whistle could be sounded. It can be heard for miles. I talked to the foreman to see if he'd agree to it bein' part of the plan."

Gavin waited for the other shoe to fall, the spectre of Cutter provoking Malloy recurring. "And?"

"He said sure."

Dana's eyes met Gavin's. Characteristic hollowing in her cheeks betrayed the mirth she strove to suppress. One corner of his own mouth twitched in response.

"Good work, LD."

Later in the cab of her truck, at her insistence he read her minutes by the overhead light. While he read, she sat quietly beside him. He was conscious of her lithe thigh close enough to touch. Twice he had to make himself refocus on reading. "I don't know how you did it, but you managed to extract the kernels of business from all that haggling," he said, when he finished.

"They're okay then?"

He felt drawn in by those shimmering green eyes. Her rosebud mouth puckered in a question mark. "You're amazing," he said earnestly.

Her cheeks dimpled, a feature he was beginning to find enchanting. She leaned her head back against the seat with a sigh. "Let's just hope we don't have occasion to need the emergency plan," she replied.

"I want to take a look from the air again, now the snow in the valley is gone. Care to come along?"

She brightened. "I'd love to."

———

Alone in his cabin an hour later, Gavin turned out the light and crawled into bed. Weary though he was, sleep would not come. He lay with an arm folded under his head, staring at the shadows of tree branches cast by the moon on the sloped cabin ceiling. His senses were stirred by thoughts of two women, one who didn't seem to want him, and one he couldn't have.

He hadn't spoken to Celeste in weeks. He argued with himself he'd been busy. He thought she would call in time, missing him as he missed her. But she had not called. A strong-willed woman, Celeste had shown her mettle before, waiting for him to bend. And he had bent, aching for closeness. He could recall the fragrance of her hair when he made love to her, burying his face in it. But lately those impressions were masked by the scent of another woman. The impulse to kiss those puckered lips tonight almost undid him.

Unbidden, the photograph of Dana with her Jeremy, the one that sat on his desk, sprang into sharp focus. How happy she looked. He remembered her reluctance to dwell on Jeremy's departure, the day she'd come with the horses. But that thought brought back the picture of her standing in his cabin doorway, slick with mud and looking like a drowned kitten. A surge went through him, remembering the sense of unexpected intimacy. Listening to the shower run, gathering up her discarded clothes, the way she looked when she emerged, clean and fresh in his shirt with the too-long arms rolled up at the wrist. She made him feel something he hadn't felt for too long now.

He rolled onto his stomach, groaning. *Get hold of yourself, man. You've just been away from your wife too long.* He resolved to call Celeste in the morning and begin to mend fences. He fell at last into a restless sleep, vivid with dreams and woke in the morning chagrined, for he woke with a stiff cock. He did not call Celeste.

———————————

He reined himself in to spend the morning with Dana in another flight. Again the pilot placed her behind him in the plane. Gavin asked the pilot to fly a circuit, catching small tributaries upstream from Withers. They got a good view of swollen streams spewing into the river, which eddied and churned well up on its banks. Next he had the pilot fly north of town so he could get a continuous view of the dike. He looked intently at one spot. Turning to Dana, he pointed down.

"You see that jog in the dike?" he shouted. She nodded. He turned to the pilot and described a circle, showing he wanted to come round again for a closer look. A few minutes later they were at the same place at a lower altitude.

"There," Gavin shouted. To the pilot, he said, "One more time. Can you go any lower still? I want to get a picture."

"That's Councillor Logan's ranch," Dana called. Gavin snapped off several shots with the camera he'd brought along. Twenty minutes later they were back on the ground.

"You're certain that section is on Logan's place?" he asked when they were on the highway headed back into town.

"Yes. His house and outbuildings are down river from there. Is there a problem, Gavin?"

"That kink in the dike is right on the river-bend. I don't know why someone would have angled it like that, but they couldn't have done it in a worse place. If the river jumps the bank, it's going to hit the dike hardest as it comes around the bend. With the dike hooking away from the river right there, it's weak at the exact spot it needs to be strongest."

"Can anything be done?"

"Well, it may look worse from the air than it actually is. I want to see it from the ground. It can be reinforced if necessary." He dropped her off at her truck, close to his office and headed over to Town Hall. Logan's Ram occupied his parking spot.

Lorraine Connor looked up from her keyboard when Gavin appeared at the counter. "I'd like to see Councillor Logan," he said.

"Do you have an appointment?" she asked, her officious air barely short of rude.

"No. But if he can see me, I'd appreciate it."

"He's quite busy. I doubt if he will see you without an appointment."

"It's quite important. Would you mind asking him if he has time today? I can come back."

With a look of disapproval, she picked up her phone and punched a number. "Hello Councillor. Mr. McLeod is asking to see you. I told him you couldn't see him without an appointment but he insisted I ask." There was a pause. "Oh. All right then."

She put down the phone. "He'll see you now. You know where his office is."

Logan didn't get up when Gavin appeared at his open door. Instead the councillor clasped his hands expansively behind his head and leaned back in his leather executive chair. "Well, if it isn't Noah," he grinned. "Can't catch those darned unicorns to get them on board?"

"Ah yes, the unicorns," Gavin replied, taking the chair opposite him. "Well, they may yet be very sorry, if they don't stop their silly games." He looked evenly at Logan, who raised an amused brow. "In fact, Councillor, there *is* a problem. There's a section of dike I'm concerned about. I flew over it this morning."

Blake's chair rocked forward a fraction, his mirth evaporated. "What section is that?"

"I believe it's on your land, upriver from your house at the river-bend."

"What's the problem?"

"There's a kink in it. I think it could give us trouble if the water gets high enough to hit it hard."

Logan lowered his hands to the arms of his chair and chewed on the inside of his cheek. His eyes grew black as storm clouds. "The dike has served us well for many a year," he declared. "But if you're concerned, I'll have it inspected."

"I'd like to see it myself, from the ground, if you don't mind, Councillor."

Logan spoke through gritted teeth. "Well now see, I do mind. Council agreed to have you come in here and prepare an emergency plan for our town. It's not a bad idea to have a plan—not that I think Withers is going to flood. It's far more likely we could have an emergency because of a train derailment, toxic spill, or severe winter weather. The town could use a plan. But your job is getting this document put together with some input from townsfolk. The integrity of the dike is not your area of expertise, now is it, Mr. McLeod?"

"I'm not an authority on dikes, but I've been involved in disaster work for some time."

"Look McLeod, let's be clear about one thing. This is my town. Those jokers in Victoria pay no attention to the north, year in and year out. We've been asking for help to upgrade the highway, incentives for doctors to practice medicine and half a dozen other projects we desperately need. They insult us by sending lackeys like you up here from the city to tell us about our river and what she'll do. We *live* here. We watch her rise and fall every year. We're familiar with high water. We know all about flooding. My father lived through the one in '48. It was *my family* that built the dike in the first place. No one could have more of a stake in it than I do. I'll be damned if I'm going let you traipse across my land to tell me what to do with my dike. As you've said, you're not an authority. If you're so concerned, I'll have it inspected and a copy of the report sent to you. If upgrades are recommended, I'll see to it myself. Good day, Sir."

There was nothing else to be done. Gavin rose. "I urge you to act quickly. If it needs reinforcing, the earlier you get started, the better." He rose and walked out.

Chapter Six

Todd's long lashes drooped as he forced his eye to track the pipe from the wall through the maze of other pipes and valves. His sight came to rest on a particular tap. He pointed to it and looked hopefully up at his dad. Blake gave a curt nod. Todd grasped the tap and turned it sharply.

"Not like that!" Blake barked.

"Sorry," Todd blurted.

"How many times do I have to tell you, boy? You've got a mind like a sieve. Turn slowly. A sudden flow of water will break the seal and cause a leak."

"Sorry," Todd repeated. He wished he could be out in the hills, riding, but his father insisted on drilling him lately on how to care for the ranch house's complex water system. It required attentive management. Neither of two wells provided a sufficient flow of water in the dry season. By turning a tap the right amount, a trickle from one well emptied into a cistern while the other well built up a reserve. Then they had to be switched before the first well drained dry. In the rainy season forgetting to turn a tap off would lead to a flooded basement.

Mary called down the stairs that Noel Connor had arrived.

"Noel," Blake gripped his hand when he came up from the basement. "Thanks for coming. I'll saddle up a couple of horses and we'll ride out along the dike so you can have a look."

"Can I come?" Todd implored.

"No. It's men's business," Blake answered, his voice quelling further entreaty. As he led the Manager of the Engineering Department out the door, he caught Mary's penetrating look and wondered if she knew he was banging the other man's wife.

When Dana arrived at the Dream-Catcher, Foster occupied the head of the committee's usual table. He sat alone, his face a study of officious discontent. He drummed his fingers and made a show of checking his watch. LD as always, dogged Mandy's heels while she busied herself with closing details. A half-finished glass of amber liquid rested on the bar but no one was sitting there. By a central pillar, Will examined the native artifacts hanging there.

Rebuffed by Foster's gruff response to her greeting, Dana joined Will, finding him more congenial. Sadie arrived with her bag of wool. With a nod to Foster, she parked herself opposite him, pulled out a length of crocheted material and began hooking.

The door to the men's room opened. Cutter emerged and headed to the bar. Sadie's eyes flew wide, tracking him as he crossed to the bar, her head swivelling like an owl's. Mandy shot a nervous glance at the two of them.

Sadie stood, her chair scraping the floor. She huffed past Dana and Will, still clutching her crochet work. "Mr. Johnson," she trumpeted, "I want a word with you."

He gave an irreverent smirk. "Just one, little lady?"

All five feet of her ballooned with indignation. "You had no business representing yourself as a member of this committee!" she excoriated him hotly. "I *demand* you apologize to the camp foreman."

His lips twisted in a sneer. "And who are you? The manners police?"

Her voice ratcheted up to shrill. "You ought to be arrested, causing public mischief like that!"

He pressed the back of his wrist to his forehead. "Oh the shame of it," he wailed.

"Don't you mock me," she rebuked, brandishing her crocheting.

His countenance surrendered to full-blown amusement. "D'ya know, Cupcakes, you're downright charming when you're aroused. It's enough to incite a man to passion."

"You drunken, foul-mouthed guttersnipe! How dare you speak to me that way!" She took an ineffectual swipe at him with her fist full of wool, boffing him on the shoulder. Cutter grinned evilly. He picked up his glass, extending it slowly in her direction.

Will read malevolent intent. "Mrs. Millhouse!" he cried, lunging toward them.

Gavin entered the Dream-Catcher to a scene from Bedlam. Everyone was shouting at once. Everyone, that is, but Cutter and Sadie. They stood frozen, in tableau, confronting one another, he holding a glass of whiskey above her, a grin pasted on his face; her eyes bulged in horrified expectation.

But instead of upending the glass, he folded his other arm in front of him and executed a little Bo Jangles dance shuffle. "Madam," he said, "I will do you one better than apologizing to that motherless hoser. I'll get you that camp for your committee. For a price."

Foster charged toward him. "You bum. You're not getting a dime. You got gall trying to chisel cash out of your trouble-making shenanigans. Besides, the committee *has* no money."

"Take is easy, you tight-ass old geezer. I don't want money and b'sides, I ain't talking to you." Cutter's eyes hadn't left Sadie. "What do you say, Mrs. Millhouse? Would you like that camp?"

"You've already seen to it that it isn't going to happen?" she retorted archly.

"And if I reverse that?"

"What is it you want?" she huffed.

The hand holding the glass motioned to the front of the restaurant, index finger pointing. "For you to accompany me to that shin-dig." All eyes looked where Cutter was pointing. It was the Starry Night poster in the window. Incredulous, she whirled on Cutter.

"The Enhancement Society's fundraiser?" She barked a laugh. "You must be mad! I wouldn't go to a dance with you if you were the last man on earth."

"M'lady," he answered with a courtly bow, "you wouldn't have a prayer. You'd be trampled in the stampede."

Sadie eyes bugged out, steam fairly emanating from her nostrils. "Get out of here, you brazen rapscallion. You're holding up a meeting of respectable citizens."

Cutter shrugged, a resigned smile hovering about his lips.

Foster gripped Sadie's elbow. "Wait! What if he can get us the camp?"

Sadie twisted round and shot a look of vexation at Foster, who still had her elbow clamped in his hand. But then she pursed her lips in thought. She turned back to Cutter. "I know your kind. You're too damn arrogant to grovel. It's a safe bet you won't deliver."

"It's a deal then?"

"You nasty old curmudgeon. You're on!"

With the flourish of a French musketeer, Cutter bowed low before her, then toasted her with his glass. He drained it and plunked it loudly on the bar. Before he exited, he gave Sadie a wink. "Witnesses," he rasped.

———

"Where's your Jeep?" Dana asked as she and Gavin left the Dream-Catcher.

"At my office. I walked."

"Can I give you a lift?"

He was about to decline her offer, thinking *It's a five-minute walk,* when another part of him remonstrated, *Turn her down? Are you nuts?* "Thanks," he said.

"Good. There's something I want to talk to you about. Can you spare a few minutes?"

"Sure. I have to do a few more things at my office anyway before I call it a night."

It had been yet another evening of personalities butting up against one another, as Gavin laboured to steer them into solidifying plans around communication, dike patrol, and reception duties. It was hard slogging. Foster and Sadie accepted the task of soliciting donations of material and services. Gavin lectured them on how to approach potential donors, what to say and more importantly, what not to. On the way to his office, Dana filled him in on the lead-in to the confrontation between Sadie and Cutter.

"I wonder what that cuss is up to and if I should warn Malloy," he remarked.

"Getting between the Martin's and the McCoy's isn't a good idea in this country," she laughed.

Vehicles filled The Winchester parking lot to overflowing. They spilled down the street's angle-parking beyond Gavin's office. Dana found an empty space beyond his office opposite it. They walked back up to his office. He let them in and flicked on the lights. They dissected the meeting and joked about the antics of the committee.

"What did you want to talk to me about?" he said finally.

"It's my mother," she sighed. "I've tried broaching the subject of moving her somewhere safe till the risk is passed, but she effectively avoids discussing it. I know she doesn't want to leave; Withers has been her home her whole life. It's not just me who visits her. People from around town drop in to see her on a regular basis. I think, too, she doesn't like the idea of me being here on my own in case there *is* a problem."

"What do you want from me?" he asked solicitously.

"I was hoping to persuade you to visit her with me. If *you* talk to her, she might listen. She regards you as an authority on the matter. Maybe you can get through to her."

"I don't know if I can make a difference but I'd be glad to try."

"Thank you, Gavin. You don't know how much this means to me."

"When shall I come?"

"I'm seeing her Wednesday afternoon. If that's not convenient..."

"Wednesday's fine."

"Alright then," she smiled, "I'll meet you there? Say...one fifteen?"

He nodded.

"I must be going. I've taken enough of your time." She stood.

"I'll walk you to your truck." He half rose from his chair but she motioned him to stay.

"Don't be silly. It's a few steps away. This isn't the big city, you know."

"Okay Miss Independence," he said with a wry smile. "I get the message."

The faint twang of country music from The Winchester reached Dana as she crossed the street. It had been a long day and she was eager to get home and crawl into bed. She threaded between the tailgates of her own truck and the neighbouring one.

A shadow moved. The sound of a footfall brought her up short with a cry. In the poor light it took her a moment to recognize Blake Logan beneath his Stetson. *Damn, why must the man always waylay me like this?*

"Evening, Miss Oleson," he purred, stepping close to her. "You're in town rather late. I might wonder what an engaged woman like yourself is up to at this hour, in the company of a handsome man from out of town. And your fiancé so recently en voyage."

She didn't answer, reaching instead for the handle of the cab but he moved to block the door, leaning against it with his hand. She recoiled, her heart lungeing. She wished she'd let Gavin accompany her after all and considered back-pedalling into the street, but thought better of letting Blake know he frightened her.

"Indeed," she retorted, her chin rising. "A man with your reputation might well think *everyone* behaves as you do."

His eyes roved down her body and back up to meet hers, his leer penetrating. He shifted his weight. She felt a scream gather in her throat, but then the latch clicked. He drew open the door, motioning in a chivalrous gesture for her to get in. She didn't wait for a second invitation. As he pushed it closed with both hands, he stared through the window, lascivious eyes never leaving her. She turned the key and stepped on the gas pedal making the engine roar. Shifting into reverse, she gunned out into the street. As she peeled away, her body gave way to uncontrollable shaking.

She entered the darkened farmhouse and clicked on the kitchen light. Despite the warmth of the evening, she felt a chill. She longed to hear Jeremy's voice. He always made her laugh, jabbering about his frenetic daily round of activity in that manic way he had. Immersed in the athletes' world, he thrived on the culture of competition. When he wound down a little, he'd ask what was happening at her end. The glow she felt after his call always lasted for hours.

It had been nearly a week since they'd spoken. When he'd first gone away, he'd called her every other day. This last time he told her what long hours he was putting in. He sounded fatigued. It was too late to be phoning him but Blake's lewd insinuation that she was having an affair behind his back fuelled her need to reach out to him. His phone rang four times. She was just thinking guiltily about how she was hauling him out of a sound sleep, when he came on.

"Jeremy. Darling, it's me."

"Dana! What are you.... It's late. Is something wrong?"

"No. Well, not really, I just hadn't heard from you for a while and..."

"Gee Dana, it's been really hectic. I was in bed." He didn't sound pleased.

"I'm sorry. I just wanted to hear your voice."

"I'm sorry, Dana. I can't talk now; I'm exhausted. It's been a gruelling day. You sure you're okay?" he added, "You don't sound so good."

"No, I'm fine. Really. Go back to sleep."

"Yeah, I'll call you when I can."

"Okay. I love you."

He said goodbye and she hung up. Guilt compounded her loneliness and she berated herself for giving in to it at his expense.

Gavin hung up from the second of the morning's calls from a committee member. Sadie and Foster appeared to have absorbed his stern advice. They had some successes to boast. Sadie lined up a rancher willing to supply bedding and reels of hay if it became necessary to board horses at her place. She also secured the volunteer services of a veterinarian should a mass evacuation of Withers result in many pets being lodged with her.

Foster managed to find several hotels in the nearest towns north and south of Withers willing to accommodate displaced families. He gained pledges of supplies from several retailers for a refugee camp. They could have them as soon as the committee obtained storage space.

It was nearly noon. Gavin was thinking of grabbing a bite to eat before meeting Dana at the nursing home when the door opened. A young man in bottle-green work pants, besmirched tee shirt, steel-toed boots and bronze tan presented himself. A boyish face with rumpled blond hair contrasted with muscular shoulders and arms.

"You Mr. McLeod?" he asked, his voice remarkably soft for the hard-bodied look of him.

"That I am," Gavin replied, coming forward to meet him.

"I'm Jeff Nash."

Gavin extended his hand. "How can I help you, Jeff?"

Jeff reached for Gavin's hand and then noticing the grime on his own, pulled it back. "I...uh, sorry sir, I'm kinda grubby from work."

Gavin clasped it anyway. "Looks like honest dirt from honest work." Jeff's mouth turned up a modest smile.

"Can I talk to you, Sir?" Gavin waved to the chair by his desk and took the other. "I'm here for my uncle," Jeff said.

Gavin shook his head and shrugged his lack of comprehension.

"Bert Malloy?"

"Ah," Gavin said, the spark of recognition igniting. "Did your uncle have another visit from a certain Mr. Johnson?"

"Cutter!" Jeff lit up. "Yes."

Gavin wagged his head with a sigh. "Has Mr. ah, Cutter given your uncle cause for grief?"

"Oh no, Sir! On the contrary. Cutter apologized." Gavin's face registered surprise. "When Uncle Bert saw him, he was ready to throw Cutter bodily off the place. Least that's what he told me later. But Cutter said right off he owed him an apology for all the trouble he'd caused. Uncle Bert told him he had to do more than apologize to *him* though. That's when he sent for me. When I walked into the office and saw Cutter with my uncle, I thought, 'Uh oh, there's gonna be trouble.' Uncle Bert said to Cutter, 'Here's the person you really owe an apology.'

"Then Cutter said he was sorry for being hard on me when I was on his crew. Said I didn't deserve it and he'd only done it 'cause he was mad at my uncle. He seemed truly remorseful. He said right out to both of us the accident had been his fault, he'd been drunk and wasn't paying attention."

A slow smile stole over Gavin's face as he listened.

"Cutter's not so bad, Mr. McLeod. I never did think so. There was just this personality clash between him and my uncle. They can both be hard headed. When Cutter lost his wife, the guys say his whole world fell apart and the drink made him ornery. They think it's too bad he got injured and can't work as a logger anymore, 'cause he's a decent fellow, a skilled woodsman and a hard worker."

Gavin pictured the scene at the camp, with Cutter kowtowing to Malloy. It must have cost his pride something. "What now?" he asked.

"Oh, I almost forgot. That's the whole reason I'm here. Cutter asked Uncle Bert if he would reconsider your request to access the camp in case there's a flood in Withers. And Uncle Bert said yes. He sent me to tell you."

"Well I'll be damned. There's a God after all."

Jeff's face broke out in a sunny smile. "So I guess you'll be calling my uncle."

"You can bet on it."

"I gotta get back to work, Mr. McLeod. It's been nice talking to you."

"The pleasure's mine, Jeff. I'm indebted to your uncle. Thanks for coming."

Once again, it was Viola Cameron's eyes that arrested Gavin's attention. They were intelligent and gave the impression she saw more than surface appearances. When he and Dana found her in the lounge, she greeted him with robust friendliness, asking how his work was progressing.

She lifted the lap-secretary from her knees, where she'd been writing a letter and set it on the coffee table. "I was writing one of my boys," she informed him. "He lives in New Zealand now with his wife and two little boys of his own. I got a letter from him last week and was just answering him."

"It's a beautiful day, Mom," Dana said. "Would you like to get out for a walk?"

"That would be grand."

Although she was ambulatory, Viola was too frail to go far on her own. A 'walk' meant wheeling her in the park-like setting of the grounds. The home sat on a pleasant estate beside Stayner Creek, the same one that ran by the cabin Gavin occupied in the hills. The creek burbled gently here. A concrete path, shaded by trees, bordered it. Residents and their guests could stroll or, as with Viola, roll a wheelchair. They came to a bench. Parking the chair beside it, Dana and Gavin sat.

"Mom, I asked Gavin to come so we could talk together about a temporary move for you."

"I'm sure the operators of the nursing home will look out for our best interests, Dana dear. I don't want to move unnecessarily and go to some far-off place where I don't know anyone."

Dana looked distressed. "I know how hard on you that would be. But I'm thinking of your safety."

"Of course you are. But the staff are *paid* to be concerned for our safety. There's been no talk of moving anyone. I'm sure they'll make arrangements if they deem it necessary. Besides, why talk of dire circumstances on such a lovely day. Oh look," she pointed off behind them, "there's a chipmunk. I wish I'd save a crust from lunch. They're so tame here they'll come right up to you."

"*Mom*, we *need* to talk about this." A note of desperation crept into Dana's voice.

"Dana," Gavin spoke for the first time since sitting down, "would you mind terribly if your mother and I talked privately?" Dana looked relieved. With a glance to check if her mother was all right with that, she stood and stepped between them to walk back inside.

Once she was out of earshot, he leaned his elbows on his knees. "I must confess, Mrs. Cameron, I came along when Dana asked me because I had an ulterior motive."

The woman gave a hearty laugh, the crinkly lines around her eyes deepening. "You've been collared into a conspiracy to manipulate a stubborn old woman, I'll wager. But I'll listen to your ulterior motive."

"The truth is, I haven't had significantly improved success since I last spoke to you, at persuading the people of Withers to appreciate the very real risk of flood. Tragedy is something we human beings tend to think of as something that happens to other people—till it's too late. I'm not surprised there's been little talk of planning at the nursing home," he went on. "There hasn't been at Town Hall either, or at the local elementary school, or the mill, or in your friend's newspaper. I fear people may bury their heads. If a flood comes, it will wreak havoc. *You* understand this. But if people are prepared, their chance of recovery will be much greater, the potential for loss of life greatly reduced.

"Mrs. Cameron, if you were to take the lead here, move to temporary lodgings elsewhere, you would signal others, staff and other residents in the home that at least one person takes the threat seriously. It would make people think. These things tend to start snowballing once one person commits to action."

Viola didn't answer right away. She seemed to ponder his words. "When you're old, your values change. Familiar faces and places are a comfort. At my age, death is not what frightens one. It's the loss of the familiar."

"There's one other perspective I think you might consider then," he said, his gaze direct and grim. "It's obvious to anyone who knows her, Dana is devoted to you. She is distraught, worrying about your safety, knowing full well that people like yourself are the most likely victims. I have no doubt Dana will put herself in harm's way to get to you, if the dike bursts. And chances are good, she won't succeed in even saving herself." He locked eyes with her until her own broke away.

"I'm surprised you're having so little luck with folks in Withers. There's nothing weak about your tactics," she said with irony. "I'm feeling a little tired now, Gavin. I wonder if you would be so kind as to wheel me back."

They found Dana flipping through a magazine in the lounge. "There you are, my dear," Viola chirped, sounding anything but weary. "We've had a lovely talk. He's such a fine man, Gavin is, don't you think?" Dana looked expectantly at him, his hands still on the handles of the wheelchair. He shrugged and shook his head with uncertainty. She looked despondent.

"Have you seen yesterday's newspaper, Dana? It was here a while ago. Now where did it get to?" She struggled out of the chair and went over to the shelves at the side of the room.

"Mom," Dana cried with exasperation, tossing the magazine aside.

"Yes dear," Viola answered sweetly.

"I want to know if you're going to agree to let me move you."

"Oh! Well, it depends."

Dana rolled her eyes at Gavin, who grimaced back.

"Here it is," she seized the folded paper and brought it back to the couch, sitting down beside her.

"It depends on what?" Dana said, ignoring the distraction.

Viola didn't answer right away, but turned the pages of the newspaper, looking for something. "Here it is." She looked up. "What are you doing Saturday night, Gavin?"

It was his turn to search illumination in Dana's face, but she frowned in mystification. "I'm probably holed up in my cabin as usual," he said. "Why?"

"Wonderful. You two want me to move. Then I have something I want you to do for me."

Gavin and Dana exchanged bewildered glances and turned to Viola for an explanation. She grinned triumphantly at each of them, letting the suspense build. She poked the paper finally and said, "I want you two to take me to this. It would be too much for Dana to take me by herself."

Gavin recognized the advertisement even upside down. It was a duplicate of the poster in the Dream-Catcher for Starry Night, the fund-raiser dinner and dance on Saturday night.

"It will be such fun," Viola exulted.

Gavin picked up his mail at the post office early Friday morning, two letters and a package. He tossed the package on the seat in his Cherokee without bothering to open it. It would be the pamphlets he'd requested from PEP. On one of the envelopes, he recognized Celeste's handwriting. He tore it open.

It was hot in the city, she complained. The air conditioner had broken down and she'd had to call a repair person. She'd also had to pay for a new pool pump. The youth she'd hired to do the gardening broke it, she claimed. A friend in New York had called. Her husband had just split and the poor woman was beside herself. She felt she should go, to give her support. Could Gavin send the air fare? And extra for shopping. Her friend needed a pick-me-up. She'd be gone ten days. Amber would stay at a girlfriend's.

That was all. He dropped her letter on top of the package and stared, unseeing out the Jeep's windshield. He felt a pang, wistful at the fact that there was no reference, good *or* bad, about their relationship, in her letter. It was always thus with Celeste. It made it hard to tell if she were softening.

With a sigh, he opened the other envelope which bore the official logo of the Town of Withers in the top corner. The letter stated that the Engineering Department had been requested to inspect the dike on a certain section of private property, for which it gave the legal description. It went on to say no structural concerns were found and was signed, Noel Connor, Manager of Engineering.

He saw red. He pulled a U-turn in the street and made tracks for Town Hall. He *demanded* to see Mayor Hale. For once, Lorraine Connor complied, chastened by his obvious pique.

"Asking a Town employee to find fault with a section of dike on a Councillor's land is like asking a peon to declare the emperor has no clothes," he fairly shouted when Hale dismissed his concerns. The proper authority was the Inspector of Dikes, located in Kamloops, but Hale repeated what Blake himself had claimed, no one had a greater interest in ensuring the integrity of the dike than Councillor Logan.

Back at his office, Gavin sat at his desk, drumming his fingers. Perhaps he should call Perce, tell him what was happening and ask his advice. He reached for the phone but his hand hesitated on the receiver. Perce already thought he was mishandling things. He might agree with the mayor and order him to leave well enough alone. His boss might even see his conflict with Logan as further evidence of his bungling and take him off the job. If only he could see the dike for himself. He picked up the phone and punched a local number.

Todd was coming in from a private lesson in the outdoor arena with Dana when Gavin arrived. "Turn Caesar out in the south paddock after you take his saddle off," she instructed him. Todd nodded and led the chestnut gelding into the barn.

"Phew, it's hot," she greeted Gavin, swiping her forehead with the back of her wrist. "Come to the house, I'll pour you some iced tea." She led him round to the kitchen door, picking up Todd's bicycle that had fallen across the path and propping it against the house.

Inside, she poured two tall glasses and motioned for them to sit at the kitchen table. The front of her white tee shirt just above her breasts was damp. Catching himself staring, he wrenched his gaze away. He took a fast gulp of the amber liquid to cool a heat surge not caused by the outside temperature.

"What did you want to talk to me about?" she asked.

"Blake Logan." He wondered if he only imagined her pupils dilate at the name. Maybe they were just adjusting to the interior light after being out in the sun. Still he was cautious. Though he was increasingly comfortable with Dana, he never knew who was friends with whom in this town and where the minefields were. "Councillor Logan appears to have quite a following."

"His family is a big name in this town," she said. "A lot of people look up to him." His hopes sank at her response.

"Still," she added, "there are, you might say, two camps when it comes to opinion of Blake Logan. Not everyone thinks he is a paragon. Few say so to his face, but there are those who think he's something else that starts with 'p'."

Mirth pulled at Gavin's mouth. "And which camp are you in?"

She snorted and rolled her eyes. When she didn't commit verbally, he raised his brows in enquiry. "The man's a beast," she spat.

A slow smile spread across his face. He began to recount the mounting conflict between himself and Logan, leading up to and including the stand-off over the fault in the dike.

"I hate to report the matter to the Inspector of Dikes and have him come up and check it, only to say it's fine. It would be the final nail in my coffin. Logan will have me for breakfast and my boss will pull me off the job. If I could just see it up close, I could take pictures and email them. Maybe the Inspector will think there's a case for intervening."

"Are you planning on trespassing?" she asked. He shrugged but with an apologetic look that said he was definitely thinking of it. "What if Logan sees you?"

"Well that's a problem. He doesn't seem to keep a regular schedule at his office. I never know when he's working on his ranch."

"What if I can guarantee you he won't be home?"

He gave her a sidelong look. "I'm listening."

She sighed and looked away to the window above the sink facing the barn. Yellow gingham curtains were being sucked out into the hot morning. "Todd desperately wants to compete in an equestrian show coming up this July, a dressage show. He's got the aptitude for it. He asked his father for the outfit he would need to show in the saddle classes but apparently Blake told him this kind of riding is for sissies. It's not like the Logan's can't afford it. I was thinking of talking to Blake myself to see if I can persuade him to support Todd's ambitions. I'll call him and ask him to come over Sunday afternoon to discuss Todd."

"You think he'll come?" he asked.

"Oh he'll come," she answered, with a certain knowing look. They sketched out a plan and then turned to discussing the logistics of getting to Starry Night. Neither of them heard the soft creak of Todd's bicycle as he crept away from under the kitchen window.

———————

Gavin fussed in front of the mirror, running the brush through his hair again needlessly. He adjusted the collar of his black shirt and pulled at his cuffs. By prior agreement, he would pick Dana up first. Together they would fetch Viola.

He pulled into her lane just before dusk. She must have been watching for him for she came out before he reached her porch steps. Her blond hair, so often pulled back in a pony-tail, grazed her shoulders in soft waves. A yellow, off-the-shoulder dress gave her a daisy-fresh 1950s look. His gaze lingered a second or two too long to be discreet. "You look lovely," he said, his throat thick. In the last rays of the sun, he thought he caught a blush tinge the highest points of her cheeks over those perfectly chiselled bones.

———————————

They wheeled Viola into Elks Hall. Great rolls of newsprint painted in swirls of blue, violet and grey were strung across the ceiling, larruped over bamboo poles. Blue lights twinkled through tiny star-shaped holes, creating the effect of a moody night sky. A continuous mural lined the walls, depicting villages and pastoral countryside at dusk in Van Gogh style.

A six-piece band in tuxedos played a lively swing number on a half-moon dais at the front. The dance floor was seeing some action, as half a dozen couples revisited their youth. A buffet table laden with a banquet stretched the length of one side of the hall. Nearly every table, filling the back three quarters of the hall, was occupied. "There's Floyd and Elsie," Viola said. Floyd waved them up, making room at their table.

After he introduced Gavin to his wife, Floyd and the two older women fell into a friendly exchange about who else had turned out. Gavin looked over at Dana but she was turned away, seemingly taking in the décor. As the band took up a new score, he asked Dana and Viola what they wanted to drink, then wended through the throng to the bar at the end of the buffet table. The man in front of him collared two bottles of beer in one hand and balanced two glasses in the other. He turned in Gavin's direction.

"Jeff!"

"Oh hi, Mr. McLeod. You having a good time?"

"I just got here."

"Great. You'll enjoy yourself. I know Cutter is."

"Cutter?"

Jeff pointed with the hand that held the bottles. Gavin searched the crowded dance floor. It writhed with gyrating bodies. He spied the familiar figure expertly executing a modified swing dance step. The lady in the blue dress, evidently having a ball, was none other than Sadie.

"Well I'll be damned." Gavin broke into a broad grin. He turned to say something else but Jeff was already out of range. He placed the women's order and for himself, as designated driver, a ginger ale.

The dance score ended. Just as he got back to the table, Mayor Hale stepped up to the microphone. With a proprietary air, he announced he'd been asked to provide the official welcome. He made a brief speech about the purpose of the function.

The mayor praised the Withers Enhancement Society for their determination to preserve a landmark building and enrich the town culturally. He credited one person in particular for being the driving force behind the enterprise, Mary Logan.

"Come on up here, Mary," he boomed over the loudspeaker, searching the crowd. "Where are you?" Several helpful voices in the crowd drew attention to her. Gavin recognized the elegant carriage of the woman in a sleek burgundy, floor-length gown, her hair swept up off her long, ivory neck. It was obvious she had not been expecting the attention and would prefer to remain behind the scenes. But Hale was insistent. With gestures from several around her, she capitulated and approached the stage.

Hale spoke of Mary's patronage of the arts. He informed the crowd in a confidential tone that she was a gifted musician in her own right. Many knew her, he noted, as the organist at Trinity Church but she was rarely coaxed to play to the public on a fine piano. He gestured to the concert grand on stage behind him and asked the crowd if they'd like to hear her. Applause and shouts greeted his suggestion.

"Mary," he implored, turning to her. "Would you indulge us?"

She looked as if she would demur, but clamours and whistles prohibited this option. She took a seat at the keyboard. In the pause that followed, she seemed to draw into herself. In a moment, music enveloped the hall and a hush fell over the audience. The music was an elixir, evocative of the spectrum of human emotion. Gavin searched the crowd for her husband. He spied him, a drink in hand, in the back corner with his cronies, Clint Murdock and Seth Colville. A peculiar expression overtook Logan's face, a mixture of yearning and jealousy. Fascinated, Gavin watched him, while all other eyes converged on the stage, till finally the passion of the music pulled his own attention to the incredible artistry of the performance. When the last notes ended, she remained still on the bench, hands folded in her lap. Seconds passed in silent awe. And then someone, somewhere clapped and tripped an avalanche of thunderous applause.

Dana fought down a bad case of nerves. Her mother appeared to be having a marvellous time. A constant stream of people Viola knew stopped at their table to chat with her. Gavin was getting on well with Elsie and Floyd. She strove to appear as if she was enjoying herself, purportedly admiring the décor and watching people dance. But she would rather have been anywhere else. In her whole life she'd never danced with anyone but Jeremy. After the hurtful taunts she'd endured in school she never left herself open to any other man making her feel like a chicken with a broken leg. Thanks to her mother's machinations, here she was, attending a dance in the company of Gavin McLeod. Was she expected to be polite and dance with him?

A familiar face emerged from the crowd heading toward their table. Mandy came up behind Gavin and touched his shoulder. He looked up. "Come on, Gavin, you look like you could use some exercise. Come dance."

He turned to the others at the table and with an apologetic grin, excused himself. As she watched Mandy lead him onto the dance floor, Dana felt confused by the dejection washing over her.

What if he *didn't* ask her to dance? That might be just as awful. He might not ask her out of scrupulousness, thinking it improper, what with her being engaged and him being married. After all, he'd always kept a respectful distance...even the time she showered at his cabin when she slipped in the mud. But if he didn't ask her to dance, she would never know whether it was out of propriety or because he didn't want to embarrass himself on the dance floor with a gimp. Suddenly, the distinction mattered a great deal to her.

Exercise was what Gavin got, trying to keep up with the dynamic energy of Mandy in a '60s rock 'n roll. "I'm surprised LD doesn't have your dance card filled," he shouted.

"He'd like to," she laughed.

"Is he here?"

"Sure." She gestured to the sidelines as the music segued into the next score. He spied LD at a table with another couple. Mandy waved and he waved back at them, looking envious in a benign sort of way.

"You come together?" Gavin asked. She nodded, hands held high, executing some pretty interesting moves. "He really digs you."

"*I* know."

The room temperature seemed to climb a degree every minute. He felt the heat at his temples and was winded by the time the piece ended. "What's with you and him?" he asked good-naturedly. "You're not telling him to get lost, but you're damn near making him sit up and beg."

"Ha, ha," she retorted, her head tilted sideways in a saucy cant, but her expression bore no hint she'd taken offence. They both looked in LD's direction at once. He straightened hopefully, looking so much like a faithful mutt whose ears perk up at the sight of his mistress that both Gavin and Mandy laughed.

"Come on, Mandy. How could you not love a face like that?"

"Aah! It's not Lionel's fault. You're right, he's a sweet guy. It's just me. I've got cold feet."

"I can't believe it. You seem like a woman who likes men."

"I do. I guess I'm just afraid they won't stick around once I let my guard down."

There was something about her expression, a sudden downturn at the corner of her mouth that came and just as quickly disappeared behind her broad smile. It told Gavin not to go there. He danced another set with her, then begged off. He walked her back to her table where LD fairly wagged his tail at their approach. Gavin chatted with them a couple of minutes, then zigzagged back to his table, passing barn-like doors open to the night air. They faced the library across a park. Paper lanterns shedding soft light in varied colours lined a meandering path that led to a gazebo.

Dana's back was to him when he approached and Elsie was regaling her with a bit of gossip. He paused till Elsie's upward glance caused a break in her story. Dana turned. "It's kind of warm in here," he addressed her. "The lights by the pond outside look inviting. Would you care to take a walk, Dana?"

He was gratified that she looked pleased. She touched Viola's arm. "You'll be okay, Mom?"

"Of course I'll be okay. Go on, get some air."

He shielded her from being buffeted by couples dancing to a lively number, till they reached the exit opening onto the patio. Gavin sucked the cooler air into his lungs. "Oh that's better," he sighed.

A few couples lounged along the railing, some smoking, others just taking the air. They followed a walkway bordered by flowers whose perfume saturated the senses. The coloured lanterns swayed from a wire strung from the branches of trees lining the path. They strolled along in silence, Dana's pumps clicking an asymmetrical cadence. The path came to the pond. The still surface reflected the lanterns' glow. A small bridge arched over a narrowing in the pond, beyond which stood a gazebo. The music followed them, softened by the distance.

"Can I ask you something personal?" he broke the silence between them.

She hesitated then replied, "I'll refrain from committing myself till I hear the question."

"I've always had a healthy respect for women walking about on those tiny spikes. Is it a trial for you?"

She made a soft sound of mirth. He caught the dimple in her cheek with his sidelong glance. "Only when I go up and down stairs."

When they reached the bottom of the steps to the gazebo, he offered his arm. Her dimples deepened and she took it. As they climbed the steps, the pressure on his arm confirmed her reliance on his assistance. He recalled the one other time she had taken his arm—to negotiate the stairs in the church on Easter Sunday.

They were alone in the gazebo. The music drifting out from the hall changed from fast to ballroom. He turned to her. "Would you dance with me?"

She blinked a sober, almost frightened look. "I...I'm not much of a dancer."

"Good. Then you'll hide the fact that I have two left feet," he smirked. She laughed, the sound of it tinkling like wind chimes. She let his arm encircle her, drawing her to him. She lay her head on his shoulder. His heart beat so fiercely he feared she would feel it.

Beyond the series of arches enclosing the gazebo, their own starry night illuminated their private ballroom. He wondered if he should talk to her for propriety's sake, but he craved the intimacy of their silence and said nothing. He listened instead to the whisper of her breathing. He wanted it to go on forever but inevitably the score came to an end and was replaced by something more upbeat.

He knew if he kept her there he would kiss her, so to save them both from awkwardness he suggested they return to the hall. She took his arm again to descend the steps. An ancient spiraea bush with cascading white flowerets grew by the railing, lacing the air with its heavy scent. For a single moment, Dana thought she caught another odour, but they moved on and it was gone. As they crossed the little arched bridge, though, she had an uncanny sensation of being watched.

Neither of them saw or heard the figure on a park bench tucked up against the gazebo. He slouched with his arm outstretched along the backrest, while his smouldering eyes stalked the woman with the uneven gait and the man whose arm she held. The end of Blake Logan's cigarette glowed orange as he took another long pull, then ground out the butt under his heel.

CHAPTER SEVEN

Maps of the local area covered Dana's kitchen table the next day. She showed Gavin how to get to the dike unobserved. On a survey map, she pointed out an infrequently used track, passable in a four-wheel drive. He would have to hike the last half mile. He folded the maps, sticking the survey map in his back pocket. The rest went into his briefcase.

Blake had readily agreed to come to discuss Todd's riding. Shortly after Gavin left, he knocked on her door. She escorted him into her office, motioning to a chair. She sat behind the big oak desk, feeling safer with it between them. By one o'clock, the mercury had climbed to an unseasonable eighty-five degrees. Blake removed his Stetson and mopped his brow with his sleeve.

"Thank you for coming, Mr. Logan. Todd is doing very well with his riding. He has an intuitive understanding of horses." While she spoke about what he was learning, Blake's eye roved lazily around the room. Just when she decided he wasn't listening, he turned to her with a look that made her feel undressed. She momentarily lost her concentration, petering out mid-sentence. She felt her face flush under his stare.

"He wants to compete," she blurted, to fill the silence, then forced herself to focus. "There are several events this season I think he would do well in, but he needs the attire for the classes."

"My son is well clothed," Blake answered. "I have the where-with-all to see to that. He doesn't need for anything."

"To enter these classes, he requires a good English riding habit…a show jacket and shirt, jodhpurs, high-top riding boots and an English helmet."

Blake snorted. "Ma'am, my boy is a rancher's son. That type of riding is done by the privileged brats of millionaires who like to put on airs. They wouldn't know cow shit if they stepped in it. What do I want him learning that for?"

She felt her ire beginning to rise. "Todd hardly can be thought of as a brat, and it *is* what he wants. He pays for his lessons by working in my stable. He works hard and does a good job. You have every reason to be proud of him."

His voice hardened, his upper lip curling into something approaching a snarl. "I think I know my son. He's scatterbrained and unreliable in his chores at home. He's a bit of a momma's boy too. So if he's working his little tail off for something he wants, even though I don't see much point to it, I'm inclined to let it go. At least it's teaching him a work ethic. Truth is, I'd rather see him putting his time and energy into helping run the ranch."

"Mr. Logan, he's only an eight-year-old boy."

"My father set me on a horse when I was three," Blake retorted. "I was working a herd of cattle before I was Todd's age. He didn't let me ease up on school either. I was expected to get good grades and a university education. Todd has a tendency to lallygag and daydream. I ought to lean harder on him, not support a frivolous pastime. But I'll think on it, Miss Oleson. How's that?" The muscle in his jaw that had bunched, relaxed just as quickly.

Dana sensed this was as much as she would get from him and pushing any harder just now would result in him balking permanently. He drew his sleeve across his damp forehead again. "Say, would you have a cold drink?"

"Iced tea?"

He nodded. She jumped up to fetch it from the kitchen. She took the pitcher from the fridge. As she poured, she heard his boots clicking on the hardwood floors, leisurely following her. She held out the glass to him. He tossed his Stetson on the table and accepted it. She retreated back against the counter. He gulped down most of the brown liquid in one long pull then stood swishing the remainder around the bottom. She crossed her arms, uptight and anxious for him to leave. His inquisitive scrutiny took in the room. Realizing his stare had zeroed in on something, she followed his line of sight. With a heart skip, she spied Gavin's briefcase, where he'd left it, his initials GM clearly embossed on the side.

Blake tipped the glass up and drained it. He stepped toward her, reaching to set it on the counter beside her. His eyes remained fixed on her. "When the cat's away, the mice will play," he gloated. "Having a last fling before tying the knot, are you?" He towered over her, the side of his mouth twisted in a leer.

"I don't know what you're talking about," she stammered, her heart pounding.

"Sure you do," he said, trapping her between his hand on the counter and the corner of the fridge jutting out several inches from it. She could feel the heat of him and was too terrified to look up. She moved to squeeze past but he anticipated her move and caught her in a rough embrace.

"Stop!" she cried.

He laughed and pressed against her. "If you're gonna fool around on your intended, you might as well give a real man what you're giving away free to McLeod."

She pushed him with all her might, arms up-folded in front of her. "Stop!" she repeated, finding her voice and her rage. He laughed again but did not exert the full strength she knew he possessed. She managed to break away from him, putting several yards between them.

"I think you'd better go, Mr. Logan," she said coldly, trembling uncontrollably. He sighed as if with disappointment, stepped to the table and picked up his Stetson. He placed it deliberately on his head and flicked the brim with his forefinger in a kind of mocking salute. He left without another word. She collapsed into a chair at the table, certain her legs would not hold her up another second. Her breathing came fast and shallow and in her whirling confusion she tried to determine whether she was more frightened or outraged.

It wasn't yet two o'clock by the time Gavin reached the dike. The first thing he noticed when he climbed to the top was the roiling chalky-brown current of the river. Already, it brimmed its banks, threatening to spill. Tree branches and the occasional driftwood log swept around the bend at an alarming rate.

The dike angled away from the river for more than two dozen yards for no discernible reason, then straightened out. He pointed his camera to capture the line and snapped off several shots.

Todd wheeled his bike around the yard in circles, looking up when his father's truck skidded to a halt on the gravel. He watched him slam the truck door and stride into the barn. On his bike, Todd continued circling.

His mother came out of the house. "Where's your father, Todd?"

He pointed to the barn. She headed toward it just as Blake emerged with his horse saddled. "Blake, where are you going? You said you'd help me with the clean-up at Elk's Hall."

"I won't be long. I'm going out to check the dike by the river bend."

Todd's head shot up. He dropped his bike and ran to them.

"Dad! You should go that way," he said, flinging his arm in the opposite direction.

Blake frowned. "What are you talking about?" he growled.

"Uh…uh. The fence! It's down. Cattle broke through."

Blake glowered. "You been down that way today already? Since church?" he demanded.

"Um, no. Yesterday."

"Yesterday!" he roared. "And you're just telling me *now*?"

"Blake, don't yell at him," Mary snapped. He ignored her.

"Answer me, boy. Why didn't you tell me yesterday?"

Todd crimsoned. "I...I...forgot."

"Jesus H. Christ!" He tugged his horse around and swung his leg over the saddle. With a rough yank on the reins he pulled round to face Todd. "You go inside. You're grounded to your room till further notice." He was gone before Mary could veto him, cantering in the direction Todd had pointed.

———

In his report to Perce, Gavin omitted mention of the photos he emailed the Dike Inspector. He hoped the Inspector wouldn't contact head office in Vancouver. Perce would be livid.

The weekly Withers Gazette came out. An article on page two stunned him. *Ark or Ship of Fools?* While no names were mentioned, it lampooned the Emergency Preparedness Committee, taking cheap shots at each and every volunteer. It missed nothing, Mandy's flaky new ageism, Foster's dithering fastidiousness, LD's illiteracy, Sadie's monomania over animals, Will's anti-social tendencies, even Dana's disability. It was low, crass and insensitive. His blood boiled.

Whipping the paper closed, he strode from his office with it gripped in his fist. Stomping along the plank sidewalk to the shop next door, he burst into Floyd's office.

Floyd's head jerked up from his desk in alarm.

"What is this crap?" Gavin almost shouted, shaking the paper at him.

Floyd floundered to his feet, his face scarlet. He extended his hands in front of him, as if to ward off a blow. "I'm sorry, Gavin. It wasn't my idea. It...it was supposed to be a bit of fun," he ended lamely.

"FUN?" he thundered. "Whose idea of fun is this?"

Floyd shrugged, shamefaced.

"Did you write this, Floyd?"

"No! I told you, it wasn't my idea. I wouldn't have." He hung his head. "Honest. I didn't write it."

"Then who did?"

Floyd squirmed. "I can't say."

"You can't say," Gavin echoed in disgust. "Why not? The scum who wrote this ought to at least sign his name."

Floyd shrugged again but said nothing. Gavin studied him, breathing heavily. He believed Floyd. Clint Murdock owned the paper. He was friends with Logan. Did Murdock write it? Maybe Logan himself. He wondered briefly how the writer knew who was on the committee, never mind their idiosyncrasies. Then he remembered Seth Colville had been in the bar when he'd bawled them out after Sadie and Foster's ill-conceived appeal to Council. Would he ever get savvy at dealing with small town politics?

Floyd peered up with abashed eyes. "I truly am sorry, Gavin. I don't have any animosity toward you. You gotta understand, freedom of the press is just an ideal. In a small town, this is *our* reality." Gavin made a sound somewhere between disgust and defeat. He dumped the paper on Floyd's desk and stalked out.

Back in his office, his phone rang. It was the Dike Inspector. He'd flown in by helicopter the day after he got Gavin's email and photos to examine the dike for himself. He informed Gavin he'd issued a writ to have it reinforced and inspected. It was being faxed to the mayor at that very moment. He also said he would fax Gavin authorization empowering him to arrange for the Withers Public Works Department to start the job as soon as possible.

Gavin was jubilant. He went to the Public Works office as soon as the fax came through. Neither the receptionist nor the supervisor seemed surprised to see him. Both however, were less than cordial. After some wrangling, it was agreed the work would begin in a couple of days.

Next he stopped by Town Hall to inform Logan that crews would be out three days hence. At reception, Lorraine was, if anything, even more frosty than the staff at Public Works. Councillor Logan, she informed him had already gone home.

Blake gripped the steering wheel of his truck, blood pounding in his temples. Rage boiled inside him. That bastard McLeod had out-foxed him. What's more, he'd trespassed and taken photos. And there wasn't a damn thing he could do about it. Now he was being ordered to allow modifications to the dike on his own land. He'd instructed Noel to take his time sending McLeod the notice certifying the dike as sound. McLeod could not have received it any earlier than Friday. The Inspector had flown up on Tuesday. Sometime between Friday and Monday McLeod had snuck onto his ranch. The monogrammed briefcase in Dana Oleson's kitchen suddenly sprang to mind. *That bitch!*

Todd jumped down from the school bus and ran up the lane. It was a glorious day. There was time for a ride before dinner, if his mother didn't insist he do his homework first. When he heard the piano, he knew luck was with him. He tiptoed past, giving her an unobtrusive wave. She acknowledged him with the merest nod. He threw his book-bag on his bed, changed from his school clothes into denims and hurried back outside.

The pinto pony he rode on the ranch gave him a bit of a chase in the paddock but was soon coaxed into being caught. He tied him to the fence and went to fetch the saddle from the tack room. He tugged the pony saddle off its rack. Turning around, he almost dropped it in fright.

His father's huge frame blocked the doorway.

"Put that back." His voice was full of gravel and threat. Todd's heart skipped. He did as he was told and turned to his father again.

"Sunday you told me cattle broke the fence in the south pasture. That was a lie." Todd stood rooted, struck dumb.

"Wasn't it?" Blake demanded.

He couldn't meet his father's terrible eyes.

"Well?" Blake's voice rose.

Todd couldn't muster breath to speak aloud. In the doomsday hush of his father's judgment, his whispered 'yes' sounded loud.

"You didn't want me to go to the dike, did you?" Miserably Todd shook his head, unable to lift his eyes from the dusty floor boards. "You knew Mr. McLeod would be there." He didn't know how his father knew all this, but grown-ups had a way of finding things out. Caught like a rabbit in a snare, he could only nod. There was a dreadful, drawn-out silence. Then Blake stepped into the room and picked up something.

"Pull down your trousers."

Todd jerked up his head in horror to see the whip in his father's hand. His legs turned to rubber. Never before had he been physically punished. Tears glazed his eyes, blurring his father's shape. He fumbled with his jeans, pushing them to his knees with trembling hands. His father spun him by the shoulder and bent him over a tack trunk, pinning him there with a huge hand in the middle of his back.

He meant to be brave. He meant to not cry. But when the whip bit into his flesh, the scream that ripped from him was not of his volition. The blows rained down like strings of molten metal across his buttocks. The pain was worse than anything he'd imagined possible.

Gavin came straight from Town Hall to deliver the edict to Logan. He heard the first scream when he stepped down from his Cherokee and it rent something deep inside him. He raced to its source.

He caught Logan's arm in mid-air, raised for the next lash. The man wheeled on him in shocked rage. Gavin's grip held. "You strike that boy again and I'll use that whip on *you*," he growled through gritted teeth.

"Bloody hell!" Logan bellowed, wrenching his arm free. He glared fire. "You have a bad habit of meddling in other people's affairs, McLeod," he snarled in a voice thick with menace.

Gavin's burning gaze never strayed from Logan's, but he spoke gently to the sobbing boy. "Todd, go up to the house to your mother."

"Stay where you are!" Blake roared. Not breaking eye contact with Gavin, he hissed, "How dare you interfere with me disciplining my son."

"Discipline?" Gavin sneered. "Perhaps the child welfare authorities would be interested in your *discipline, Councillor* Logan. Go on, Todd. Your father and I have business."

The boy couldn't stop his jerky hiccups but he needed no further invitation. Tugging at his pants, he fled the barn. Blake's eyes narrowed to slits.

"You're trespassing, McLeod—again. I suggest you leave while I'm inclined to let you. I find you here again, you may be looking down the business end of my rifle."

"I came to give you a message," Gavin responded evenly. "Work will begin shoring up the weak spot in the dike on your land this Saturday. And now I have another message for you. If I hear of you abusing that child again, I *will* report you to the authorities." Without waiting for a reply, he spun on his heel and left.

As he climbed into the Jeep, he looked to the house. Mary Logan crouched on the porch, her son folded in her arms.

The road back to town led past Dana's place. His mind beyond clear thought, the Jeep turned of its own accord, scarcely slowing. He skidded to a stop in her yard, raising a dust cloud. He sat staring straight ahead through blood-shot eyes, knuckles whitening on the wheel.

Hearing a vehicle screech to a halt outside her barn, Dana hurried out. She could tell something was wrong from the way he sat rigid in the driver's seat. She approached the open window. "Gavin?" He didn't respond but kept his fixed stare unseeing on the horizon.

"What's wrong?" she asked, apprehension clutching her throat.

"I'd like to take that son-of-a-bitch into the ring," he hissed.

As she would with a frightened colt or frustrated riding student, she waited, attentive and patient for him to come around. Gradually, in a voice reedy with emotion, he told her what happened. She eased the door open and coaxed him out. Laying her hand lightly on his arm, she shepherded him to her kitchen, brewed a pot of tea and made him sit and sip it till he was rational. Neither could bring themselves to speak of Logan again.

After leaving Dana, Gavin drove to a trailhead where he left his Jeep and hiked up into the hills. He clambered up steep paths and over rocks as if pursued by the devil, letting the toil first numb his mind and then cool the searing heat behind his eyes. Gradually the exertion bled his driven energy. In the retreating tide of emotions, a familiar despairing sense of isolation washed over him.

Reluctantly, he turned around, knowing he had to get back for the committee meeting. There'd be no time for supper, but that was no matter for he had no appetite. He wondered how he would dredge up the strength to contend with the volunteers tonight after the drubbing they'd taken in the newspaper. They would be a belligerent and obstreperous lot. He had no stomach for another confrontation today.

He was late pulling into the Dream-Catcher. A hasty scan of the parking lot told him all were present. Inside, silence and long faces awaited. He offered a general greeting and received a couple of mumbled responses. No eyes met his but Dana's, and hers signalled woe. A copy of the Gazette lay on the table.

He took the empty chair opposite Foster and searched from one bent head to the next. "You've seen the article, I see," he said.

Foster cleared his throat and folded his hands in front of him on the table. "Yes, we have. We've been talking while we waited for you and we all feel the same way. We think it best we resign from the committee."

His heart sank. He looked to Dana. Her expression beseeched him. He sighed, then reached for the paper. He spoke in a low, even voice. "I owe each of you a profound apology." Some faces tipped up to steal a glance, other eyes remained stolidly glued to their laps. "Though I myself was spared in this article," he went on, "by stepping forward to volunteer for what appears to be an unpopular cause in this town, you have become the target of an attack meant for me. I take full responsibility for putting you all in the line of fire."

Mandy looked up, her eyes brimming with tears. "People think we're a bunch of misfits and have no business organizing an emergency plan for the town. And it's true," she squeaked, on the verge of breaking down.

"Is that what you think?" he said. He looked from one to the other. "All of you?"

"Wahl it's true I cain't read," LD drawled despondently.

"We just think you ought to have the right people working for you," Foster explained, then muttered. "People who know what they're doing."

"I tried to overcome my hermit tendencies and consider myself part of the community, but I guess I was just deceiving myself." Will mumbled.

"Fiddlesticks. If the truth be told," Foster sniffed, "my whole life I've never done anything worthy of recognition. My own grown-up kids think

I'm a nincompoop. I thought it was a chance to do something decent, maybe even admirable. I was just swollen-headed. Now the whole dang *town* thinks I'm a nincompoop. Probably always have."

"And I just wanted to look out for the animals," Sadie wailed.

Gavin turned to the one person who had not yet spoken. "Is there anything you want to say, Dana?"

She mused. "I hear people think you're objectionable too, an over-zealous, fear-mongering outsider. What do they call you? Noah?" He felt a pang, thinking himself betrayed. "Then there was the time someone swore at you, calling you an urban cowboy pretending to be a Marlborough man." Her eyes wide, she puckered her lips, as if holding back a smirk. He could have hugged her. She was including him.

He raised his brows and canted his head. "True," he acknowledged. He surveyed the others, who continued to regard him woefully, then rattled the newspaper still in his hand. "This article wasn't written by 'the people' in town. It was written by one person—and by the way, it wasn't Floyd Hancock. It was written by someone, or a friend of someone, who wants this whole business of a possible dike failure to go away; a person who wants *me* to disappear.

"I could do that. I might even be forced to leave. But there's one thing I can't change. The snowmelt in the hills will come down. It will fill the river to overflowing. The water will be higher than at any time in your memories. I have grave concerns about the dike. If it is properly reinforced, it may hold. But know this! It may not. If it fails, the difference between an emergency and catastrophic disaster is being prepared. If you quit now, and if nature is unkind, the people of Withers will be as lambs to the slaughter."

He regarded them grimly.

For a moment, no one spoke. Then Foster smacked his palm on the table. "Then it's our duty to carry on." This was met with a chorus of cheers. Some back-slapping, jokes and self-congratulations ensued, followed by a contented lull.

Sadie took advantage of it to address Gavin. "Cutter says you refused him as a volunteer on the committee." This drew a tense silence.

"I did," he said quietly.

"I think we need all the help we can get."

"Aw, now Sadie," Foster interjected fussily, "why would you want that old souse on the committee? I thought you despised him."

"She's sweet on him now," LD grinned. "Ever since he took her to the dance."

"I am *not* sweet on him!" Sadie retorted, blushing. "He's handy with tools is all. His back isn't strong enough to be a logger anymore, but the camp will need some carpentry work, won't it? I could use a handyman to get the barn up to snuff if horses need to be sheltered at my place. Anyway, he wants to help."

Gavin shrugged and turned his palms up. "This is your committee, folks, your town. You make the decision." They voted with a show of hands. Mandy, LD and Will readily sided with Sadie. With a cantankerous huff, Foster went along and Dana duly recorded the decision.

The day had been an emotional roller-coaster. By the time the meeting ended, Gavin was dog-tired. There'd been lively discussion about readying the camp. Everyone wanted to know about the problem with the dike and what was being done to rectify it. They guessed at the conflict between Councillor Logan and Gavin but he kept the details to a minimum.

Everyone climbed into their own vehicles, noisy and happy. Gavin waved as they filed out of the lot. He had a brief final interchange with Dana and said good-night to her too. He waited till she pulled out before starting the engine, but before he released the brake, something under the wiper caught his eye. He retrieved it. By the map light he read a note, written in graceful script.

> *Mr. McLeod: I did not wish to interrupt your meeting but I am anxious to speak with you tonight. I will wait for you outside your office.*
>
> *Mary Logan*

At first he thought it might be a trap set by Blake. But the script was fine, unlike what he imagined would flow from that massive fist. It was exactly what befitted his elegant wife. He fired the ignition and a minute later pulled into a space in front of his office beside a car. He saw her in the shadows under the overhang. He slipped out of the Jeep and leapt up the steps. Even in the dark, one could tell what a handsome woman she was.

"Mrs. Logan, I hope you haven't been waiting long. Our meeting went quite late."

"It's no matter. You didn't know, and it was important enough to me to wait."

"Please, come inside." He hastened to unlock the door. Under the glare of the interior lights, he wished he had blinds to pull. He felt an uncanny urge to protect her privacy. "Won't you sit down?" he said, offering a chair.

She shook her head. "No, I won't take much of your time."

How tall she was, he realized, looking into her eyes on the level. They were fine, dark eyes, which met his with frank directness. But they were mysterious and tragic too, somehow. "Mr. McLeod, I came to thank you for stopping the beating my son was subjected to today."

Words failed him. The emotion he'd been fleeing since it had happened, threatened to undo him.

"I knew Blake had come home and I saw you drive up. I was astonished to see you run into our barn. From inside the house, I didn't hear Todd. It was not until I saw him run from the barn that I knew anything was amiss."

"Todd's a good boy," Gavin said. "He doesn't deserve what he got."

"He's a wonderful boy," she responded. He could hear her love for him in the way she said it. "He's never been whipped before." Her spine, impossibly, seemed to become even straighter and she added, "And I can assure you, he never will be again."

"I hope you're right. I must confess I threatened your husband with the child protection authorities if I learned that he beat him again."

Her voice was resonant when she answered. "In that event, you will have to stand in line behind me in making such a report."

He offered a wry, sad smile. "I believe you." There was fire and steel in this woman. He had no doubt she possessed the ferocity of a bear to protect her child.

"I must go now," she said and turned away. At the door, she paused with her hand on the knob, not looking at him. "You haven't asked why Todd was whipped."

Gavin cleared an obstruction in his throat. "I don't see what difference it makes."

"In this case, you might be interested. He overheard your plans with Dana Oleson to keep Blake occupied while you viewed the dike on our ranch. When Blake came home and said he was going there, Todd diverted him by telling him cattle had broken a fence in the south pasture. Blake realized he'd been fooled."

Gavin heard this with a brand to his heart. "Oh God!" he croaked, his voice cracking with emotion. "You don't know how sorry I am."

"Todd admires you, Mr. McLeod. He didn't want you to come to harm."

She opened the door.

"Mrs. Logan, wait." He forced himself to bring his feelings under control. "No doubt you're well aware of the conflict between your husband and me. You also know why I'm here. The dike on your land represents a threat to the entire community, but no one is more at risk than your own family. In a week or so, when the river rises to new heights, take your son and go somewhere safe."

She paused in the doorway, gazing outward. After a moment, she half turned to him. She spoke in a resigned tone, "There is only so far I will go to antagonize my husband, Mr. McLeod. If I were to side against him concerning the dike on his land, it would be his undoing."

She left, leaving Gavin mystified as to what she meant.

The logging camp mushroomed into a hive of volunteer activity. Timing for once, worked in Gavin's favour. The logging company was embroiled in a legal wrangle with the First Nations band over logging rights in the area. A court order curtailed work, resulting in a major layoff.

Malloy made Jeff available on payroll to help out with the modifications. Jeff commandeered some lumber and helped Cutter and LD build bunks to quadruple the capacity of the bunkhouses. When laid-off workers knew Cutter was on the project, more than a dozen volunteered to help. Foster followed up on promises of donated bedding. A storage room down the hall from the camp's office was emptied and Will went to work there setting up a communications centre.

In the kitchen, Mandy was loading in food supplies. She took inventory in the walk-in freezer. Realizing the amount of storage they'd need for food would require auxiliary freezers, she went in search of Gavin. She headed to the office, entering the back door by the communications centre. Will lay on his back stringing wires up through holes in the desk.

"Have you seen Gavin?" she asked.

"He took a call in the office."

She approached the office door, which was slightly ajar. Her knuckle was poised to rap when Gavin's tone caused her to hesitate. Judging by his placating tone, he was dealing with an irate caller. Vacillating, she heard his end of the exchange and realized he was defending his decision to involve the Dike Inspector. He addressed the person on the line as, 'boss'. Feeling awkward, she was about to retreat, but his next words, spoken in rising anger, burned her ears. "It's the Withers Gazette for God sakes, a local rag."

Then she heard him defend the committee members and felt a warm rush of gratitude. His boss must have a copy of the article, for Gavin was forced to answer for some very specific inferences. Someone must have faxed it, she thought. If they were looking to undermine Gavin, the tactic proved successful. In dismay she understood that he was combating the threat of being recalled.

She tip-toed away, overcome with guilt. He was paying the price for their short-comings. She had to *do* something, but what? She needed someone to confide in who would know how to help. But who? LD? No. Foster? Definitely not. Dana! Of course. If anyone would know what to do, it would be her. Back in the communications room, she said, "Gavin's tied up, Will. I'll catch him later."

It was after sunset by the time she quit the camp. Mandy was acquainted with the location of Dana's riding academy but had never been there. House and stable were in darkness when she arrived. She wondered if Dana was away but her truck was in the yard. She climbed the porch steps and found the inside front door open. She knocked on the screen door but no one came. A second knock and a querying 'halloo' also produced no result.

The hair on Mandy's arms stood up, her psyche telling her something was wrong. Faintly, she thought she heard sounds—human sounds. She drew open the screen door, its squeak quickening her pulse. The sound she thought she heard stopped. She froze, wondering what on earth she was doing creeping into a strange house in the dark. Then she heard the distinct sound of a sniff, a human sniff.

"Dana?" she called softly. She crept to an entrance of a room, a living room. In the dark, she could barely make out a small form, sitting sideways in the corner of a couch. She crept over and crouched down beside her. Crying soundlessly, Dana hugged her knees. Mandy recognized the condition of one who has been lost in tears for hours.

"Honey, whatever is the matter?" she crooned. Glancing aside, she could barely see on the carpet the open folds of a letter, not typed, but with cursive handwriting. In a knowing voice, she gently summed up the evidence. "Girl, looks to me like some man has gone and broke your heart." Inviting response, she finished with a questioning, "Hmh?"

She was rewarded with the barest of nods. "Well now," she mused without rancour, "isn't that just like men. They go and steal your heart and then mail it back in pieces in an envelope." She groped around in her pockets and came up with a clean, though crumpled tissue. "Here now, there's a good girl, blow your nose."

Dana accepted the tissue in a dainty hand, though the clarion sound of blowing her nose was anything but dainty. "What are you doing here?" she croaked.

"Well, it just might be karma. Seems like you needed a woman to happen along to give you some motherly support." Dana stared straight ahead, eyes glazed.

"You mind if I turn on a lamp?" Mandy asked. "It's pretty gloomy in here." She clicked on the lamp beside her. The ravages of the last several hours were evident in Dana's reddened eyes and nose. Mandy regarded her pensively.

"You were engaged to Dr. Robbins, weren't you?"

Dana nodded and added. "The whole town knew the handsome, athletic doctor was engaged to the cripple," she said bitterly, her voice hoarse from crying.

"Hey now," Mandy murmured. "You've no need to dump on yourself like that."

"Well, he dumped *me*—for a woman who's able-bodied. A rising-star athlete in fact."

"Dana, I know for a fact you're a fine athlete yourself. I visited Dr. Robbins professionally. I've seen your picture. You're a superb equestrian."

Dana made a derisive sound. "He gave me his horse, you know. In his letter…he told me I could have his mare. I guess it's supposed to be a consolation prize. Kind of ironic, don't you think? Both the horse and the woman he abandoned are lame."

"Men are fools, honey. They don't know a good thing when they've got it."

Dana drew a shuddering breath and exhaled. She turned to look at Mandy for the first time. "You sound experienced. Did someone break *your* heart?"

The question caught Mandy off guard. Coupled with the palpable grief of the other woman, it touched off a pain she'd thought was history. "A long time ago."

Dana gave her a searching look. "Would you tell me about it?"

Mandy held those pained eyes a long moment. Years suddenly telescoped. A vivid vision of a face appeared. "His name was Wayne Ashton," she found herself saying. "A free spirit. A *kindred* spirit, or so I thought." A bittersweet smile played around her mouth. "He arrived in town one summer from heaven knows where and got a job playing gigs on his guitar at The Winchester. I waited tables in the bar. We hit it off right away. It was the first time in my life I ever felt really special to a fella. We just seemed to understand one another without having to explain. And we laughed. Boy did we have some laughs!" Her gaze lingered on some indefinite place in the middle distance.

"I flipped head over heels. He was the *one*, you know what I mean? When he looked into my eyes and said, 'I love you', I was so convinced. No one had ever said that to me." She fell silent, her face alight with remembered happiness.

She sighed audibly and the light was extinguished. "I was so naïve. I guess I didn't know what love was. I was so hungry for it, I didn't know when I was being conned."

"What happened?"

"He left. Packed up and left without so much as goodbye. I never heard from him again."

Silence hung between them a moment, a shared grief. "I'm sorry," Dana whispered finally.

"Oh never mind. Like I said, it was a long time ago."

"There's never been anyone else?"

Mandy gave a self-deprecating laugh. "I never let there be anyone else. Don't get me wrong, I like men. I could be happy settled down with one. I'm just afraid if I let myself fall in love again, the same thing will happen; the guy will take off."

Dana nodded as if in fellowship, then drew another long breath. "Mandy, please don't tell anyone about Dr. Robbins."

"Honey, you've got nothing to be ashamed of."

"I need time to deal with it. I'm not ready for people's questions… or sympathy. Promise me."

"Sure, honey. Whatever you want. I won't tell a soul."

"Why *did* you come tonight?"

"I came about Gavin."

Dana's eyes flew wide. "What about him?"

"He's in trouble with his boss on account of us—the committee, I mean." She explained how she'd inadvertently eavesdropped and what she heard. "We owe it to Gavin to make sure he doesn't get pulled from this assignment because of us."

Dana said, "We'll just have to prove his boss wrong."

An urgent call from the First Nations band thrust the priority of the work at the camp to a back seat. The river was rising rapidly, the current now sweeping through the marshy lowland and creeping toward the nearby homes on the reserve. Gavin left Cutter in charge of construction at the camp, with the help of the loggers who were volunteering.

He instructed Foster to arrange immediate delivery of truckloads of sand. A load of sandbags, recently ordered by Foster was routed to the reserve as well. On his way there, Gavin pulled off the highway just past the bridge. He walked back onto it to observe the river. He had not had time to look at it in over a week. He was shocked by the change. Water, the colour of liquid mud churned and roiled, cascading upward in places, in boiling waves. A log carried down on the current thrust up a branch like the hand of a drowning soul, green leaves still clinging to it. It swept under the bridge at an alarming speed.

The first delivery of sand was being dumped when he arrived. Every able-bodied man and a number of women from the reserve congregated, ready to work, some with shovels over their shoulders. LD proved resourceful again. He arrived at the head of a convoy of four vehicles with a dozen mates he'd rounded up from his shift at the mill to work alongside the people from the reserve.

All morning, crews worked efficiently in groups, filling and laying bags like brickwork in walls around the perimeter of the houses. LD slogged with the rest of them yet always found energy to crack a joke and laugh. He winked at the girls, who giggled in return. His bonhomie was infectious, the physical labour satisfying. Though Gavin's arms and shoulders ached and blisters broke on his hands, he knew these badges were worn by everyone. By mid-morning, Mandy appeared, honking her horn. She brought coffee and sandwiches. Emma Toms rode with her. The two women handed out refreshments.

The back-breaking work continued for the next three days, each day hotter and more humid than the preceding one. Clouds gathered and threatened rain. Mandy faithfully appeared twice a day with food and drink to succour the workers. Gavin enjoyed the sense of community among them. Each night he dropped into bed, every fibre in his body hurting.

It was from Mandy that he learned Dana had found a place for her mother in Kamloops. She would take her on Friday. He tried calling Dana to say he'd come by the nursing home to see her mother once more before she was gone. But every time he called, Dana's phone rang unanswered.

The sandbagging crews finished just in time, for after the fourth day, the rains came.

Flood tide reached first alert level. Withers Engineering Department initiated daily monitoring of the gauges. Gavin received a copy of a certificate, filed with the department, serving notice that reinforcements on the dike on the Logan ranch passed inspection. He wished he could see for himself, but in his last heated call from his boss, Perce issued a direct order for him to stay off Logan's land.

Daily dike patrol would now begin. LD volunteered for the duty, happy to be able to put his ATV to important official business. Gavin briefed him on what to watch for.

Viola Cameron knew her daughter. Dana was covering up something. In the twenty-three years since she had come to live with her and Mr. Cameron, Dana had never been cold or rude. No, her daughter, for she had thought of her as her daughter from the beginning, was a warm and affectionate individual. But when troubled, she pulled into a shell. Nothing and no one could coax her out until she sorted out whatever was bothering her.

Something was wrong now. First there'd been her inability to reach Dana on the phone these last few days. Then when Dana called to give her the news of the move, her voice on the phone was flat. Inquiry as to whether something was troubling her was met with bland denial. Now, in person, she was distant.

Dana folded Viola's clothing neatly and packed them into the two suitcases she'd brought. Viola tried to help but Dana insisted she not exert herself. The trip would be long and tiring. It was with a sense of relief then that Viola looked up to see Gavin McLeod hesitating in the doorway.

"Mr. McLeod! Come in. What a pleasure to see you."

Dana whirled at hearing his name. The smile Viola expected to appear, did not. "Gavin! Is... is something wrong?" Dana stuttered.

"No. Not at all," he answered, hat in hand. "I came to see you off, Mrs. Cameron," he said, turning to her. "Since it was me who instigated your leaving, I thought it was the least I could do. I don't mean to hold you up." This last was aimed at Dana. He shifted under her stare, clearly uncomfortable.

Perplexed by the tension between them, Viola wondered if the pleasure they had seemed to take in each others' company the night of the dance had tumbled toward something more. Was this the reason for Dana's remoteness?

In some ways, Viola thought grimly, an affair might be good for her. She'd never dated anyone but Jeremy. In the years they'd been together, he'd always been the perfect gentleman. He'd been the best of the crop at the time they got together. Yet Viola never warmed to him. His driving ambition left little room for Dana's own expression. She deferred to him too much, her spirit muffled. This McLeod, there was more depth to him. Too bad he was married, but if Dana could only see what was possible, maybe she wouldn't settle for shallow.

"That's very thoughtful of you," Dana addressed him, her tone and manner formal. "I'm sure Mother would much rather visit with you in the lounge than watch me pack her things."

"Dana, dear, wouldn't you like to take a break and come have tea with Mr. McLeod and me?"

"I think it best I finish here. Besides, Mother, he came to see you." She turned away, making her intent clear.

"Come, Mrs. Cameron," McLeod said to her, gallantly offering his arm. "We've been scuttled. Shall we make the best of it over a cuppa?"

They ambled down the hall at a snail's pace. A door opened abruptly and a middle-aged woman in a white uniform darted across in front of them. Viola called to her. "Rosalind. This is Mr. McLeod."

The woman halted. She regarded Gavin over glasses pulled low on her nose, her countenance stern. "Ah, Mr. McLeod," she said, her genial tone belying the look. "You've been causing quite a stir here."

"Here?" Gavin answered, with sinking dismay. "What have I done?"

"Ever since you persuaded Viola to leave Withers during the crisis, other residents and their families have talked and come to the same decision. Last week the Board voted to ensure *all* residents have alternate accommodations arranged in case the river surpasses safe levels. We've been very busy here. In fact, I must go take a call right now about moving someone. I'm pleased to have met you." She shook his hand warmly and hurried down an intersecting corridor.

The large bay window in the lounge afforded a view of the lawns where rain puddled in low spots and bounced off patio furniture. "Gavin, how fortunate you've come just now. I wonder if I could impose on you for a favour?"

"Of course, if I'm able."

"I have two pieces of furniture of my own here, a rocking chair and a bureau. Dana will be taking them with us to Kamloops. They're the vestiges of an old woman's home," she explained. "They mean a lot to me. Dana will borrow a dolly from storage. Would you help her load them onto her truck?"

"Mrs. Cameron! You'll be more than an hour on the highway. Your furniture will be ruined in the rain."

"Well… she brought a tarp. It's a shame about the weather but—"

"I have a better idea," he interrupted. "Leave it to me."

Over tea, she told him about the small, private family care facility Dana had found for her in Kamloops.

He said, "I can't tell you how grateful I am to you for your leadership in this. You obviously mounted a very effective campaign here."

She patted his knee. "Some people just need a nudge. I'm grateful you'll be here. I know you'll look out for my Dana."

"Gavin is very busy, Mother. Looking out for me is not part of his responsibility." Dana stood unsmiling, in the doorway.

He rose. "It's my duty to look out for all Wither's residents," he remarked, with a slight bow. "Your mother informs me you're moving a couple of pieces of her furniture. The weather isn't being very co-operative."

She looked out at the rain and grimaced. "No, it isn't."

"Trade vehicles with me. My Cherokee will take the furniture and her suitcases and keep everything dry."

Dana's countenance lost some brittleness. "You're too kind."

The interchange made Viola wonder if she'd been mistaken about something transpiring between them to occasion Dana's asperity. Perhaps she wasn't upset with *him* after all. Experience had taught Viola that no amount of questioning would pry from Dana an explanation for her mood. It had been Jeremy who divulged, years after the fact, that it was bullying classmates who caused Dana's periods of remoteness.

Chapter Eight

Dana's mood threw Gavin off balance. When he first arrived at the nursing home her reaction made him think he had done something to upset her. But she seemed grateful for his offer to trade vehicles and his help with the furniture. As he mulled it over on his way up to the camp, he thought of other reasons for it.

She was devoted to her mother. It must be very distressing to have to send her to a strange place. Moreover, her riding academy, her childhood home and beloved valley all stood in harm's way. All this at a time her fiancé was away. It had to be taking a toll. He felt foolish for imagining her preoccupation had anything to do with him.

He had no time to think more about it once he arrived at the camp. He joined the small army of volunteers sawing wood and hammering additional bunks together in the bunkhouses. Rain kept up a steady pounding on the roof. He stayed till the last of the workers left, well after dark. He slogged through heavy mud to Dana's pick-up, driving with care down the mountain road. Still, the truck slithered around a couple of turns.

He was bone-weary by the time he reached his cabin. As he came in, the phone rang. He made a dash for it, cursing the muddy track it caused him to make across the floor.

"Hey, boss."

"LD! How'd it go today?"

"Wahl, that's just the thing. I've been trying t' get a hold o' you since this afternoon."

"Why, what's up?"

"Wahl, that there jog in the dike you told us about on the Logan spread…you said they was 'sposed to fix it. In my opinion, they just did some window dressing. The way the river's tearing past there now, if the water gets any higher, that spot's gonna take a shit-kicking."

Gavin swore under his breath. "What do you mean by window dressing?"

"There's sand pushed up against the side away from the river. A bit of gravel was dumped on the river side, but the current's already eating away at it."

"That sounds bad. It should have been sandbagged at the very least."

"I gotta go, boss. I'm on my break at the mill and I gotta get back to work now."

"Okay, LD. Good work. Thanks for calling."

"Okey-doke. Bye."

"LD wait! I got a favour to ask."

"Shoot."

"Can I borrow your ATV tomorrow?"

"Sure thing."

"Thanks. Goodnight LD."

Trading vehicles with Dana turned out to be fortuitous because he was able to load the ATV in her pick-up. LD laid planks against the truck bed and gunned it up. Gavin slid the planks in after. He backed the ATV out at the head of the same route across Logan's ranch Dana had shown him on the map previously, and headed to the dike.

The situation was pretty much as LD described it. Several days ago the river had jumped its banks and was creeping up the dike. Several loads of gravel had been dumped on the vulnerable flank but the current swung hard around the opposing bend in the river and chewed at it. As Gavin watched, tiny avalanches occurred at the water's edge, testimony to the voracious appetite below the eddies. *God damn it to hell.*

To return the ATV, he had to pass by Dana's. He spied her leading a horse into the barn. He wheeled in. After asking about getting Viola settled, he remarked, "You should be getting your stock moved, Dana."

"I know. I've been holding off because of lessons. I worked out an arrangement with Sadie to keep them. I planned to start shipping them tomorrow."

"Start?"

"It's a big job to load and unload, settling them in two at a time."

He studied the ground, scuffing his boot in the dirt. "Look, Dana, the sooner this is done the better. If I help you," he looked up, "can you ship them in a day?"

She hesitated. "There must be so many other things you need to do."

"I'll feel better if I know your horses are out of here."

"Well... alright. Thank you. I'd be grateful for your help."

After restoring everyone's vehicles to their owners, Gavin arrived at his office in a state of grim determination. He went straight to the phone and called his boss. Perce came on right away.

"So this is what comes of making terms with the devil!" Gavin seethed.

"McLeod? That you? What's got the wind up your kilt? You sound pissed."

"I AM pissed," he fairly shouted into the receiver. "Logan foiled us. The dike wasn't properly reinforced. I got a copy of a pretty little certificate showing it passed inspection. Now how hard do you think it is for a town councillor to get a certificate from his own engineering department? The first day I have a man on dike patrol, he informs me all they did was cosmetic alterations."

"Jesus," Perce swore softly. "You think it'll breach?"

"I don't know, Perce, I'm not clairvoyant. But it's going to take a pounding and it's not in good shape for it."

"Who'd you have out on patrol?"

"LD Metcalfe."

"Metcalfe... Metcalfe. Isn't he the one who can't read or write?"

"He's not blind!" Gavin did yell this time. As the insult to LD hit him, he added in a surly afterthought, "He's not stupid either. Anyway, how do you know his name? The newspaper article printed no names."

"I did some investigating." Gavin's pent-up breath whistled through gritted teeth. "How do you know for sure what shape the dike's in? This Metcalfe might just want to seem important."

"I *saw* it, Perce. It's a mess."

"What do you mean, you saw it? I told you to stay off Logan's land."

"I know you did but—"

"God damn it, McLeod. You defied a direct order. I'll have your ass."

"And in the investigation after this town is wiped out, who'll be left in the department to point the finger to, once you've fired me?" He didn't wait for Perce's response, slamming the receiver into the cradle.

In for a penny, in for a pound, he muttered to himself as he picked it up again. He punched the long-distance number for the Dike Inspector in Kamloops. He explained his concerns; told him what he'd seen. Stepping carefully around the politics, he said, "I know it passed inspection, sir, but I am pretty worried about the erosion."

"Inspection?" the man's voice cut in, heavy with suspicion.

Gavin smirked to himself. *Bingo!* "Yes sir," he continued innocently. "I got a copy of the certificate."

"Certificate! Who issued it?"

"Uh, it says here," he paused, "Withers Engineering Department."

"*I'm* the Inspector of Dikes. *I* ordered this improvement." Gavin waited for the information to take effect. "Listen Mr. McLeod, thank you for your information. I need to make some calls. I'll get back to you, say, in an hour. Will you be there?"

"I'll be here." He hung up and rubbed his hands together in satisfaction. Perce would find out he was right to raise the alarm. His boss wouldn't fire him. He could expect a letter of discipline though. Perce hated dealing with crap.

The return call came in less than an hour. In that time the Inspector spoke with Mayor Hale twice. Logan was supposed to have had the Public Works Department do the work. They were to notify the Inspector so he could come up and see it for himself. But Logan had arranged through Noel Connor to lend him one of the town bulldozers. He did the work himself. He wangled this new certificate out of the Connor's department.

"I'm preparing an order for repairs to be done by the Public Works Department independent of Logan," the Inspector told him. "The 'dozer is to go out tomorrow morning."

The following morning, thunderstorms moved in. Pounding rain mired the gravel roads. Work on the dike was postponed. Dana called. She couldn't move horses in a thunderstorm. They would be spooky. Loading them would risk injury to horses and humans.

Gavin stood staring out his office window where the water sheeted off the overhang. *We don't need this,* he thought.

It rained the next day too; work on the dike was delayed again. The rain eased up to a fine mist by the following morning. By now, Dana was anxious to move her horses. She was putting travel pads on Jake's legs when Gavin arrived. A bay mare stood patiently in cross-ties, already booted up.

"I thought you'd want to move Nefarious first," he said.

"No," she said without looking up. "I don't want to contend with the more inexperienced travellers or high strung animals first. They'll settle better when they find their buddies already there."

"Makes sense."

She led the mare out first. A large puddle had formed overnight behind the trailer's ramp. "Damn," she swore. "I'll have to move the trailer." Gavin didn't understand what the big deal was, but the mare danced sideways in the mud, snorting.

"You can always count on horses having their own ideas," Dana grumbled. "This one hates water. If I try to walk her through that puddle, I may never get her trailered."

"I'll pull the truck ahead," he offered. "Key's in it?" She nodded. Soon they had the mare aboard. Jake followed like a lamb. The roads were slick and they took it slow.

Sadie's nervous Shih Zhu, Barney, snuck out while they were unloading and darted at the mare's heels, yapping. The mare exploded, dragging Dana sideways off the ramp. Sadie, in her baseball hat, chased Barney, hollering at him to come, but he dashed hither and yon barking up a storm. The mare tracked him, the whites of her eyes showing, while Dana clung to the halter. Gavin grasped the other side. They let her face the shaggy little fury. Eye to eye, both creatures seemed to come to terms with the other.

"You okay?" Gavin asked.

"Yeah. She gave my shoulder a good yank but nothing terminal."

"You get her settled in the barn. I'll unload Jake."

It was already lunch time before they got back to her place. She heated some canned soup and tossed Gavin a towel to dry his hair. "How's your shoulder?" he asked.

She rubbed it. "It's sore but not serious."

"You want to leave the others till tomorrow?"

She rolled her eyes. "You're the one who thought time was of the essence."

He grimaced. "Yeah but I don't want to see you get bashed up."

"I'll be fine. Let's make another couple of trips."

They ferried two more horses without mishap.

Back at her stable, Dana explained that the big black mare could be a fiend to trailer. "Her previous owner let her fall off the ramp once. Naturally, she was nervous after that. He was very forceful and every trip was accompanied by whips, ropes and shouting." It took her forty-five minutes to reassure the mare and coax her to join Bongo in the trailer. No sooner was the tailgate latched when thunder rumbled across the ridge and it began to rain in earnest again.

"Great," Dana moaned at the sound. "Let's not hang around."

The gravel roads had gotten worse. Lightning cracked across the sky. From the trailer, they heard crash, boom, thud as the mare kicked and thrashed. "Jesus Murphy," Dana exclaimed. "We're gonna have to stop so I can settle her down. She'll hurt herself or put a hole through the side."

They crested a hill; there was nowhere safe to stop. The syncopated percussion increased as they reached the bottom and began rounding a curve. "Look out!" Gavin hollered. An orange and black bus from the opposite direction crowded toward them. Dana pumped the brakes. The trailer began to jack-knife, the truck juddered. They skidded to a halt. Both sat frozen a second or two.

"You didn't tell me you were a stunt driver," he said, straight-faced.

"Listen, you can take over here anytime."

"Hey," he said, cocking an ear. "Do you hear anything?"

"No." They exchanged knowing looks and jumped out of their respective doors. She hopped up on the trailer hitch, peering inside, rain dripping off her hat brim.

"Can you see anything?"

"Yeah," she said disparagingly. "The pig is eating as if she hadn't a care in the world."

"Everything okay?" the bus driver hollered. Dana stepped into the centre of the road.

"We're fine," she answered.

A window near the back of the bus was pushed down. A small face appeared. "Miss Oleson. Are you taking the horses to Mrs. Millhouse's?"

"Todd! Hi. Yes, I am."

"Oh." He sounded disappointed. "I guess you don't want me to come on Saturday then."

"There won't be any stalls to clean, Todd."

They heard the driver holler at him to sit down. On the far side of the van, Gavin stayed out of sight. The last time he'd encountered the boy was that awful day he'd stopped the beating. He would have liked to have said 'Hi', but suspected the feeling might not be mutual.

"Wait, Todd," Dana called, "if you want to ride your bike over to Mrs. Millhouse's on Saturday, you could turn the horses out and muck out stalls. That would be a big help."

"Okay," he brightened. The bus driver hollered a second order. "I gotta go now, Miss Oleson." He started to put up the window, then pushed it down once more. "Is it okay if I ride Nefertiti?"

"Of course it is."

As they pulled away, Gavin asked, "He's still coming to your place on weekends?"

"Yes."

"I'm surprised Blake lets him after what happened. I thought you'd be in his bad books now too."

She didn't answer instantly. Finally she said, "When he isn't abusing his son, he pretty much ignores him. I'm not sure he cares much *what* Todd does as long as he doesn't get in the way." She failed to tell him about Blake coming on to her.

They settled the horses in their new stalls and headed back once more. "Six down, six to go," he remarked, getting behind the wheel for the return trip. She slid down in the seat till her head rested on the back. "You look all done in," he said. "Why don't we do the rest tomorrow?" Too beat to even answer, she nodded.

At the farm, he helped her feed the remaining horses. "You should be staying in town by now," he observed. "I don't like the idea of you out here overnight by yourself."

"I can't leave the horses."

Though her response made him uneasy, he left it at that.

The river rose overnight to the second level alert. Twenty-four-hour dike patrol was implemented. The Department didn't have enough staff, but again LD came to the rescue. He enrolled a crew from the mill to help him with the duty. The river was expected to crest in three days. It was still raining.

Gavin called Public Works. Again he was told there was no point sending a 'dozer out. The weight of the machine on a water-logged dike would do more harm than good.

On his way to Dana's, he detoured around to the bridge to view the river. What he saw chilled him. Twice as wide as normal, it swept toward him in a swollen rampage. Debris bobbed in the churning, mud-like flow. Ridiculously, an empty punt shot by, its trailing tie-rope testimony to the river's theft from its mooring. A huge tree trunk, propelled at high velocity, struck the bridge abutment like a battering ram, ringing it like a gong.

With a sense of urgency, he hastened on to Dana's. She came out of the house in her slicker to meet him.

"I tried calling you but you'd already left."

"What's wrong?"

She pointed to the trailer. "It's got a flat. We must have picked up a nail or something yesterday."

"We'll have to unhitch it to put on the spare," he said, hating the thought of changing a tire in the rain.

"Well, that's the thing," she said lamely. "I don't have a spare."

"You don't have a spare!" he echoed.

She gave him an embarrassed look. "One of the horses chewed on it the last time I took it to a show."

He gave a sardonic laugh. "Bet that gave him a belly ache."

"Yeah, it cost me a vet bill. I meant to get the tire replaced but never got around to it."

"We'll just have to get this one repaired."

They unhitched and jacked the trailer. Gavin took the tire into town and waited for it. It was noon before he was back. Dana had lunch made.

They took Nefarious and Nefertiti first. The docile mare followed Dana up the ramp but Nefarious was in high spirits and itching to stretch his legs. The horses had been kept in their stalls for several days, the paddocks too slick to let them out. Unlike the mare yesterday who balked and rolled her eyes in fear, Nefarious simply cavorted like an over-excited kid, prancing and begging for a good gallop. In the end, Dana took him to the indoor ring and lunged him on the long-line for twenty minutes. This time, when he saw his dam's familiar rear, he rushed eagerly up the ramp to be with her.

It was dark by the time they unloaded the last animal. They unhitched the trailer and left it. Again Gavin drove the return trip. The rain had let up a few times during the day but now came down in torrents. A wind blew up. He thought of the scene by the bridge that morning, imagining the river's ominous power in the dark. He pitied whoever was out there this night riding LD's ATV along the dike.

"You should stay in town tonight," he said.

He felt her look askance at him in the darkness of the cab. "The town is in the flood plain too, you know," she countered wearily.

"But it's closer to evacuation routes. And you won't be alone."

"I'd have to stay at The Winchester. Ugh! Above that bar? I'd rather sleep in Sadie's barn."

He peered hard out the windshield. Through the watery smear the wipers made, it was hard to tell where the edge of the road was. They drove in silence a while longer. The same restraint he'd felt from her at the nursing home had pervaded the last two days. He wanted to shake her and say, *Look to your own safety. You've put your mother and your horses out of harm's way, now what about yourself?* No, he didn't want to shake her, he wanted to shield her, protect her from whatever was weighing down upon her.

"I saw the river today," he said finally, the sound of his voice grim and magnified by the silence that had gone before. He thought of all the arguments—logical, rational arguments to persuade her, but instead he said with far more feeling than he intended, "Don't go home tonight." He tried to recover. "It's a bad night. It's too risky."

When she didn't answer, he added, "If you've nowhere else to go, stay at my cabin. I can sleep on the couch." He found himself holding his breath, afraid that even breathing would pressure her into refusal from which she would not likely retreat.

"Okay," she answered, so softly, at first he wasn't sure she'd spoken. Relief flooded him, slackening his vice-like grip on the steering wheel. She asked him to take her home first. She would come up later in her own vehicle.

The floodlight came on in the yard when they drove in, stirred to life by the motion of the truck. "I'll be a half hour or so," she said. "I'm going to take a shower."

By the time the headlights of her pick-up appeared in his yard, Gavin too had showered, devoured microwaved stew and built a fire against the damp chill. He held the door open as she made a dash for it, holding her slicker above her to fend off the incessant rain.

He took the dripping garment from her and closed the door. She had a satchel slung over her shoulder. "You'll be staying in that room," he motioned across the way. "Want me to put your bag in there?" She gave a slight nod and let him slip it off her shoulder.

When he came out of the bedroom she was still at the door, looking wan and timid. She hugged herself, her delicate fingers peeking out from the sleeves of her grey sweater. "Go over by the fire and get warm," he urged. She stepped out of her boots and approached the hearth. "Have you eaten?" he asked.

"Yes," she answered, her tone spiritless.

"Would you like some coffee? Tea?"

She shook her head vaguely, her back to him, but turned a moment later. "Would you have anything stronger?"

"Hmh. My wet bar is kind of Spartan. Southern Comfort?"

She nodded, her expression tense, distracted. He poured two glasses and handed her one. She took a strong swallow, shuddering as it hit her throat. For a moment her eyes closed. Lightning flickered at the windows and after a lapse, thunder rumbled.

"How's your shoulder?"

"What? Oh." She touched it, as if she'd forgotten about hurting it. "It's okay."

With the hand holding his glass, he pointed toward the snug, inviting her to sit down. She took the end of the couch; he, the armchair. He tried to engage her in conversation but she responded in monosyllables. In the long pauses, the fire crackled. He sought to fill the silence by telling her how things were going at the camp, but her mind was elsewhere, her eyes restless and more grey than green. As the storm grew closer, the windows flickered with persistent lightning. She started at a thunderclap.

Just as he asked, "Does the storm scare you?", she jumped to her feet.

"No," she said, biting off the word. She made a beeline for the bottle on the counter. "Do you mind if I have another?"

"Help yourself."

She poured and threw back a swallow at the counter, her body taut. His unease amplified. What would make a woman—a woman like Dana, take a shot like that? *Like a man*, he thought.

"Dana, what's wrong?"

"Nothing," she contended, her voice brittle. She left her glass on the counter and turned to face him. "Why do you ask?"

"You're so edgy."

She lowered her gaze "I'm sorry," she murmured. "I'm not good company tonight. I guess I'm just tired."

"You've had a lot to contend with," he acknowledged. "You must be worried about the threat of flood…about your farm." The wind picked up. Rain pinged against the window. He got up and knelt to poke the fire, adding another block of wood. "Moving your mother has to have been difficult. Moving your horses has exhausted you."

"I'm grateful for all your help. You've been very kind."

Her expression of appreciation did not sound empty, yet she remained remote. Her mood troubled him. He stood and turned to her, his face grim. "You shouldn't have to shoulder all this alone."

She shrugged dismissively.

"Jeremy ought to be here, helping you," he said, the reproach he felt toward the man transparent in his tone.

Something disintegrated in her face. He cursed himself instantly for speaking out. Her eyes clouded, tears gathering in her lashes. The working of her mouth laid bare her struggle for composure. He felt punched in the stomach with dawning awareness.

"Jeremy broke off with me..." Her throat caught, the rest came out in a croak. "...for another woman." He stared slack-jawed, not knowing what to say, damning himself for his blundering. Awkwardness hung between them.

A sizzle, then a blinding flash fused with an ear-splitting crack, rent the night. The cabin plunged into darkness. Dana screamed. Gavin took two strides and engulfed her in his arms, his need to protect her eclipsing propriety. Thunder reverberated like a dropped bucket of gargantuan marbles. A whimper sounded in her throat. She shrank against him. The scent of her hair and Southern Comfort, the carnal warmth of her intoxicated him. He forgot how she got there. She pressed her face to his chest, her fingers clutching his shirt. He pulled her closer, finding her unresisting. He felt her silent sobs. "It's okay," he whispered. "Sh...sh, it's okay."

She tipped her face up, exposing the tracks of her tears in the firelight. Tears reached her lips. He bent to kiss them away. Her lips were wet and soft and yielding. He felt drunk with his mouth pressed to hers. He kissed her harder, hunger for her exploding, igniting a long-denied yearning. He felt the length of her against every part of him, heard her moan. For one redemptive moment, he pulled back, seeing himself a scoundrel. She was drunk and wounded.

But she clung to him as if drowning. "Hold me. Please!"

He held her, fighting his emotions. But her arms slid up, encircling his neck, pulling his mouth down to hers again. Her kiss hinted of hunger. Abandoning restraint, he kissed her back.

He stooped and gathered her up in his arms. She was light as an angel. He carried her across the dark cabin to the bedroom, laying her ever so gently on his bed.

Her arms refused to relinquish his neck. "Don't leave me! Stay with me."

"Hush now, I'm here. I won't leave you." She lay back, pulling him down with her. He lay beside her, holding her against him.

"No one will ever want me," she wept, pain wringing the words from her.

"Oh God, Dana, you don't know how wrong you are."

"It's true!"

"How can you think that?"

"Because I'm a *cripple*!" she cried, flinging the word viciously, as if it were a life sentence.

"Don't," he pleaded. "Don't do that to yourself. You're beautiful. God, you're *so* beautiful." He traced her hip with his hand as if to convince her, and passion welled up in him again. He felt himself go hard. He kissed her wet cheek, then found her mouth once more, tasting salt and Southern Comfort. She arched into him, moulding to his touch.

He explored the length of her with his hand, tenderly, worshipfully. Gently, with infinite care, he unwrapped her till she lay naked on his bed. He unbuttoned his shirt, shedding it and wrestled out of his pants.

He took her slowly, lovingly, in an unhurried ascent, till her moans turned to gasps, then subsided to satiated sighs. When she wrapped her arms round him, he suffered an emotional meltdown and a physical release.

Long afterward, she lay in the crook of his arm, breathing deeply. Gingerly he drew his arm away, reaching for the duvet to cover her. The storm passed, moonlight streamed through the window. He lay on his side watching her sleep, a swell of emotion filling his chest. A wisp of her blond hair lay against her cheek, pasted there by the now dried tears. He wanted to brush it away but resisted, afraid she would stir and turn away. He imagined he discerned a ghost of a smile on her full and slightly parted lips. He longed to kiss them again.

But as he watched her, his wondrous elation gave way to self-reproach. He now understood the melancholy he'd sensed since encountering her at the nursing home. Jeremy's betrayal had shattered her. Heart-sick till she was half out of her mind, she had asked only to be held. Perhaps she'd felt safe with him, believing him a man of integrity, a *married* man. But what had he done? In the heat of his desire, he'd deluded himself into thinking she returned his feelings.

In your dreams, McLeod, he castigated himself.

If he'd been honourable, he'd have responded to *her* need, *her* wishes. Instead, he'd delivered her another betrayal.

In the realm between sleep and wakefulness, Dana felt light. Her hand reached across the bed, searching, but closed on the bed-sheet. The airiness faltered and she opened her eyes. It was morning and he was not there. She swung her legs off the bed and looked out the window. His Cherokee was gone.

Wrapping his bathrobe around her, she went out to look for a note in the kitchen or on the door, but there was none.

She scolded herself for wishing he could dally in bed with her. In these days of high water, there were many demands on the Emergency Co-ordinator, and Gavin had sacrificed two days to her horses. She showered and dressed languidly, feeling buoyant for the first time in weeks.

The yard was bathed in sunshine and the scent of damp earth met her nostrils as she left the cabin and climbed into her truck. As she put the key in the ignition, she saw the note tucked under the wiper. She smiled and retrieved it.

But as she read, all happiness drained away and she slid down onto the running board.

> *Dana,*
>
> *What I did last night was a terrible mistake. I acted impulsively, permitting myself to take advantage of your vulnerable state. The fact I am married should have been enough for me to desist. Would it make a difference to you to know I have never before been guilty of adultery? No, I suppose not. But I need to confess, in the light of day, I deeply regret what I have done. The only decent thing for me to do is accept that I should not see you again.*
>
> *Gavin*

She buried her face in her hands. *A married man*, she thought bitterly *How could I have thought he was in love with me?* She had *wanted* to believe it. Now she saw her denial. He loved his wife, felt guilty for cheating on her. The realization delivered a crushing fresh rejection. She felt stupid, a foolish schoolgirl.

Harshly, she brushed away her tears against her sleeve on the underside of her wrist. She sniffed and lifted her chin. She still had her pride. Vowing not to let him think her a pathetic victim of her own naïveté, she pulled herself together and went back inside to the phone. She would call him at his office and dispel any notion that she'd allowed herself to be used.

Todd spread jam on his toast at the kitchen table. At one end of the table his mother read a book, at the other, his father sipped coffee behind a newspaper.

"Mom?"

There was no sign he'd been heard.

"Mom?"

"Mmh?"

"Can I have a sandwich?"

She looked up with a perplexed expression. "For breakfast?"

"No. To take on my bike." His eyes darted nervously at the newspaper.

"Will you be longer than usual at Miss Oleson's?"

He winced at the name, fearful of its effect on his father's ears.

"I… I'm not going there. She took her horses to Mrs. Millhouse's. I promised to go muck out stalls." His demeanour brightened as he added, "She said I could still ride Nefertiti."

The paper rattled. Todd jumped. Over the top, his father's eyes skewered him but he said nothing. Mary got up, squeezing Todd's shoulder and began making a sandwich. He tip-toed past his dad to go brush his teeth. When he finished, his mother had the sandwich wrapped in a brown paper bag. Just when he thought he'd escaped, his father's voice collared him.

"Aren't you forgetting something?"

He froze, trying to think what his father meant. These 'quizzes' had the power to paralyze his brain. He regarded the stern face glaring at him over the paper and shook his head dumbly.

"You start a job, you finish it."

A light bulb flashed in his mind. "The cistern!" He'd endured the usual Saturday morning lesson on the water system.

"Turn off the tap at eight thirty." Todd checked the clock on the kitchen wall. There were twenty minutes till then. He resigned himself to the delay.

"What the hell?" Blake exclaimed half rising out of his chair. Todd recoiled in fright, then realized his father's attention was focused out the window. A large piece of equipment was making its way toward them from the direction of town along the dike. In a few minutes, it would come within a hundred metres of the house.

Logan thrust the paper aside and strode from the kitchen. His footsteps could be heard going into his study. A distinct click, followed a moment later by a louder snap made the back of Todd's neck prickle. His dad had loaded a rifle. Blake went out the door. Through the window, Todd watched him stride toward the dike. Mary stood, rigid, at the sink, clutching the edge of it.

On top of the dike, Logan blocked the advance of the caterpillar churning toward him, his stance wide, his rifle slung across the crook of his elbow. The machine halted, the blade ten paces from him. The driver cut the engine.

Noel Connor pushed up the brim of his baseball hat. "Come on now, Blake," he coaxed, his voice a study of authority mingled with timidity. "Let's not have any trouble."

"You're on my land," Blake proclaimed, offering no sign of recognition.

"Aw now, you know I gotta do this."

"I know I got a certificate of inspection with your signature on it."

"God damn it, Blake," Connor snapped, "it's out of my hands now."

Logan stood like a rock. "This is my ranch. I built this dike. It protects me and mine. Whatever fortifications it needs, I'll see to it personally."

"There's other people involved now," Connor blustered.

"I'm not going to trust the safety of my home and family to some damned rookie from the city."

"Who you talkin' about?"

"You know who I mean."

"Who? McLeod?"

"Yeah, him."

"Shit, Blake, why get into a pissing contest with some civil servant over this? What harm can it do to shore up the dike a bit? You can see how high the water is." He swung his arm toward the current rushing past a few feet away, but Blake kept his sights on Connor.

"Like you said, he's a civil servant."

"Christ sakes, man," Connor cursed, pulling something from his pocket. "I got an order from the office of the Inspector of Dikes." He held up a paper. "I got no choice. *You* got no choice."

"No lackey from Victoria is dictating to me what I gotta do in my valley…on *my* ranch. McLeod's out of his league."

"The whole town's watched you carry on your cock-fight with this guy all spring," Connor bristled. "His predictions have been pretty accurate up to now. People are getting nervous about the run-off. Now I'm telling you Blake, get out of my way. I got a job to do." He turned the key and the machine roared to life.

Blake levelled the rifle barrel at him.

Connor blanched and cut the engine once more. They eyed each other for long seconds, a cord in Connor's neck bulging. Then he growled between gritted teeth. "You're not the king of this valley. You think you are. But you're not! Don't think I don't know that you're screwing my wife," he charged, his face choleric.

Blake didn't flinch. Only the pupils of his eyes grew, but the other man was too far away to detect it.

Connor held up the paper. "The law applies to you too, *Councillor Logan.*"

Blake cocked the trigger.

Connor's eyes bulged. "You wouldn't shoot me," he said, his voice shaky.

"I'll tell the police you tried to run me down," Blake answered coolly.

For several seconds neither moved. Connor capitulated. "You crazy son-of-a-bitch. Have it your way! But it'll be the cops next time." The engine roared to life and the cat reversed.

Blake waited till it retreated a hundred metres or so before turning back to the house. Seeing him about face, Todd fled. He wanted no part of his father in this mood. By the time Blake restored the rifle to its rack, Todd had pushed his bicycle halfway up the hill behind the barn, in the direction of Sadie's place.

———————————

Blake closed the door to his study, unloaded his rifle and set it on its rack. He sat at his desk staring into space. The panic pumping through his veins denied the iron nerves he'd displayed in his stand-off with Connor. Under normal circumstances, he'd have laughed off the man's whining about being cuckolded. Now that accusation, as much as the confrontation, left him shaken.

Nearly twenty years had elapsed. Years of trying to forget. It happened the summer between his undergraduate and postgraduate studies. Mooning over Mary's rejection, infuriated by Mandy Sky's rebuff, he vented his frustration on the drifter Mandy took a shine to. After getting the goods on his drug dealing and threatening him with the law, he figured he'd seen the last of Ashton. When he went to Mandy's to claim his prize, it didn't go like he expected. Though he damn near took her by force, when there was no fight in her, he couldn't do it. He didn't know his departure had been witnessed.

That spring had been another year of high run-off. He'd persuaded his father, Hugh Logan, to construct a dike. Hugh put him in charge. Blake recruited the crew, mostly buddies like Seth Colville, and operated the heavy machinery himself. The day after his encounter with Mandy, he was working alone in the early evening after the crew left for the day. A pick-up crossed the prairie, kicking up dust along the track they'd graded to bring equipment in from the road.

It was Ashton. Blake climbed down from the bulldozer and with his characteristic swagger, approached him. Ashton came out of the truck, his face a mask of cold fury. Not bothering to waste energy on words, he caught Blake off guard, slugging him hard on the jaw. Blake had fought his share of fights. He had the grit and power to come out on top most of the time. But Ashton gave a good account of himself. They minced round each other, fists poised, looking for an opening. Between punches, he cussed Blake out for stealing his girl when Blake didn't even want her. He realized Ashton didn't know that Mandy hadn't put out for him. Blake gave a satisfied smirk, making a flippant remark about Mandy being happy to give a real man a blow job. That's when the knife appeared. Ashton lunged. Blake somehow fended him off. He managed to kick the knife-wielding arm. The weapon arced through the air. Ashton kicked at his groin but Blake caught his foot and threw him. They both ended up in the dirt. Ashton reached and grabbed the knife again. They struggled, rolling around in the dust. Then the man grunted and lay still.

He remembered the blood seeping out from under the inert form. He didn't remember how he got to the ranch house. Panicked, he sought out the only person alive whom he feared, the only person whose power seemed greater than his own—Hugh Logan. He would know what to do.

The senior Logan returned to the scene with him. It was dusk. He kicked the body over with his toe. *Put the corpse in his truck,* he ordered his son with cold disgust. He told him to put the truck into the line of the dike and bury it. He left him to do the dirty work. Blake worked throughout the night, not daring even to use the headlights for fear someone, somewhere would see them. By dawn, he scraped clear all signs of tracks. Luckily it was Sunday. The crew was not due back for another day. He worked on to extend the dike, putting as many yards of earth as he could between the buried hulk and the raw end of the dike. His buddies gaffed him when they saw his work, with the sloppy jog he had put in the bulwarks.

Hugh Logan survived another ten years, sharing the house with him and Mary after their wedding. He didn't live to see his grandson, only Mary's three miscarriages. Now, because of that damned McLeod, the carefully buried secret threatened to become unearthed.

Gavin rose at dawn. He slipped out quietly while Dana slept, leaving her the note on her windshield. In a vain effort to flee the emotions tormenting him, he escaped in his Cherokee up into the hills, hiking trails till hunger drove him down. He didn't want to return to the cabin in case she was still there. Neither did he relish Mandy's cheerful morning patter so he ended up at the only other café in town open for breakfast.

Afterward, he headed over to the Department of Engineering to learn the morning reading on the river. The overnight rain had pushed it to nine metres. The river was expected to crest within twenty-four hours.

Next, he dropped by Public Works to see if dike reinforcement work would proceed. Equipment was on its way there now, he was told. He swung by his office to pick up his phone messages before heading up to the camp. One from Celeste, wanting him to call home, pricked his conscience. He didn't have the stomach to return it. There were four other messages, nothing urgent, then Dana's. Even before he heard her out, the ice in her voice devastated him.

Gavin,

Thank you for informing me how smitten by guilt you feel for breaking your marriage vows. You seem to fear you may have wounded me last night. Don't flatter yourself. You served as a convenient distraction.

That was all. If he'd felt remorse earlier, he now felt sick. He slouched at his desk savaging himself for giving in to his baser urges.

Suddenly he sat up and pressed the play button again. This time he focused not on her tone but on her words. It wasn't the sex she was reacting to. It was his *note!* This time he grasped the hurt behind her cold anger. She felt betrayed by what he'd *said.* What the hell *had* he said? Something about cheating on his wife. She must have thought he meant he was sorry for the adultery, instead of for hurting her. *Christ!* What a mess he'd made.

With no consciousness of having made a decision and forgetting his pledge not to see her again, he leapt up and left his office. He jumped in the Jeep and was soon accelerating in the direction of her farm.

When Todd arrived at Sadie's, her car was gone. The horses had already been fed and turned out in the paddock. Nefertiti greeted him with a nicker. Without the aid of Miss Oleson's movable steps, Todd couldn't manage to saddle the mare. He led her to a fence, bridled her and climbed on bareback.

His destination was a ridge above the river, north of the Logan ranch house. To reach it, he doubled back toward home, then veered north on a trail through the woods. It emerged in an open meadow. From there, he surveyed the tremendous sweep of the river. He was stunned by how much wider it was than normal. He imagined the scene if the river spilled over the lip of the dike. It would be unstoppable. Like the Sorcerer's Apprentice, he thought, remembering the Disney classic his mother had bought for him on video. She'd told him the names of the musical scores and composers, but it was the images which mesmerized him, especially Mickey's disastrous flirtation with sorcery.

Nefertiti nickered and flicked an ear. Todd turned to see what alerted her. At the edge of the woods, a horse grazed. That was odd. It hadn't been there when they passed by. Nefertiti whinnied. The other animal raised its head and answered.

"Nefarious!" Todd exclaimed. The young stallion trotted up to them. "How did you get here?" The two horses touched noses. "Oh man, you must have jumped the fence! Guess you didn't want your mom to leave you in a strange place, eh boy." Nefarious snorted like freight train, then apparently satisfied, dropped his head to graze.

Todd studied the landscape once more, the music from the Sorcerer's Apprentice playing in his head. He saw it all. Mickey's desperation, his losing battle to stem the flood from buckets of water hurled down the staircase by proliferating renegade brooms, the rescue by the Sorcerer, then the awful moment of truth when he had to face his cold wrath. Like Dad. *Dad! Oh jeepers, the tap! He told me to turn off the tap!*

Panic exploded in his chest. He kicked his heels into Nefertiti. Nefarious would follow her. He'd have to return them both after he took care of the tap. He prayed the cistern would not overflow before he got there.

———————

The strains of Beethoven being played on the piano floated in under the study door, seeping into Blake's consciousness. It called to him, his anxiety giving way to yearning. There were times in a man's life when he needed—*needed* to lose himself in his wife's arms.

He left his study and strolled past her, idling behind her. Facing the opposite wall, he stood beyond her line of sight. Fists jammed in his pockets denied the casual mien he wanted her to perceive. The music shifted to a slower movement, evoking a melancholy mood. He turned to observe her. She leaned into the phrases of the piece, bending from her narrow waist. He crept over and perched on her bench, putting his mouth near her ear. He breathed into it. She twisted her head away from him without breaking stride at the keys, acute irritation in her expression.

"Mary," he murmured, as if beckoning to someone in a coma. She played on. He bent to kiss her neck.

"Leave me alone," she whispered fiercely.

"Mary," he intoned again. The scent of her raised a hunger in him. He nuzzled again, wetting her flesh with the tip of his tongue.

A dissonant crash reverberated from the keyboard. "Stop it!"

He turned full face to her, for once letting his mask drop. "Please Mary, I just want to hold you. I need you." His voice disintegrated to a whisper. "I love you."

"Today you love me. Today things aren't going your way. But I don't return your feelings. I've lost all respect for you, Blake. If people get in your way, you abuse them. Like this Mr. McLeod. Like your own son."

His breath rushed audibly through his nostrils as anger boiled up inside him. "Fuck McLeod! Leave him out of this."

She made a sound of pity.

"This is about us," he argued, "about our marriage."

"We don't have a marriage."

"How can you say that? Mary!" He slipped an arm around her waist. "I want you," he croaked huskily.

"Well, I don't want you!" She leapt up.

In a lightning move, he grabbed her upper arm and forced her back down. "You're a bully," she hissed.

"And you're a frigid bitch." She winced as he tightened his grip. "I've told you before, you're my wife and I expect to be able to have sex with my wife."

She glared at him, defiance burning in her eyes. "Then you'll have to take what you want by force."

He rose, dragging her up with him, clear of the bench. He gripped her arms. "Mary," he beseeched her, "I don't want to hurt you. I just want to hold you, I want you close to me. Come to bed."

"No."

He shook her. "Why can't you give me a little love?"

She eyed him with disgust. He saw her look and thrust her roughly away. "You know what the trouble is," he snarled. "You've got a lover."

She barked a laugh. "Now that's rich, Blake. Me... a lover? Look in the mirror."

"Yeah you! You goddamn high-class snob, you think you're so much better than me. You're nothing but a whore, a goddamn fucking WHORE!" He raised his arm pointing at the piano. "*There's* your lover!"

He whirled and picked up a porcelain lamp from an end-table, wrenching the cord from the wall. Mary threw out her arms to stop him. "No-o-o!" she screamed. He hurled it at the piano, her cry obliterated by the crash.

"You want your lover?" he roared. "Fine! Let you be bound in matrimony." He strode to the window, where heavy drapes were swagged by a braided cord. In one violent wrench, he yanked it free. He lunged for her. She backed away, extending her hands in front of her to fend him off. He grabbed an arm and viciously twisted it behind her. She cried out in pain. Forcing her to the floor, he looped the cord expertly around a wrist.

She struggled. "Ow! Stop it, Blake, you're hurting me."

He ignored her protests, shoving her back against the piano leg. He secured her arms around the leg with the cord, trussed so she couldn't move. He stood then and looked down on her, panting.

"There. You two lovebirds can *fornicate* to your heart's content," he growled. He moved toward the door.

"Don't think I don't know what's *really* eating you, Blake," she shot at him, her voice strident. He ignored her. "You're afraid!"

He halted, his back to her. Malevolently, he twisted around and pinioned her with a dangerous look. But she failed to heed the threat. Her voice tight with disgust, she blundered on. "You're afraid of what people may find in the dike. What *you* put there."

His face went ashen. For long seconds they stared each other down. Then his mouth twisted cruelly. "You don't know shit."

She raised her chin, belligerent. "I know you killed a man. You buried his body in the dike." Thunderstruck, he could only gape. "That's right, Blake, I know what you are. A murderer!"

"How do you know this?" His voice betrayed how shaken he was.

"You once meant to confide in me. You revealed your intentions to your father one night in his study. He thought you a fool and forbade you to do it. But I heard everything from the garden through the open window. Whatever Daddy dictated, you obeyed," she mocked him, her tone rich in condescension.

His mouth curved in a sneer. "Then my dear, I guess that makes you an accessory after the fact. I'll leave you for the afternoon to consider whether or not you want to turn me in." He wheeled about on his heel.

"Blake!" she cried, panic rising in her voice. "Release me. Don't leave me like this!"

He paused once more, then approached and knelt by her. He cupped her breast in his hand, squeezing it. She writhed and he gave a rough laugh. "Why darling, you're not alone. You have your lover to keep you company."

He stood and turned from her.

"Blake!" she shrieked after him. He kept on walking.

A murderer! His hand frozen on the doorknob, Todd reeled at the word. He'd been racing up the steps when he heard his mother's scream and a crash. He opened the door a crack and peered through. In horrified fascination he watched his father tie her to the piano. Appalled, he absorbed her shocking accusation, his father's failure to deny. Todd felt his insides sucked out, leaving a vacuous hole where they'd been.

In stark terror of being caught, he ran to the corral where he'd left the horses. Moments later, his father appeared on the porch.

Blake stormed over to him. "Why are these horses here?" he growled.

"I...I...was riding Nefertiti. Nefarious must have jumped the fence. I didn't know he followed us. I...I'm taking them back. I was coming to get a rope to put around his neck," he lied.

"Never mind the stallion. I'll take care of him. You get that mare back where she belongs."

Todd thought of the tap running, of his mother tied up. If his dad would just leave he could turn off the water and maybe untie her. His mind whirled.

"Move!" his father bellowed.

"But I—"

"What?"

"I...I..." he gestured helplessly toward the house.

"Stop stuttering you little ninny! You forgot to shut off the water, didn't you? I don't know what's the matter with you, boy. You're always wool-gathering. Never mind the damn tap! I'll do it myself."

Resigned to his inability to rescue his mother just yet, Todd climbed the fence and slipped onto Nefertiti's withers. He headed back to Sadie's, up the steep hill protruding like a spur into the prairie. As he rode up the switchback path, he felt the world slipping on its axis, making him dizzy.

Blake saddled the stallion. He led him round to the back door, looping the reins over the garden fence and hurried inside, down the stairs to turn off the water. He ignored Mary's entreaties when she heard him. Moments later he cantered out of the yard.

———

Gavin sped past farms and rural homes toward Dana's. On his left, the dike hid the river from sight. A caterpillar churned toward him along the top of the dike. *What the hell?* he muttered aloud. He wheeled over to the shoulder, jogged across the road, leapt the ditch and climbed the bank. A minute later Connor pulled up.

"Aren't you supposed to be working on repairs a few miles up?" Gavin hollered over the machine's din.

"Yeah," Connor shouted back, not elaborating.

Gavin motioned to him to kill the engine. His ears buzzed in the resulting silence. "Is there a problem?"

"Yeah there's a problem," Connor growled.

Gavin could see the man was steamed. "What it is?" he asked, feeling more than a little steamed himself. Would there be no end of resistance from people in this town?

"The sumbitch is crazy. Pointed a rifle at me and ordered me off his property."

"Who? Logan?"

"Well who else?" he shouted.

He'd figured Connor to be on Logan's side, but his ire seemed genuine. The part about the rifle rang true. He recalled Logan's threat when he'd stopped Todd's beating.

"You have a writ to proceed with this work, do you not?"

Connor pulled the folded sheet from his pocket once more and held it aloft. "I do. And I got no quarrel with it, 'cept I don't care to play chicken with a hot-headed, gun-toting screwball."

Logan had balls, that was for sure, and the arrogance to think he could make his own rules. But shoot someone? "Listen, this work has *got* to get done, and soon," he warned. Connor shrugged as if to say it wasn't his problem. "Look, I'll go there myself right now and talk to him. If I can get him to see reason, will you come back?"

"Suit yourself," Connor said. "I'll come back if I know that bugger's disarmed or has had a major change of heart."

"Where will I find you?"

"I'll be in the office at the Works yard."

Gavin clambered down the bank. The engine roared to life behind him and the treads began chewing their way along the top of the dike once more.

He bypassed Dana's. Personal matters would have to take a back seat.

After leaving the curt message on Gavin's office voice mail, Dana went home. But she was at loose ends, no horses to demand her attention, no students wanting lessons. She could have gone to Sadie's and fussed with her animals, but she wasn't up to encountering anyone. The house was stark and empty downstairs, her household possessions crowded onto the second floor in hopes of keeping them dry if the river came through.

She sat on the stairs between floors, hugging her knees and fighting to stave off tears that even now exerted pressure behind her eyes. She was truly alone now. Alone, unloved and defective. Unbidden, a memory crept into her mind of dancing with Gavin in the gazebo. It mocked her. He'd seemed so gallant. For the first time in her life, she'd danced without feeling clumsy. It was then she'd fallen in love with him. Somehow he'd made her feel special that night. Last night, she'd mistaken his passion for love.

Desperate to act, to do anything but dissolve into desolate weeping, she rose and climbed the stairs. Rooms were crammed with furniture. In one, she shoved aside boxes piled in front of a closet door. She opened it, avoiding her image in the full-length mirror on the inside of the door. Finding what she was looking for, she tugged her sweater over her head and dropped it to the floor, unzipped her jeans and slid out of them. She put on a dress, the one she wore to Starry Night. Stepping into her heeled sandals, she turned finally to the mirror. This is what Gavin had seen that night. Not bad. Attractive actually. A little more make-up of course. It wasn't till she walked—or danced, that she looked like a gimp.

She gazed round the room, choked with furniture and boxes of household contents from downstairs. This had been her room when she was a little girl. On too many occasions, she'd hidden out here when others tormented her. The air in the room was stuffy. Suddenly she felt claustrophobic. She fled downstairs, but the empty rooms and blank walls depressed her. Instinctively she retreated to the one place she always felt whole and at peace. In the stable she breathed deeply, drawing in the soothing scents of horse, liniment, saddle soap and hay.

When he reached the boundary of the ranch, Blake dismounted to open the by-pass gate around the cattle-guard in the road. A vehicle hove into sight, barrelling toward him, splashing through puddles from last night's rain. It rumbled over the cattle-guard and skidded to a halt.

McLeod got out.

"You!" Logan snarled. "I warned you to stay off my land."

Gavin held up a hand in a gesture of conciliation. "Go easy, Logan. Let me talk to you."

"We've got nothing to say to each other."

"Listen to reason, man. I'm here trying to protect people in this valley from disaster, yourself included."

"You're nothing but Victoria's stable boy, sticking your nose where it doesn't belong."

Gavin gritted his teeth. He didn't want to sink into a heated...and useless argument. "Okay Logan, let's agree that you don't like me and I don't like you. But there's a writ requiring you to allow the—hey that's Dana's horse! What the hell are *you* doing with it?"

"None of your damn business."

"I should say it *is*. I helped her move that horse yesterday."

Blake bored a hateful stare at McLeod, his eyes narrowing to slits. "For a married man, you're pretty friendly with our local women?"

Gavin winced as the remark struck a raw nerve. "No more than yourself, *Councillor*," he shot back.

Logan's fist connected with Gavin's temple with the force of a sledge-hammer, too fast even for his father's training to dodge. Everything went black.

LD rode dead slow along the dike, scrutinizing the water's edge and soil just above it. For the first time since volunteering so whimsically for the committee, he felt a full appreciation of the threat Gavin had warned about. On one side, water surged past only a foot or so down the embankment, the river wider than he ever remembered. On his other side, the bank fell away five metres to flat prairie.

One thing the high water accomplished was rousing people from their complacency. Folks had begun to talk in sober comprehension of the sheer volume draining from the snowfields and run-off from heavy rains. They read notices, assembled emergency kits and discussed contingency plans with family members for where to meet should a sudden evacuation order catch them separated. Moreover, the committee finally began getting responses to its call for volunteers.

Trees with nine or ten-foot root wads careened past him. LD approached the place where the dike took its unaccountable jog away from the river. He stopped just beyond it and climbed off his ATV, leaving the engine idling. The earlier patrol reported the spot had held through last night's rain. LD watched the current tearing into the bank. He wondered what was happening below the surface.

He walked across the dike to check the other slope. What he saw made his eyes bulge. The early morning patrol could not have seen this. If he had, LD would have received a very different report. An irregular V-shaped scar of erosion started near the top, widening to nearly five feet. It was three or four feet deep at the bottom. What's more, something protruded from the gaping wound.

He slithered down, digging his heels in. Below, he studied the damage, hands on his hips. A low whistle escaped through his teeth. The rusted-out fender and grill of a vintage truck poked through the gravel. Scores of such vehicles lay scattered about the country-side, relics of long ago, some in places where old logging roads had grown over; others, peculiarly, where no roads had ever been. But buried here in the dike?

He reached down and fingered the license plate. The paint had long since rusted away. He tugged at the plate but corroded bolts held it fast. He climbed up to the idling ATV and flipped open the toolbox lashed to the back. He reached for the cell phone in his breast pocket, then decided to get the plate before calling in.

He grabbed a hammer and chisel and climbed back down the bank.

Blake looked down on Gavin's inert body with grim satisfaction, adrenalin pumping through his veins. The bastard's apparent success at scoring with that sensational looking Oleson woman was the final insult. He stepped over his legs and climbed in the Cherokee, whose engine was still running. He reversed, spitting gravel and rumbled back across the cattle-guard. The Jeep spun around and sped toward the public road.

Dana heard a vehicle charging down her lane. With dismay, she saw through a dusty stable window that it was Gavin's Cherokee. If he saw her wearing this dress, he'd know she was wounded. Loathe to be caught, she cast about wildly for a place to hide, but there were only empty stalls. She'd be more humiliated than ever if he found her hiding in one. She opted to hold her ground in the corridor, raising her chin, ready to bluff her way through.

The Jeep halted in the shadow under the overhang. Backlit by bright sunlight, the face was obscured. A Stetson's silhouette sent a second wave of dismay over her. The immense frame blocking the entrance did not belong to Gavin. Blake said nothing, but treated himself to a full, frank and familiar examination of her.

Her heart missed a beat. In the soirée dress, she felt more vulnerable than ever. "What are you doing here?" she spluttered, instantly regretting how defensive she sounded. His mouth curved at one corner in some private amusement. The back of her neck prickled. He moved toward her and she resisted the urge to retreat.

"Why do you have Gavin's Jeep?" she demanded, suspicion giving rise to fear. He took another stride toward her. The blood drained from her face and in spite of herself, she took a step back.

"It suits me to have it," he gloated, innuendo hanging in the air. "Like it suits me to have McLeod's whore."

"Get out!" she cried, in full-blown panic.

"You're willing to put out for him," he crooned silkily. "Why not for me? Hmh?" As he spoke, he closed in on her. "I know what you *really* want. Come on, Sweetcakes, I'll give it to you."

———

It took LD several minutes to chip away the rusted plate but finally it came loose. He tried tracing the relief of the lettering but it was in pretty rough shape. He heard a gurgling sound and looked down. Water puddled around his boots. It hadn't been there a minute ago. He stared. Bubbles rose around his toes. He looked at the bottom of the erosion wound. A circle of soil was damp...and spreading.

In a bolt of realization, he lunged at the bank, scrabbling on hands and feet. He leapt onto the ATV. His backward glance caught an awesome, horrifying sight. A twenty-metre section where he had just stood, heaved like a gigantic boil, and with a hurricane roar he would never forget, the river burst through.

He cranked the accelerator so hard the quad skidded in an S before straightening out. He fled north along the dike. He reached for the cell phone in his breast pocket, pressing the pre-programmed digit with his thumb. It was answered immediately. He screamed into the phone. "It broke! It broke! Sound the alarm. The dike's been breached!"

———

Like cornered prey, Dana tensed, eyes wide, searching for an escape. She would risk giving Blake a good laugh at her expense, just to get out in the open. She bolted for the door, but with a lightning strike he caught her in his arm, his Stetson knocked to the floor. His arms wrapped her in a bear hug, trapping hers and lifting her off the ground. She kicked and writhed. He slammed her into the wall, body-checking her so hard it knocked the wind out of her. Her head struck the boards with a sickening crack. She went limp. He dragged her through the open stall door and thrust her away from him. Propelled backward, she fell heavily in the straw, unable to scream or even draw breath. Despite the physical shock, she summoned every ounce of strength to try to get up, but he was upon her, straddling her. She clawed at his face but he grabbed both wrists, pinning them under his knees, crushing them. His hand fumbled at the scoop of her dress. In one violent wrench, he tore the front to her waist. With barely a flick of his wrist, he severed the thin strap that clasped her bra at the front. He ripped the fabric aside with both hands, exposing her breasts. Shifting his knees, he grabbed her wrists and forced them over her head, clamping them with one hand. His free hand swept up her dress and clawed at her panties, shredding them. She sucked in her breath at last and screamed.

"Go ahead, Sweetcakes. Make all the noise you want. No one's gonna hear you but me." She fought. With everything that was in her she fought, but his strength was impregnable. His knee bruised her thighs, forcing them apart. He unzipped himself and thrust into her like a battering ram. With the knowledge she could not keep him out, she turned her face aside and bit her bottom lip, refusing to cry. For a time, she was conscious only of the jarring of her whole body with his heaving, grunting, rutting. He tensed, holding his breath and releasing it in gasps in her ear, finally exploding inside her. After a moment, his body went slack and he lay with his full weight on her, panting.

A far-off sound penetrated her consciousness. She didn't know if it just started or if it had been there the whole while. A far-off whistle, like a train. A long blast and several short, followed by another long. Blake heard it too, for he raised his head, cocking an ear to it. Suddenly he jerked up on his arms, eyes wide and staring, and croaked a single strangled word.

"Mary!"

The first sense that returned to Gavin was taste—the taste of gravel in his mouth. He raised his face an inch or two and spit. His head throbbed. He couldn't remember where he was or why he hurt. In his confusion, he couldn't make sense of the sound he heard. Then he remembered the argument with Logan and…. What *was* that sound? Thinking it was his ears ringing, he shook his head, then groaned at the pain it caused. He drew his knees up under him. The sound was still there, a whistle, intermittent. It was—God! The mill whistle! He jerked upright on his knees, reeling. How long had he been lying here? He lumbered to his feet, dizziness making the landscape undulate for several seconds. The Jeep was gone. So was Logan. Nefarious grazed nearby, oblivious to any calamity.

He spoke to the stallion. It turned an ear to him. Steadier now, he edged toward the horse. Nefarious raised his head to regard him. Then Gavin heard a vehicle. Looking down the road, he saw his own Jeep careening toward the gate. He watched it get closer till he was able to see the set of Logan's jaw above the steering wheel. He didn't slow even for the cattle-guard and bounced past with no sign of having seen Gavin. Heading in that direction, he had to be racing to rescue his family. Gavin felt weak at the knees as he realized the peril they were all in.

He held out his hand to the stallion. "Easy boy," he murmured. He hoped the animal would not elude him now. But Nefarious merely eyed him curiously as he approached and took hold of the reins. "Thank God for Dana's training," he muttered, putting a foot in the stirrup and hauling himself into the saddle.

He could only hope Dana, if she'd returned home this morning, was at this moment evacuating. What of Logan? The Jeep disappeared over the slight rise just ahead. From there, he knew, the ranch house was visible down in the flat prairie. Movement high on the spur of land jutting toward the ranch caught his eye. It was a child on a bicycle. Todd! He was riding hell-bent-for-leather *toward* home.

No, Todd. Run away! He kicked Nefarious. The horse leapt forward. Gavin pointed him in a line around the base of the spur to intercept Todd. He gave Nefarious his head, grabbing a fistful of mane to steady himself. This was no time to fall off. They topped the rise. The horse threw up his head and sat on his heels, skidding to a halt so sudden it nearly sent Gavin over his head.

Where there had been flat prairie, an angry brown tide surged past, mere metres away. The Logan buildings were awash. Logan had abandoned the Jeep half way across the yard, up to the floorboards in the rising tide. He was fighting his way on foot to the house. Gavin glanced uphill. Todd dropped his bike and hurtled pell-mell down the steep slope, toward the house. He fell hard on his face, but jumped up and kept running.

Again he kicked Nefarious' flanks, steering him across the side of the hill. He called to Todd but the boy was oblivious to him. He hauled Nefarious to a sliding stop and leapt off in a single motion. He caught the boy in his arms, helicoptering around with the momentum of his flight. Todd kicked and writhed with the desperation of a wild animal. He shrieked over and over, "MOMMY! MOMMY!" Gavin struggled to hold him.

Logan reached the porch, the water half way up the steps. He disappeared inside. Todd twisted in Gavin's arms, trying to push them away from his trunk. "No Todd!" he cried, "You can't help. The water's too high." But the boy was deaf to him. He fought like a wildcat, collapsing at the knees to slip out of his grasp but Gavin tightened his grip, lifting him off the ground to deprive him of a foothold. Still Todd fought, squirming and howling.

It took a minute or more for Logan to reappear. He had Mary by the hand but she shrank in terror on seeing the foaming torrent. He tugged and she leaned away. Roughly, he swept her up in his arms. He descended the hidden stairs one cautious step at a time. For once, Todd stopped struggling to watch.

Away from the stairs, the current sucked hungrily at Logan's legs. He took another unsteady step. He staggered under the combined force of the river and weight of his burden. He advanced deliberately, step by step. A dozen feet from the house, he swayed in the current. He hesitated, fighting for balance. Lifting his foot for his next step, the force of the river toppled him and rent Mary from his arms.

Todd's scream pierced Gavin's ears. Hysteria gave the boy strength. He flung himself backward and broke Gavin's grip. He gained his feet and lunged, but Gavin clamped a vice-like grip on his arm. "MOMMY!" Todd shrieked, his other hand outstretched toward her. The speed with which the two were swept along was shocking. Mary disappeared, then Blake. For a brief moment, he surfaced again. Then nothing. The torrent claimed them both.

Gavin hauled Todd, keening in the madness of grief, into his arms, crushing him to his chest. As he sat on the hillside holding him, all life drained from the boy. He lay limp, mewling achingly in his throat. Numbly Gavin saw the Jeep shift, begin to drift and finally turn over, swept along in the growing tide.

Water lapped at his boots and he scrabbled backward uphill on his behind, cradling Todd. He searched to see if the stallion was anywhere in sight. Miraculously, Nefarious stood twenty paces or so uphill, alert, ears flicking back and forth at the churning water. Gavin clambered to his feet. Carrying Todd, he picked his way across the slope to the horse. Once more, Nefarious let him approach. Gavin again gave thanks for Dana's superb training. He lifted the boy into the saddle and led Nefarious up the steep trail to the top. There he swung up behind Todd. Holding him against him, he took one last look at the devastation below, searching for what he knew would not be there. Then he turned Nefarious' head and began the long trek up to the camp.

Chapter Nine

Dana pulled herself into a corner of the stall, huddling there. She listened indifferently to the whistle, wondering numbly what it would be like to drown. Unbidden, from somewhere in the deep recesses of her mind she heard a gentle rap of knuckles on a door. "Come now, Dana, it's time to come out." It was her mother's voice, calling her from the seclusion in her room after some painful incident at school or on the bus. The voice was kind but matter-of-fact, and not to be disobeyed.

She pushed herself up using her hands on the boards behind her. She pulled up the useless flap of fabric in an effort to cover her nakedness. Her torn panties lay in a ball in the straw. She'd lost a shoe. She kicked off the other and hobbled to the exit.

There was no time to go to the house. An emergency kit bag Gavin advised her to keep in the truck at all times was tucked behind the seat. It contained two changes of clothes, some toiletries and other emergency items. She hauled herself up into the cab, reached under the seat for the spare key and started the engine.

The evacuation route led past the north slope of 'the hill' away from town. She drove with one hand holding the torn dress in front of her. At higher elevation, she turned onto another road leading away from the camp. A couple of kilometres along, she pulled into a turn-around at a trail-head. Retrieving the duffel bag from behind the seat, she changed, dazed, into jeans, jersey and sneakers. Outside, she balled up the dress and threw it in a trash can placed there for hikers.

The trail traversed both east and west from the road. She floundered down the path heading back toward the valley. In a few minutes she came to an overlook and a scene of spectacular destruction. Farms, fields and roads so familiar to her had disappeared beneath a brown lake. Marooned barns and homes, trees and telephone poles were all that was visible.

She located her own farm. Grief struck a blow to her stomach. Her knees threatened to buckle. Her mouth, sucked dry of all moisture lost its power to express. She stared, hollow, empty, destroyed.

A sound, foreign and at first unaccountable, drifted up from the chaos below. It sounded like a violin whose strings were snapping, slowly one after another. Eventually she identified the cause. As the flood spread across fields bounded by wire fences, posts were being sucked from the ground, one by one, the wire playing its desultory dirge of destruction.

She turned away and hobbled back to the road. Only then did she turn the truck around and point it in the direction of the camp.

––––––––––––––

Will was at work in his repair shop, when he heard the mill whistle. He ran outside. His view afforded no northward line of sight toward the Logan ranch, where he suspected the trouble was. Activity in town resembled a hornet's nest hit by a big stick. People ran every which way. Vehicles charged in all directions, several nearly colliding. Some fled north over the bridge, some south up the hill. Others scattered about town, likely to fetch loved ones.

He raced back inside and patched through to the emergency numbers he'd kept handy. Within minutes, he notified the Provincial Emergency Program, highway patrol and nearest heliport. He remained at his station, answering return traffic, reporting what he saw from his window. Activity in town dwindled, then ceased. He watched in appalled helplessness when a surge of muddy water half a kilometre wide rolled across the highway cutting off the bridge.

––––––––––––––

Foster backed his car up to the trailer holding his five-metre fishing boat and outboard motor. He'd never revealed to anyone his intention to grab his boat. It just seemed logical to him in a flood a boat might come in handy.

Sadie was shopping at Overwaitea when the evacuation signal sounded. Panic erupted as patrons ran screaming from the store. She made her way calmly to the front of the store and exited the parking lot in her station wagon. She didn't follow the signed evacuation route. Instead she headed up the street several blocks from the centre of town. There was no sign of anyone at the house. She made her way to the back property where the stink of ill-kept dog kennels assaulted her. Several kennels housed bedraggled weaned puppies of various breeds and two pathetically thin, nursing bitches with their litters. Sadie withdrew from her extra large handbag a pair of wire-cutters she'd put there last week, imagining just such a necessity. She carted puppies, two under each arm and several more in her bag, to her car and shoved them in. She returned for more. On the second trip, a pup got away from her. She left it but kept an eye on its whereabouts.

When all the weanlings had been retrieved, she broke into the first compound with the bitch and litter. She spoke to the anxious mother and petted her, depositing the pups in her bag. The last she held under the bitch's nose and led her to the car, stowing them all safely away. She transported the last litter the same way.

Then she tried to capture the loose puppy. Nervous and unused to gentle handling, he had other ideas. She coaxed and called, but to no avail. She tried to box him in against the house but he raced past her into the street. She followed as hastily as possible while trying not to frighten him further. He cowered against the curb. She didn't hear the car approach till it honked right behind her. It gave her a fright and she jerked up.

The driver leaned out the window and hollered. "Sadie, what the hell are you doing? Get yourself in gear and get out of town!"

It was Foster.

"I can't leave this pup to drown. Help me, Foster."

"Sadie, for God's sake, it's a dog. This is the real thing. You could get killed."

She thrust out her considerable chest and announced, "I'm not leaving the poor thing to fate. You can help me or you can carry on."

With a sound of disgust, Foster clambered out and slammed the door. "Jesus, jumping Jehoshaphat!"

They herded the pup back across the road and cornered it between the steps and the side of the house. Sadie lunged for it and it ran straight into Foster's arms. "Gotcha, ya little renegade." Sadie got in her car and Foster stuffed him in to her through the window. "Now let's skedaddle. There's nobody around but us two nut cases."

———————————

At the Dream-Catcher, the lunchtime rush had not yet started. Several patrons idled over coffee, most of them travellers passing through. Mandy was the first to realize the significance of the mill's blowing whistle. She began yelling orders.

"Anyone from out of town get in your car now and get over the bridge. This is an emergency. Now!" she shouted when some stared stupidly at her. "Never mind your bill," she cried to a customer who pulled his billfold from his pocket. "Run for your life. That whistle means judgement day is coming. Billy!" she shouted to the cook in the kitchen. "Kill the switches in the breaker and get out. Rosie, you come with me," she ordered the girl who helped out in the dining room. "Don't forget your emergency kit bag." She'd made her staff bring their kits to work every day for the last couple of weeks. She and Rosie struck the evacuation route eastward toward the logging camp.

Cutter and a crew of six were working at the camp when the call came. He took charge, briefing the men to handle the tide of people who would soon begin converging on the camp. He assigned several to handle vehicle traffic and parking. He left another two to answer the phone and run messages. Grabbing a box of pens and stack of blank registration forms from the office, he led the last man to the dining hall to set up a reception centre.

Will watched in horror as the river chewed through town in a ferocious brown wave. Power lines snapped off amid showers of sparks as abandoned vehicles were flung against them by the tide. The leading edge of the surf bouldered through town sweeping everything in its path not rooted down—cars, trailers, lawn furniture, whole sheds, a trampoline. It crashed like surf against the railroad embankment at the south end. With no exit, the water level rose, churning in eddies.

Then a reverberating explosion shook the ground. Fire in the general area of the gas station shot dozens of feet in the air. Flames ate into the building next to it. The whole block down to The Winchester would burn.

Foster, with Sadie right behind him, gained a safe elevation on the outskirts of town. He spotted a small crowd gathered in a knot at the hydro substation parking lot. A woman, shouting frantically, tugged at a man's shirt front. Wondering what the commotion was, he pulled in. Sadie followed. The man, barely less agitated, gripped the woman by her upper arms and seemed to be trying to communicate with her. Foster demanded of a bystander what was going on. A number of people had pre-arranged with family members to use this lot as a meeting place if they were separated when the evacuation order came. The couple at the centre of the disturbance had done likewise, but apparently each had thought their two children were with the other.

Foster shoved his way to the centre and addressed the man. "Where are your kids?"

Tearfully the man answered, "Bonnie thought I took them with me to the hardware store. But I didn't. She last remembers them in the tree house."

"Could they still be there?"

"It's possible."

"Where do you live?"

He gave an address. Foster gave a single decisive nod. "I have a boat. We'll get them."

The man admonished his wife to stay put and dashed to Foster's car with him. As they got in the front seat, Sadie jumped in behind Foster. "What the hell are you doing now?" Foster yelled.

"You might need an extra pair of hands."

Foster wasted no time arguing. He peeled out of the lot, spitting gravel. They approached the rising tide on the downhill slope. He wheeled into a driveway and backed out around to the water's edge. "Sadie," he barked, "get behind the wheel. When we unload the boat, pull the car well up the hill."

They worked with the speed of a well-drilled team. Sadie sped uphill, then trotted back with uncommon haste for her squat bulk. They donned life jackets. Foster climbed aboard to man the motor. Sadie followed post-haste. But the father hesitated, his eyes wide. "Get in, man! We've no time to waste," Foster yelled. The father gave a shove then and scrambled aboard. Just before the motor roared to life, he shot a plaintive look at Sadie. "I can't swim," he said.

The current caught the boat, duelling Foster for control of their direction. He dodged all kinds of debris. After donning life jackets, the others each used an oar to fend off flotsam that threatened to bash the boat. Idiotically, an intact manure pile floated by. They motored past homes, with Foster trying to steer along what he guessed was the middle of the roadway. The father pointed the way along streets turned into canals. Pushing against the current, progress was lethargic.

The flood was louder than what she would have imagined, Sadie thought. Above the motor, one could hear sucking, surging sounds of flowing water, cracks and bangs of objects crashing into buildings. They felt, as well as heard the explosion from the direction of downtown. An orange fireball, swallowed by billowing black smoke, roiled into the sky. Foster dared not look more than a second. He steered clear of obstructions, his face grim.

After a few minutes, the father waved excitedly and pointed. A small pair of arms waved frantically from a rude tree-house—a boy, Sadie thought. His bare legs hung over the side. A little girl jiggled up and down beside him.

"Daddy, daddy," the girl cried as they chugged up beneath the ancient cottonwood. Dirty tear tracks lined her cheeks. Foster manoeuvred them up to the trunk. Boards had been nailed vertically to the tree with cross-pieces attached to serve as a ladder. With a monkey's agility, the boy scampered down. The current kept pushing the boat away. With shouts and hand signals the men communicated with each other and the boy, till a moment when the gunwale was just beneath him. He leapt toward his father's outstretched hand. The man caught him, but the boat rocked dangerously, water splashing over the gunwale. The boat drifted a couple of metres away from the tree trunk as Foster fought to regain control.

Again he nudged them up to the ladder. The father beckoned to the girl with his arm, but she stood rooted, wide-eyed and shaking her head. The boat lunged and floundered like a wild horse on a rope.

"Clarisse! Climb down. I'll catch you."

"I'm sca-a-ared!" she cried, her voice strangled with near hysteria.

"Come down right now!" he shouted, almost equally frantic.

But she bobbed up and down, crying, "No-o-o-o."

Sadie reached across the space between benches and laid her hand on the man's knee, giving him a quick shake of her head. Then she looked up and spoke calmly. "Clarisse, we're going to get you out of here. Your Mum's waiting for you just over there." She pointed in the direction from which they had come. "You need to help us and use your courage. All you have to do is get onto the top step of the ladder. You do it every time you come down from the tree house so I know you can do it."

Clarisse stopped crying.

"Go ahead, now. Just put one foot on the ladder. Good girl, I knew you could do it. Now then, hang on tight with your hands and climb down a step. Good. Now one more. We can reach you soon."

Foster pushed the prow of the boat diagonally across the current till the ladder was mid-way alongside it. Gingerly, Clarisse backed down the ladder at Sadie's urging, one step, then another, her legs shaking violently. Just beyond her father's reach, she ran out of nerve and clung there whimpering.

"Use your courage, Clarisse," Sadie spoke calmly but firmly. "Just one more step." The girl eased a trembling bare foot from the rung and extended it down to the next. Her father grasped her ankle in a tight grip, preventing any last second retreat. "I've got you, honey. Keep coming."

None of them saw the log. It hit just off-side the prow. The boat swung violently around. Clarisse screamed as her father's grip peeled her off the ladder. She fell into the water, ripped from his hand. He gave an anguished cry as she disappeared from sight.

Her head bobbed above the surface already a half dozen feet below the boat. In a flash, Sadie was over the side. She stroked strongly in her bulky life-jacket. Ahead of her, Clarisse disappeared once more, then surfaced again, flailing her arms in a supreme effort to swim. Sadie closed the gap but not before the girl had gone under a third time.

Foster swung the boat wide to come alongside. Sadie had stopped swimming. They caught up to her. He shouted to the father to grab hold of her. Everyone in the boat realized it at the same time. Sadie had the child in her arms. The father grasped one small arm and handily lifted her out, while Sadie gripped the side. Clarisse's brother leaned to the far side, helping to keep them level. The man deposited the girl in the bottom of the boat and turned to help Sadie. There was no question of trying to haul her aboard in this current. They would all be swamped. He grabbed a section of nylon rope and slipped a loop through the shoulder of her life preserver and fastened it to the seat.

By the time all this was accomplished, Foster had guided them out of the heavy current and back toward their entry point. Their return took a fraction of the time it had taken to push upstream.

The crowd from the parking lot was gathered around Foster's car, the water closer to it than when they had left. A cheer went up when they hove into sight. The mother rushed forward. Half a dozen people surged into the shallows as Foster cut the engine. They held the boat, lifted the children to safety and reeled Sadie in. With all the hands to help, the boat was rapidly stowed on the trailer. No one hung around to debrief.

Foster argued with Sadie that she should come up to the camp with him to get checked over by a medic but she insisted he head up to the camp and she would drive herself home. "I've got animals to care for, some in my car. 'Sides I don't need your mollycoddling. I'll get cleaned up by myself, thank-you very much."

"You are one tough old bird," he carped, but with a generous tinge of admiration.

People queued in rows at the table where Cutter and three more volunteers filled out registration forms. Other volunteers explained where to pick up blankets and find their assigned bunkhouse. Mandy, Billy and Rosie set up the kitchen as soon as they arrived. Already they were dispensing tea, coffee and cookies. Evacuees huddled numbly around the long dining tables, sipping coffee.

Several times when he looked over, Cutter caught Mandy come from the kitchen and peer anxiously out the dining hall window. Seeing her again, backing through the swinging door hefting a large coffee urn, he motioned to a volunteer nearby to spell him off. He nudged his way through the throng, greeting the occasional acquaintance with a sympathetic nod or hand on their shoulder. He picked up a mug from a tray of clean ones. "How are things going in there, Mandy?"

"We're getting organized. We've got as much help as the kitchen can hold." She checked the entrance. "How many have registered so far, Cutter?"

"I figure about four hundred. Could be another four hundred before we're done."

She glanced nervously out the window again.

"He'll come," he said to her over the lip of his steaming mug.

"Who?"

"The fella you're waitin' for," he said softly.

She gave him a despondent look. "Does it show?"

"You've only been at that window every two minutes looking for him." He took another swallow. "LD knows how to take care of himself."

"I talked to the fellow from the mill who took the call," she remarked. "He said Lionel sounded pretty freaked out when he gave the alarm. There's been no word from him since. If he was south of the breach when it happened…" She let her sentence trail off, the implications too horrible to voice.

Cutter put his hand on her forearm. "There's no reason to think the worst yet. I bet he's on his way here right now."

Dana huddled on a bottom bunk in a bunkhouse set up for forty women, but holding nearly sixty including the children with the women. Mothers sought to settle keyed-up children. Babies cried and women swapped casualty stories. Several tried to engage her in conversation but soon gave up after her monosyllabic responses. Two of her young riding students spied her. They too tried to tell her their harrowing tales. Incapable of responding, she pulled the blanket around her, mumbling something about needing to sleep. She blocked out all commotion around her.

Hours may have passed when someone called her. "Miss Oleson!" It was her students again. "Nefarious is here. A man is riding him."

She shook her head. "It must be some other horse. Nefarious is being boarded at a farm."

"It *is* Nefarious," the other girl insisted. "I've seen the man at the stables."

"A student's father?"

The girl gave an exaggerated shrug and tugged the first by the sleeve. "Come on, let's go see Nefarious." Dana pulled the blanket up around her ears, but almost immediately they were back.

"Miss Oleson, Miss Oleson, he wants to talk to you."

People loitered in clots at the camp. Several recognized Gavin. They gathered round firing questions. Why was he arriving so long after the others? And why on horseback? "Isn't that's Logan's boy?" one exclaimed. Gavin ignored their questions. Only the two girls who dashed up, shouting, "Isn't that Nefarious?" got his attention.

In the hours it had taken to ride to the camp, sorrow and guilt weighed heavily on him. He felt keenly the tragedy meted out to the boy in his arms. Not knowing if Dana had made it out safely had been a torture. He almost wept with relief when the girls exclaimed Dana was inside.

When she appeared, he nudged the horse forward. She took Nefarious muzzle in her hands, then almost reluctantly it seemed, lifted her eyes. She studied Todd, frowning. The boy stared vacantly, oblivious to his surroundings. Unable to put it all together—Nefarious, Todd, and Gavin, she shook her head in confusion.

He stroked Todd's bangs off his forehead. "Blake and Mary were caught in the flood." He tried to say more but his voice failed him.

Nearby, someone reacted in shock. "They drowned?"

He turned to the speaker. "For God's sake, man, have a care," he reproached. "This is their son." Dana wore an inscrutable expression. "Dana," he pleaded, "will you take care of him?" Her eyes met his but he could read nothing in them. Silently, she reached up her arms.

"Okay cub," he murmured, "go with Dana now." He lifted him from the saddle, handing him down. Todd wrapped around her like a sleepy toddler. Without a word, she turned and hobbled back into the bunkhouse. Gavin had a score of questions, but swallowed them. They would have to wait.

As soon as she disappeared inside, he was deluged with queries. He waved them away with his hand and headed over to the office. The two girls followed him, peppering him still with questions about what happened to Todd and why he had Nefarious. He side-stepped the difficult ones with bland responses. Dismounting stiffly, he looped the reins over the railing. "Would you girls mind keeping an eye on Nefarious while I take care of some business?" They eagerly agreed. Behind him, he heard an argument break out over who would hold the reins.

No one was in the office. He picked up the phone; the line was dead. He continued down the narrow hall to the communications room. He was relieved to find Will there, wearing a set of headphones. Will's face broke into a relieved smile. He held up his forefinger, signalling he was listening to someone on the other end. Scribbling furiously, he responded to the person on the line. He recited names off a stack of forms, signing off when he finished.

"Boy, am I glad to see you," he said, pulling the headset down around his neck. "We were beginning to wonder if something had happened to you."

"I lost my Jeep in the flood."

"How'd you get here?"

"It's a long story. Later. Fill me in on what's been happening here. Any reports of casualties?"

"None so far. People took off north and south on the highway. Lots of calls pouring in looking for folks who might be here. People here are looking for others. We've been able to match up a lot of inquiries. There should be a runner here any minute to pick up this latest list of confirmed names." He held up the paper he'd been scribbling on.

"I saw it from my house," Will added, his expression sombre. "I called all the emergency numbers right away. Minutes later I picked up movement on the roof of The Winchester with my binoculars. It's a good thing the helicopters were on their way. There were three people. We found out later they were guests on the top floor. They hadn't understood the significance of the mill whistle. When the water came, they were trapped. They went up to the roof but then there was an explosion down the street. In no time the whole block was on fire. I got a message out and a helicopter moved in for a rescue. I watched them lower someone in a basket but the smoke got so bad I couldn't see anymore. They got them though; we got word. They were flown south to a hospital."

Just then footsteps hurried down the hall. Cutter burst in. Seeing Gavin, he thrust out his hand with a relieved grin. "Hey boss, glad you made it. We been limping along here as best we can without your able direction."

Gavin gave a wan smile. "Looks like you've been handling things just fine."

"Heard you arrived on that horse outside."

"News travels fast. You heard the rest of it then?"

"Just that you had a kid with you."

He nodded glumly. "Todd Logan. His parents drowned. He saw it happen."

Cutter dropped his head. "Lord ha' mercy," he murmured. "That's rough. Where's the kid now?"

"With Dana."

"How'd you get him?"

"I was nearby. He was running toward the house for his mother. I had to head him off; he'd have drowned too."

"You saw it happen too then?" Will asked softly.

Gavin couldn't speak for the lump in his throat. He nodded, avoiding their eyes. "There was nothing I could do," he rasped.

Cutter shook his head, "Hell of a thing."

Gavin cleared his throat and forced a business-like tone. "What are the rest of the committee up to?"

"Mandy's in the kitchen with her staff from the Dream-Catcher and her other volunteers," Cutter answered. "She's had lots of additional offers of help. She's doin' a helluva job gettin' everyone organized. They're serving dinner in shifts."

"How many are we talking about?"

"Close to eight hundred. We've put up the tents and spread out cots. Foster's in charge of lodgings."

"How's he behaving? People need sensitivity at times like this. It's not exactly his strong suit."

Cutter chortled and winked at Will. "He's a cantankerous old bugger all right. A drill sergeant. But nobody minds. Foster's a hero. Sadie too."

Gavin's eyebrows arched in scepticism. Will and Cutter took turns recounting the now-famous dramatic rescue by Sadie and Foster. "I'll be damned," he said at the end. "People sure surprise you in a crisis. How about LD?" he asked. "Where's he?"

The other two sobered. Cutter told him what they knew.

A renewed sense of grief washed over him. "Christ," he whispered. "Has an air search been organized?"

Will nodded. "We're doing everything we can, Gavin."

He gave a resigned nod. "Where do you need me most?"

Cutter responded. "I'll take you around to the duty stations. You can give advice on any wrinkles. There are veteran and new volunteers. Most folks just want a pat on the back. They'll appreciate it, coming from you."

"Okay. What about you, Will? You've been going at it pretty steady without a break. How can we help you?"

"Oh hey, I forgot," Cutter broke in, "what with you bein' here an' all. A fellow who just registered says he has experience with short-wave radio. He offered his help."

"Send him over," Will said. "I'd be glad of extra hands."

Turning to Gavin, Cutter asked, "What are you gonna do about the stallion, boss?"

Gavin looked toward the door as if he'd forgotten him. "Good question. He can't stay here. I've got to get him back to Sadie's somehow."

"A farmer and his wife came up here in their cattle truck. Said their car was in the repair shop. Guess by now it's in the car *wash*. I could ask to borrow their truck this evening. I wouldn't mind checking on Sadie anyhow, after her tumble in the water and all. There's no power either. The flood knocked everything out. She probably could use some help with all those animals. We sent quite a few pets her way that people brought here with them. Then there's that carload of puppies she rescued."

"Puppies?" Gavin echoed.

Cutter recounted Foster's version of the tale. Gavin rolled his eyes and shook his head. "Now that sounds like the Sadie *I* know. You sure she wants your help, Cutter?"

"Don't worry, boss. I know how to handle Sadie."

Gavin clapped him on the shoulder. "Go ahead then. Whenever you're ready."

"I'll hunt up the guy with the truck. We can load the horse. It'll be fine in the truck while I show you around. I'll drive it down after dinner."

Cutter followed Gavin outside. "Boss, what happened to your Cherokee?"

"It washed away at the Logan ranch," he said with finality. Feeling the way he did about their deaths, he had no wish for anyone to know about his altercation with Logan.

LD kept to the top of the dike till it ran out. He headed in what he figured was generally a north-east direction through the woods. Eventually he should come out onto an old logging road. He bounced over deadwood and through scratchy underbrush. A few meandering deer trails seemed promising but each eventually petered out. After zigzagging around trees and deadfalls, he was no longer sure which way was north. The sun filtering through the trees high overhead was no help. It was shortly past noon. Doggedly he kept going in what he hoped was the right direction. He splashed through soggy, grassy openings in the trees. Another hour passed. He should have come to the road but now everything looked the same. He stopped. Several times he tried using the cell phone but each time the screen displayed a 'no service' message.

By two o'clock, clouds moved in. He could no longer tell exactly where the sun was in the sky. Shortly after three, he crossed his own tracks in one of the swampy areas. He'd been in the woods all his life, but for the first time felt the foreboding sense of panic that comes of knowing you are lost in the Canadian bush. What's more, the last anyone had heard from him, he'd been at the site of disaster. No one knew for sure he was alive.

He forced himself to stop. He killed the engine and assessed his situation. He was out of the way of the flood. Of that much he was certain. It was early summer; he wouldn't freeze to death, only spend an uncomfortable night in the forest with no blanket. He had no food. He wouldn't starve to death in a day. But how long could a man last without food and water? Water. He never thought after this morning he'd be wishing for water this afternoon, but he suddenly realized how thirsty he was. Ah! But he'd come through puddles. Rain water. Not the best but it would do. The last one was just a hundred feet or so back the way he'd come. His tracks were fresh and he followed them on foot.

He found it easily. The mud, stirred by his splashing through, had settled. He knelt and leaned his face to the water, sipping like a deer. His thirst slaked, he walked back to the ATV and checked the gas level. He was three-quarters down. Not good unless he came to the road soon. He checked the sky but there was complete cloud cover by now. If he'd learned one thing about being in the bush it was this. If you know you're lost, stay put. Don't wander aimlessly.

He spent the next hour gathering branches to make a rough lean-to and bough bed to keep himself as warm as possible when night set in.

———————————

Gavin jerked awake, jolted by horrible images. In his dream, he saw Dana walking away from him, carrying Todd. He tried to warn her of a tumultuous wave rolling toward them but when he opened his mouth, no sound came out. The breaker washed over them and swept them away into the ocean.

He'd fallen asleep over the desk in the office. He heard the sonorous breathing of Will sawing wood on a cot behind him against the wall. His watch read three twenty a.m. He clicked off the lamp. He ought to be more frugal. They had plenty of generators. Still, with all these people, power was precious. Tomorrow, they would air-lift out maybe a hundred and fifty, next day, the same again. The camp couldn't accommodate this number for long without problems.

Down the hall he heard the muffled voice of the fellow Cutter had rounded up to help Will. Radio traffic was steady. He wandered down and waited till Oscar signed off.

"That was the Armed Forces," he remarked. "They'll start evacuating first thing in the morning. We're to prioritize. Anyone in poor health, the elderly and families with young children first. After that, they'll take anyone with relatives or friends who will put them up."

"Right. Any more names on the missing list been accounted for."

"Yeah, we're doing good. I've checked off quite a few. While you were sleeping several worried folks stopped by. I was able to give good news to most."

"I slept through people passing through the office?"

Oscar chuckled. "Like a baby."

"More like an old man. Gave myself a stiff neck," he said, rubbing it. "You need a break?"

"Not yet. Let Will sleep another hour. Could use some coffee though."

"Sure thing. I'll hop on over to the dining room and get you one."

Outside, the night sky was brilliant with stars. The earlier cloud cover had moved off. You never saw stars like this in Vancouver, he thought absurdly. Most of the camp lay in darkness. A light glowed inside one of the large tents. Across the yard, the bloom of a cigarette attested to some poor soul unable to sleep. He wondered how many others lay awake on cots or mats on the ground throughout the camp. Mandy left a coffee station open for just such circumstances. A single light winked at one end of the dining hall. Two more sleepless individuals sat at a darkened table, talking softly. He went up to the coffee urn and poured a cup.

"Long night, isn't it?" a female voice spoke to him from the shadows.

"Mandy! I thought you'd be sleeping long since."

"I can't," she answered.

She sat at a table alone. He joined her on the bench, both of them leaning back against the table. "Any word from the reserve?" he asked.

"They're doing fine according to the Red Cross choppers that were here earlier. Will sent a message out. Hopefully someone will get into the reserve to let Grandmother know I'm okay." In the dim light, he saw her smile pensively. "Maybe her spirit guides will already have told her."

"You'll have a long day tomorrow, Mandy, starting early too. You should try to get some rest."

She didn't answer. He felt the weight of her silence.

"You're thinking about LD."

She turned her face away but he sensed her tears. He put his arm around her shoulders and gave a gentle squeeze. She sniffed and lifted the apron on her lap and dabbed at her eyes. "Truth is, I'm awfully fond of the silly gomer," she laughed through the apron.

"I know," he said, his own throat thick. "They'll start searching again at first light."

Gavin had his work cut out for him next morning, supervising the evacuation process. Choppers began arriving at dawn bringing perishable food and other supplies and air-lifting people out. He settled disputes about priority status, reassured people and persuaded those with a fear of flying to trust the able pilots and their flying machines.

The kitchen staff worked overtime, with breakfast blending into lunch. A continuous parade of people streamed past serving tables. A dozen helpers bussed loads of dirty dishes into the kitchen; a growing pile of garbage accumulated in bins outside the kitchen's back door.

The media flocked to the camp in their own helicopters. Throughout the morning, Gavin was plagued by hungry reporters looking for an angle on the human tragedy. He'd been busy directing people, assuring nervous seniors, answering people's anxious questions only to find a microphone repeatedly thrust in his face. They besieged him with questions about the flood's two presumed victims, the collapse of the dike, who was responsible. All the while, a camera's huge eye trained on him for his responses. He bridled his irritation. They had a job to do, he knew, just as he did, but they made him think of vultures drawn by the scent of death.

By three o'clock, a hundred and nine people were evacuated. He slipped away to get his first food of the day, leaving an assistant in charge. Afterward, he checked in at the communications centre.

"How's it going?" he asked Will, handing him one of the Styrofoam cups of coffee he'd brought.

"Everyone reported missing has been accounted for," Will answered, with an appreciative nod for the coffee, "except of course the Logans and LD."

Gavin sighed. "That's good news," he said, sounding anything but happy.

"There's still hope for LD," Will said, mirroring Gavin's mood. They avoided eye contact. Will fiddled with the equipment, Gavin leaned far back in the chair, his long legs stretched out in front of him. Will broke the silence, saying, "You look exhausted Gavin. Why don't you hole up somewhere and get some shut-eye?"

He stared at the floor, in a daze. "Ever wanted to tell someone something, missed the opportunity, then wondered if it was too late?"

Will's answer was soft. "Yes, I have." Gavin made no sign of having heard. It wasn't LD he was thinking about. It was Dana.

He got up wearily. "Maybe I'll take your advice. I *am* pretty shagged." He headed across the compound toward the supply centre in hopes of cabbaging a sleeping mat. Couples milled around, families strolled about letting their children run and play. Kids are so resilient, he thought. At that moment, he spied Todd at a picnic table under a lone pine. Dana sat beside him, her back to him. The third person, facing his way, was Mandy.

The question he'd just asked Will was fresh in his mind. Mandy would keep an eye on Todd. Would Dana speak with him alone? Yesterday when he asked her to take Todd, she had not said a word to him.

Mandy noticed him. "Hi Gavin," she said warmly. Dana's head snapped up.

"Hi Mandy," he answered, his attention seemingly focused on Todd.

He straddled the bench, where Todd sat hunched, and gently rubbed his back. "Hi, cub. How ya doin'?" But Todd stared at the table top, unresponsive. Gavin lifted his eyes to meet Dana's over Todd's head. She dropped hers back to Todd. Gavin looked across to Mandy, who shook her head with a doleful expression. A half-eaten peanut butter sandwich lay on a plate in front of Todd. A special effort by Mandy, no doubt.

"Did he sleep last night?" he addressed Dana.

"Yes, some," she said very, very softly. He rejoiced that she spoke at all. She stroked Todd's bangs out of his eyes. His only acknowledgment was a blink.

"Dana," Gavin said. "Could I speak with you, privately?"

A look of fright—or maybe resistance—widened her eyes. She glanced at Mandy as if for help, but Mandy said, "Go ahead. I'll stay with the boy."

She shimmied down the bench to extricate her legs from under the picnic table. Gavin sprang up and caught her elbow to steady her. She let him, but pulled away as soon as she gained her feet.

They strolled toward the trees at the edge of the camp, neither speaking until well out of ear-shot. She spoke before he could marshal the words he wanted to say. "How did you come to be riding Nefarious?"

It came close to a question he desperately wanted to ask her. *Why did Blake Logan have your horse? The horse I helped you move to higher ground the day before.* But he didn't want to let on he knew Blake was riding him in case he'd have to explain things he didn't want to get into.

"Didn't Todd say?" he said, fishing.

"Todd hasn't uttered a word since he arrived."

He frowned. This troubled him. "He's suffered a terrible trauma. I wasn't surprised he said nothing all the way up here yesterday. But I thought...I hoped he'd talk to you."

"Perhaps it would help if you told me what exactly happened."

He felt a great weight pressing upon him. Reluctantly, he nodded. He told her about encountering Connor. Noel and Lorraine were among the people who had evacuated south out of town. Connor would have told his staff about his own confrontation with Blake on the dike. Sooner or later, Dana would learn of it from another source if he didn't tell her. She listened to that part but did not seem particularly surprised. He explained how he decided to go out and try to talk to him. He left out the part where he'd met Logan at the gate and Blake had knocked him out. He skipped to where he'd witnessed Logan struggling through the flood waters to the house. He told her about Todd running toward the house, about stopping him. He described how Blake tried to carry Mary to safety, how Todd reacted when they were swept away.

As for Nefarious, he merely said the horse was nearby, saddled and bridled. He told her his Jeep was overcome by the flood. He couldn't get to it, so Nefarious became their transportation to the camp.

She took all this in, saying nothing when he finished. He wished she would volunteer an explanation about why Blake had her stallion but perhaps she didn't know. Perhaps Todd had taken him from Sadie's. He'd promised to go muck out stalls and ride Nefertiti. Had he taken the stallion instead? It didn't seem likely. Where was Blake going on the horse? Where did Blake go in his Jeep while he lay unconscious?

"Dana, I want to explain about my note."

She turned her face away.

A shriek from behind him cut short his next words. He spun around. Mandy was running in the opposite direction. Coming up the road purred an ATV. A grin split LD's face from ear to ear. He leapt off, catching Mandy in a bear hug. She covered his face with kisses. Then he kissed her full on the mouth, long and hard. She made no attempt to pull away. A cheer went up from people around, for his safe return, as well as for the warm welcome Mandy gave him. He came up for air, his grin irrepressible.

Spying Gavin, he waved and tugged Mandy by the waist over to meet him. They converged at the picnic table.

"You're a sight for sore eyes," Gavin returned his grin. LD let go of Mandy to shake his hand. But Gavin pulled him into a hug instead.

"Damn happy to be here, boss."

He leaned to the side to look around behind Gavin. "Hi Dana," he called.

"Welcome back, LD."

"Where'd you get to?" Gavin asked.

"I hightailed it when the dike bust. I thought I'd come out at a logging road I knew to the north but I got all turned around. Ended up goin' in circles. Felt like a darn greenhorn tourist." He spoke in a rush, regaling them.

"In the morning the skies were clear, so I could get my bearings. I came out way west of where I thought I was. Found a farmer who gave me some gas. He told me all the phone lines round here were out. Sketched me a map to get back, mostly on logging roads and, well... here I am!"

Gavin clapped him on the back. "You had us all pretty worried."

LD grinned at Mandy, whose waist his arm had found again. She hung on pretty tightly too. "I guess absence really does make the heart grow fonder," he quipped. She punched him gently with her free hand. He kissed her temple.

"Oh hey," he exclaimed, turning again to Gavin, "I got something to show you!" He let go of her and strode back to the ATV, retrieving something. He handed Gavin the rusted license plate.

"Found it on a vehicle buried in the dike right at the spot you was worried about. The storm night before last must have softened up the ground. The side away from the river was badly eroded, exposing the front end of a rusted out truck. The truck is why there was a bend in the dike. Not much wonder the whole thing gave way."

Gavin gaped at the bent, rusted piece of tin, absorbing the meaning of LD's revelation. "This is what it was all about?" he exclaimed in a shocked murmur.

"It's tough to read the numbers but I had a lot of time to kill after I quit ridin' yesterday. You can trace the ridges with your finger."

Setting the plate on the table, Gavin pulled a pencil and small writing pad from his breast pocket. "Tell me the numbers, Lionel." He leaned his foot on the picnic bench to write on his knee. He saw Dana tug Todd's hand. She led him away. He caught her eye and felt ashamed. This news certainly would not help the boy's state of mind.

He scribbled down the license number LD recited. "Do you know the year?"

"No. That number's too small and it's bent there. The truck was a real oldie, though. From the '40's or '50's judging by what I could see of the grill."

Mandy picked up the plate. "What make was it, Lionel?"

"Dunno. Ford maybe. Why?"

"Nothing. Just curious." She handed it to Gavin.

"Can I hang onto this?" he asked.

"'Spected you'd want to," LD answered.

"I'll try to find out who it was registered to. Till then, I'd just as soon this doesn't become public information. Can you two keep this under your hats?"

"Sure, boss. Whatever you say," LD said.

Mandy nodded.

"Gavin," LD said tentatively, "I told the farmer who gave me gas for the ATV." He scuffed his boot in the dirt. "But their phone was out."

"Maybe it'll buy us some time."

In the office, Gavin set the plate down, pulled out a sheet of paper and laid it on top. He began rubbing the side of a pencil tip over it. In less than a minute he confirmed the license number LD had given him. He worked in the corner till a number emerged. It was the same year the dike was built. Had the truck been an old jalopy finally giving up the ghost? Rather than pay to have it towed to a junk-yard, a rancher with lots of room might well bury it, especially if he's in the midst of an earth moving project, like building a dike.

Why had Logan been so determined to keep it from being discovered? The answer could be as simple as fear of a lawsuit. If it had been found by workers stabilizing the dike and collapsed despite reinforcements, he might have been held liable. In addition to his home sustaining flood damage, a lawsuit could have ruined him financially and politically.

Gavin put the piece of tin in a drawer and took the paper down the hall. He dictated to Will a message for Perce. *Find out from the motor vehicle branch in whose name the license had been registered.*

Clouds scudded across the moon. Shivering, Mandy pulled her sweater across her ample chest as she crossed the compound. The chill, replacing the heat of the day, was a relief after fourteen hours in the steamy kitchen. Even as the moon hid behind the clouds, she found her way without the aid of her flashlight. No one could afford to squander battery power.

Inside the bunkhouse, blackness swallowed her. She clicked on the beam, hooding it with her fingers. As she crept along rows of sleeping forms, sounds of breathing and snoring filled the air. She counted bunks till she came to the one she was looking for. The army blanket covering a still form was coarse under her fingers. The sleeper jerked awake with a cry.

"Sh-sh. Dana, it's me, Mandy."

Dana bolted upright, gasping with fright. "Mandy? What is it?"

"Can you come outside?"

"What's wrong?"

"I need to talk to you."

"Give me a minute," Dana answered, reaching for her clothes. She checked the top bunk. Todd breathed softly but evenly. Outside, she followed Mandy to the picnic table. Climbing the bench, she turned and sat on the table top facing Mandy. She shivered. "What is it?"

Mandy bit her lower lip. "Maybe I'm just letting my mind run away with me."

"For heaven sake's Mandy, you scared me half to death. You woke me to tell me something, so tell me!"

Mandy drew a shaky breath. "Were you there when LD told Gavin the truck he found in the dike was '40's or '50's vintage?"

"I don't know. I just wanted to get Todd out of there. Why?"

"You remember me telling you about a man who was special to me years ago?"

"Of course."

"He drove a truck that was real old even then, maybe thirty years old."

"So?"

"Dana, Blake built the dike the summer Wayne was in Withers."

"What are you saying, Mandy? That the truck LD found belonged to your old boyfriend? Why would it be buried in the dike on the Logan ranch? You said he left."

"I said he was gone, suddenly. Cleared out of his cabin without a word."

Dana shook her head, wanting to scream. She was barely coping as it was. She didn't need Mandy dragging her out of bed in the middle of the night to listen to her flaky rumination about a fizzled romance years ago.

"What I didn't tell you," Mandy said, lowering her voice, "Was that before Wayne, I had a regular thing with Blake Logan. Oh, I never had any illusions he cared for me. I was just a convenient romp in the hay, one of many he had up and down this valley. But even though he didn't give a fig for me, he couldn't abide anyone else moving in on what he considered to be his territory.

"That night, Blake came to my house wanting to jump in the sack. I was lovesick over Wayne and refused. He got pretty rough."

Dana felt a cold chill creep up her spine. She wanted to put her hands over her ears. She wanted to shout *Stop!* but the word strangled in her throat. She gripped her upper arms in a supreme effort to mask the emotions she feared her face might betray. Mandy continued, oblivious to the war going on inside her.

"In the end, Blake took off in a temper. I never saw Wayne again."

The women stared at each other. The moon came out from behind the clouds, accentuating the pallor in their faces.

"Dana! What if Blake killed him?" Mandy whispered. "And buried him and his truck in the dike?"

She wanted to scoff at the idea. She wanted to chalk it up to Mandy's gullibility. "It's probably a coincidence," she allowed, without conviction.

Mandy sat down heavily on the bench, beside Dana's legs. "I tried to tell myself the same thing all evening. Wayne was here in 1978. I told myself I could toss my theory out the window, if the license plate was older than that. Lionel told me Gavin did a rubbing on it with a pencil and paper to determine the year."

Dana's heart pumped furiously. "And...?"

"It was '78."

"Oh my God," Dana whispered. Both kept silent a moment as the implications hung between them.

"I keep thinking about Todd," Mandy said despondently. "If the shock of losing his parents has struck the poor waif dumb, what will it do to him if it *is* Wayne's truck and his dad is posthumously accused of murder?" In that moment, Dana realized Mandy was telling her all this not just out of concern for herself, but for Todd. "You've been so kind, taking him under your wing. I thought if you knew... if you had some advance warning, you could do something to buffer the shock."

Dana hunched over her knees for warmth. "Thank you, Mandy," she said after a bit. "It's made up my mind for me. I thought about taking him out of here for the time being. I have a foster brother in Vancouver who would put me up for a few weeks. He has kids about Todd's age. It would be good for him to be away from here awhile, be around kids his own age."

Mandy stared off into the blackness. "Yeah," she answered vaguely, her tone suggesting her mind strayed elsewhere.

Dana laid her hand on her shoulder. "I'm really sorry, Mandy. This must be awfully hard for you."

"You know what's even weirder?" Mandy said, her voice shaky. "Not long ago, my grandmother had a vision. The river spirit spoke to her. It told her the answer to my heart's longing…how did she put it? *'Tarries at the water's edge. A wound will heal my wound'*, she said. All these years I believed Wayne lied about loving me. After him, I didn't trust myself to fall in love again. The water's edge, Dana! A wound in the dike. It *has* to be Wayne."

Dana shuddered at the possibility.

––––––––––––––––––

Withers lay submerged beneath a shallow lake stretching north for seventeen kilometres. Gavin saw it almost immediately once the chopper was airborne. The raised railway bed at the south end of town acted like a dam. The errant river swept around it, meeting up with Stayner Creek and in a tumult together with it, rejoining the main stream.

The Winchester and entire block south of it had burned to the water-line. All other buildings stood like forlorn islands in a sea of red-brown water. The destruction hit him on an achingly personal level when he saw the peaked roof of the gazebo where Dana had danced with him. Virtually the only building untouched by the flood was the old train station. It hunkered on its narrow marooned island beside the tracks.

The chopper swung across the river. Surveying the impact on the reserve, he was gratified to see all the houses they'd sandbagged were secure. Boats were tied up outside several of these sunken, man-made islands. At his request, the helicopter banked around so he could get a closer look. Yes, everything seemed okay. It looked like people were just checking to ensure there were no leaks. A couple of arms waved. He waved back.

As they flew north, over 'the hill' he spotted Will's car in his driveway. He'd requested leave of his post to go feed Macbeth.

Dana's farm came into view, or what was left of it. The house and barn were awash. It hammered home the devastation. How would she ever rebuild on her own? Guilt seeped in around the edges of his distress. He should have dealt with Logan decisively. Hell, the man would be alive today, he and his wife, and all this destruction might be but a frightful dream.

He wondered again why Blake had Dana's horse. Returning from helping Sadie this morning, Cutter confirmed that Sadie never saw Todd the morning of the flood. Until the boy spoke, they would not learn if he took the stallion. Why did Logan take his Jeep? Where had he gone? How far had Logan driven before turning around? Did Dana have answers to any of this? LD's joyous arrival was frustratingly ill-timed. Afterward, Gavin didn't feel he could go to Dana and pester her, not with his questions or to explain his note. The latter was probably the last thing on her mind. Still, he wanted her to know he'd never meant to hurt her. He resolved to try again as soon as he got back to the camp.

They were flying now over drowned woodlots. The 'lake' spread out three kilometres wide north of 'the hill'. Only rows of telephone poles suggested where the roads were. Emotion choked him as they drew near Logan's ranch house. He couldn't stop himself from morbid wondering about how far their bodies had been carried. Idly he scanned for his Cherokee, but it was nowhere to be seen. What he did see, wrenched his heart. Todd's bicycle lay where he'd dropped it on top of the spur. *God damn it to hell! I should have dealt with Logan's resistance.*

The breach came into view. The foaming surge racing through the opening gave witness to the river's awesome power. It had ripped open a swathe now sixty metres wide. A sense of futility bore down on him with punishing intensity. It was all for nothing. All his efforts. He had failed.

His hope of searching out Dana when the chopper landed died on the vine. Mayor Hale, who'd escaped the flood by the southern route, had just flown in on a Canadian Air Force Labrador. He came to visit the camp and boost morale among his constituents. Appointing Gavin to take him on a tour of the camp, he asked to be briefed on their needs. He would do whatever was necessary, he promised, to get them anything they required. *A little like shutting the gate after the cows are out,* Gavin thought, remembering the times he really could have used the mayor's support. But he buried his sentiment, as it was plain Hale felt pretty glum about Councillor Logan and Mary.

It was three in the afternoon before Gavin helped the mayor climb aboard the Labrador with three evacuating families, including a hugely pregnant woman and an asthmatic child. It seemed he was in demand by one person after another, volunteers with various problems, a Red Cross worker needing supplies, a farmer anxious about his dry but un-fed stock and a myriad of other concerns.

He checked in at the communications centre to see if there was any response yet from Perce, but there was nothing. Afterward, he grabbed a few minutes to wolf down some food, searching the dining hall for any sign of Dana or Todd, but he couldn't spot them.

Finally he caught a quiet moment to head over to the bunkhouse where she and Todd were assigned. He rapped at the door. He asked the woman who answered if Dana was inside. After several minutes she returned, reporting Dana wasn't there. He wondered if it were true. Perhaps Dana told the woman to lie because she didn't want to talk to him.

Depressed and tired, he returned to the office to handle messages still pouring in. It was nearly dark by the time he finished up. He strolled across the compound, breathing in the cool evening air after the heat of the day. He wasn't the only one seeking peace for some private thoughts out of doors. Singly or in pairs, people milled around the yard, or smoked, or sat at the several picnic tables.

He spied someone moving purposefully from the direction of the dining room toward Dana's bunkhouse. He recognized her walk, and called out.

"Mandy."

She spun in a startle response as if caught in a misdemeanour. "Gavin! Oh, hi."

"You heading for bed?"

"No. I ran out of cigarettes. I have a fresh pack in the bunkhouse. I gotta get back to the kitchen. We're not ready for tomorrow."

"Since you're going to the bunkhouse, could you do me a favour?"

There was hesitancy in her eyes that made Gavin wonder if she had Dana's confidence. It hurt somehow. "Sure. What is it?"

"Would you see if Dana's asleep? If she's awake, would you mind asking her if I can see her?"

Mandy's expression clouded. "Gavin, Dana's gone."

"Gone! What do you mean? Gone where?"

She gave him a look which might have been sympathy. "She said she was going to take Todd away for a while. They left this morning on a helicopter."

His face fell. Mandy did not fail to notice. "I see," he said quietly, struggling to recover. "Did she…leave a forwarding address?"

"No," she lied, unable to keep contact with his eyes. "Uh, I'm sorry. Maybe I should have asked."

"That…that's alright. Thanks, anyway. Goodnight, Mandy."

He turned on his heel. Something tugged at her heartstrings as she watched him walk away. She wondered what was between these two. She'd observed the tension between them yesterday at the picnic table. This morning, she chalked up Dana's hasty exit to her concern for Todd. Asking if she didn't want to wait and say goodbye to Gavin, she was puzzled when Dana said it was best she leave immediately. *Best for whom?* she wondered now.

Dana asked her to write as soon as she found out whether the truck was Wayne's. She gave Mandy an address but was very particular she not tell *anyone* she had it. This morning, Mandy thought it was to keep Todd's whereabouts a secret. Now she wasn't so sure.

"Oh Gavin, I almost forgot," she called after him. "Here," she said, digging something from her pocket.

He held out his hand to accept what she extended. "What's this?" he asked.

"The keys to Dana's truck. She figured you might need to get around. Since you lost your vehicle in the flood, she said you could use hers." He narrowed his eyes at Mandy as if assessing the veracity of her message, then nodded and thanked her.

He headed over to stores, picking up a gas lantern and a flashlight. Next, he stopped in to tell Will where he was going and when he'd be back. With the flashlight, he searched the parking lot till he found Dana's truck.

It was a relief to leave the camp. For the first time in three days, he was alone. Twenty minutes later he pulled into the driveway at Foster's cabin. There was no power of course. He used the flashlight to find the keyhole. Inside, he didn't bother with the lantern, but headed straight into the bedroom.

He stripped his clothes, crawling naked between the sheets. The last time he was here was with *her*. It seemed a lifetime ago. He pulled the second pillow to his face, hungry for her scent. But too much time had passed.

He would be here a few more scant weeks. When the floodwaters receded, the townsfolk would begin the onerous task of clean up and rebuilding. His job would be finished and he would be recalled. The thought that he might never see her again hit him full force. The cavity in his chest felt sliced, as if by a razor, his insides raw and bleeding. Exhaustion finally took its course. He fell into a sleep troubled by disturbing images.

When Gavin arrived in camp next morning, he knew instantly something was up. The press were in front of the office, jockeying for position with their expensive camera equipment. Standing on the porch, LD seemed to be fielding questions. Before he was out of the truck, reporters rushed him. "Mr. McLeod! Is it true the dike collapsed because a vehicle was buried in it?"

"Who did the vehicle belong to?"

"Is it true the man who died in the flood obstructed reinforcements to the dike?"

He faced this last questioner, a female reporter. "There are two people still listed as missing. I know of no confirmed fatalities." Cameras whirred in his face. He cut through the throng and climbed the steps. LD stuffed his hands in his pockets, giving him a hangdog look. Gavin took him by the arm and backed him away none too gently.

"What's going on?"

"They came in on a coupla helicopters. Bin buzzing round like a swarm of hornets."

"What'd you tell them?"

"Nothin'," LD countered.

Gavin scowled sceptically.

Cameras and microphones closed in on him. "Mr. McLeod, PEP headquarters says a vehicle was found buried in the dike. Who found it?"

Gavin regarded LD with new respect. He'd been so sure LD had been lapping up attention at centre stage. Chastened, he turned to the press, "Give me twenty minutes and I'll take your questions."

He led LD inside and addressed the volunteer behind the desk. "Stand guard outside the door and keep the press from coming in." The fellow nodded and went out.

"Any idea how they found out?" he asked LD.

"No, Boss. Mandy and me was havin' a coffee on her break in the dining hall when they arrived. Somebody tole 'em I was the one who was on patrol when the dike went. Soon's Mandy spotted them heading our way, she figured they musta heard something about what I found. She told me to play dumb, so I did. Played the village idiot." He grinned. "I've had a lot of practice. They soon buggered off when they couldn't get nothin' from me. That's when they started lookin' fer you. I hightailed it over here to the office to give the others the heads up and barely beat them to the door. Good thing you got here when you did."

"They must have got the news at the other end," Gavin said. "I'm surprised. It's not Perce's style to involve the media."

LD hung his head. "Maybe it was the farmer I told, the one who helped me when I was lost."

"Maybe so. Don't beat yourself up, LD. Anyway, I suppose there's no reason to keep this from them. First I'd like to know if we've got an ID yet on the plate owner."

He led the way down the hall and stuck his head in the radio room. "Morning Will. Did we hear from Perce yet?" Will flipped through some sheets on the desk and picked up a scrap. He held it up. Gavin took it, glanced at it and asked, "This mean anything to you?" Will shook his head. He handed it to LD. "How about you?"

LD studied it, sounding out the words. "Nope."

Just then a familiar voice hollered from the front office. "Where the dickens is everyone? Great Scott, it's a three-ring circus outside!"

"Sadie!" Gavin hollered, striding out to meet her. "Hey, old girl," he grinned, "I hear you're quite a hero."

"Poppycock! It's about time my husband's swimming lessons came in handy. One of the few useful things he done for me. How's the little girl anyway?"

"She's fine. Her family chose to take the opportunity to evacuate. They've already left."

"Smart move."

"What brings you to camp?"

"Thought I better see for myself if things are being run properly up here," she said with a scowl.

He knew she was teasing. "We're barely managing without you," he grinned.

"Humph! I thought as much. I'm also looking for that derelict veterinarian. Cutter asked him to come down to check out my charges yesterday but seems he figures he's on vacation. Cutter also said there were a couple of teenagers who'd offered to help me with all the critters."

"Well, I'm glad you're here. I was just thinking about calling the committee together for a quick conference."

"Well, let's get crackin'."

LD went off in search of Foster and Cutter and to pull Mandy away from the kitchen. Within ten minutes they were assembled in the communications room. Will remained seated at the station. The rest stood.

Gavin surveyed them. "You've all seen the press scramble outside."

"They're acting like a pack of starved dogs fighting over a bone," Sadie said. "Asked me what I knew about the dike breaching. Something about a vehicle stuck in it."

"Yes. LD, fill the others in on what you found."

When he finished, Cutter whistled through his teeth. "Whoo-ee! Why would somebody do a dumb thing like that?"

"We don't know," Gavin said. "But those guys outside already know about the truck in the dike. They may or may not know LD got the license. I now have the name it was registered to." He held up the piece of paper. "People from Withers may have known this person, may even know the answer to Cutter's question. But before I go making a statement to the press, I want to ask the rest of you. Does the name Wayne Ashton mean anything to you?"

Sadie and Cutter looked to one another and shook their heads. Foster responded in the negative. Gavin could have sworn Mandy blanched. She said nothing.

"Mandy?" he queried. She shrugged with the merest of headshakes.

"If this Ashton lives around here now," Foster remarked, "one of us would more than likely know of him."

"Can anyone think of a reason to withhold the name from the press?" Gavin asked.

Mandy, who had bowed her head, looked up. "Maybe we should wait a few days. I mean, it might be important to someone. We could ask people around the camp on the QT."

Gavin regarded her, then the rest of the group. "If it's been in the dike these twenty years," Will offered, "surely a couple more days can't hurt."

"Fine," Gavin said. "Then your task, all of you, is to speak to people, one on one, and casually, to see if anything pops up. Don't mention the name in connection with the breach in the dike. Meantime, I'll feed the piranhas outside. Thanks, everyone. You can go back to what you were doing."

They filed out. Gavin followed as far as the office. He asked Foster to hang back a minute. "Now that your home is no longer habitable, Foster," he observed, "I imagine you'll want your cabin back."

"I thought you might ask. Fact is, I'm settled in here at the camp. I figured to hang in here a couple of weeks till things simmer down. Then I'm gonna give in to my daughter's nagging to go south and live with her, permanent. Winter's are milder. My old bones will be grateful. If you want to keep on using the cabin, you're welcome to it." Gavin thanked him and said he'd be glad to have the use of it till he was recalled.

Mandy hurried away. No one noticed her slip over to stores a short while later, and deposit a letter in the mailbag.

CHAPTER TEN

The floodwaters took a full month to recede. In the fifth week, Blake Logan's bloated corpse was discovered washed up on a strip of sand two kilometres downstream from the town. The following day, the body of Mary Logan was found snagged on a barb wire fence on their ranch.

Gavin was with Mandy and LD at the Dream-Catcher when the news came about Mary. Mandy had wanted to look the place over. They drove down in Dana's truck, dodging all manner of debris littering the streets. Several times they nearly got mired in the stinking, oozy mud coating everything.

Mandy wandered about the Dream-Catcher, listlessly up-righting chairs. She picked up a carved Indian mask which had hung on the wall and fingered the destroyed basket cradle, in tatters on a post. LD traced the water mark on the wall a foot above his head with his finger. He asked Gavin for the pen in his breast pocket and, along the mark, scratched the date the flood had swept through.

Someone burst in the door, announced the discovery of Mary Logan's body, then rushed out to deliver their grisly news along the street. None of the three spoke. LD found a janitor's broom still in the closet and began sweeping the mess into piles. Mandy pushed tables out of his way.

Gavin slipped out the back door. He climbed to the top of the raised railway bed skirting the back lot and stood facing the river. It was still swollen but flowing now within its banks. He heard Mandy puffing as she laboured up the incline behind him. He offered no acknowledgment when she reached the top and stood beside him. They stood gazing at the river, not speaking. After a bit she said quietly, "Why do I feel like you're blaming yourself?"

"Because it's my fault," he growled through clenched teeth.

"Really? Just what part is your fault?"

"Look at this!" he practically shouted, flinging an outstretched arm in an arc behind them. "It's a town in ruins. I was sent here to prevent this."

"You tried, Gavin."

"I should have tried harder," he muttered. He didn't look at her, couldn't look, though he felt her eyes on him. He heard a deep sigh, but she said nothing more. She turned to go and started down the bank, then stopped. Without turning, she said, "I'm alive to tell about it." She left him wrestling with his guilt.

Power and telephone service were restored to some areas surrounding Withers. That night the phone in Foster's cabin rang for the first time in five weeks. Gavin answered.

"So the phones *are* working," observed a voice, laced with astringent.

"Celeste? Is that you?"

"You've forgotten your wife's voice?"

He had to admit it had been a while. If only she could have sounded happy to hear him. "You know I couldn't contact you directly. I sent you a message."

"Yes. Let's see…that would be a month ago. Or was it more? But it's alright, Gavin. At least I knew my husband was fine since I could see you on TV."

"I suppose I deserve that," he answered. "Can't we talk without tearing at each other?"

"I wrote you, telling you how worried I am about Amber. I asked you to come home."

"You know I couldn't."

"We need you, Gavin…Amber and I. *We're* your family. What about us? You give everything of yourself to strangers."

Strangers? The people he'd come to know over the last several months no longer felt like strangers.

"You *need* me?" He hoped she meant it. "How, Celeste?" He didn't know what he expected to hear. He was surprised by a muffled sound of sniffling at the other end. She didn't answer. "Are you crying?" he asked, solicitous.

Another sniff, louder now, was followed by a plaintive cry, "What do you think?" He wasn't sure how to proceed, feeling lousy as he heard muffled sobs.

"Celeste?"

"What?" she said, in a perfect pout.

"What's wrong?" he asked, trying to be gentle.

"It's Amber," she wailed with a trace of hysteria. "She's run off."

"Run off! What do you mean? What happened?"

"She went with that boyfriend of hers. He's way too old for her and…he's got a record. She's been picked up by the police in Kamloops. He was arrested for breaching probation and they're holding her. Gavin, you have to go get her and bring her home. She needs a firm hand. You've got to talk to her."

He felt something drain out of him. It left behind a residue of frustration mixed with bitterness. "I have no influence on Amber, Celeste. I've never had a relationship with her. You made sure of that."

"What's that supposed to mean?"

"Never mind. It's water under the bridge," he sighed wearily, thinking instantly what an ironic metaphor that was. "How old *is* this guy anyway?"

"Twenty-five."

"Jesus. You think he's a pimp?"

"No! Amber's no prostitute! How can you say such a thing?"

He hoped not, but recruitment crossed his mind.

"Will you go and get her or not?" she demanded.

"Why can't you fetch her?"

"She won't listen to me. She needs *a man* to lay down the law."

He pulled back from the retort on his lips, *Like your ex*? The man had been a brute to Celeste and left her with this primitive benchmark for the masculine gender. "I'll go, Celeste. I'll try to talk to her—but on one condition. You meet me there. You'll take her home. I have to return here."

She tried to change his mind but when it was clear he would not budge, she reluctantly agreed.

An hour after Dana stepped down from the Greyhound bus in Withers, with Todd in tow, she sat behind the wheel of Mandy's Toyota with the boy beside her. She headed up to Sadie's to check on her horses.

Mandy had been able to call her just hours after they got the news about Mary, thanks to restored phone service. Dana made an instant decision to bring Todd back for the funeral. Mandy explained that she and LD were staying in a borrowed cabin, since both their homes had been flooded. She suggested to Dana that she and Todd could stay with her. LD would bunk in at Will's house.

Mandy met them at the bus and threw their suitcases full of new clothes in the trunk. They stopped at the Dream-Catcher where LD was tearing out damaged interior walls. He and Mandy filled her in on changes since she'd gone. It was Cutter's cabin Mandy and LD had taken over. Their ease with one another, the tender glances they exchanged, revealed the intimacy that had grown in the weeks since LD's harrowing disappearance.

Was Cutter still up at the camp then, Dana asked. LD flashed a wolfish grin. "Nah. The old fox has taken up residence in the hen-house."

Dana gave an uncomprehending frown.

"They're shacked up."

"Who?"

He leaned toward her with a conspiratorial look and whispered. "Cutter and Sadie."

"Cutter and Sadie!" she echoed, a little too loudly. She checked Todd, sitting at a table, to see if he were listening, but he never looked up from his book. "I thought Sadie was a lot older than Cutter."

LD reared back with an indignant look. "So what's wrong with a guy bein' interested in an older woman?"

Dana laughed and laid a hand on LD's arm. "Oh Lionel, I'm sorry. I guess all this news is a little much to take in all at once."

She accepted Mandy's offer of her car when LD assured her they had wheels to get home. He pointed out the window at his ATV. She teased Mandy about how she'd been so reluctant at one time to get on that thing.

As for LD bunking in with Will, it seemed that here too, new relationships had burgeoned from surviving a shared disaster. LD had accompanied Will a time or two when he went home to feed Macbeth. He'd been awed by the rows and stacks of books everywhere. With his eyes aglow, LD told Dana how Will had regaled him with stories, from Greek mythology to Shakespearean plays, inspiring him with his own love of classical literature. Will assured LD he could learn to read well enough to enjoy books on his own. In fact, he was tutoring him.

Dana resisted the urge to ask about Gavin. During her stay in Vancouver, if she had not had Todd to care for and worry about, she'd have been utterly consumed by the tangle of emotions she suffered over Gavin. She even borrowed her brother's car one time, looked up the address in the phone book and drove past his large and lovely home in upscale West Vancouver. It both dismayed her and grounded her in the realization that she must move on.

Now that she was back in Withers, she was assailed by thoughts of him, hoping she would encounter him, yet at the same time, fearing it. So when she drove into Sadie's yard and saw her own truck she had lent him, she felt heart-pounding anticipation. Todd ran to the paddock where the horses were turned out. He climbed the board fence and whistled. Nefertiti lifted her head, pricking her ears toward the sound. Gratified, Dana watched the gentle mare plod toward him.

Cutter came out of the house. She got out of the car to meet him. "There's a sight for sore eyes," he greeted her. "It's not every day a pretty young lady comes calling."

"Hello Cutter," she smiled, extending her hand. He took it in the wrong hand and pulled her into his arms to embrace her. Tears welled up at the warmth of the welcome. "There, there," he said gruffly. "We're all gonna survive these times." He held her away from him. With surprising tenderness, he asked, "How's the boy?"

She glanced toward Todd, who by now was reaching over the fence to scratch Nefertiti under her forelock. The mare pushed her muzzle through the fence, nosing about his pockets. He produced a lump of sugar, squirrelled away from the tray of coffee and milk Mandy served them at the Dream-Catcher. "As well as can be expected. He's happy to see the horses."

"Hmph!" Cutter grunted. "Looks like that one's happy to see him too."

"Is Gavin here?" she asked, nodding toward her truck and striving to sound casual.

"Huh?" he looked where she gestured. "Oh! No. He went to Kamloops. He didn't feel right taking your vehicle so he asked to borrow mine. He's spending a couple of days with his family. Can't blame the poor fellow. He hasn't seen much of them for months. I wondered how he managed being separated from his wife all this time. Ought to get isolation pay if you ask me."

Vertigo threatened to topple her. It felt like falling from a great height. She wanted to run away and give release to her pain and sorrow but she forced her face to produce the semblance of a smile. She heard herself stringing words together, telling Cutter she wanted to spend a little while checking out her horses. He made her promise to come up to say hello to Sadie before they left. He turned back toward the house and she fled to the seclusion of the barn.

Gavin was ushered into a sitting room by a worker in the receiving home in Kamloops and left alone. He stood gazing out the window of the large house into a once-elegant back yard whose overgrown shrubbery and worn lawn spoke of neglect. He heard the skipping of agile feet pedalling down the stairs just beyond the arched doorway he'd recently entered. He turned as Amber flounced into the room and threw herself carelessly onto the threadbare chesterfield.

He took in the ring piercing her eyebrow, new since he'd seen her. It augmented the stud above her left nostril, over which they'd had words five months ago. Her jeans hung low and snug on her hips. The skin-tight top clinging to her bosom stopped six inches above her jeans. Several inches to the left of her navel, she sported a skull tattoo.

Her potentially pretty face poured into a resentful moue, slamming him with the resemblance to the mother. He regarded her steadily with his hands in his pockets till she grew tense at his silence.

"What?" she challenged him.

He shook his head slowly and resolutely. "I'm not going to deliver the lecture you're just waiting to fight about." Her brow creased in angry confusion as she sorted through his meaning. "I *am* here because it matters to me that you're making mistakes harmful to your future and threatening to your safety."

She snorted. "Yeah, aren't you're just Mr. Disaster Prevention."

He bridled his temper. "Tell me about this man you were picked up with."

"What about him?" she retorted, jutting out her chin.

"What does he want with you?"

"He loves me."

"Enough to care about your best interests?" She refused to answer, picking at the frayed slash in the thigh of her jeans. He sighed and sat down on the edge of an armchair opposite her. "Right now you should be writing exams at school. By not writing, you'll lose your year."

She barked a humourless laugh. "Like I was passing or something."

He kept his gaze steady. "I'm not surprised. But you need an education to have any kind of a life. I'm not telling you something you don't know somewhere back there in your own head."

She thrust her chin out. "Quentin can support me."

"Quentin? As in San?"

She pulled a face. "Very funny."

"A good name for someone likely to spend periods of his life in jail." She scowled, sour but unable to debate this point. He bowed his head, wanting to offer her a chance to de-escalate, looking for a way to come around her defences from the side. "Amber… consider this. Don't answer me, just turn it over in your own mind. What does a twenty-five-year-old man want with a fifteen-year-old girl in high school? How does a guy… a guy with a record no less, think he's doing right by the girl he claims to care about, if he encourages her to drop out of school and run away from home, causing her mother no end of heartache and worry?"

She drew in a breath to make a retort but he headed her off saying, "Don't answer *me*. Answer it for yourself."

She rolled her shoulder. "Yeah, whatever."

"Your Mom will come and get you tomorrow."

"What! I'm not staying in this fucking pig-sty another night."

"Sorry, kid," he said, "but I'm afraid you're gonna have to."

She lunged up. "Oh, that's just fucking great! Thanks for nothing." She stormed out, hissing, "Bastard!" and took the stairs two at a time.

The next morning he found the hotel Celeste told him she would check into and enquired at the desk for her room number. He took the elevator to the third floor and knocked on the door. It was a fashionable few moments before it was opened. He stood there with his hands in his pockets.

"Hello, Celeste."

"Well, come in" she chirruped, standing aside for him to enter. He stepped across the threshold. "It's a fright to come up-country," she chattered as she closed the door. "They're so *primitive*. I couldn't get a no-smoking room. Can you imagine!" She swished past him with a feminine flourish of her wrist, her manner breezy. "I wanted a two-bedroom suite, but this one-bedroom with twin beds is the best they could offer," she complained. "We'll have to make do, I guess," ambiguous as to whether "We" meant him, or Amber.

She turned to face him, presenting a vacuous expression of amiability. She wore a chic white calf-length dress which showed off her slender curves to advantage. He wondered briefly if this was a New York City acquisition. He stood with hands still in his pockets, taking a long look at her. "Well," she exclaimed as if to break his stare, "Here you are." She came up to him and planted a brief kiss on his lips, then retreated to the bar. "Shall I mix you a drink?"

His lips burned where hers had touched them. "No—thanks."

"You're sure? I'm having one." She fanned herself with her hand. "It's so hot. It's taking forever for the air conditioner to cool the room down."

He'd come from a rustic camp with hundreds of displaced people who'd lost everything and she was fretting about air conditioning. "Don't you want to know how Amber is?"

She mixed her drink with a swizzle stick. "Of course, I do. But we can be civilized. Sit down, Gavin. You're making me nervous standing there like that." He glanced at the sofa to his side and perched on the thick arm. She sank into an armchair, crossing one long leg over the other. A side slit in her dress revealed leg up to her thigh. "Well, what about Amber? I imagine she's as fractious as a cat in a rain barrel."

He stifled the urge to laugh at the accuracy of her description. He kept his voice and expression sober. "I think you should arrange to place her in a private school. Find the best and do it immediately. Don't wait till fall."

"Oh Gavin," she groused. "I don't want to do *that*. She'll think we're just shipping her off and don't love her."

"Taking such a step *is* an act of love, Celeste," he said firmly. "She's out of control. A good private school will ensure she studies, maintains a routine, dresses in a way that doesn't imply she's selling her body. And they'll make her take that metal out of her face."

"Oh goodness, you're such a fuddy-duddy. She's just following today's fashions."

"She's not *following* them, Celeste. She's pushing them to the limit. This stunt exhibits some very risky behaviour."

"She'll settle down when things get back to normal. She needs a firm hand. I can't do it all myself." She set her drink on the table beside her with an irritated clink.

"She wasn't *settled down* before I left. You admit you can't manage her; then do the responsible thing. Get her into a private school before the decision is taken away from you and she's put in a group home—or worse, winds up on the street."

"I can't send her away. She's my *baby*! She just needs a man's firm hand. Come home."

He puffed his cheeks out and exhaled slowly. He got up and went to the window and stared across the city. For fully half a minute, neither of them spoke. Then he turned and faced her.

"I want a divorce, Celeste."

Her mouth gaped open but nothing came out. "But... What...?" she sputtered finally. "You can't mean that!"

He answered, quiet and determined. "I mean it."

Her breath exploded in shock. She launched out of the chair. She paced across the room, furious, then whirled to face him, eyes blazing. "Is there another woman?" she ripped into him. "That's it, isn't it!"

He stood as stolid as she was enflamed. "I have no woman waiting in the wings," he replied, feeling regret. "This is about you and me, Celeste."

"How can you do this to me? To us, to Amber and me?" She had reverted to a pathetic whine and it left him cold. He didn't answer.

"What will we do?" she demanded. "Gavin!"

"You'll be fine, Celeste. You don't need me. You never needed me. That's the problem. You've treated me as if I'm superfluous, useful only to pick up the tab for your extravagant indulgences. I can't stay. I won't live any longer with being humiliated; belittled for not being able to give you, what you don't want anyway, another child. You'll survive, Celeste. As for Amber, I invested well in an education fund for her. I only hope she gets to use it."

Before she could descend into useless histrionics, he crossed to the door and pulled it open. "Goodbye, Celeste." He left her with her mouth open, searching for words to forestall him, but unable to find any.

It was dusk by the time he left the city behind. It had taken a while to stock up on the supplies and special requests of people in the camp. Even a bag of potato chips meant a lot to a displaced kid whose family had lost everything.

As the shadows spread purple up the hillsides, he replayed in his mind his conversation with Viola Cameron. He'd got the name of the family who operated the care home where Dana had taken her from a nurse at the camp who was among the refugees. He'd telephoned and received a hearty invitation from Viola to come by for a visit. In a cosy sitting room, he answered her many questions. She asked after numerous people, some he knew, some he didn't.

It was from her he learned Dana and Todd had just returned to Withers for the funeral that would take place in two days. It jolted him to realize they'd visited her, having stayed at a motel the same evening he'd taken a room in another part of town.

"What brings you to Kamloops?" she asked him, smoothing the woollen throw covering her knees. From his lower seat on a couch, he had to look up at her in her straight-backed arm-chair.

"A family matter."

Her mouth pursed in concern. "Not trouble I hope."

Feeling awkward, he made a weary grimace. "An end to trouble, one might say."

"Really? You have the look of a man who's just quit a battlefield. In defeat, I might add." He peered up at her through narrowed eyes, as if to discern the source of her knowledge. "I daresay," she added gently, "long months away from home puts a strain on family life."

"Truthfully, Mrs. Cameron, the strain was there before."

"And have you made amends with your wife?"

Only the elderly could get away with such directness. Perhaps they knew time had run out for tip-toeing around the truth, or maybe they realized there were few sanctions left to restrain them from speaking their mind. "I've done what I should have done long ago. I've asked for a divorce."

Her frank appraisal lingered so long he felt himself squirming, wondering why on earth he'd confided in this elderly woman he barely knew.

"What is there between you and my daughter?"

It was not said unkindly, but he could only stammer, "What do you mean?"

"Come now, Gavin. I wasn't born yesterday. I'm frail but I'm not blind. I've seen that candy-through-the-store-window way you look at her."

He dropped his head and tried to swallow the painful lump in his throat. "Mrs. Cameron, I might wish there was something between Dana and me," he allowed, his voice husky, "but my feelings are of no consequence." He looked up. "She's in love with Jeremy Robbins."

"Jeremy Robbins jilted her."

"I didn't think you knew," he said softly.

"Humph! I suspected. The way Dana moped around for days like a lost puppy. Still, I thought he'd be frantic about her with the news of the flood. As soon as I got her message saying she was safe, I called him to let him know. Oh, he was concerned alright, but not the way you'd expect from a fiancé. I asked him outright if he'd broken off their engagement and he admitted it."

"So she still hasn't told you herself."

"No. Dana pretty much keeps her deepest feelings to herself. Always has. She wouldn't likely share her feelings about *you* with me either."

"I doubt she has any special feelings about me. In any case, I'm not the man for her."

"More's the pity. You're twice the man Jeremy Robbins is."

Her final comment on the subject played over and over in his mind as the highway unfolded before him and darkness fell. Would she think the same if she knew he couldn't produce children? He flipped on the radio in a vain attempt to distract himself from his misery. The only clear station he could pull in played a string of cowboy hurtin' songs that dragged his mood lower still. He spun through the frequencies searching for something else… anything else, and tripped across a news broadcast. He stiffened in shock at what he heard.

"A grisly discovery today brings a new twist to the flood disaster in Withers. A crushed and rusted truck discovered several miles below where the river breached the dike is believed to be the one found buried at the site just before the dike collapsed. Human remains were found inside. The investigation continues. In Israel today, an explosion rocked a crowded shopping centre… "

A blaring horn jolted him back to awareness. He swerved to miss the oncoming car into whose path he had drifted. Noel Connor's description of Blake barring his passage on the dike with his rifle loomed before his eyes; the confrontation of his own at the cattle-guard and Blake's violent reaction. It all began to make sense. These were acts of a desperate man, a man with something to hide.

It was nearly midnight when he pulled into the yard at Foster's cabin. Weary and depressed, he stopped only long enough to listen to his messages. There was just one, from Perce. It was the long-expected recall. He was to report to work in Vancouver five days hence.

The events of the day kept him tossing and turning till nearly dawn and then he overslept. He arrived at the camp late in the morning and spent the first hour or so delivering the various packages and items he'd picked up in the city. Over three hundred people still bunked at the camp, though during the day, most were down below, beginning the long, onerous task of mopping-up and reconstruction. He met up with Cutter, who dismissed his attempt to return his truck, saying he'd get by with Sadie's car for now. Dana had retrieved her truck.

"Is she here at the camp?" he asked, trying not to sound too eager.

"No. Some folks are fixing up the train station to use it for the funeral. She's organizing it with Rev. Hildebrand."

"Is Todd with her?"

"Negative. Mandy took a much-needed day off and is looking after the kid at home, that is, at my place."

After lunch, he did some paperwork in the office, picked up and responded to messages from the now-operational telephone voice mail. Several people came by to talk to him, asking his advice on how to deal with various issues surrounding disaster recovery.

The door to the office opened yet again while he was down on one knee, pawing through the bottom drawer in search of some information for someone who'd come by earlier. "I'll be with you in a moment," he said, without looking up. "I've just got to find this—ah, here it is."

He stood and found himself facing a scowling Seth Colville. The Logan ranch bordered Colville's but much of the latter on higher ground. Seth had not needed to evacuate.

With his guard up, Gavin asked, "What can I do for you, Mr. Colville?"

"I'm here about Logan's boy," Colville announced gruffly. "I'm hoping you can make that Oleson woman see sense."

Alarm stiffened Gavin's spine. "What do you mean?"

"I tried to talk to her about the boy's future but she wouldn't even hear me out."

"What about the boy's future?" He knew he sounded more defensive than he had any right to be. Colville had been a long time friend of Logan, with children of his own. It would make sense he might want to step in to assume responsibility for raising Todd.

"Well see here, I've got Blake's herd. They didn't get caught in the flood, 'cause he'd put them out on higher ground, but they didn't have much pasture left after a couple of weeks, so I moved 'em to my place. They'll be part of the estate of course but it's not likely to get settled for a while. I can work with the estate lawyer and see they get sold while the market is prime and get the best price for them. Blake would have wanted his boy to get a university education. The money from the sale of his stock could go into a fund for the boy."

Gavin appraised the man with new eyes. He motioned to the chair opposite him. "Why don't you take a seat, Mr. Colville?" They both sat. "What exactly did you tell Ms. Oleson?"

"I didn't have a chance to tell her anything. I went to where she's staying with Mandy Sky. I heard she'd taken him down to the city. I wanted to talk to her before she might take off with him again after the funeral. I said, same as I did to you, I wanted to talk about the boy's future."

"Miss Oleson has stepped in to look after Todd. Perhaps she is more concerned just now about helping him get through the emotional trauma of this difficult time."

Colville looked tense and angry. "See here," he argued. "It's trying for all of us who were friends of the Logan's. This talk about a body and possible murder has got me riled up. I knew Blake Logan all my life. He got into his share of scraps when he was younger. Hell, who didn't? But he's a decent man. He served this town for years and his daddy before him. He was a good friend, and I can tell you *one* thing for sure. He loved his wife. Never mind all the chin-wagging about him tomcatting around. He did what a man needs to do when his wife won't meet his physical needs. But he loved Mary. Lord Almighty, he worshipped her!"

Gavin leaned back in his chair, nodding thoughtfully. "I don't doubt or dispute anything you say, Mr. Colville. I can personally vouch for his valiant effort to save Mary Logan's life. You said you didn't get a chance to explain your intentions to Miss Oleson. Why is that?"

"'Cause she stood at the door, holding it ajar, just so," he held up his callused hands inches apart. "She said it wasn't a good time to talk. Before I could say my piece she closed the door on me."

"It's possible the boy was inside. Perhaps it *wasn't* the best time. I can try to talk to her if you'd like."

Colville gave a curt nod. "I'd be obliged." He stood and without a further word, departed.

Three vehicles sat outside the train station. Seeing Dana's truck among them made his heart race. He stepped through the station's open door. Reverend Hildebrand, in jeans and an old shirt, stood on a step-ladder with a broom, sweeping cobwebs from the rafters. He recognized Nettie, the librarian. Armed with rags and a spray bottle, she was polishing windows.

"Good day, Mr. McLeod," Hildebrand greeted him. He climbed down the ladder and approached with an outstretched hand. Gavin shook it. "Molly Maid duties don't usually fall under my job description," Hildebrand smiled affably, pointing the broom toward the ceiling. "But these aren't exactly normal times, are they? Are you here on business?"

"Actually, I'm looking for Dana Oleson. Is she here?"

The Reverend pointed his chin toward the end of the building. "She's over yonder setting up a quiet room for refreshments for tomorrow. Gavin thanked him and headed for the room Hildebrandt pointed out. He hesitated in the doorway. Her back was to him. She was arranging paper cups and plastic spoons for beverages on a linen-draped table. She must have heard something, for she straightened and turned toward him.

"Hello, Dana."

"Gavin! I didn't..." she stammered, "I didn't know if I would see you here."

"I *won't* be around after the weekend. I've been recalled."

"On to the next crisis, I suppose," she said too brightly, her smile brittle.

"I…can we…? " he pointed across himself toward the exterior door, "Can I talk to you…outside?"

She hesitated, then gave a brief nod. They passed Nettie and Reverend Hildebrandt. "I'll just be a minute," she said.

They meandered along the road, Dana with her arms folded tightly across her chest, the remoteness still evident in her body. "You've heard yesterday's news?" he asked.

"About the truck with human remains." She nodded, turning her face even farther away.

"I guess there'll be an investigation," he remarked. She didn't respond. "Does Todd know?"

"I don't think so. I haven't told him yet. He needs to get through the funeral first."

"Has he talked about what happened?"

She halted and faced him, her expression accusatory. "Todd hasn't spoken since it happened."

"Not spoken!" he echoed, incredulous. "That's shocking. The boy needs help. You should take him to a child psychologist."

She bristled. "And you should just butt out! What business is it of yours? None of this is your affair anymore," she hissed. "You've completed your assignment. You said yourself you'll be gone in days. The rest of us will still be here putting our lives back together. Todd needs love and time and people who will be here for him. So why don't you go back to your tidy life and your mansion in the city and stop interfering in matters that don't concern you."

Every word cut him like a knife. He felt justly chastised. As she turned on her heel and stalked away, he could only watch her, feeling clumsy and heartsick. He was half-way back to the camp when he realized he hadn't delivered Seth Colville's message. Or explained about his note.

The day of the funeral dawned grey and overcast. The bodies of Mary and Blake Logan, flown south for forensic identification, returned to Withers in two black limousines.

By the time Gavin arrived, cars filled the parking lot and lined the road for two blocks. People stood around in clots. As he made his way through, a few familiar faces nodded. Inside, two closed caskets dominated one end of the room, faced by rows of rented chairs either side of a wide aisle, some already occupied. People gathered in hushed clusters, their conversation muffled by solemn background music played on a piano which had materialized since the day before.

He spotted Dana immediately. With sombre body language, she and a couple who were contemporaries of Logan conversed in front of the caskets. She looked straight at him, then turned away as if he were invisible. Todd was nowhere in evidence.

He retreated to the room at the other end of the building where he'd found her the day before. It was crowded with people sipping coffee and talking quietly, among them Mandy and LD. Todd sat by himself on a chair, his hands tucked under his knees, swinging his feet. He wore a blue serge suit, white shirt and red tie. Gavin threaded through unnoticed, toward him. Todd looked up with a spark of recognition as he took the chair beside him.

"Hi cub," he murmured, stroking the boy's back. Todd's feet stopped swinging. Gavin struggled to think of something to say, some message that would comfort. But nothing seemed adequate. Instead, he wove his fingers through the boy's hair, leaned over and kissed his head.

"Gavin. I didn't notice you come in." It was Mandy. "Can I see you for a minute?" She led him outside. "I didn't want to say anything in front of Todd. I gather he's fond of you and he has enough loss to deal with right now. I hear you're leaving in a few days."

"Yes. My job here is pretty well finished."

"We're going to miss you."

"I'm going to miss all of you too."

"Sure you are," she smiled with gentle mockery. "I bet you'll be relieved to see the last of the bad-news-bears committee."

It was his turn for a sad smile. "Don't be so sure."

She laid a hand on his jacket sleeve. "You've changed our lives, you know."

He gave a self-deprecating shrug.

"You mustn't just disappear," she said, giving his arm a squeeze. "You make sure you come by and say goodbye to us before you go."

"I will. I promise."

Mandy's gaze was arrested by something behind him. He turned to see Dana standing on the deck of the station house, with a worried frown. "Mandy," she called, "where's Todd? I thought he was with you. Pastor Hildebrand is ready to begin the service."

"He's in the back room with LD."

"No, he's not. I looked. LD said he *was* there but he didn't see him leave."

"He can't be far," Gavin said. "I'll help you look."

"Maybe he went to my truck," she said. "I'll check there."

"I'll tell the Reverend to hold off till we find him," Mandy offered.

Gavin scouted around the end of the building, re-entering from the side facing the tracks. He asked several people; no one had noticed Todd leave. He returned to the coffee room. It was vacant. A Vancouver newspaper lay on the chair where Todd had been. Someone must have brought it from out of town. He was about to turn and leave when the headline caught his eye.

Flood victim a murderer? He snatched up the paper and raced through the story. It was all there, Blake's obstruction of work on the dike, the buried truck and the discovery of human remains. The details were deliberately crafted to cast suspicion of murder. That Logan and his wife were the only flood fatalities was presented as a final twist of irony.

He folded the paper and rushed out, pushing past people to get outside. "Dana!" he shouted to her, returning from the parking lot. He held the newspaper aloft. Her look of worry turned to alarm as he rushed to her and thrust the paper into her hands.

"He must have seen it," he announced breathlessly. "It was right where he was sitting."

Dana's eyes skimmed the article. She paled, "Oh my God. We've got to find him!"

"We'll split up," he said. "I'll head north along the tracks. He won't likely have gone south through the mill yard. It's a soggy mess in there. Get some help. He's probably wandering around town somewhere. He can't have got far." He turned on his heel, circling the end of the station once more and struck out along the tracks where it angled in to flank the river.

He used the elevation to scan the streets and buildings to the east. On his other side, the water streamed past at a ferocious rate, still brimming its banks. He tried not to dwell on the possibility Todd might have gravitated to the river. Still, he scanned the left slope for small footsteps in the mud.

He was behind the Dream-Catcher now. Since Dana was staying with Mandy, she may have taken Todd there a time or two. He might head for a familiar place. In the rough triangle formed by the tracks, dike and highway, truckers had been accustomed to parking their rigs. The lot was strewn now with trailers that had been caught in the flood, some on their sides. He started down the slope toward the restaurant. Just before he dropped below eye-level of the tracks, something made him turn.

His throat constricted. There on the trestle, mid-way across the river, Todd straddled the railing. Gavin lunged up the bank, forcing down the urge to shout. He was behind Todd's direct line of sight. Tentatively, Gavin crept toward the trestle on uneven ties. Just as he reached it, Todd swung his other leg over the railing, perching precariously. His feet dangled out over the river. He'd not yet seen him, but if Gavin made any sudden move, the boy might catch it in his peripheral vision. If only he could get close before Todd became aware of him, then God willing, he'd find the words to keep him from leaping.

He inched forward onto the trestle. Railway ties stretched away from him like rungs on a ladder. Below, through the gaps, he saw the brown torrent racing past. He fought a dizzying sense of vertigo. Twenty feet away, his foot scraped a tie. The boy's head torqued, his eyes wild…wary, locking Gavin in his sights.

"Todd."

He spoke his name as an entreaty, extending it like a life-buoy across the space between them. "I've come for you," he said, easing onto the next tie. "Let me help you get down from there." Todd watched him without response. Gingerly, Gavin felt for his footing and Todd turned away, leaning toward the water. Gavin's arm shot out. "Todd, wait! I have…something to tell you."

He blurted words without knowing what to say next. His mind whirled, desperate for words that would *mean* something to hold the boy back. Todd stared down into the river, leaning recklessly over it. "Everyone…" Gavin risked another step forward. "Everyone is waiting for you. They don't want to start without you."

Another step.

"People back there care about you."

Todd's head shook vehemently. Gavin scarcely dared to breathe, feeling how thin was the thread between them.

"Yes they do, Todd. They care."

An anguished drawn-out cry, spilled from the boy. "No-o-o! They *hate* me!"

"You think people hate you? Why? Because of your father?"

He nodded, misery and despair eloquent in his body. He turned his face to Gavin, tears streaming down it. "It's my dad's fault the flood happened."

"The flood happened because there was too much water, cub. It was too strong for the dike."

Todd refuted this with another fierce head-shake "He ruined *every-thing*. They'll say he deserved to drown. They'll be happy if I'm drowned too." Great choking sobs welled up from deep within him.

"No! No one wants anything bad to happen to you."

Todd nodded his head with dogged conviction and turned to the roiling river again. Gavin measured the distance between them. Too far to lunge for him.

"Todd, I promise you, there are people who care about you, who feel sad for you. All those people back there came out of respect for your dad."

"I don't believe you. They're *glad* he's dead."

"What makes you think they're glad?"

"Because!" he howled, his next words disintegrating to a whimper. "He's a murderer."

"Just because the newspaper makes it sound like that, doesn't make it true."

"It's true! *I know* it's true!" he bawled.

"*How* do you know?" There was a long pause, while the boy seemed to waver on the point of a decision. Gavin edged closer, still out of reach. "How do you know, cub?"

"My Mom said so."

Gavin felt his breath sucked out. "Your mother *told* you that!"

Todd shook his head again, tears wringing from eyes squeezed shut. Gavin inched closer. "I heard her," Todd cried, blinking through a river of tears. "The day the flood happened.

"I rode Nefertiti that morning. Then I remembered I was s'posed to turn off a tap to the cistern, so I rode her home. Nefarious followed us. He must've jumped the fence." A piece of the puzzle that had plagued Gavin fell into place. "I heard my Dad yelling. They were having a really bad fight. My Mom screamed. I got scared for her."

Todd sobbed bitterly, unable to go on. Five feet separated Gavin from him.

"What happened, son?" he asked softly.

Todd cried harder. "He tied her to the piano. She yelled at him. She said she knew he killed a man and put him in the dike." Between hiccups, he blurted, "He got real mad. I thought he was coming so I ran. He came out and saw the horses. He told me to take Nefertiti back but he wouldn't let me take Nefarious. I wanted to help my Mom but he made me go. I hurried as fast as I could. I was riding my bike home when the whistle blew." He tried to say something else but his throat squeezed it off as grief overwhelmed him. Gavin closed the gap in two strides and grasped him around the waist. Todd sagged against him without a struggle. Gavin plucked him from the railing, knelt and gathered him in. Two small arms clung round his neck. Wet tears fell on his collar and neck.

"There was nothing you could have done, cub. It was a terrible accident." He held him, waiting for the storm to subside, stroking his hair.

In a thin voice, Todd wept, "He killed her too."

"Todd, your dad didn't mean for your mom to die. He loved her. He loved her very much. He went back to save her. He died trying to." Todd pulled back to study Gavin's face. "We don't know what happened between your dad and that man years ago. But you *saw* your dad fight his way through the flood to try to rescue your mom. You need to hang onto that."

Gavin pulled the poof from his breast pocket and handed it to Todd. He took it and rubbed the end of his nose.

"You'll feel better if you blow your nose."

Todd shook his head. "Sometimes when I blow my nose, it bleeds."

Gavin stroked the tie Todd wore. "Hey, nobody will notice with this red tie," he said softly. Todd peered down at the tie, dazed, then at him. He blew his nose, calmer now but infinitely sad. Gavin brushed the bangs off the boy's forehead. "Nothing that happened is your fault, son. And believe me, there *are* people who care about you. Dana cares about you. Mr. Colville cares about you. *I* care." Gavin stood, lifting him in his arms as he did so. The boy's legs wrapped around his waist. He turned and carried him back along the tracks.

A crowd gathered outside the train station watching them approach. Dana pushed her way through to the front. When they got close, Gavin lowered Todd to the ground. He put his hand on his shoulder and shepherded him to her. She waited for them to draw near, her expression mixed worry and relief. When they reached her, Gavin knelt, his eyes below the level of Todd's. "I want you to tell Dana what you told me. Okay?"

Todd nodded.

"Promise me."

He nodded again. Gavin gently shook Todd's shoulder, then stood and faced Dana. "I suggest you take him to your truck where you can talk quietly." She regarded him with wide-eyed wonder, then simply nodded. She took Todd's hand and led him away.

Gavin heard little of the eulogy. He scarcely registered where he was; a grief he could not easily have explained, gripped him. When the caskets were wheeled to the door by twelve pallbearers, he felt numb until he watched Todd, holding Dana's hand, follow them. Then pain ripped through him.

Mary and Blake Logan were buried in the cemetery tucked into a hillside overlooking the town. Todd, who had been sober and subdued through the funeral, came undone when the caskets were lowered into the ground. He tipped back his head and keened, limp and unresisting as Dana pulled him to her side. She stood erect, her expression granite, her colour ashen. Her gaze rested on Gavin, opposite them across the graves, and on the stricken expression on his face. She looked for him at the reception held at the camp dining hall, but he never came.

He returned to the cabin, changed clothes and went out again, seeking solace in the hills. *What business is it of yours? None of this is your affair anymore. You've completed your assignment.* There was nothing here for him. There was nothing back in the city for him but a job. Here he was again, adrift, connected to no one, a failure, not part of the town he'd let down, not a part of anything or anyone.

Gavin spent the next morning at his cabin packing. At noon he headed into town. He stopped at his office, or what was left of it after the flood. A few maps, high on the walls, were untouched. Everything else had peeled or disintegrated. The telephone still sat on the desk, though it had been submerged. He picked it up and put it to his ear, then wondered what he had expected and dropped it back in its cradle.

He left Cutter's truck in front of his office and walked over to the Dream-Catcher. Will's car and LD's ATV were parked out front. The door was slightly ajar. It was so warped, it wouldn't close all the way.

"Hullo," he hollered when he didn't see anyone in the outer area.

"In here." It was LD.

Gavin pushed the swinging door into the kitchen. Will worked at the fuse panel with the cover off, fiddling with wires. A pair of trousered legs protruded from beneath the sink. Their owner scrabbled out and LD grinned up at him from the floor. "Howdy, Gavin. Help yerself to a beer," he said, pointing with a pipe wrench to a Styrofoam cooler. "One of the guys from the mill just came back from Prince George and brought a few dozen cases."

"How's it going in here?" Gavin asked, pulling out a bottle and twisting off the top.

"Mandy's got new appliances on order. Will and me should have the kitchen ship-shape by the time they arrive," he said. "'Course we can't use the water supply. Hopefully, by the time the town takes care of it, we'll have the dining room ready to go. We figure there'll be looky-loos coming to town to check out the damage. Plus a lot of folks from town may come for the occasional meal or a gossip break while they get their own place fixed up. Mandy wants to capitalize on traffic."

"She's got good business sense that woman," Gavin said pointing the neck of his bottle at LD. "You make sure you hang on to her."

Will grinned while he twisted some wires together. "By the time I'm through with him, he'll be reciting Keats and Browning under her bedroom window at night."

"I plan on bein' *in* her bedroom, dork."

The other two laughed at LD's self-satisfied grin. They laughed harder when his grin slipped at Mandy's call, "Yoo hoo! Lunch is here." She burst through the swinging door. "Hi, Gavin! You're just in time. I've got lunch from the campground. What's so funny? LD, you look like the cat that ate the canary. In fact, you all do."

"It's hunger you see in our eyes, Sugar," LD said, scrambling to his feet. He put his arms around her, pipe wrench and all and gave her a loud smack on the cheek.

"Humph. I can believe it's hunger in *your* eyes, you horny old goat, and not just for lunch," she said, smiling happily all the same. "I never got around to telling you, Gavin. Remember my grandmother's vision the day I introduced you to her?"

"I remember," Gavin replied, thinking of the old woman's strange message. *The answer to your heart's longing tarries at the water's edge. A wound will heal your wound.*

LD set aside the wrench and clasped Mandy around the waist from behind. She hooked her thumb over her shoulder at him. "I think it means him."

"That's a *good* thing, ain't it?" he replied.

"Yeah, it's a good thing. Okay, let go of me now. You two wash up," she gestured to Will and LD. "There's a jug of non-potable water outside the back door. Come with me, Gavin," she tugged his elbow. "Help unpack the food."

With his beer in one hand, he let her haul him out through the swinging doors, where he stopped dead. In the middle of the room, Dana set a box on a table. They stared at each other awkwardly.

"Hello Dana," he finally managed.

She forced a thin smile. "Hi." She began unpacking the contents of the box. "I want to thank you for what you did for Todd yesterday."

"I got lucky."

"No, not just lucky; you were awesome with him."

He shrugged. "How's he doing?"

"Okay, I think. At least now he responds verbally when spoken to. He's up at Sadie's. He wanted to help Cutter with the horses."

"That's good."

She smiled. "Sadie gave him a puppy, one that she rescued. The one that tried to run away from her. She named it Renegade—something to do with Foster it seems. She told Todd it needs extra special love. Isn't that sweet of her?"

"And she had us believing she was such a crusty old dame," he grinned in return.

Just then LD and Will came through the door. Mandy ordered everyone to take a place at the table. Talk was of the work to be done and news of how other folks were faring, who had returned and who decided to move away for good. The incident the day before with Todd was not raised again.

Mandy was pouring everyone a second cup of coffee from thermal jugs, when the warped front door scraped open.

Gavin jumped to his feet. "Amber! What are you doing here?"

"Hi, Dad. I've been looking all over for you. Someone told me I might find you here." She wrestled uselessly with the door, then gave it a kick. She made a face and waved her hand in front of her nose. "Jeez, how do you stand the stink in this place? The whole town smells like an outhouse."

Her observation irritated him but he ignored it. "Why have you come looking for me?"

Her expression switched to round-eyed pathos. "Mom told me you're getting a divorce." Gavin felt four pairs of eyes on him. He didn't answer her. Amber tossed her backpack on a nearby table. "I'm ravenous," she said. "Where is there to eat around here?"

"This is the best restaurant in town," he answered. "Of course it was under seven feet of water recently, so you might be out of luck."

Dana reached into the box, pulled out a wrapped sandwich and took it to her.

"What kind is it?" Amber asked, crinkling her nose.

"Tuna."

"I hate tuna," she said.

"Suit yourself," Dana answered, leaving it on the table and returning to her place.

Amber picked it up, unwrapped it and took a sizeable bite.

"How did you get here?" Gavin asked her.

"On the bush," she slurred, her mouth full of sandwich.

"The bus doesn't arrive for another hour."

She rolled her eyes. "Yeah, whatever."

"You still haven't told me why you're here."

She wrapped the remains of the sandwich and stuffed it into her backpack. "Well, Dad, since you're not going to be coming home, like, you know, to live, you won't be around to sign for stuff."

"Stuff?"

She spoke rapidly and dug in the pocket of the backpack. "I went to the bank and got some papers. All you have to do is sign them."

"What are you talking about?"

"My money! I can't get my money out of the bank unless you sign."

"Amber, that money is for your education."

"Well, you're not exactly gonna to be around when I'm in college," she retorted, growing surly.

"We don't need to discuss this here."

"I don't care about them," she cried in a pique. "I want my money! We drove eight hours to get here."

"Drove? I thought you said you came on the bus. Who'd you drive with? Quentin?"

"No!" she spat in hot denial. Denial he didn't believe. She found the paper she was looking for and yanked it out of the pocket. "Here, just sign this and you won't have to see my face again."

He stood looking at her for several long seconds while she stood with her hand outstretched. "That fund is for your future, Amber. I hope you'll be able to make use of it someday. In the meantime, it's staying right where it is."

"Oh, that's fucking grand! It's just what you'd expect from a *limp dick*."

A muscle in Gavin's jaw rippled. There was not a sound in the restaurant. Suddenly he strode toward her. She yelped and jumped behind a table but he swept past her and wrenched open the door. He paused. Without turning, he said, "If you need bus fare to get home, you'll find me at my office. Someone will give you directions." He walked out, leaving the door open.

Amber snapped, "Fuck you, you bastard."

Dana and Mandy exchanged stunned looks. Dana got up and walked over to her. She stood with her arms folded, confronting the girl.

"Who are you?" Amber challenged. "The other woman?"

She ignored the jab. "I don't know what else you expected from your father when a daughter shows such utter disrespect."

Amber barked a laugh. "Hah! That's a laugh. He's not my father. He's not *capable* of being anyone's father." She grabbed her backpack, threw it over one shoulder and headed for the door. She turned on the sill. "Gavin shoots blanks... if you get my drift."

Gavin busied himself at his office for the next hour and a half, handwriting notes to incorporate in his report. Realizing Amber was not going to show up, he closed the door behind him for the last time.

Before making his way up to the camp, he went by Sadie's house. It was with a sense of letdown he discovered Dana had already picked up Todd. It was probably for the best, he thought, thinking of her remonstrance. *Todd needs love and time and people who will be here for him.* She was right.

He told Cutter he'd return his truck in the morning and asked if he'd give him a lift to the Greyhound then. At the camp, there were enough loose ends to tie off to keep him busy the rest of the day and into the evening. A constant flow of people dropped by to ask his advice. They lingered, seeming as reluctant as he to say goodbye. He was glad for the busyness, for he dreaded going back to the cabin with its silence. For the last hour, he knew he was just fending off yawning emptiness stretching out before him. It was full dark when he departed.

He saw the light on inside the cabin before he noticed Dana's truck. His first instinct was to back out and lay low till he was sure she'd be gone. He did not know if he could face this final goodbye at the mercy of his hammering emotions. But he knew she must have seen his headlights and he went in.

She stood by the kitchen table, rigid and erect. The silence between them amplified the ticking of the clock over the sink. It was she who broke it.

"Is it true you're getting a divorce?" Her tone was cold.

He gave the barest of nods.

"At her initiation or yours?"

"Mine," he owned.

"Why didn't you ever say you were unhappy in your marriage?"

His gaze flicked to the side. "I never said I was happy."

"Amber implied that you're sterile. Is that true, too?"

His jaw hardened, but he returned her stare. "It's true."

"Your wife wanted more children."

His brow furrowed in contradiction. "No."

The cant of her head challenged his veracity.

"It was part of why I thought it would work between us. I'd been open with her, that I…couldn't. Another child was the *last* thing Celeste wanted."

"I thought you pulled back after you slept with me because you felt guilty for cheating on her."

"I *did* feel guilty. Not for betraying her…for betraying *you*. I felt like a beast for acting on my feelings for you when you were hurting."

"Your feelings for me?" She gave him a penetrating look. "What *exactly* are you saying, Gavin?"

He wavered on the brink of such raw exposure but then in a ragged voice, he confessed. "I've never loved anyone the way I love you."

Nothing in her demeanour acknowledged this declaration. Her next words cut like shards of glass. "It was *you* who hurt me, Gavin. You took me to bed, then told me you'd never see me again."

"I thought you wouldn't *want* to see me."

"How noble."

"God, Dana, I never meant it like that."

"You could have told me your feelings for me," she rebuked him, sounding haughty.

"When?" he countered. "While you're engaged? When you're heart-broken because the man you've loved for years breaks up with you?" He wagged his head with regret. "I should have shown more restraint. I should have offered you the comfort you wanted."

"Don't tell me what I want!" she shrilled, silencing them both.

Collecting herself like a ruffled bird, she remarked bitterly, "His breaking up with me hurt because of how he made me feel about *myself*. I thought *you* were made of different stuff. I'd come to think of you as heroic. But what kind of man sleeps with a woman and then just slinks out of town?"

He made a grim sound. "A man who's told to go back to his tidy life and his mansion in the city."

"How was I to know how you felt?" she cried accusingly. She held his eyes defiantly while rearranging her features into a mask. "This is my home," she declared abruptly. "I will never leave here. I plan to adopt Todd and raise him where he belongs."

He sensed her iron resolve and mumbled. "I see."

"No!" she shouted. "You don't." He detected a tremor in her voice. "You still don't understand, do you?" Her green eyes glittered with moisture. "I *wanted* what happened between us that night. I wanted *you*. I'd fallen in love with you."

He stared slack-jawed, his breath caught short. His next words hurt his throat. "Then don't send me away."

The muscles in her face, her whole body, twitched as if enduring acute torture. Whatever it meant, it warned him to be still. He feared even breathing, as if to do so would shatter something vital in her.

"There's something you need to know," she choked. A long pause ensued then finally she said, "The morning of the flood, Blake Logan came to my farm. I gather you encountered him, since he came in your Jeep and you ended up with my stallion."

With a shock, another puzzle piece fell into place.

"I did," he acknowledged.

"What happened between you?"

"I was coming to you after I heard your message at my office. I knew you'd got it wrong...about my note." As he spoke, her vision fell away from him, unfocussed.

"When I met Connor on the 'dozer, I had to go to Logan's first, to get him to cooperate. We met at his cattle guard. He had Nefarious, saddled and bridled. We had words. He flew into a rage and slugged me. He knocked me out. When I came to, my Jeep was gone and the mill whistle was blowing. He returned but sped past me like a madman toward the ranch house. I got on Nefarious to follow but that's when I saw Todd running toward home. You know the rest."

She continued to stare into the middle distance, distracted, tense. "I asked Blake why he had your Jeep. He told me it suited him..." Colour drained from her face. "...like it suited him...", the rest came out in a whisper, "...to have McLeod's whore."

The room tilted. He felt sick.

"He raped me."

An indecipherable sound escaped him. He reached out to her but she forestalled him with her upraised hand. "You need to know it all, Gavin." She spoke now with steel in her voice, meeting his eyes. "I'm pregnant. I hoped this child in me was yours. I know now that's not possible."

He reeled at the layers of shock and pain. Pain for her.

Again, he moved to embrace her but she shook her head, halting him. "You were ready to walk out of my life. How can I believe you're ready to stay? Ready for this child? I won't wipe it out of existence; it's not in me to get rid of it."

He clenched his fists against the ache to hold her. Her revelations threatened to bring him to his knees and rip out his throat. "You don't *know* how much I love you. It doesn't matter about the child."

"Oh, it matters. If you love me, how can you *not* hate Blake for what he did to me? He did it to get even with you. I can't let Todd be raised by a man who hates his father. I can't risk letting the child growing within me being rejected by you."

He knew in his heart she needn't fear this in him, but what words would convince her? "On that long ride up to the camp," he ventured, "with his traumatized son in my arms, any animosity I felt toward the father drained away. No one knows better than I, the desperation to which Todd was driven by his fear of others' hatred. The man is dead; what use is hate? As for this unborn child, she is innocent and deserves only to be loved."

He kept talking, while a kaleidoscope of emotions vied for supremacy in her countenance. "I'm not heroic, Dana. These last few weeks, ordinary people showed me that being a hero is nothing more than stepping up to the plate when there's no one else to do it. The measure of a man—or a woman—is in still standing after the high water mark, picking up the pieces of one's shattered life and rebuilding."

Playing his last card, he offered up his soul to her examination. "In this moment, for this man, it's telling the woman you can't live without, that you love her and risking she'll say it's too late."

Bitter reproach laced her response. "You *should* have told me you were in love with me. These past weeks I thought I'd *die* of hurt, believing I'd been nothing to you but an indiscretion. If Amber hadn't spilled the beans about you seeking a divorce, I might never have learned—"

"Dana, stop." He said it gently, but commanded her none-the-less. She broke off abruptly on a hiccup.

"I'm guilty as charged," he admitted. "I *should* have found a time and place to tell you my feelings. But I'm telling you now. If I'd had the barest inkling that you were in love with me, the river in full flood would not have had the power to sweep me away from you. To spend my life here with you, help you rebuild, be a father to these children would make me happier than I have ever been."

He arched a bemused brow. "And what about you, Dana? Are you not just as guilty. If not for Amber's revelation you would have *let* me walk out of your life, never telling *me* how *you* feel."

She clutched her elbows as if she would fly into pieces.

He took a step toward her. "Do you? Love me?"

Her granite features gave way then, tears spilling unchecked. She nodded on another hiccup.

He closed the gap between them and folded her in his arms. He longed to kiss those wet lips, but held back long enough for her to speak past the gravel in her throat, "I do, Gavin. I do."

Acknowledgments

Many thanks to Ward Edwards, without whose help in the myriad logistics of going from manuscript to publishing, this book would never have 'arrived'. Thanks to Bonnie Branton who provided helpful feedback and editing on the manuscript. Here's to my husband, who patiently kept himself occupied while I spent long hours writing and who cheered me on through the many steps of launching this book.

I also want to acknowledge and laud that dedicated army of people, both professionals and volunteers, who help out in disasters.

About the Author

Donna Gannon is a retired social worker.

Her passion for writing began in childhood.

In her role as a social worker, her delight in the power of the written word took the form of creating promotional material, manuals, curriculum and dialogue for video presentations and writing policy and protocols for government and non-government organizations.

She lives with her husband in British Columbia in her beloved mountains, where they enjoy their two beautiful granddaughters.

Front cover design by Gayll Morrison — www.gayllery.biz